W9-AEX-652

The Beginnings of Love

They knew not how long they had sat — the storm had soon passed over. The sweet smell of the hay in the barn grew stronger.

"Now must I go," said Kristin; and Erlend answered: "Ay, 'tis like you must." He took her foot in his hand: "You will be wet — you must ride and I must walk — out of the woods . . ." and he looked at her so strangely.

Kristin shook — it must be because her heart beat so, she thought — her hands were cold and clammy. As he kissed her vehemently she weakly tried to push him from her. Erlend lifted his face a moment — she thought of a man who had been given food at the convent one day — he had kissed the bread they gave him. She sank back upon the hay . . .

KRISTIN LAVRANSDATTER

by
Sigrid Undset

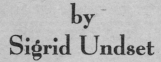

I
The Bridal Wreath

Translated by Charles Archer
and J. S. Scott

*This low-priced Bantam Book
has been completely reset in a type face
designed for easy reading, and was printed
from new plates. It contains the complete
text of the original hard-cover edition.*
NOT ONE WORD HAS BEEN OMITTED.

RL 7, IL 10-up

KRISTIN LAVRANSDATTER
I: THE BRIDAL WREATH

*A Bantam Book / published by arrangement with
Alfred A. Knopf, Inc.*

PRINTING HISTORY

*Original title: Kransen; Copyright 1920 by
H. Aschehoug & Company, Oslo
Translated by Charles Archer and J. S. Scott
Knopf edition published February 1923
18 printings through October 1976
Bantam edition / September 1978
2nd printing*

*All rights reserved under International
and Pan-American Copyright Conventions.
Copyright 1923 by Alfred A. Knopf, Inc.
Renewal Copyright 1951 by Alfred A. Knopf, Inc.
This book may not be reproduced in whole or in part, by
mimeograph or any other means, without permission.
For information address: Alfred A. Knopf, Inc.,
201 East 50th Street, New York, N.Y. 10022.*

ISBN 0-553-10936-7

Published simultaneously in the United States and Canada

*Bantam Books are published by Bantam Books, Inc. Its trade-
mark, consisting of the words "Bantam Books" and the por-
trayal of a bantam, is registered in the United States Patent
Office and in other countries. Marca Registrada. Bantam
Books, Inc., 666 Fifth Avenue, New York, New York 10019.*

PRINTED IN THE UNITED STATES OF AMERICA

THE BRIDAL WREATH

PART ONE

JÖRUNDGAARD

WHEN the lands and goods of Ivar Gjesling the younger, of Sundbu, were divided after his death in 1306, his lands in Sil of Gud-bransdal fell to his daughter Ragnfrid and her husband Lavrans Björgulfsön. Up to then they had lived on Lavrans' manor of Skog at Follo, near Oslo; but now they moved up to Jörundgaard * at the top of the open lands of Sil.

Lavrans was of the stock that was known in this country as the Lagmandssons. It had come here from Sweden with that Laurentius, Lagmand † of East Gothland, who took the Belbo Jarl's sister, the Lady Bengta, out of Vreta convent, and carried her off to Norway. Sir Laurentius lived at the Court of King Haakon ‡ the Old, and won great favour with the King, who gave him the Skog manor. But when he had been in this country about eight years he died in his bed, and his widow, who belonged to the Folkunga kin-dred, and had the name of a King's daughter among the Norwegians, went home and made matters up with her relations. Afterwards she made a rich marriage in another land. She and Sir Laurentius had no children, so the heritage of Skog fell to Laurentius' brother, Ketil. He was father's father to Lavrans Björgulfsön.

Lavrans was married very young; he was three years younger than his wife, and was only twenty-eight when he came to Sil. As a youth he had been in the King's bodyguard, and had enjoyed a good upbringing;

---

* Jörundgaard, see Note 2.
† Lagmand, see Note 3.
‡ King Haakon, see Note 4.

but after his marriage he lived a quiet life on his estate, for Ragnfrid was something strange and heavy of mood, and seemed not at home among the people of the south. After she had had the ill-hap to lose three little sons, one after the other, in the cradle, she grew yet more shy of people. Thus it was in part to bring his wife nearer to her kinsfolk and old acquaintance that Lavrans moved to Gudbrandsdalen. When they came there, they brought with them the one child that was left, a little maid called Kristin.

But when they had settled at Jörundgaard they lived for the most part just as quietly there, keeping very much to themselves; it seemed as though Ragnfrid did not care much for her kindred, for she saw them no oftener than seemly use and wont required. This was in part because Lavrans and Ragnfrid were more than commonly pious and God-fearing folk, diligent in churchgoing, and always pleased to give harbour to God's servants, to messengers sent on the Church's errands, or to pilgrims on their way up the valley to Nidaros; and showing the greatest honour to their parish priest — who was also their nearest neighbour, living at Romundgaard. Other folk in the valley were rather given to think that the Church cost them quite dear enough in tithes and in goods and money; and that there was no need to fast and pray so hard besides, or to bring priests and monks into their houses, unless at times when they were really needed.

Otherwise the Jörundgaard folk were much looked up to, and well-liked too; most of all Lavrans, for he was known as a strong man and a bold, but peace-loving, quiet and upright, plain in his living, but courteous and seemly in his ways, a rarely good husbandman and a mighty hunter — 'twas wolves and bears and all kinds of harmful beasts he hunted most keenly. In a few years he had gotten much land into his hands; but he was a good and helpful landlord to his tenants.

Folk saw so little of Ragnfrid that they soon gave

up talking much about her. In the first time after she came back to the valley many people had wondered, for they remembered her as she had been at her home at Sundbu in her youth. Beautiful she had never been, but she had looked kind and happy; now she had fallen off so that you might well believe she was ten years older than her husband, and not only three. Most folk deemed she took the loss of her children harder than was reason, for but for this she was better off in every way than most wives — she lived in great plenty and in high esteem, and things were well between her and her husband, so far as people could see; Lavrans did not go after other women, he took counsel with her in all affairs, and, sober or drunk, he never said a harsh word to her. Besides she was not so old but she might yet bear many children, if it were God's pleasure.

It was somewhat hard for them to get young folks to take service at Jörundgaard, the mistress being thus heavy of mood and all the fasts so strictly kept. Otherwise it was a good house to serve in; hard words and punishments were little in use; and both Lavrans and Ragnfrid took the lead in all the work. The master, indeed, was glad of mood in his own way, and would join in a dance or lead the singing when the young folk held their games on the church-green on vigil nights. But still it was mostly older folks who came and took service at Jörundgaard; these liked the place well, and stayed there long.

When the child Kristin was seven years old, it so fell out one time that she got leave to go with her father up to their mountain sæter.

It was a fine morning; a little way on in the summer. Kristin was in the loft-room, where they were sleeping now summer had come; she saw the sun shining outside and heard her father and his men talking in the courtyard below, and she was so joyful that she could not stand still while her mother put on her clothes, but hopped and jumped about as each piece of clothing was put on her. She had never been up in the mountains before; only across the pass to Vaage, when she was taken to visit her mother's kinsfolk at Sundbu, and sometimes to the woods near by the manor with her mother and the housefolk, when they went out to pluck berries for Ragnfrid to mix with the small beer, or to make into the sour paste of cranberries and cowberries that she ate on her bread in Lent instead of butter.

The mother twisted up Kristin's long yellow hair and tied it into her old blue cap, then kissed her daughter on the cheek, and Kristin sprang away and down to her father. Lavrans was in the saddle already; he lifted her up behind him and seated her on his cloak, which he had folded up and placed on the horse's loins for a pillion. Kristin had to sit there astride and hold on to his belt. They called out "Good-bye" to Ragnfrid; but she came running down from the balcony with Kristin's hooded cape — she handed it to Lavrans and bade him look well to the child.

The sun shone, but it had rained much in the night, so that everywhere the becks came rushing and singing down the grassy slopes, and wreaths of mist clung and drifted under the mountain-sides. But over the hill-crest white fair-weather clouds were swelling up in the blue air, and Lavrans and his men said among themselves that it was like to be hot as the day went on. Lavrans had four men with him, and they were all well armed; for at this time there were many kinds of outlandish people lying up among the mountains — though a strong party like this, going but a short way, was not like to see or hear aught of such folk. Kristin was fond of all the men; three of them were men past youth, but the fourth, Arne Gyrdsön, from Fins-brekken, was a half-grown boy, and he was Kristin's best friend; he rode next after Lavrans and her, for it was he that was to tell her about all they saw on their road.

They passed between the Romundgaard houses, and changed greetings with Eirik priest.* He was standing outside chiding with his daughter — she kept house for him — about a web of new-dyed cloth that she had hung out and forgotten the day before; it was all spoilt now with the night's rain.

On the hill behind the parsonage lay the church; it was not large, but fair and pleasant, well kept and newly tarred. By the cross outside the churchyard gate Lavrans and his men took off their hats and bowed their heads; then the father turned in the saddle, and he and Kristin waved to Ragnfrid, whom they could see down below at home standing out on the sward by the houses; she waved back to them with the fall of her linen headdress.

Up here on the church-green and in the churchyard Kristin was used to come and play near every day; but to-day, when she was setting out to go so far, the sight she knew so well — home and all the parish round it — seemed new and strange to the child. The clusters of houses at Jörundgaard looked, as it were, smaller and greyer, lying there down on the flats, courtyard and farmyard. The river wound shining on its way, the valley spread far with broad green meadows and marshes in its bottom, and farms with ploughland and pasture stretched up the hillsides under the grey and headlong mountain walls.

Far below, where the mountains came together and closed the valley, Kristin knew that Loptsgaard lay. There lived Sigurd and Jon, two old men with white beards; they were always for playing and making merry with her when they came to Jörundgaard. She was fond of Jon, for he would carve out the fairest beasts in wood for her, and once she had had a gold finger-ring of him; nay, the last time he came to them, at Whitsuntide, he had brought her a knight so sweetly

---

* Priests, see Note 5.

carved and coloured so fairly that Kristin thought she had never had so fine a gift. She must needs take the knight to bed with her every single night; but when she woke in the morning he was always standing on the step in front of the bed she lay in with her father and mother. Her father said the knight jumped up at the first cockcrow; but Kristin knew well enough that, after she had fallen asleep, her mother took him away, for she had heard her say that he was so hard, and hurt so if he got underneath them in the night. Sigurd of Loptsgaard Kristin was afraid of, and she did not like him to take her on his knee; for he used to say that when she grew up he meant to sleep in her arms. He had outlived two wives, and he said himself he was sure to outlive the third, and then Kristin could be the fourth. But when she began to cry at this, Lavrans laughed and said he had no fear that Margit would give up the ghost so speedily; but if the worst came to pass and Sigurd should come a-wooing, let Kristin have no fear — he should have No for his answer.

A bowshot or so north of the church there lay by the roadside a great block of stone, and around it a thick, small grove of birch and aspen. Here the children were wont to play at church, and Tomas, the youngest son of Eirik priest's daughter, stood up in the person of his grandfather and said mass, sprinkled holy water, and even baptized, when there was rain-water in the hollows of the rock. But once, the autumn before, this game had fallen out but sadly for them. For first Tomas had married Kristin and Arne — Arne was not so old but he would go off and play with the children when he saw a chance. Then Arne caught a baby pig that was going by, and they brought it into church to be baptized. Tomas anointed it with mud, dipped it into a pool of water, and, copying his grandfather, said mass in Latin and chid them for the smallness of their offerings — and at this the children laughed, for they had heard their elders talk of Eirik's exceeding greed of money. But the more they laughed the worse Tomas got in the things he hit on: for next he said that this child had been gotten in Lent, and they must pay penalty for their sin to the priest and the Church. The great boys shouted with laughter at this; but Kristin was so ashamed that she was all but weeping, as she stood there with the little pig in her arms. And just as this was going on who must chance to come that way but Eirik himself, riding home from a sick visit. When he understood what the young folks were about, he sprang from his horse, and handed the holy vessels to Bentein, his eldest grandson, who was with him, so suddenly that Bentein nearly dropped the silver dove with God's body in it on the hillside, while the priest rushed in among the children belabouring all he could reach. Kristin let slip the little pig, and it rushed shrieking down the road with the christening robe trailing after it, while Eirik's horses reared and plunged with terror; the priest pushed her, too, so that she fell down, and he knocked against her with his foot so hard that she felt the pain in her hip for many days after. Lavrans had thought when he heard of this that Eirik had been too hard with Kristin, seeing she was but a little child. He said he would speak to the priest of it, but Ragnfrid begged him not to do so, for the child had gotten but what she deserved, for joining in such a blasphemous game. So Lavrans said no more of the matter; but he gave Arne the worst beating the boy had ever had.

So now, as they rode by the stone, Arne plucked Kristin by the sleeve. He dared not say aught for fear of Lavrans, but he made a face, then smiled and clapped his hand to his back. But Kristin bowed her head shamefacedly.

Their way led on into thick woods. They rode along under Hammerhill; the valley grew narrow and dark here, and the roar of the river sounded louder and more harsh — when they caught a glimpse of the Laagen it ran ice-green and white with foam between walls of rock. The mountains on either side of the valley were black with forest; it was dark and narrow and ugly in the gorge, and there came cold gusts of wind. They rode across the Rostaa stream by the log-bridge, and soon could see the bridge over the great river down in the valley. A little below the bridge was a pool where a kelpie lived. Arne began to tell Kristin about it, but Lavrans sternly told the boy to hold his peace in the woods about such things. And when they came to the bridge he leaped off his horse and led it across by the bridle, while he held the child round the waist with his other arm.

On the other side of the river was a bridle-path leading steeply up the hillside, so the men got off their horses and went on foot; but her father lifted Kristin forward into the saddle, so that she could hold on to the saddle-bow, and let her ride Guldsveinen all alone.

New greystone peaks and blue domes flecked with snow rose above the mountain ridges as they climbed higher up; and now Kristin saw through the trees glimpses of the parish north of the gorge, and Arne pointed and told her the names of the farms that they could make out down there.

High up the mountain-side they came to a little croft. They stopped by the stick fence; Lavrans shouted, and his voice came back again and again from the mountains round. Two men came running down, between the small tilled patches. These were both sons of the house; they were good men at the tar-burning, and Lavrans was for hiring them to burn some tar for him. Their mother came after them with a great bowl of cooled milk, for the day was now grown hot, as the men had foretold.

"I saw you had your daughter with you," she said, when she had greeted them, "and methought I must needs have a sight of her. But you must take the cap from her head; they say she hath such bonny hair."

Lavrans did as the woman asked him, and Kristin's hair fell over her shoulders and hung down right to the saddle. It was thick and yellow like ripe wheat.

The woman, Isrid, took some of it in her hand, and said:

"Ay, now I see the word that has gone about concerning this little maid of yours was nowise too great — a lily-rose she is, and looks as should the child of a knightly man. Mild eyes hath she too — she favours you and not the Gjeslings. God grant you joy of her, Lavrans Björgulfsön! And you're riding on Guld-sveinen, as stiff and straight as a courier," she said laughingly, as she held the bowl for Kristin to drink.

The child grew red with pleasure, for she knew well that her father was held to be the comeliest man far around; he looked like a knight, standing there among his men, though his dress was much of the farmer fashion, such as he wore at home for daily use. He wore a coat of green-dyed wadmal, somewhat wide and short, open at the throat, so that the shirt showed beneath. For the rest, his hose and shoes were of un-dyed leather, and on his head he had a broad-brimmed woollen hat of the ancient fashion. For ornaments he had only a smooth silver buckle to his belt, and a little silver brooch in his shirt-band; but some links of a golden neck-chain showed against his neck. Lavrans always wore this chain, and on it there hung a golden cross set with great rock-crystals; it was made to open, and inside there were shreds of the hair and the shroud of the holy Lady Elin of Skövde, for the Lagmandssons counted their descent from one of that blessed lady's daughters. But when Lavrans was in the woods or out at his work he was used to thrust the cross in next his bare breast, so that he might not lose it.

Yet did he look in his coarse homely clothing more high-born than many a knight of the King's household in his finest banqueting attire. He was stalwart of growth, tall, broad-shouldered, and small waisted; his head was small and sat fairly on his neck, and he had comely features, somewhat long — cheeks of a seemly fullness, chin fairly rounded and mouth well shaped.

His skin was light and his face fresh of hue; he had grey eyes and thick, smooth, silky-yellow hair.

He stood there and talked with Isrid of her affairs; and asked about Tordis too, a kinswoman of Isrid's that was tending the Jörundgaard sæter this summer. Tordis had just had a child; Isrid was only waiting for the chance of a safe escort through the woods before taking the boy down to have him christened. Lavrans said that she had best come with them up to the sæter; he was coming down again the next evening, and 'twould be safer and better for her to have many men to go along with her and the heathen child.

Isrid thanked him. "To say truth, 'twas even this I was waiting for. We know well, we poor folk under the uplands here, that you will ever do us a kind turn if you can, when you come hither." She ran up to the hut to fetch a bundle and a cloak.

It was indeed so that Lavrans liked well to come among these small folk who lived on clearings and leaseholdings high up on the outskirts of the parish; amongst them he was always glad and merry. He talked with them of the ways of the forest beasts and the reindeer of the upland wastes, and of all the uncanny things that are stirring in such places. And he stood by them and helped them with word and deed; saw to their sick cattle, helped them with their errands to the smith or to the carpenter; nay, would sometimes take hold himself and bend his great strength to the work, when the worst stones or roots were to be broken out of the earth. Therefore were these people ever glad to greet Lavrans Björgulfsön and Guldsveinen, the great red stallion that he rode upon. 'Twas a comely beast with a shining skin, white mane and tail and light eyes — strong and fiery, so that his fame was spread through all the country round; but with his master he was gentle as a lamb, and Lavrans used to say that the horse was dear to him as a younger brother.

Lavrans' first errand was to see to the beacon on

Heimhaugen. For in the hard and troubled times a hundred years or more gone by, the yeomen of the dales had built beacons here and there high up on the fells above them, like the seamarks in the roadsteads upon the coast. But these beacons in the uplands were not in the ward of the King's levies, but were cared for by the yeoman guilds,* and the guild brothers took turns at their tending.

When they were come to the first sæter, Lavrans turned out all but the pack-horse to graze there; and now they took a steep footpath upwards. Before long the trees grew thin and scattered. Great firs stood dead and white as bones upon the marshy grounds — and now Kristin saw bare greystone peaks rising to the sky on all hands. They climbed long stretches amid loose stones, and at times the becks ran in the track, so that her father must carry her. The wind blew strong and fresh up here, and the ground was black with berries amidst the heather, but Lavrans said they could not stop now to gather them. Arne sprang now in front and now behind, plucked berries for her, and told her whose the sæters were that they saw below them in the forest — for there was forest over the whole of Hövringsvangen in those days.

And now they were close below the highest round bare top and saw the great pile of timber against the sky, with the watch-house under the lee of a crag.

As they came up over the brow the wind rushed against them and buffeted their clothing — it seemed to Kristin as though something living, that dwelt up here, met and greeted them. It blew gustily around her and Arne as they went forward over the mosses, till they sate them down far out on a jutting point, and Kristin gazed with great eyes — never before had she dreamed that the world was so big and wide.

Forest-shagged ranges lay below her on all sides; the valley was but a cleft betwixt the huge fells, and

---

* Peasant Guilds, see Note 6.

the side-glens still lesser clefts; there were many such, yet was there little of dale and much of fell. All around grey peaks, flaming with golden lichen, rose above the sea of forest, and far off, on the very brink of heaven, stood blue crests flashing here and there with snow, and melting, before their eyes, into the grey-blue and pure white summer-clouds. But north-eastwards, nearer by — just beyond the sæter woods — lay a cluster of mighty slate-coloured domes with streaks of new-fallen snow down their slopes. These Kristin guessed to be the Boar Fells she had heard tell of, for they were indeed like naught but a herd of heavy boar wending inland that had just turned their backs upon the parish. Yet Arne told her 'twas a half-day's ride to get even so far.

Kristin had ever thought that could she but win over the top of the home-fells she would look down upon another parish like their own, with tilled farms and dwellings, and 'twas great wonder to her now to see how far it was betwixt the places where folks dwelt. She saw the small yellow and green flecks down below in the dale-bottom, and the tiny clearings with their grey dots of houses amid the hill forests; she began to take tale of them, but when she had reckoned three times twelve, she could keep count of them no longer. Yet the human dwelling-places were as nothing in that waste.

She knew that in the wild woods wolves and bears lorded it, and that under every stone there dwelt trolls and goblins and elfin-folk, and she was afraid, for no one knew the number of them — but there must be many times more of them than of Christian men and women. Then she called aloud on her father, but he could not hear for the blowing of the wind — he and his men were busy rolling heavy stones up the bare mountain-top to pile round the timbers of the beacon.

But Isrid came to the children and showed Kristin where the fell west of Vaage lay. And Arne pointed out the Grayfell, where folk from the parish took reindeer in pits, and where the King's falcon-catchers lay in stone huts. That was a trade Arne thought to take to some day — but if he did he would learn as well to train the birds for the chase — and he held his arms aloft as though to cast a hawk.

Isrid shook her head.

" 'Tis a hard and evil life, that, Arne Gyrdsön. 'Twould be a heavy sorrow for your mother, boy, should you ever come to be a falcon-catcher. None may earn his bread in those wild hills except he join in fellowship with the worst of men — ay, and with them that are worse still."

Lavrans had come toward them and had heard this last word. "Aye," says he, "there's more than one hide of land in there that pays neither tax nor tithe—"

"Yes; many a thing must you have seen," said Isrid coaxingly, "you who fare so far afield — "

"Ay, ay," said Lavrans slowly. "Maybe — but methinks 'tis well not to speak of such things overmuch. One should not, I say, grudge folks who have lost their peace in the parish, whatever peace they can find among the fells. Yet have I seen yellow fields and brave meadows where few folk know that such things be; and herds have I seen of cattle and small stock, but of these I know not whether they belonged to mankind or to other folk — "

"Oh, ay!" says Isrid. "Bears and wolves get the blame for the beasts that are missed from the sæters here, but there are worse thieves among the fells than they."

"Do you call them worse?" asked Lavrans thoughtfully, stroking his daughter's cap. "In the hills to the south under the Boar Fells I once saw three little lads, and the greatest was even as Kristin here — yellow hair they had, and coats of skin. They gnashed their teeth at me like wolf-cubs before they ran to hide. 'Twere little wonder if the poor man who owned them were fain to lift a cow or two — "

"Oh, both wolves and bears have young!" says Isrid

testily; "and you spare not them, Lavrans, neither them nor their young. Yet they have no lore of law nor of Christendom, as have these evil-doers you wish so well to — "

"Think you I wish them too well, because I wish them a little better than the worst?" said Lavrans, smiling a little. "But come now, let us see what cheer Ragnfrid has sent with us to-day." He took Kristin by the hand and led her with him. And as they went he bent and said softly, "I thought of your three small brothers, little Kristin."

They peeped into the watch-house, but it was close in there and smelt of mould. Kristin took a look around, but there were only some earthen benches about the walls, a hearth-stone in the middle of the floor, and some barrels of tar and faggots of pine-roots and birch-bark. Lavrans thought 'twould be best they should eat without doors, and a little way down among the birches they found a fine piece of green sward.

The pack-horse was unloaded, and they stretched themselves upon the grass. In the wallets Ragnfrid had given them was plenty food of the best — soft bread and bannocks, butter and cheese, pork and wind-dried reindeer meet, lard, boiled brisket of beef, two kegs with German beer, and of mead a little jar. The carving of the meat and portioning it round went quickly, while Halvdan, the oldest of the men, struck fire and made a blaze — it was safer to have a good fire out here in the woods.

Isrid and Arne gathered heather and dwarf-birch and cast it on the blaze. It crackled as the fire tore the fresh green from the twigs, and small white flakes flew high upon the wisps of red flame; the smoke whirled thick and black toward the clear sky. Kristin sat and watched; it seemed to her the fire was glad that it was out there, and free, and could play and frisk. 'Twas otherwise than when, at home, it sat upon the hearth and must work at cooking food and giving light to the folks in the room.

She sat nestled by her father with one arm upon his knee; he gave her all she would have of the best, and bade her drink her fill of the beer and taste well of the mead.

"She will be so tipsy she'll never get down to the sæter on her feet," said Halvdan, laughing; but Lavrans stroked her round cheeks:

"Then here are folk enough who can bear her — it will do her good — drink you too, Arne; God's gifts do good, not harm, to you that are yet growing — make sweet, red blood, and give deep sleep, and rouse not madness and folly — "

The men, too, drank often and deep; neither was Isrid backward. And soon their voices and the roar and crackle of the fire were but a far-off hubbub in Kristin's ears, and she began to grow heavy of head. She was still aware how they questioned Lavrans and would have him tell of the strange things he had met with when out a-hunting. But much he would not say; and this seemed to her so good and so safe — and then she had eaten so well.

Her father had a slice of soft barley-bread in his hand; he pinched small bits of it between his fingers into shapes of horses, and, cutting shreds of meat, he set these astride the steeds and made them ride over his thigh and into Kristin's mouth. But soon she was so weary she could neither open her mouth nor chew — and so she sank back upon the ground and slept.

When she came to herself again she was lying in a warm darkness within her father's arm — he had wrapped his cloak about them both. Kristin sat up, wiped the moisture from her face, and unloosed her cap that the air might dry her damp locks.

The day was surely far spent, for the sunlight was golden, and the shadows had lengthened and fell now toward the south-east. No breath of wind was stirring, and gnats and flies buzzed and swarmed about the group of sleeping men. Kristin sat stock still, scratched her gnat-bitten hands and gazed about her. The mountain-top above them shone white with moss and golden with lichen in the sunshine, and the pile of weather-beaten timber stood against the sky like the skeleton of some wondrous beast.

She grew ill at ease — it was so strange to see them all sleeping there in the naked daylight. At home if by hap she woke at night, she lay snug in the dark with her mother on the one side, and on the other the tapestry stretched upon the wall. And then she knew that the chamber with its smoke-vent was shut and barred against the night and the weather without, and sounds of slumber came from the folk who lay soft and safe on the pillows 'twixt the skins. But all these bodies, lying twisted and bent on the hillside, about the little heap of black and white ashes, might well be dead — some lay upon their faces, some upon their backs with knees updrawn, and the noises that came from them scared her. Her father snored deeply, but when Halvdan drew a breath, it piped and whistled in his nose. And Arne lay upon his side, his face hidden on his arm, and his glossy, light brown hair spread out amongst the heather; he lay so still Kristin grew afraid lest he be dead. She had to bend forward and touch him, and on this he turned a little in his sleep.

Kristin suddenly bethought her, maybe they had slept through the night and this was the next day — and this frightened her so that she shook her father; but he only grunted and slept on. Kristin herself was still heavy of head, but she dared not lie down to sleep again. And so she crept forward to the fire and raked in it with a stick — there were still some embers aglow beneath. She threw upon it heather and small twigs which she broke off round about her — she dared not pass the ring of sleepers to find bigger branches.

There came a rattling and crashing in the woods near by, and Kristin's heart sank and she went cold with fear. But then she spied a red shape amidst the trees, and Guldsveinen broke out of the thicket. He

stood there and gazed upon her with his clear, bright
eyes. She was so glad to see him, she leapt to her feet
and ran to the stallion. And there, too, was the brown
horse Arne had ridden, and the pack-horse as well.
Now she felt safe and happy again; she went and
patted them all three upon their flanks, but Guldsveinen
bent his head so that she could reach up to fondle his
cheeks, and pull his yellow-white forelock, while he
nosed round her hands with his soft muzzle.

The horses wandered, feeding, down the birch-
grown slope, and Kristin went with them — she felt
there was naught to fear so long as she kept close to
Guldsveinen — he had driven off a bear before now,
she knew. And the bilberries grew so thick in here,
and the child was thirsty now, with a bad taste in her
mouth; the beer was not to her liking any more, but
the sweet, juicy berries were good as wine. Away, on
a scree, she saw raspberries growing too, so she grasped
Guldsveinen by the mane, and sweetly bade him go
there with her, and the stallion followed willingly with
the little maid. Thus, as she wandered farther and
farther down the hillside, he followed her when she
called, and the other two horses followed Guldsveinen.

Somewhere near at hand she heard the gurgling and
trickling of a beck; she followed the sound till she
found it, and then lay out upon a great slab and washed
her hot, gnat-bitten face and hands. Below the slab
the water stood, a still, black pool, for over against it
there rose a wall of rock behind some small birches
and willows. It made the finest of mirrors, and Kristin
leaned over and looked at herself in the water, for she
wished to see whether 'twas true, as Isrid said, that she
bore a likeness to her father.

She smiled and nodded and bent forward till her
hair met the bright hair about the round, great-eyed
child-face she saw in the beck.

Round about grew a great plenty of those gay, pink
flower clusters they name valerian — redder far and

finer here by the fell-beck than at home by the river. Of these Kristin plucked, and bound them about with grass, till she had woven herself the finest, thickest wreath of rose-pink. The child pressed it down on her head and ran to the pool to see how she looked now she was decked out like a grown maid who goes a-dancing.

She stooped over the water and saw her own dark image rise from the bottom and grow clearer as it came to meet her—and then in the mirror of the pool she saw another figure standing among the birches opposite and bending toward her. In haste she got upon her knees and gazed across. At first she thought it was but the rock and the bushes clinging round its foot. But all at once she was aware of a face amid the leaves — there stood a lady, pale, with waving, flaxen hair — the great, light-grey eyes and wide-pink nostrils were like Guldsveinen's. She was clad in something light, leaf-green, and branches and twigs hid her up to the broad breasts, which were covered over with brooches and sparkling chains.

The little girl gazed upon the figure, and as she gazed the lady raised a hand and showed her a wreath of golden flowers — she beckoned with it.

Behind her Kristin heard Guldsveinen neigh loud in fear. She turned her head — the stallion reared, screaming till the echoes rang, then flung around and fled up the hill with a thunder of hoofs. The other horses followed — straight up the scree, while stones came rumbling down and boughs and roots broke and rattled.

Then Kristin screamed aloud. "Father!" she shrieked, "father!" She gained her feet, tore after the horses and dared not look behind. She clambered up the scree, trod on the hem of her dress and slipped back downwards; climbed again, catching at the stones with bleeding hands, creeping on sore bruised knees, and crying now to Guldsveinen, now to her father — sweat started from every pore of her body and ran like water into her eyes, and her heart beat as though 'twould break against her ribs, while sobs of terror choked her throat:

"Oh, father! oh, father!"

Then his voice sounded somewhere above: she saw him come with great bounds down the scree — the bright, sunlit scree; birch and aspen stood along it and blinked from their small silvered leaves — the hillside was so quiet, so bright, while her father came leaping, calling her by name; and Kristin sank down and knew that now she was saved.

"Sancta Maria!" Lavrans knelt and clasped his daughter. He was pale and strange about the mouth, so that Kristin grew yet more afraid; 'twas as though only now in his face she read how great had been her peril.

"Child, child — " He lifted her bleeding hands, looked at them, saw the wreath upon her bare head, and touched it. "What is it — how came you hither, my little Kristin — ?"

"I went with Guldsveinen," she sobbed upon his breast. "I got so afraid seeing you all asleep, but then Guldsveinen came, and then there was some one by the beck down yonder that beckoned me — "

"Who beckoned — was it a man?"

"No, 'twas a lady — she beckoned with a wreath of gold — I think 'twas the dwarf-maiden,* father — "

"Jesus Kristus!" said Lavrans softly, and crossed himself and the child.

He helped her up the scree till they came to a grassy slope; then he lifted and bore her. She clung about his neck and sobbed — could not stop for all his soothing.

Soon they met the men and Isrid. The woman smote her hands together, when she heard what had befallen:

"Ay, 'twas the elf-maiden * sure enough — she would have lured the fair child into the mountain, trust you me."

"Hold your peace!" bade Lavrans sternly. "Never

---

* Elf or dwarf-maiden, see Note 7.

should we have talked of such things here in the woods as we did — one knows not what may lie beneath the rocks and hearken to each word."

He drew the golden chain from out his shirt and hung it and the relic-holding cross about Kristin's neck and thrust them in upon her bare body.

"But see to it, all of you," he said, "that you watch well your mouths, so Ragnfrid may never know the child has been in such peril."

Then they caught the three horses, which had made off into the woods, and went quickly down to the pasture where the other horses were grazing. There they all mounted and rode to the Jörundgaard sæter; it was no great way.

The sun was near setting when they came thither; the cattle were in the pens, and Tordis and the herds were busy at the milking. Within the hut porridge stood cooked awaiting them, for the sæter-folk had spied them by the beacon earlier in the day, and they were looked for.

Now, at length, was Kristin's weeping stilled. She sat upon her father's knee and ate porridge and cream from out the same spoon as he.

Lavrans was to go next day to a lake farther in the mountains, where lay some of his herdsmen with the bulls. Kristin was to have gone with him, but now he said she must stay in the hut while he was gone. "And you must take heed, both Tordis and Isrid, to keep the door barred and the smokehole closed till we come back, both for Kristin's sake and for the poor unchristened babe's here in the cradle."

Tordis was so frighted now that she dared no longer stay with the little one up here, for she was still unchurched since her lying-in — rather would she go down at once and bide in the parish. Lavrans said this seemed to him but wise; she could go down with them the next evening; he thought he could get an older widow woman, serving at Jörundgaard, up hither in her stead.

Tordis had spread sweet, fresh mountain grass under the skins on the benches; it smelt so strong and good, and Kristin was near asleep while her father said Our Father and Ave Maria over her.

"Ay, 'twill be a long day before I take you with me to the fells again," said Lavrans, patting her cheek.

Kristin woke up with a start:

"Father, mayn't I go with you either when you go southwards at harvest, as you promised — "

"We must see about that," said Lavrans, and straightaway Kristin fell asleep between the sheepskins.

2

EACH summer it was Lavrans Björgulfsön's wont to ride southward and see to his manor in Follo. These journeys of her father were landmarks of each year in Kristin's life — the long weeks while he was gone, and the joy of his homecoming with brave gifts: fine outlandish stuffs for her bride-chest, figs, raisins and honey-bread from Oslo — and many strange things to tell her.

But this year Kristin marked that there was something more than common afoot toward the time of her father's going. 'Twas put off and off; the old men from Loptsgaard rode over at odd times and sat about the board with her father and mother; spoke of heritage, and freehold and redemption rights, and hindrances to working the estate from so far off, and the Bishop's seat and the King's palace in Oslo, which took so much labour from the farms round about the town. They scarce ever had time to play with her, and she was sent out to the kitchen-house to the maids. Her mother's brother, Trond Ivarsön, of Sundbu, came over to them more often than was his wont — but *he* had never been used to play with Kristin or pet her.

Little by little she came to have some inkling of what it was all about. Ever since he was come to Sil, Lavrans had sought to gather to himself land here in

the parish, and now had Sir Andres Gudmundsön
tendered him Formo in Sil, which was Sir Andres'
heritage from his mother, in change for Skog, which
lay more fittingly for him, since he was with the
King's bodyguard and rarely came hither to the Dale.
Lavrans was loth to part with Skog, which was his
freehold heritage, and had come to his forbears by
royal gift; and yet the bargain would be for his gain
in many ways. But Lavrans' brother, Aasmund Björgulfsön, too, would gladly have Skog — he dwelt now
in Hadeland, where he had wedded an estate — and
'twas not sure that Aasmund would waive the right his
kinship gave him.

But one day Lavrans told Ragnfrid that this year
he would have Kristin with him to Skog. She should
see the manor where she was born, and which was his
fathers' home, now that it was like to pass from their
hands. Ragnfrid deemed this but right, though she
feared not a little to send so young a child on such a
long journey, where she herself could not be by.

For a time after Kristin had seen the elf-maid she
was so fearful that she kept much within doors by her
mother — she was afraid even when she saw the folk
who had been with them on the fells and knew what
had befallen her, and she was glad her father had
forbidden all talk of that sight of hers.

But when some little time was gone by, she began
to think she would like to speak of it. In her thoughts
she told the story to some one — she knew not whom
— and, 'twas strange, the more time went by, the
better it seemed she remembered it, and the clearer
and clearer grew the memory of the fair lady.

But, strangest of all, each time she thought of the
elf-maid there came upon her such a longing for the
journey to Skog, and more and more fear that her
father would not take her with him.

At last she woke one morning in the loft-room and
saw her mother and old Gunhild sitting on the
threshold looking over a heap of Lavrans' squirrel-

skins. Gunhild was a widow who went the round of the farms and sewed fur-lining into cloaks and the like. And Kristin guessed from their talk that now it was she should have a new cloak, lined with squirrel-skin and edged with marten. And then she knew she was to go with her father, and she sprang up in bed and shrieked with gladness.

Her mother came over to her and stroked her cheek:

"Are you so glad, then, my daughter, you are going so far from me?"

Ragnfrid said the same that morning they were to set out. They were up at cock-crow; it was dark without, with thick mist between the houses, as Kristin peeped out of the door at the weather. The mist billowed like grey smoke round the lanterns, and out by the open house-doors. Folk ran 'twixt stables and out-houses, and women came from the kitchen with steaming porridge-pots and trenchers of meat and pork — they were to have a plenty of good, strong food before they rode out into the morning cold.

Indoors, saddle-bags were shut and opened, and forgotten things packed inside. Ragnfrid called to her husband's mind all the errands he must do for her, and spoke of kin and friends upon the way — he must greet this one and not forget to ask for that one.

Kristin ran out and in; she said farewell many times to all in the house, and could not hold still a moment in any place.

"Are you so glad, then, Kristin, you are going from me so far and for so long?" asked her mother. Kristin was abashed and uneasy, and wished her mother had not said this. But she answered as best she could:

"No, dear my mother, but I am glad that I am to go with father."

"Ay, that you are indeed," said Ragnfrid, sighing. Then she kissed the child and put the last touches to her dress.

At last they were in the saddle, the whole train —

Kristin rode on Morvin, who ere now had been her
father's saddle-horse — he was old, wise and steady.
Ragnfrid held up the silver stoup with the stirrup-cup
to her husband, and laid a hand upon her daughter's
knee and bade her bear in mind all her mother had
taught her.

And so they rode out of the courtyard in the grey
light. The fog lay white as milk upon the parish. But
in a while it began to grow thinner and the sunlight
sifted through. And, dripping with dew, there shone
through the white haze hillsides green with the after-
math, and pale stubble fields, and yellow trees, and
rowans bright with red berries. Glimpses of blue
mountain-sides seemed rising through the steamy haze
— then the mist broke and drove in wreaths across the
slopes, and they rode down the Dale in the most glorious sunshine, Kristin in front of the troop at her father's
side.

They came to Hamar one dark and rainy evening,
with Kristin sitting in front on her father's saddle-bow,
for she was so weary that all things swam before her
eyes — the lake that gleamed wanly on their right, the
gloomy trees which dripped wet upon them as they
rode beneath, and the dark, leaden clusters of houses
on the hueless, sodden fields by the wayside.

She had stopped counting the days — it seemed as
though she had been an endless time on the journey.
They had visited kindred and friends all down the
Dale; she had made acquaintance with children on the
great manors and had played in strange houses and
barns and courtyards, and had worn many times her
red dress with the silk sleeves. They had rested by the
roadside by day when the weather was fair; Arne had
gathered nuts for her and she had slept after meals
upon the saddle-bags wherein were their clothes. At
one great house they had silk-covered pillows in
their beds; but one night they lay at an inn, and in one
of the other beds was a woman who lay and wept

softly and bitterly each time Kristin was awake. But every night she had slumbered safely behind her father's broad, warm back.

Kristin awoke with a start — she knew not where she was, but the wondrous ringing and booming sound she had heard in her dream went on. She was lying alone in a bed, and on the hearth of the room a fire was burning.

She called upon her father, and he rose from the hearth where he had been sitting, and came to her along with a stout woman.

"Where are we?" she asked; and Lavrans laughed, and said:

"We're in Hamar now, and here is Margret, the wife of Fartein the shoemaker. You must greet her prettily now, for you slept when we came thither. But now Margret will help you to your clothes."

"Is it morning, then?" said Kristin. "I thought you were even now coming to bed. Oh! do *you* help me," she begged; but Lavrans said, something sternly, that she should rather be thankful to kind Margret for helping her.

"And see what she has for you for a gift!"

'Twas a pair of red shoes with silken latchets. The woman smiled at Kristin's glad face, and drew on her shift and hose up on the bed, that she should not need to tread barefoot upon the clay floor.

"What is it makes such a noise," asked Kristin, "like a church bell, but many bells?"

"Ay, those are our bells," laughed Margret. "Have you not heard of the great minister here in the town? — 'tis there you are going now. There goes the great bell! And now 'tis ringing in the cloister and in the church of Holy Cross as well."

Margret spread the butter thick upon Kristin's bread and gave her honey in her milk, that the food she took might stand in more stead — she had scant time to eat.

Out of doors it was still dark and the weather had

fallen frosty. The fog was biting cold. The footprints
of folk and of cattle and horses were hard as though
cast in iron, so that Kristin bruised her feet in the thin,
new shoes, and once she trod through the ice on the
gutter in the middle of the street and her legs got wet
and cold. Then Lavrans took her on his back and
carried her.

She strained her eyes in the gloom, but there was
not much she could see of the town — she caught a
glimpse of black housegables and trees through the
grey air. Then they came out upon a little meadow
that shone with rime, and upon the farther side of the
meadow she dimly saw a pale grey building, big as a
fell. Great stone houses stood about, and at points lights
glimmered from window-holes in the walls. The bells,
which had been silent for a time, took to ringing again,
and now it was with a sound so strong that a cold
shiver ran down her back.

'Twas like going into the mountain-side, thought
Kristin, when they mounted into the church forehall;
it struck chill and dark in there. They went through a
door, and were met by the stale, cold smell of incense
and candles. Now Kristin was in a dark and vastly
lofty place. She could not see where it ended, neither
above nor to the sides, but lights burned upon an altar
far in front. There stood a priest, and the echoes of his
voice stole strangely round the great place, like breath-
ings and whisperings. Her father signed the cross with
holy water upon himself and the child, and so they
went forward; though he stepped warily, his spurs
rang loudly on the stone floor. They passed by giant
pillars, and betwixt the pillars it was like looking into
coal-black holes.

Forward, nigh to the altar, the father bent his knee,
and Kristin knelt beside him. She began to be able to
make things out in the gloom — gold and silver glittered on altars in between the pillars, but upon that
before them shone tapers which stood and burned on
gilt candlesticks, while the light streamed back from

the holy vessels and the big beautiful picture-panel
behind. Kristin was brought again to think of the
mountain-folk's hall — even so had she dreamed it
must be, splendid like this, but maybe with yet more
lights. And the dwarf-maid's face came up before her
— but then she raised her eyes and spied upon the wall
above the altar Christ Himself, great and stern, lifted
high upon the Cross. Fear came upon her — He did
not look mild and sorrowful as at home in their own
snug timber-brown church, where He hung heavily,
with pierced feet and hands, and bowed his blood-
besprinkled head beneath the crown of thorns. Here
He stood upon a footboard with stiff, outstretched
arms and upright head; His gilded hair glittered; He
was crowned with a crown of gold, and His face was
upturned and harsh.

Then she tried to follow the priest's words as he
read and chanted, but his speech was too hurried and
unclear. At home she was wont to understand each
word, for Sira Eirik had the clearest speech, and had
taught her what the holy words betokened in Norse,
that she might the better keep her thoughts with God
while she was in church.

But she could not do that here, for every moment she
grew ware of something new in the darkness. There
were windows high up in the walls, and these began
to shimmer with the day. And near by where they
knelt there was raised a wondrous scaffolding of
timber, but beyond lay blocks of light-coloured stone;
and there stood mortar-troughs and tools — and she
heard folks coming tiptoeing about in there. But then
again her eyes fell upon the stern Lord Christ upon
the wall, and she strove to keep her thoughts fixed
upon the service. The icy cold from the stone floor
stiffened her legs right up to the thighs, and her knees
gave her pain. At length everything began to sway
about her, so weary was she.

Then her father rose; the mass was at an end. The
priest came forward and greeted her father. While they

spoke, Kristin sate herself down upon a step, for she
saw the choir-boy had done the like. He yawned —
and so she too fell a-yawning. When he marked that
she looked at him, he set his tongue in his cheek and
twisted his eyes at her. Thereupon he dug up a pouch
from under his clothing and emptied upon the flags all
that was in it — fish-hooks, lumps of lead, leather
things and a pair of dice, and all the while he made
signs to her. Kristin wondered mightily.

But now the priest and her father looked at the
children. The priest laughed, and bade the boy be gone
back to school, but Lavrans frowned and took Kristin
by the hand.

It began to grow lighter in the church now. Kristin
clung sleepily to Lavrans' hand, while he and the priest
walked beneath the pile of timber and talked of Bishop
Ingjald's building-work.

They wandered all about the church, and in the end
went out into the forehall. Thence a stone stairway led
to the western tower. Kristin tumbled wearily up the
steps. The priest opened a door to a fair chapel, and
her father said that Kristin should set herself without
upon the steps and wait while he went to shrift; and
thereafter she could come in and kiss St. Thomas's
shrine.

At that there came an old monk in an ash-brown
frock from out the chapel. He stopped a moment,
smiled at the child, and drew forth some sacks and
wadmal cloths which had been stuck into a hole in
the wall. These he spread upon the landing.

"Sit you here, and you will not be so cold," said he,
and passed down the steps upon his naked feet.

Kristin was sleeping when Canon Martein, as the
priest was called, came out and wakened her with a
touch. Up from the church sounded the sweetest of
song, and in the chapel candles burned upon the altar.
The priest made sign that she should kneel by her
father's side, and then he took down a little golden
shrine which stood above the communion-table. He

whispered to her that in it was a piece of St. Thomas of Canterbury's bloody garments, and he pointed at the saint's figure on the shrine that Kristin might press her lips to his feet.

The lovely tones still streamed from the church as they came down the steps; Canon Martein said 'twas the organist practising his art and the schoolboys singing; but they had not the time to stay and listen, for her father was hungry — he had come fasting for confession — and they were now bound for the guest-room of the canons' close to take their food.

The morning sun without was gilding the steep shores on the farther side of the great lake, and all the groves of yellowing leaf-trees shone like gold-dust amid the dark-blue pine-woods. The lake ran in waves with small dancing white caps of foam to their heads. The wind blew cold and fresh, and the many-hued leaves drifted down upon the rimy hillsides.

A band of riders came forth from between the Bishop's palace and the house of the Brothers of Holy Cross. Lavrans stepped aside and bowed with a hand upon his breast, while he all but swept the sward with his hat, so Kristin could guess the nobleman in the fur cloak must be the Bishop himself, and she curtsied to the ground.

The Bishop reined in his horse, and gave back the greeting; he beckoned Lavrans to him and spoke with him a while. In a short space Lavrans came back to the priest and child, and said:

"Now am I bidden to eat at the Bishop's palace — think you, Canon Martein, that one of the serving-men of the canonry could go with this little maid of mine home to Fartein the shoemaker's, and bid my men send Halvdan to meet me here with Guldsveinen at the hour of nones."

The priest answered, doubtless what he asked could be done. But on this the bare-footed monk who had spoken to Kristin on the tower stairs came forward and saluted them:

"There is a man here in our guest-house who has an errand of his own to the shoemaker's; he can bear your bidding thither, Lavrans Björgulfsön, and your daughter can go with him or bide at the cloister with me till you yourself are for home. I shall see to it that she has her food there."

Lavrans thanked him, but said, " 'Twere shame you should be troubled with the child, brother Edvin —"

"Brother Edvin draws to himself all the children he can lay hands upon," said Canon Martein, and laughed. " 'Tis in this wise he gets some one to preach to —"

"Ay, before you learned lords here in Hamar I dare not proffer my poor discourses," said the monk without anger, and smiling. "All I am fit for is to talk to children and peasants, but even so 'tis not well, we know, to muzzle the ox that treadeth out the corn."

Kristin looked up at her father beseechingly; she thought there was nothing she would like more than to go with Brother Edvin. So Lavrans gave thanks again, and while her father and the priest went after the Bishop's train, Kristin laid her hand in the monk's, and they went down towards the cloister, a cluster of wooden houses and a light-hued stone church far down by the lake-side.

Brother Edvin gave her hand a little squeeze, and as they looked at one another they had both to laugh. The monk was thin and tall, but very stoop-backed; the child thought him like an old crane in the head, for 'twas little, with a small, shining, bald pate above a shaggy, white rim of hair, and set upon a long, thin, wrinkled neck. His nose was large too, and pointed like a beak. But 'twas something which made her light of heart and glad, only to look up into the long, narrow, deep-lined face. The old, sea-blue eyes were red-rimmed and the lids brown and thin as flakes. A thousand wrinkles spread out from them; the wizened cheeks with the reddish network of veins were scored with furrows which ran down towards the thin-lipped mouth, but 'twas as though Brother Edvin had grown thus wrinkled only through smiling at mankind. Kristin thought she had never seen any one so blithe and gentle; it seemed he bore some bright and privy gladness within which she would get to know of when he began to speak.

They followed the fence of an apple-orchard where there still hung upon the trees a few red and golden fruit. Two Preaching Brothers in black-and-white gowns were raking together withered beanshaws in the garden.

The cloister was not much unlike any other farm steading, and the guest-house whither the monk led Kristin was most like a poor peasant's house, though there were many bedsteads in it. In one of the beds lay an old man, and by the hearth sat a woman swathing a little child; two bigger children, boy and girl, stood beside her.

They murmured, both the man and the woman, that they had not been given their breakfast yet: "None will be at the pains to bear in food to us twice in the day, so we must e'en starve while you run about the town, Brother Edvin!"

"Nay, be not peevish, Steinulv," said the monk. "Come hither and make your greetings, Kristin — see this bonny, sweet little maid who is to stay and eat with us to-day."

He told how Steinulv had fallen sick on the way home from a fair, and had got leave to lie here in the cloister guest-house, for he had a kinswoman dwelling in the spital, and she was so cursed he could not endure to be there with her.

"But I see well enough, they will soon be weary of having me here," said the peasant. "When you set forth again, Brother Edvin, there will be none here that has time to tend me, and they will surely have me to the spital again."

"Oh, you will be well and strong long before I am done with my work in the church," said Brother Edvin. "Then your son will come and fetch you — "

He took up a kettle of hot water from the hearth and let Kristin hold it while he tended Steinulv. Thereupon the old man grew somewhat easier, and soon after there came in a monk with food and drink for them.

Brother Edvin said grace over the meat, and set himself on the edge of the bed by Steinulv that he might help him to take his food. Kristin went and sat by the woman and gave the boy to eat, for he was so little he could not well reach up to the porridge-dish, and he spilled upon himself when he tried to dip into the beer-bowl. The woman was from Hadeland, and she was come hither with her man and her children to see her brother who was a monk here in the cloister. But he was away wandering among the country parishes, and she grumbled much that they must lie here and waste their time.

Brother Edvin spoke the woman fair: she must not say she wasted time when she was here in Bishopsha-mar. Here were all the brave churches, and the monks and canons held masses and sang the livelong day and night — and the city was fine, finer than Oslo even, though 'twas somewhat less; but here were gardens to almost every dwelling-place: "You should have seen it when I came hither in the spring — 'twas white with blossom over all the town. And after, when the sweetbriar burst forth — "

"Ay, and much good is that to me now," said the woman sourly. "And here are more of holy places than of holiness, methinks — "

The monk laughed a little and shook his head. Then he routed amidst the straw of his bed and brought forth a great handful of apples and pears which he shared amongst the children. Kristin had never tasted such good fruit. The juice ran out from the corners of her mouth every bite she took.

But now Brother Edvin must go to the church, he said, and Kristin should go with him. Their path went slantwise across the close, and, by a little side wicket, they passed into the choir.

They were still building at this church as well, so that here, too, there stood a tall scaffolding in the cross where nave and transepts met. Bishop Engjald was bettering and adorning the choir, said Brother Edvin. The Bishop had great wealth, and all his riches he used for the adornment of the churches here in the town; he was a noble bishop and a good man. The Preaching Friars in St. Olav's cloister were good men too, clean-living, learned and humble. 'Twas a poor cloister, but they had made him most welcome — Brother Edvin had his home in the Minorite cloister at Oslo, but he had leave to spend a term here in Hamar diocese.

"But now come hither," said he, and led Kristin forward to the foot of the scaffolding. First he climbed up a ladder and laid some boards straight up there, and then he came down again and helped the child up with him.

Upon the greystone wall above her Kristin saw wondrous fluttering flecks of light; red as blood and yellow as beer, blue and brown and green. She would have turned to look behind her, but the monk whispered, "Turn not about." But when they stood together high upon the planking, he turned her gently round, and Kristin saw a sight so fair she almost lost her breath.

Right over against her on the nave's south wall stood a picture, and shone as if it were made of naught but gleaming precious stones. The many-hued flecks of light upon the wall came from rays which stood out from that picture; she herself and the monk stood in the midst of the glory; her hands were red as though dipped in wine; the monk's visage seemed all golden, and his dark frock threw the picture's colours softly back. She looked up at him questioningly, but he only nodded and smiled.

'Twas like standing far off and looking into the heavenly kingdom. Behind a network of black streaks, she made out little by little the Lord Christ Himself in the most precious of red robes, the Virgin Mary in raiment blue as heaven, holy men and maidens in shining yellow and green and violet array. They stood below arches and pillars of glimmering houses, wound about with branches and twigs of strange bright leafage.

The monk drew her a little farther out upon the staging.

"Stand here," he whispered, "and 'twill shine right upon you from Christ's own robe."

From the church beneath there rose to them a faint odour of incense and the smell of cold stone. It was dim below, but the sun's rays slanted in through a row of window-bays in the nave's south wall. Kristin began to understand that the heavenly picture must be a sort of window-pane, for it filled just such an opening. The others were empty or filled with panes of horn set in wooden frames. A bird came, set itself upon a window-sill, twittered a little and flew away, and outside the wall of the choir they heard the clank of metal on stone. All else was still; only the wind came in small puffs, sighed a little round about the church walls and died away.

"Ay, ay," said Brother Edvin, and sighed. "No one here in the land can make the like — they paint on glass, 'tis true, in Nidaros, but not like this. But away in the lands of the south, Kristin, in the great minsters, there they have such picture-panes, big as the doors of the church here — "

Kristin thought of the pictures in the church at home. There was St. Olav's altar, and St. Thomas of Canterbury's altar, with pictures on their front panels and on the tabernacles behind; but those pictures seemed to her dull and lustreless as she thought of them now.

They went down the ladder and up into the choir. There stood the altar-table, naked and bare, and on the stone slab were set many small boxes and cups of metal and wood and earthenware; strange little knives and irons, pens and brushes lay about. Brother Edvin said these were his gear; he plied the crafts of painting pictures and carving altar-tabernacles, and the fine panels which stood yonder by the choir-stalls were his work. They were for the altar-pieces here in the Preaching Friars' church.

Kristin watched how he mixed up coloured powders and stirred them into little cups of stoneware, and he let her help him bear the things away to a bench by the wall. While the monk went from one panel to another and painted fine red lines in the bright hair of the holy men and women so that one could see it curl and crinkle, Kristin kept close at his heels and gazed and questioned, and he explained to her what it was that he had limned.

On the one panel sat Christ in a chair of gold, and St. Nicholas and St. Clement stood beneath a roof by His side. And at the sides was painted St. Nicholas' life and works. In one place he sat as a suckling child upon his mother's knee; he turned away from the breast she reached him, for he was so holy that from the very cradle he would not suck more than once on Fridays. Alongside of that was a picture of him as he laid the money-purses before the door of the house where dwelt the three maids who were so poor they could not find husbands. She saw how he healed the Roman knight's child, and saw the knight sailing in a boat with the false chalice in his hands. He had vowed the holy bishop a chalice of gold which had been in his house a thousand years, as guerdon for bringing his son back to health again. But he was minded to trick St. Nicholas, and gave him a false chalice instead; therefore the boy fell into the sea with the true beaker in his hands. But St. Nicholas led the child unhurt underneath the water and up on to the shore, just as his father stood in St. Nicholas' church and offered the false vessel. It all stood painted upon the panels in gold and the fairest colours.

On another panel sat the Virgin Mary with the Christ-child on her knee; He pressed His mother's chin with the one hand, and held an apple in the other. Beside them stood St. Sunniva * and St. Christina. They bowed in lovely wise from their waists, their faces were the fairest red and white, and they had golden hair and golden crowns.

Brother Edvin steadied himself with the left hand on the right wrist, and painted leaves and roses on the crowns.

"The dragon is all too small, methinks," said Kristin, looking at her holy namesake's picture. "It looks not as though it could swallow up the maiden."

"And that it could not either," said Brother Edvin. "It was not bigger. Dragons and all such-like that serve the devil, seem great only so long as fear is in ourselves. But if a man seek God fervently and with all his soul, so that his longing wins into his strength, then does the devil's power suffer at once such great downfall that his tools become small and powerless — dragons and evil spirits sink down and become no bigger than sprites and cats and crows. You see that the whole mountain St. Sunniva was in is no larger than that she can wrap it within the skirt of her gown."

"But were they not in the caves, then," asked Kristin, "St. Sunniva and the Selje-men? Is not that true?"

The monk twinkled at her, and smiled again:

" 'Tis both true and untrue. It seemed so to the folk who found the holy bodies. And true it is that it seemed so to Sunniva and the Selje-men, for they were humble and thought only that the world is stronger than all sinful mankind, and they thought not that they themselves were stronger than the world, because they loved it not. But had they but known it, they could have taken all the hills and slung them forth into the sea like so many pebbles. No one, nor anything, can harm us, child, save what we fear or love."

---

* St. Sunniva, see Note 8.

"But if a body doth not fear nor love God?" asked Kristin, affrighted.

The monk took her yellow hair in his hand, bent Kristin's head back gently, and looked down into her face; his eyes were wide open and blue.

"There is no man nor woman, Kristin, who does not love and fear God, but 'tis because our hearts are divided twixt love of God and fear of the devil and fondness for the world and the flesh, that we are unhappy in life and death. For if a man had not any yearning after God and God's being, then should he thrive in hell, and 'twould be we alone who would not understand that there he had gotten what his heart desired. For there the fire would not burn him if he did not long for coolness, nor would he feel the torment of the serpents' bite, if he knew not the yearning after peace."

Kristin looked up in his face; she understood none of all this. Brother Edvin went on:

" 'Twas God's loving-kindness towards us that, seeing how our hearts are drawn asunder, He came down and dwelt among us, that He might taste in the flesh the lures of the devil when He decoys us with power and splendour, as well as the menace of the world when it offers us blows and scorn and sharp nails in hands and feet. In such wise did He show us the way and make manifest His love — "

He looked down upon the child's grave, set face — then he laughed a little, and said with quite another voice:

"Do you know who 'twas that first knew our Lord had caused Himself to be born? 'Twas the cock; he saw the star, and so he said — all the beasts could talk Latin in those days; he cried: 'Christus natus est!' "

He crowed these last words so like a cock that Kristin fell to laughing heartily. And it did her good to laugh, for all the strange things Brother Edvin had just been saying had laid a burden of awe on her heart. The monk laughed himself:

"Ay, and when the ox heard that, he began to low: 'Ubi, ubi, ubi.'

"But the goat bleated, and said: 'Betlem, Betlem, Betlem!'

"And the sheep longed so to see Our Lady and her Son that she baa-ed out at once: 'Eamus, eamus!'

"And the new-born calf that lay in the straw, raised itself and stood upon its feet. 'Volo, volo, volo!' it said.

"You never heard that before? No, I can believe it; I know that he is a worthy priest, that Sira Eirik that you have up in your parts, and learned; but he knows not this, I warrant; for a man does not learn it except he journey to Paris — "

"Have *you* been to Paris, then?" asked the child.

"God bless you, little Kristin, I have been in Paris and have travelled round elsewhere in the world as well; and you must not believe aught else than that I am afraid of the devil, and love and covet like any other fool. But I hold fast to the Cross with all my might — one must cling to it like a kitten to a lath when it has fallen in the sea.

"And you, Kristin — how would you like to offer up this bonny hair and serve Our Lady like these brides I have figured here?"

"We have no child at home but me," answered Kristin. "So 'tis like that I must marry. And I trow mother has chests and lockers with my bridal gear standing ready even now."

"Ay, ay," said Brother Edvin, and stroked her forehead. " 'Tis thus that folk deal with their children now. To God they give the daughters who are lame or purblind or ugly, or blemished, or they let Him have back the children when they deem Him to have given them more than they need. And then they wonder that all who dwell in the cloisters are not holy men and maids — "

Brother Edvin took her into the sacristy and showed her the cloister books which stood there in a bookcase; there were the fairest pictures in them. But when one of the monks came in, Brother Edvin made as though he were but seeking an ass's head to copy. Afterwards he shook his head at himself:

"Ay, there you see what fear does, Kristin — but they're so fearful about their books in the house here. Had I the true faith and love, I would not stand here as I do, and lie to Brother Aasulv — . But then I could take these old fur mittens here and hang them upon yonder sunbeam — "

She was with the monk to dinner over in the guest-house, but for the rest she sat in the church the whole day and watched his work and chatted with him. And first when Lavrans came to fetch her, did either she or the monk remember the message that should have been sent to the shoemaker.

Afterwards Kristin remembered these days in Hamar better than all else that befell her on the long journey. Oslo, indeed, was a greater town than Hamar, but now that she had seen a market-town, it did not seem to her so notable. Nor did she deem it as fair at Skog as at Jörundgaard, though the houses were grander — but she was glad she was not to dwell there. The manor lay upon a hillside; below was the Botnfjord, grey, and sad with dark forest; and on the farther shore and behind the houses the forest stood with the sky right down upon the tree-tops. There were no high, steep fells as at home, to hold the heavens high above one, and to keep the sight sheltered and in bounds so that the world might seem neither too big nor too little.

The journey home was cold; it was nigh upon Advent; but, when they were come a little way up the Dale, snow was lying, and so they borrowed sleighs and drove most of the way.

With the affair of the estates it fell out so that Lavrans made Skog over to his brother Aasmund, keeping the right of redemption for himself and his heirs.

3

THE SPRING after Kristin's long journey, Ragnfrid bore her husband another daughter. Both father and mother had wished indeed that it might be a son, but they soon took comfort, and were filled with the tenderest love for little Ulvhild. She was a most fair child, healthy, good, happy and quiet. Ragnfrid doted so on this new baby that she went on suckling it during the second year of its life; wherefore, on Sira Eirik's counsel, she left off somewhat her strict fasts and religious exercises while she had the child at the breast. On this account and by reason of her joy in Ulvhild, her bloom came back to her, and Lavrans thought he had never seen his wife so happy or so fair and kindly in all the years he had been wed.

Kristin, too, felt that great happiness had come to them with this tender little sister. That her mother's heavy mood made a stillness about her home had never come into her thought; she had deemed it was but as it should be that her mother should correct and chide her, while her father played and jested with her. But Ragnfrid was much gentler with her now and gave her more freedom; petted her more, too; and so Kristin little heeded that her mother had much less time to tend her. She loved Ulvhild as much as the others, and was joyful when they let her carry or rock her sister, and in time there was still more sport with the little one when she began to creep and walk and talk and Kristin could play with her.

Thus there went by three good years for the Jörundgaard folk. They had fortune with them in many ways, and Lavrans built and bettered round about on the manor, for the buildings and cattlesheds were old and small when he came thither — the Gjeslings had had the place leased but for more life-times than one.

Now it fell out at Whitsuntide in the third year that

Trond Ivarsön, from Sundbu, with his wife Gudrid and his three small sons, were come to Jörundgaard to visit them. One morning the older folk were sitting talking in the balcony of the loft-room, while the children played about in the courtyard below. In the yard Lavrans had begun a new dwelling-house, and the children were climbing and creeping about on the timber brought together for the building. One of the Gjesling boys had struck at Ulvhild and made her weep; and at that Trond came down and gave his son a buffet, and took Ulvhild up into his arms. She was the fairest and sweetest child a man's eyes could see, and her uncle had much love for her, though else he cared not for children.

Just then there came a man across the court from the cattle-yard, dragging at a great black bull; but the bull was savage and unmanageable and broke away from the man. Trond sprang up upon the pile of timber, driving the bigger children up before him, but he had Ulvhild in his arms and his youngest son by the hand. Then a beam turned under his feet and Ulvhild slipped from his grasp and fell to the ground. The beam slipped after, rolled over on the child and lay across her back.

Lavrans was down from the balcony in the same instant; he ran up and was in act to lift the beam when the bull rushed at him. He tried to seize it by the horns, but was flung down and gored. But getting then a grip of its nostrils, he half raised himself from the ground and managed to hold the brute till Trond came to himself from his bewilderment, and the farm servants, running from the houses, cast thongs about the beast and held it fast.

Ragnfrid was on her knees trying to lift the beam; and now Lavrans was able to ease it so far that she could draw the child from under and into her lap. The little one wailed piteously when they touched her, but her mother sobbed aloud: "She lives, thank God, she lives — !"

It was great wonder the child had not been quite crushed; but the log had chanced to fall so that it rested with one end upon a stone in the grass. When Lavrans stood up again, blood was running from the corners of his mouth, and his clothes were all torn at the breast by the bull's horns.

Tordis came running with a skin coverlet; warily she and Ragnfrid moved the child on to it, but it seemed as though she suffered unbearable pain at the lightest touch. Her mother and Tordis bore her into the winter-room.

Kristin stood upon the timber-pile, white and stock-still, while the little boys clung round her weeping. All the house and farm folk were now huddled together in the courtyard, the women weeping and wailing. Lavrans bade them saddle Guldsveinen and another horse as well; but when Arne came with the horses, Lavrans fell to the ground when he tried to climb to the saddle. So he bade Arne ride for the priest, while Halvdan went southward for a leech-woman who dwelt by the meeting of the rivers.

Kristin saw that her father was ashy white in the face, and that he had bled till his light blue garments were covered all over with red-brown stains. All at once he stood upright, snatched an axe from one of the men and went forward where some of the folk stood holding on to the bull. He smote the beast between the horns with the back of the axe — it dropped forward on its knees; but Lavrans ceased not striking till its blood and brains were scattered all about. Then a fit of coughing took him and he sank backwards on the ground. Trond and another man came to him and bore him within the house.

At that Kristin thought her father was surely dead; she screamed loudly and ran after, calling to him as if her heart were breaking.

In the winter-room Ulvhild had been laid on the great bed — all the pillows were thrown out upon the floor, so that the child lay flat. 'Twas as though already she lay stretched upon the dead-straw. But she wailed loudly and without cease, and her mother lay bent over her, soothing and patting the child, wild with grief that she could do naught to help her.

Lavrans lay upon the other bed: he rose and staggered across the floor that he might comfort his wife. At that she started up, and shrieked:

"Touch me not, touch me not! Jesus, Jesus — 'twere liker you should strike me dead — never will it end, the ill-fortune I bring upon you — "

"You! Dear my wife, 'tis not you that have brought this on us," said Lavrans, and laid a hand upon her shoulder. She shuddered at that, and her light grey eyes shone in her lean, sallow face.

"Doubtless she means that 'twas my doing," said Trond Ivarsön roughly. His sister looked at him with hate in her eyes, and answered:

"Trond knows what I mean."

Kristin ran forward to her parents, but both thrust her away from them; and Tordis, coming in with a kettle of hot water, took her gently by the shoulder, and said, "Go — go over to our house, Kristin; you are in the way here."

Tordis was for seeing to Lavrans' hurt — he had set himself down on the step before the bed — but he said there was little amiss with him:

"But is there naught you can do to ease Ulvhild's pain a little — God help us! her crying would move the very stones in the mountain-side!"

"Nay; we dare not touch her ere the priest or Ingegjerd, the leech-wife, comes," said Tordis.

Arne came just then with word that Sira Eirik was not at home. Ragnfrid stood a while wringing her hands. Then she said:

"Send to Lady Aashild of Haugen! Naught matters now, if only Ulvhild may be saved — "

No one gave heed to Kristin. She crept on to the bench behind the bed's head, crouched down and laid her head upon her knees.

It seemed to her now as if stony hands were pressing on her heart. Lady Aashild was to be fetched! Her mother would not have them send for Lady Aashild, even when she herself was near death's door at Ulvhild's birth, nor yet when Kristin was so sick of the fever. She was a witch-wife, folk said — the Bishop of Oslo and the chapter had held session on her; and she must have been put to death or even burned, had it not been that she was of such high birth and had been like a sister to Queen Ingebjörg — but folk said she had given her first husband poison, and him she now had, Sir Björn, she had drawn to her by witch-craft; he was young enough to be her son. She had children too, but they came never to see their mother, and these two highborn folk, Björn and Aashild, lived upon a petty farm in Dovre, and had lost all their wealth. None of the great folk in Dale would have to do with them; but, privily, folk sought her counsel — nay, poor folk went openly to her with their troubles and hurts; they said she was kind, but they feared her too.

Kristin thought her mother, who else was wont to pray so much, should rather have called on God and the Virgin now. She tried to pray herself — to St. Olav most of all, for she knew he was so good and helped so many who suffered from sickness and wounds or broken bones. But she could not keep her thoughts together.

Her father and mother were alone in the room now. Lavrans had laid himself upon his bed again, and Ragnfrid sat bent over the sick child, passing, from time to time, a damp cloth over her forehead and hands, and wetting her lips with wine.

A long time went by. Tordis looked in between whiles, and would fain have helped, but Ragnfrid sent her out each time. Kristin wept silently and prayed to herself, but all the while she thought of the witch-wife and waited eagerly to see her come in.

Suddenly Ragnfrid asked in the silence:

"Are you sleeping, Lavrans?"

"No," answered her husband. "I am listening to Ulvhild. God will surely help His innocent lamb, wife — we dare not doubt it. But 'tis weary lying here waiting — "

"God," said Ragnfrid hopelessly, "hates me for my sins. 'Tis well with my children, where they are, I doubt not that; and now 'tis like Ulvhild's hour has come, too — but me He has cast off, for my heart is a viper's nest, full of sin and sorrow — "

Then some one lifted the latch — Sira Eirik stepped in, straightened his huge frame where he stood, and said in his clear, deep voice: "God help all in this house!"

The priest put the box with his medicines on the step before the bed, and went to the open hearth and poured warm water over his hands. Then he took a cross from his bosom, struck out with it to all four corners of the room and mumbled something in Latin. Thereupon he opened the smoke-vent, so that the light might stream into the room, and went and looked at Ulvhild.

Kristin grew afraid he might find her and send her out — not often did Sira Eirik's eyes let much escape them. But the priest did not look round. He took a flask from the box, poured somewhat upon a wad of finely carded wool and laid it over Ulvhild's mouth and nose.

"Now she will soon suffer less," said the priest. He went to Lavrans and tended his wounds, while they told him how the mishap had come to pass. Lavrans had two ribs broken and had a wound in the lungs; but the priest thought that for him there was no great fear.

"And Ulvhild?" asked the father fearfully.

"I will tell you when I have looked at her more nearly," answered the priest; "but you must lie in the loft-room, so that there may be more quiet and room here for those who must tend her." He laid Lavrans' arm about his own shoulder, took firm hold under the man, and bore him out. Kristin would fain have gone with her father now, but she dared not show herself.

When Sira Eirik came back, he did not speak to Ragnfrid, but first cut the clothes off Ulvhild, who now moaned less and seemed half asleep. Then carefully he felt with his hands over the child's body and limbs.

"Is it so ill with my child, Eirik, that you know not how to save her, since you say naught?" asked Ragnfrid under her breath.

The priest answered low:

"It seems as though her back were badly hurt, Ragnfrid; I see no better way than to leave all in God's hands and St. Olav's — much there is not that I can do."

"Then must we pray!" cried the mother passionately. "You know well that Lavrans and I will give you all you ask and spare nothing, if so be your prayers can win God to grant that Ulvhild may live."

"'Twould seem to me a miracle," said the priest, "were she to live and have her health again."

"And is't not of miracles that you preach late and early — believe you not that a miracle can happen with my child?" she said, as wildly as before.

"'Tis true," replied the priest, "that miracles happen; but God does not grant the prayers of all — we know not His secret counsel. And think you not, it would be worst of all should this fair little maid grow up marred or crippled?"

Ragnfrid shook her head. She wailed softly:

"I have lost so many, priest; I cannot lose her too!"

"I will do all that I may," answered the priest, "and pray with all my power. But you must strive, Ragnfrid, to bear the cross God lays upon you."

The mother moaned low:

"None of my children have I loved like this little one — if she too be taken from me, full sure I am my heart will break."

"God help you, Ragnfrid Ivarsdatter," said Sira Eirik, and shook his head. "In all your praying and fasting, you have thought only to force your will upon God. Can you wonder that it has helped but little?"

Ragnfrid looked defiantly at the priest, and spoke: "I have sent for the Lady Aashild even now."

"Ay, you know her; I know her not," replied the priest.

"I cannot live without Ulvhild," said Ragnfrid as before. "If so be God will not help her, I will seek counsel of Lady Aashild, or e'en give myself to the devil if he will help!"

The priest looked as though he would answer sharply, but checked himself again. He bent and felt the limbs of the little sick girl once more.

"Her hands and feet are cold," he said. "We must lay jars of hot water about her — and then you must touch her no more till Lady Aashild comes."

Kristin let herself sink back noiselessly on the bench and lay as if asleep. Her heart beat hard with fear — she had understood but little of the talk between Sira Eirik and her mother, but it had frighted her terribly, and the child knew well that it had not been for her ears.

Her mother rose up to go for the hot-water jars, and suddenly she burst out sobbing: "But yet pray for us, Sira Eirik!"

Soon after she came back with Tordis. Then the priest and the women busied themselves with Ulvhild, and soon Kristin was found and sent away.

The light dazzled the child as she stood without in the courtyard. She had thought that most of the day must have gone by while she sat in the dark winter-room, and yet the houses stood there light-grey, and the grass was shining like silk in the white midday sunshine. The river gleamed behind the dun and golden trellis-work of the alder-brakes — it filled the air with its gladsome rushing sound, for here by Jörund-gaard it ran swiftly over a flat bed strewn with bould-ers. The mountain walls rose into the thin blue haze, and the becks sprang down their sides through the melting snows. The sweet, strong springtide out of doors brought tears to her eyes, for sorrow at the helplessness she felt all about her.

There was no one in the courtyard, but she heard voices in the house-carls' cottage. Fresh earth had been strewn over the spot where her father had killed the bull. She knew not what to do with herself, so she crept behind the wall of the new house — two log-courses had already been laid. Inside lay Ulvhild's play-things and her own; she put them all together and laid them in a hole between the lowest log and the foundation wall. Of late Ulvhild had wanted all her toys; this had vexed her sometimes. Now she thought, if her sister got well, she would give her all she had. And this thought comforted her a little.

She thought of the monk in Hamar — *he* was sure that miracles could happen for every one. But Sira Eirik was not so sure about it, nor parents either — and she was used to think as they did. A heavy weight fell upon her as it came to her for the first time that folk could think so unlike about so many things — not only bad, ungodly men and good men, but such men as Brother Edvin and Sira Eirik — even her mother and her father: she felt all at once that they too thought not alike about many things. . . .

Tordis found her there in the corner, asleep, late in the day, and took her to her own house; the child had eaten nothing since the morning. Tordis watched with Ragnfrid over Ulvhild through the night, and Kristin lay in Tordis' bed with Jon, Tordis' husband, and Eivind and Orm, their little boys. The smell of their bodies, the man's snoring and the children's even breathing made Kristin weep silently. It was no longer ago than last evening that she had lain down, as each night of her life before, by her own father and mother and little Ulvhild — it was as though a nest had been riven asunder and scattered and she herself lay cast out from the shelter of the wings which had always kept her warm. At last she cried herself to sleep, alone and unhappy among these strange folk.

Next morning as soon as she was up, she heard that her mother's brother and all his party had left the place — in anger; Trond had called his sister a foolish, crazy woman, and his brother-in-law a soft simpleton who had never known how to rule his wife. Kristin grew hot with wrath, but she was ashamed too — she understood well enough that a most unseemly thing had befallen in that her mother had driven her nearest kin from the house. And for the first time she dimly felt that there was something about her mother that was not as it should be — that she was not the same as other women.

While she stood brooding on this, a serving-maid came and said she was to go up to the loft-room to her father.

But when she was come into the room Kristin forgot to look at him, for right opposite the open door, with the light full upon her face, sat a little woman who she guessed must be the witch-wife. And yet Kristin had never thought that she would look like this.

She seemed small as a child and slightly made, as she sat in the great high-backed arm-chair which had been brought up thither. A table had been set before her too, covered with Ragnfrid's finest, fringed, linen tablecloth. Bacon and fowl were set out upon the silver platter; there was wine in a mazer bowl, and she had Lavrans' own silver goblet to drink from. She had finished eating and was busy drying her small and slender hands on one of Ragnfrid's best hand-towels. Ragnfrid herself stood in front of her and held for her a brass basin with water.

Lady Aashild let the hand-towel sink into her lap;

she smiled to the child and said in a clear and lovely voice:

"Come hither to me, child!" Then to her mother: "Fair children are these you have, Ragnfrid."

Her face was greatly wrinkled, but as clear white and pink as a child's, and it looked as though her skin must be just as soft and fine to the touch. Her mouth was as red and fresh as a young woman's, and her large, hazel eyes shone bright. A fine, white, linen headdress lay close about her face and was fastened under her chin with a gold clasp; over it she had a veil of soft, dark-blue wool; it fell over her shoulders and far down upon her dark, well-fitting dress. She was upright as a wand, and Kristin felt more than thought that she had never seen a woman so fair and so mannerly as was this old witch-wife, with whom the great folk of the valley would have naught to do.

Lady Aashild held Kristin's hand in her old, soft one, and spoke to her with kindly jesting; but Kristin could not answer a word. Then said Lady Aashild with a little laugh:

"Is she afraid of me, think you?"

"Nay, nay," Kristin all but shouted. And then Lady Aashild laughed still more, and said to the mother:

"She has wise eyes, this daughter of yours, and good strong hands, nor is she used to be idle, I can see. You will need one by and by to help you tend Ulvhild, when I am gone. 'Twere well, therefore, you let Kristin be by me and help while yet I am here . . . she is old enough for that; eleven years is she not?"

Thereupon the Lady Aashild went out, and Kristin would have followed her, but Lavrans called to her from his bed. He lay flat upon his back with the pillows stuffed beneath his up-drawn knees; Lady Aashild had bidden that he should lie so, that the hurt in his breast might sooner heal.

"Now surely you will soon be well, sir father, will you not?" asked Kristin.

Lavrans looked up at her — the child had never said "sir" to him before. Then he said gravely:

"For me there is naught to fear; 'tis worse with your sister."

"Aye," said Kristin, and sighed.

She stood yet a little while by his bed. Her father said no more, and Kristin found naught to say. And when Lavrans after a while said she should go down to her mother and Lady Aashild, Kristin hastened out and ran across the courtyard down into the winter-room.

4·

LADY AASHILD stayed on at Jörundgaard most of the summer. Thus it fell out that folk came thither seeking her counsel. . . . Kristin heard Sira Eirik fling at this now and then, and it came into her mind that her father and mother, too, were not pleased. But she put all thoughts of such things from her, nor did she ponder over what she thought of Lady Aashild, but was with her ever, and tired not of listening to the lady and of watching her.

Ulvhild still lay stretched upon her back in the great bed. Her little face was white to the lips, and dark rings had come about her eyes. Her lovely yellow hair had a stale smell, it had been unwashed for so long, and it had grown dark and lost all gloss and curl, so that it looked like old, burnt-up hay. She looked tired and suffering and patient; but she smiled faintly and wanly at her sister when Kristin sat down on the bed-side by her and chattered and showed the child all the fine gifts that were for her from her father and mother and from their friends and kinsfolk from far around. There were dolls and wooden birds and beasts, and a little draught-board, trinkets and velvet caps and coloured ribbons; Kristin kept them all together in a box for her — and Ulvhild looked at them all with her grave eyes, and, sighing, dropped the treasures from her weary hands.

But when Lady Aashild came nigh, Ulvhild's face lit up with gladness. Eagerly she drank the quenching and sleeping drinks Lady Aashild brewed for her; when Aashild tended her hurts she made no plaint, and lay happy listening when the lady played on Lavrans' harp and sang — she had great store of ballads strange to the folk of the Dale.

Often she sang to Kristin when Ulvhild lay asleep. And then at times she would tell of her youth, when she dwelt in the South at the courts of King Magnus and King Eirik and their Queens.

Once as they sat thus and Lady Aashild told of these things, there slipped from Kristin's lips a thought she had often had in mind:

"Methinks it is strange you can be so glad at all times, you who have been used to — " She broke off and grew red.

Lady Aashild looked down at the child with a smile:

"Mean you because I am parted from all that now?" She laughed quietly, and said: "I have had my happy time, Kristin, and I am not so foolish as to murmur, if now, since I have drunk up my wine and beer, I have to put up with skimmed milk and sour. Good days may last long if one lives wisely, and deals warily with what one has; all wise folk know that, and 'tis therefore, I trow, that wise folk must rest content with good days — for the best days of all cost very dear. In this world they call him a fool who wastes his heritage that he may make merry in the days of his youth. As to that, each man may deem as he lists. But that man only do I call a fool and a very dolt who rues his bargain after it is made; and twice a simpleton and a fool of fools is he who thinks to see more of his boon-companions after his heritage is gone . . ."

". . . Is there aught amiss with Ulvhild?" she called gently across to Ragnfrid, who had made a sharp movement where she sat by the child's bed.

"Nay, she sleeps well," said the child's mother, and came over to Lady Aashild and Kristin at the hearth. Her hands on the pole of the smoke-vent, she stood and looked down into Lady Aashild's face.

"Kristin doth not understand such things," she said.

"No," answered the lady. "But she learned her prayers, too, I doubt not, before she understood them. The times when we need prayers or counsel, we are little like to be in a mood to learn, nor yet to understand."

Ragnfrid drew her dark eyebrows together thoughtfully. At such times her bright, deep-set eyes looked like tarns below a dark-wooded hillside, so Kristin had often thought when she was little — or so she had heard others say. Lady Aashild looked at Ragnfrid with her little half-smile, and the mother seated herself upon the edge of the hearth, and, taking a twig, stuck it into the embers.

"But he who has wasted his heritage upon the sorriest goods — and thereafter beholds a treasure he would gladly give his life to own — think you not he must rue bitterly his own folly?"

"No doing without some rueing, Ragnfrid," said Lady Aashild. "And he who is willing to give his life should make a venture and see what he can win — "

Ragnfrid plucked the burning twig from the fire, blew out the flame and bent her hand about the glowing end, so that it shone out blood-red from between her fingers.

"Oh! these are words, words, and only words, Lady Aashild."

"Well," said the other, "truly Ragnfrid, there is not much that's worth buying so dear as with one's life."

"Nay, but there is," said Ragnfrid passionately; and she whispered it so it could scarce be heard: "My husband."

"Ragnfrid," said Lady Aashild, in a low voice, "so hath many a maid thought when she strove to bind a man to her and gave her maidenhood to do it. But have you not read of men and maids who gave to God all they owned, went into a cloister or naked into the wilds, and repented after. Ay, they are called fools in the godly books. And 'twould sure be sinful to think God cheated *them* over their bargain."

Ragnfrid sat quite still a while. Then Lady Aashild said:

"You must come now, Kristin; 'tis time we went and gathered dew for Ulvhild's morning wash."

Outside the courtyard lay all black and white in the moonlight. Ragnfrid went with them, through the farmyard, down to the gate of the cabbage garden. Kristin saw her mother's thin dark figure leaning there, while she was shaking the dew from the big, icy-cold cabbage leaves, and the folds of the lady's-mantles, into her father's silver goblet.

Lady Aashild walked silent at Kristin's side. She was there only to watch over her, for it was not well to let a child go out alone on such a night. But the dew had more virtue if gathered by an innocent maid.

When they came back to the gate Ragnfrid was gone. Kristin was shaking with the cold as she gave the icy silver cup into Lady Aashild's hands. She ran in her wet shoes over toward the loft-room, where she slept now with her father. She had her foot upon the first step when Ragnfrid stepped out of the shadow of the balcony. In her hands she bore a steaming bowl.

"Here, I have warmed some beer for you, daughter," said the mother.

Kristin thanked her mother gladly, and put the bowl to her lips. Then Ragnfrid asked:

"Kristin — the prayers and all the other things that Lady Aashild teaches you — you are sure there is naught sinful or ungodly in them?"

"That I can never believe," answered the child. "There is Jesus' name and the Virgin Mary's, and the names of the Saints in them all — "

"What is it she teaches you?" asked her mother again.

"Oh! — about herbs — and charms to stop running blood and cure warts and sore eyes — and moth in clothes and mice in the store-room. And what herbs one should pluck in sunshine, and which have virtue in the rain. . . . But the prayers I must not tell to any one, for then they lose their power," said she quickly.

Her mother took the empty bowl and put it upon the step. Then suddenly she threw her arms around her daughter, and pressed her tightly to her and kissed her. . . . Kristin felt that her mother's cheeks were wet and hot:

"May God and Our Lady guard and shield you from all evil — we have naught else but you, your father and I, that has not been touched by our ill-fortune. Darling, darling — never forget that you are your father's dearest joy — "

Ragnfrid went back to the winter-room, undressed and crept into bed beside Ulvhild. She put an arm about the child and laid her cheek close to the little one's, so that she felt the warmth of Ulvhild's body and smelt the keen odour of her damp hair. Ulvhild slept heavily and soundly, as she ever did after Lady Aashild's evening draught. The lady's bedstraw, spread beneath the bedding, gave out a drowsy scent. None the less did Ragnfrid lie long sleepless, gazing at the little spot of light in the roof where the moon shone upon the smoke-hole's pane of horn.

Over in the other bed lay Lady Aashild, but Ragnfrid never knew whether she slept or waked. The lady never spoke of their having known each other in former days — this frightened Ragnfrid. And it seemed to her she had never known such bitter sorrow and such haunting dread as now — even though she knew that Lavrans would have his full health again — and that Ulvhild would live.

* * *

It seemed as though Lady Aashild took pleasure in talking to Kristin, and with each day that passed the maid became better friends with her. One day, when they had gone to gather herbs, they sat together high up the hillside on a little green, close under the scree. They could look down into the farm-place at Formo and see Arne Gyrdsön's red jerkin: he had ridden down the valley with them, and was to look after their horses while they were up the hillside seeking herbs.

As they sat, Kristin told Lady Aashild of her meeting with the dwarf-maiden. She had not thought of it for many years, but now it rose before her. And while she spoke, the thought came to her strangely that there was some likeness betwixt Lady Aashild and the dwarf-lady — though she knew well all the time they were not really like. But when she had told all, Lady Aashild sat still a while and looked out down the Dale; at length she said:

"You were wise to fly, since you were only a child then. But have you never heard of folk who took the gold the dwarfs offered, and after bound the troll in stone?"

"I have heard such tales," said Kristin, "but I would never dare to do it. And methinks it is not a fair deed."

" 'Tis well when one dares not do what one doth not think a fair deed," said Lady Aashild, laughing a little. "But it is not so well when one thinks a thing to be no fair deed because one dares not do it. . . . You have grown much this summer," the lady said of a sudden. "Do you know yourself, I wonder, that you are like to be fair?"

"Ay," said Kristin. "They say I am like my father."

Lady Aashild laughed quietly.

"Ay, 'twould be best for you if you took after Lavrans, both in mind and body, too. Yet 'twould be pity were they to wed you up here in the Dale. Plainness and country ways let no man scorn; but they think themselves, these big folk up here, they are so fine that their like is not to be found in Norway's land. They

wonder much, belike, that I can live and thrive, though
they bar their doors against me. But they are lazy and
proud and will not learn new ways — and they put
the blame on the old strife with the King in Sverre's
days. 'Tis all lies; your mother's forefather made
friends with King Sverre and received gifts from him;
but were your mother's brother to become one of our
King's men and wait upon his Court, he would have
to trim himself up both without and within, and that
Trond would not be at the pains to do. But you,
Kristin, — you should be wedded to a man bred in
knightly ways and *curteisie* — "

Kristin sat looking down into the Formo yard, at
Arne's red back. She scarce knew it herself, but when
Lady Aashild talked of the world she had once moved
in, Kristin ever thought of the knights and earls in
Arne's likeness. Before, when she was little, she had
always seen them in her father's shape.

"My sister's son, Erlend Nikulaussön of Husaby, *he*
might have been a fitting bridegroom for you — he has
grown comely, has the boy. My sister Magnhild looked
in on me last year as she passed through the Dale, and
he with her. Ay, 'tis not like you could get him, but
I had gladly spread the coverlid over you two in the
bridal bed — he is as dark-haired as you are fair, and
he has goodly eyes. . . . But if I know my brother-in-
law aright, he has bethought him already for sure of a
better match for Erlend than you."

"Am I not a good match, then?" asked Kristin, wondering. She never thought of being hurt by anything
Lady Aashild said, but she felt humbled and sad that
the lady should be in some way better than her own
folks.

"Ay, you are a good match," said the other. "Yet
you could scarce look to come into my kindred. Your
forefather in this land was an outlaw and a stranger,
and the Gjeslings have sat and grown moulded on their
farms so long that soon they'll be forgotten outside

the Dale. But I and my sister had for husbands the nephews of Queen Margaret Skulesdatter."

Kristin could not even pluck up heart to say it was not her forefather, but his brother, who had come to the land an outlaw. She sat and gazed at the dark hillsides across the Dale, and she thought of the day many years gone by, when she had been up on the upland wastes and seen how many fells there were 'twixt her own valley and the outer world. Then Lady Aashild said they must go home now, and bade her call on Arne. So Kristin put her hands to her mouth, and hallooed and waved her kerchief, till she saw the red spot in the farm-place move and wave back.

Not long after this Lady Aashild went home; but through the autumn and the first part of the winter she came often to Jörundgaard to spend some days with Ulvhild. The child was taken out of bed in the daytime now, and they tried to get her to stand, but her legs gave way beneath her when she put her feet to the ground. She was fretful, white and weary, and the laced jacket of horsehide and thin withes which Lady Aashild had made for her plagued her sorely, so that she would rather lie still in her mother's lap. Ragnfrid had her sick daughter for ever in her arms, so that Tordis had the whole care of the house now; and, at her mother's bidding, Kristin went with Tordis to learn and to help.

Kristin longed for Lady Aashild between whiles, and sometimes the lady would chat much with her, but at other times the child would wait in vain for a word beyond the other's greeting when she came and when she went. Lady Aashild sat and talked with the grown-up folk only. That was always the way when she had her husband with her, for it happened now at times that Björn Gunnarsön came with his wife. Lavrans had ridden to Haugen one day in the autumn to take the lady her leech's fee — it was the very best silver tankard they had in the house, with a plate to match. He had slept there the night, and ever since he praised the farm mightily; it was fair and well ordered, and not so small as folks would have it, he said. And within the house all spoke of well-being, and the customs of the house were seemly, following the ways of great folks' houses in the South. What he thought of Björn, Lavrans said not, but he welcomed him fairly at all times when he came with his wife to Jörundgaard. But the Lady Aashild Lavrans liked exceeding well, and he said he deemed most of the tales that had been told of her were lies. He said, too, 'twas most sure that twenty years since she could have had small need of witchcraft to bind a man to her — she was near the sixties now, yet she still looked young and had a most fair and winning bearing.

Kristin saw well that her mother liked all this but little. Of Lady Aashild, it is true, Ragnfrid said naught; but once she likened Björn to the yellow, flattened grass one sometimes finds growing under big stones, and Kristin thought this fitted him well. Björn looked strangely faded; he was somewhat fat, pale and sluggish, and a little bald, although he was not much older than Lavrans. Yet one saw he had once been a very comely man. Kristin never came to speech with him — he spoke little, and was wont to sit in the same place where he first settled down, from the time he stepped into the room till he went to bed. He drank hugely, but one marked it but little on him; he ate scarce any food, but gazed now and again at one or another in the room with a fixed, brooding look in his strange, pale eyes.

They had seen naught of their kinsfolk at Sundbu since the mishap befell, though Lavrans had been over at Vaage more times than one. But Sira Eirik came to Jörundgaard as before; and there he often met Lady Aashild, and they were good friends. Folk thought this was good of the priest, for he was himself a very skilful leech. That, too, was doubtless one cause why the folk of the great estates had not sought Lady Aashild's counsel, at least not openly, as they held the priest to be skilful enough, nor was it easy for them to know how they should bear themselves toward two folks who had been cast off, in a manner, by their own kin and fellows. Sira Eirik said himself they did not graze on one another's meadows, and as to her witchcraft, he was not her parish priest — it might well be the lady knew more than was good for her soul's health — yet one must not forget ignorant folk were all too ready to talk of witchcraft as soon as a woman was a bit wiser than her neighbours. Lady Aashild, on her side, praised the priest much, and was diligent at church if it chanced she was at Jörundgaard on a holy day.

Yuletide was sorrowful that year; Ulvhild could not yet put her feet to the ground, and they neither heard nor saw aught of the Sundbu folk. Kristin knew that it was talked of in the parish and that her father took it to heart. But her mother seemed to care naught; and Kristin thought this wrong of her.

But one evening, toward the end of Yuletide, came Sira Sigurd, Trond Gjesling's house-priest, driving in a great sledge, and his chief errand was to bid them all to a feast at Sundbu.

Sira Sigurd was ill-liked in the parishes about, for it was he who really managed Trond's estates; or, at the least, he got the blame for Trond's hard and unjust dealings, and there was no denying Trond was something of a plague to his tenants. His priest was most learned in writing and reckoning, versed in the law, and a skilful leech — if not quite so skilful as he deemed himself. But from his ways, no one would have thought him otherwise; he often said foolish things. Ragnfrid and Lavrans never liked him, but the Sundbu folk, as was but reason, set great store by their priest, and both they and he felt very bitter that he had not been called in to Ulvhild.

Now by ill-fortune it fell out that when Sira Sigurd came to Jörundgaard, Lady Aashild and Sir Björn were there already, besides Sira Eirik, Gyrd and Inga of Finsbrekken, Arne's parents, old Jon from Lopts-gaard, and a Preaching Friar from Hamar, Brother Aasgaut.

While Ragnfrid had the tables spread anew with Christmas fare, and Lavrans looked into the letters brought by Sira Sigurd, the priest wished to look at Ulvhild. She was already abed for the night and sleeping, but Sira Sigurd woke her, felt her back and limbs, and asked her many questions, at first gently enough, but then roughly and impatiently as the child grew frightened. Sigurd was a little man, all but a dwarf, with a great, flaming, red face. As he made to lift her out upon the floor to test her feet, she began screaming loudly. On this Lady Aashild rose, went to the bed, and covered Ulvhild with the skins, saying the child was so sleepy she could not have stood upon the floor even had her legs been strong.

The priest began then to speak loudly; he too was reckoned to know somewhat of leech-craft. But Lady Aashild took him by the hand, brought him forward to the high-seat and fell to telling him what she had done for Ulvhild, and asking his judgment on each and every matter. On this he grew somewhat milder of mood, and ate and drank of Ragnfrid's good cheer.

But as the beer and wine began to mount to his head, Sira Sigurd's humour changed again and he grew quarrelsome and hotheaded — he knew well enough there was no one in the room who liked him. First he turned on Gyrd — he was the bishop of Hamar's bailiff in Vaage and Sil, and there had been many quarrels 'twixt the Bishop's see and Trond Ivarsön. Gyrd said not much, but Inga was a fiery woman, and then Brother Aasgaut joined in, and spoke:

"You should not forget, Sira Sigurd, our reverend Father Ingjald is your overlord, too — we know enough of you in Hamar. You wallow in all good things at Sundbu, never thinking that you are vowed to other work than to do Trond eye-service, helping him in all wrong and injustice, to the peril of his soul and the minishing of the rights of Holy Church. Have you never heard how it fares with the false and unruly priests who hatch out devices against their spiritual fathers and those in authority? Wot you not of that time when the angels took St. Thomas of Canterbury to the door of hell and let him peep in? He wondered much that he saw none of the priests who had set themselves up against him, as you have set yourself against your bishop. He was about to praise God's mercy, for the holy man begrudged not salvation to all sinners — but at that the angel bade the devil lift his tail a little, and out there came, with a great bang and a foul smell of sulphur, all the priests and learned men who had wrought against the good of the Church. Thus did he come to know whither *they* had gone."

"*There* you lie, monk," said the priest. "I have heard that tale too; only they were not priests, but beggar-monks, who came from the rear of the devil like wasps out of a wasp-nest."

Old Jon laughed louder than all the serving-folk, and roared:

"There were both sorts, I'll be bound — "

"Then the devil must have a fine broad tail," said Björn Gunnarsön; and Lady Aashild smiled, and said:

"Ay, have you not heard that all evil drags a long tail behind it?"

"Be still, Lady Aashild," cried Sira Sigurd: "do not you talk of the long tail evil drags after it. You sit here as though *you* were mistress in the house, and not Ragnfrid. But 'tis strange you could not help her child — have you no more of that strong water you dealt in once, which could make whole the sheep already boiling in the pot, and turn women to maids in the bridal-bed? Think you I know not of the wedding in this very parish where you made a bath for the bride that was no maid — "

Sira Eirik sprang up, gripped the other priest by the shoulder and thigh, and flung him right over the table, so that the jugs and tankards were overturned and food and drink ran upon the cloths and floor, while Sira Sigurd lay his length upon the ground with torn garments. Eirik leaped over the board, and would have struck him again, roaring above the tumult:

"Hold your filthy mouth, priest of hell that you are — "

Lavrans strove to part them, but Ragnfrid stood, white as death, by the board, and wrung her hands. Then Lady Aashild ran and helped Sira Sigurd to his feet, and wiped the blood from his face. She poured a beaker of mead down his throat, saying:

"You must not be so strict, Sira Eirik, that you cannot bear to listen to jesting so far on in a drinking bout. Seat yourselves now and you shall hear of that wedding. 'Twas not here in the Dale at all, nor had I the good fortune to be the one that knew of that water — could I have brewed it, I trow we would not be sitting now on a hill-croft in the wilds. I might have been a rich woman and had lands in the great, rich parishes — nigh to town and cloisters and bishop and chapter," and she smiled at the three churchmen.

"But 'tis said, sure enough, that the art was known in the olden days."

And the lady told a merry tale of a misadventure that befell in King Inga's time, when the magic wash was used by mistake by the wrong woman, and of what followed thereon.

Great was the laughter in the room, and both Gyrd and Jon shouted for more such tales from Lady Aashild. But the lady said: "No! Here sit two priests and Brother Aasgaut, and young lads and serving-maids; 'tis best we cease before the talk grows unseemly and gross; let us bear in mind 'tis a holy day."

The men made an outcry, but the women held with Lady Aashild. No one saw that Ragnfrid had left the room. Soon after, it was time that Kristin, who sat lowest on the women's bench among the serving-maids, should go to bed — she was sleeping in Tordis' house, there were so many guests at the manor.

It was biting cold, and the northern lights flamed and flickered over the brows of the fells to the north. The snow crackled under Kristin's feet as she ran over the courtyard shivering, her arms crossed on her breast.

Then she was aware of a woman in the shadow of the old loft walking hurriedly to and fro in the snow, throwing her arms about, wringing her hands, and wailing aloud. Kristin saw it was her mother, and ran to her affrighted, asking if she were ill.

"No, no," burst out Ragnfrid. "But I could not stay within — go you to bed, child."

As Kristin turned away, her mother called her softly:

"Go back to the room and lie beside your father and Ulvhild — take her in your arms so that he may not roll upon her by mischance; he sleeps so heavily when he has drunk deep. I am going up to sleep in the old loft-room to-night."

"Jesus, mother," says Kristin, "you will freeze to death if you lie there — alone, too. And what think you father will say if you come not to bed to-night?"

"He will not mark it," answered her mother, "he was all but asleep when I left, and to-morrow he will waken late. Go and do as I have said."

" 'Twill be so cold for you," said Kristin, whimpering; but her mother sent her away, a little more kindly, and shut herself into the loft-room.

Within it was as cold as without, and it was pitch dark. Ragnfrid groped her way to the bed, pulled off her headdress, undid her shoes, and crept in among the skins. They chilled her to the bone; it was like sinking into a snowdrift. She pulled the skins over her head, and drew her knees up to her chin, and thrust her hands into her bosom — so she lay and wept; now quite low, with flowing tears; now crying aloud and

grinding her teeth. But in time she had warmed the
bed around her so much that she grew drowsy, and
at last wept herself to sleep.

5

THE YEAR that Kristin was fifteen in the spring, Lavrans Björgulfsön and Sir Andres Gudmundsön of Dyfrin made tryst at the Holledis Thing. There 'twas
agreed between them that Andres' second son, Simon,
should wed Kristin Lavransdatter and should have
Formo, Sir Andres, mother's udal estate. This the two
men shook hands upon; yet it was not put in writing,
for Sir Andres had first to settle with his other children
about their heritage. And for this reason no betrothal
feast was held; but Sir Andres and Simon came to
Jörundgaard to see the bride, and Lavrans gave them a
great banquet.

By this time Lavrans had ready his new dwelling-
house of two storeys, with corner fireplaces of masonry
both in the living-room and the loft-room above; richly furnished and adorned with fair wood-carvings. He
had rebuilt the old loft-room too, and bettered the
other houses in many ways, so that he was now housed
as befitted an esquire bearing arms. He was very
wealthy now, for he had had good fortune in his under-
takings and was a shrewd and careful husband of his
goods; above all was he known as a breeder of the
finest horses and the goodliest cattle of all kinds. And
now he had been able so to order things that his
daughter was to wed into the Dyfrin kindred and the
Formo estate, all folks deemed he had brought to a
happy end his purpose to be the foremost man in the
countryside. He, and Ragnfrid too, were well pleased
with the betrothal, as were Sir Andres and Simon.

Kristin was a little cast down when she first saw
Simon Andressön; for she had heard great talk of his
good looks and seemly bearing, so that she had outrun

all measure in her hopes of what her bridegroom would be.

Truly Simon was well favoured, but he was something fat to be only twenty years of age; he was short of neck and had a face as round and shining as the moon. He had goodly hair, brown and curly, and his eyes were grey and clear, but lay deep and as it were shut in, the lids were so fat; his nose was over small and his mouth was small too, and pouting, but not unsightly. In spite of his stoutness he was light, and quick, and nimble in all his ways, and was skilled in all sports. He was something too brisk and forward in his speech, but Lavrans held he showed both good wit and learning when he talked with older men.

Ragnfrid soon came to like him, and Ulvhild was taken at once with the greatest love for him — he was more gentle and kind with the little sick maid than with any other. And when Kristin had grown used a little to his round face and his way of speech, she grew to be well content with her betrothed, and happy in the way her father had ordered things for her.

Lady Aashild was at the feast. Since Jörundgaard had opened its doors to her, the great folk in the parishes round about had begun to call to mind her high birth and to think less of her doubtful fame, so that the lady came much out among people. She said when she had seen Simon:

" 'Tis a good match, Kristin; this Simon will go forward in the world — you will be spared many cares, and he will be good to live with. But to my mind he seems something too fat and too cheerful —. Were it now in Norway as it was in days gone by, and as it is still in other lands — that folk were not more hard to sinners than is God Himself, I would say you should find yourself a friend who is lean and sorrowful — one you could have to sit and hold converse with. Then would I say, you could not fare better than you would with Simon."

Kristin grew red, though she understood not well

what the lady's words might mean. But as time went on and her bridal chests filled, and she evermore heard talk of her wedding, and of what she was to take into the new household, she began to long that the betrothal-knot should be tied once for all, and that Simon should come north; thus she thought much about him in the end, and was glad at the thought of meeting him again.

Kristin was full-grown now and very fair to look upon. She was most like her father and had grown tall; she was small waisted, with slender, fine limbs and joints, yet round and plump withal. Her face was somewhat short and round, her forehead low and broad and white as milk; her eyes large, grey and soft, under fairly drawn eyebrows. Her mouth was something large, but it had full bright red lips, and her chin was round as an apple and well shaped. She had goodly long, thick hair; but 'twas something dark in hue, almost as much brown as yellow, and quite straight. Lavrans liked nothing better than to hear Sira Eirik boast of Kristin — the priest had seen the maid grow up, had taught her her books and writing, and loved her much. But the father was not so pleased when the priest sometimes likened his daughter to an unblemished, silken-coated filly.

Yet all men said that had not that sorrowful mishap befallen, Ulvhild had been many times more comely than her sister. She had the fairest and sweetest face, white and red as lilies and roses; and light yellow hair, soft as silk, which waved and clung about her slender throat and small shoulders. Her eyes were like those of her Gjesling kin; they were deep set, under straight, dark brows, and were clear as water and grey-blue; but her glance was mild, not sharp like theirs. Then, too, the child's voice was so clear and lovely that it was a joy to hearken to her, whether she spoke or sang. She was most apt at book-learning and all kinds

of string-instruments and draughts, but had little mind
to work with her hands, for her back soon grew weary.

There seemed little hope, indeed, this fair child
should ever have full use of her limbs. It is true she
had mended a little after her father and mother had
been to Nidaros with her to St. Olav's shrine. Lavrans
and Ragnfrid had gone thither on foot, without man
or serving-maid to attend them; they bore the child
between them on a litter the whole way. After the
journey Ulvhild grew so far well that she could walk
a little with a crutch. But they could not hope that
she should grow well enough to be wedded, and so it
was like that, when the time came, she must be given
to a cloister with all the wealth that should fall to her.

They never spoke of this, and Ulvhild herself scarce
knew how much unlike she was to other children. She
was very fond of finery and pretty clothes, and her
father and mother had not the heart to deny her anything; so Ragnfrid stitched and sewed for her, and
decked her out like any king's child. Once some pedlars
passing through the parish lay overnight at Laugarbru;
and Ulvhild got a sight of their wares there. They had
some amber-coloured silk-stuff, and she set her heart
on having a shift of it. Lavrans was not wont to deal
with such folk, who went around against the law, selling wares from the market-towns in the country
parishes; but now he bought the whole bale at once.
He gave Kristin some of the stuff, too, for a bridal
shift, and she was sewing on it this summer. Until now
all the shifts she owned had been of wool, or of linen
for best wear. But now Ulvhild had a shift of silk for
feast days and a Sunday shift of linen with silk let
in above.

Lavrans Björgulfsön owned Laugarbru too now, and
Tordis and Jon were in charge there. With them was
Lavrans' and Ragnfrid's youngest daughter, Ramborg,
whom Tordis had nursed. Ragnfrid would scarce look
at the child for some time after it was born, for, she

said, she brought her children ill-fortune. Yet she loved the little maid much and was ever sending gifts to her and Tordis; and later she went often over to Laugarbru and saw Ramborg, but she liked best to come after the child was asleep and sit by her. Lavrans and the two older daughters were often at Laugarbru to play with the little one; she was a strong and healthy child, but not so fair as her sisters.

This was the last summer Arne Gyrdsön was on Jörundgaard. The Bishop had promised Gyrd to help the youth on in the world, and in the autumn Arne was to set out for Hamar.

Kristin knew well enough that she was dear to Arne, but she was in many ways still a child in mind, and she thought little about it, but bore herself to him as she had always done from the time they were children; was with him as often as she could, and always stood up with him when there was dancing at home or upon the church-green. That her mother did not like this, seemed to her something of a jest. But she never spoke to Arne of Simon or of her wedding, for she marked that he grew heavy-hearted when there was talk of it.

Arne was a very handy man, and was now making Kristin a sewing-chair * as a keepsake. He had covered both the box and the frame of the chair with fair, rich carving, and was now busy in the smithy on iron bands and a lock for it. On a fine evening well on in summer Kristin had gone down to him. She had taken with her a jacket of her father's she had to mend, and sat upon the stone threshold sewing while she chatted with the youth in the smithy. Ulvhild was with her; she hopped about upon her crutch, eating the raspberries which grew among the heaps of stone around the field.

After a while Arne came to the smithy door to cool himself. He made as though to seat himself beside

---

* Sewing-chair, see Note 9.

Kristin, but she moved a little away and bade him have a care not to dirty the sewing she had upon her knee.

"Is it come to this between us," said Arne, "that you dare not let me sit by you for fear the peasant boy should soil you?"

Kristin looked at him in wonder, and answered:

"You know well enough what I meant. But take your apron off, wash the charcoal from your hands and sit down a little and rest you here by me — " And she made room for him.

But Arne laid himself in the grass in front of her; then she said again:

"Nay, be not angry, my Arne. Can you think I could be unthankful for the brave gift you are making me, or ever forget you have been my best friend at home here all my days?"

"Have I been that?" he asked.

"You know it well," said Kristin. "And never will I forget you. But you, who are to go out into the world — maybe you will gain wealth and honour or ever you think — you will like enough forget me, long before I forget you — "

"You will never forget me?" said Arne, smiling. "And I will forget you ere you forget me? — you are naught but a child, Kristin."

"*You* are not so old either," she replied.

"I am as old as Simon Darre," said he again. "And we bear helm and shield as well as the Dyfrin folk; but my folks have not had fortune with them — "

He had dried his hands on the grass tufts; and now he took Kristin's ankle and pressed his cheek to the foot which showed from under her dress. She would have drawn away her foot, but Arne said:

"Your mother is at Laugarbru, and Lavrans has ridden forth — from the houses none can see us where we sit. Surely you can let me speak this once of what is in my heart."

Kristin answered:

"We have known all our days, both you and I, that 'twas bootless for us to set our hearts on each other."

"May I lay my head in your lap?" said Arne, and as she did not answer, he laid his head down and twined an arm about her waist. With his other hand he pulled at the plaits of her hair.

"How will you like it," he asked in a little, "when Simon lies in your lap thus, and plays with your hair?"

Kristin did not answer. It seemed as though a heaviness fell upon her of a sudden — Arne's words and Arne's head on her knee — it seemed to her as though a door opened into a room, where many dark passages led into a greater darkness; sad, and heavy at heart, she faltered and would not look inside.

"Wedded folk do not use to do so," said she of a sudden, quickly, as if eased of a weight. She tried to see Simon's fat, round face looking up into hers as Arne was looking now; she heard his voice — and she could not keep from laughing:

"I trow Simon will never lie on the ground to play with my shoes — not he!"

"No, for he can play with you in his bed," said Arne. His voice made her feel sick and powerless all at once. She tried to push his head from off her lap, but he pressed it against her knees, and said softly:

"But *I* would play with your shoes and your hair and your fingers, and follow you out and in the live-long day, Kristin, were you ever so much my wife and slept in my arms each single night."

He half sat up, put his arm round her shoulder and gazed into her eyes.

" 'Tis not well done of you to talk thus to me," said Kristin bashfully, in a low voice.

"No," said Arne. He rose and stood before her. "But tell me one thing — would you not rather it were I — ?"

"Oh! I would rather" — she sat still awhile — "I would rather not have any man — not yet —"

Arne did not move, but said:

"Would you rather be given to the cloister then, as 'tis to be with Ulvhild, and be a maid all your days?"

Kristin pressed her folded hands down into her lap. A strange, sweet trembling seized her — and with a sudden shudder she seemed to understand how much her little sister was to be pitied — her eyes filled with tears of sorrow for Ulvhild's sake.

"Kristin!" said Arne, in a low voice.

At that moment a loud scream came from Ulvhild. Her crutch had caught between the stones, and she had fallen. Arne and Kristin ran to her, and Arne lifted her up into her sister's arms. She had cut her mouth, and much blood was flowing from the hurt.

Kristin sat down with her in the smithy door, and Arne fetched water in a wooden bowl. Together they set to washing and wiping her face. She had rubbed the skin off her knees, too. Kristin bent tenderly over the small, thin legs.

Ulvhild's wailing soon grew less, but she wept silently and bitterly as children do who are used to suffering pain. Kristin held her head to her bosom and rocked her gently.

Then the bell began to ring for vespers up at Olav's Church.

Arne spoke to Kristin, but she sat bent over her sister as though she neither heard nor marked him, so that at last he grew afraid and asked if she thought there was danger in the hurt. Kristin shook her head, but looked not at him.

Soon after she got up and went towards the farmstead, bearing Ulvhild in her arms. Arne followed, silent and troubled — Kristin seemed so deep in thought, and her face was set and hard. As she walked, the bell went on ringing out over the meadows and the dale; it was still ringing as she went into the house.

She laid Ulvhild in the bed which the sisters had shared ever since Kristin had grown too big to sleep by her father and mother. She slipped her shoes off and lay down beside the little one — lay and listened for the ringing of the bell long after it was hushed and the child slept.

It had come to her as the bell began to ring, while she sat with Ulvhild's little bleeding face in her hands, that maybe it was a sign to her. If she should go to the convent in her sister's stead — if she should vow herself to the service of God and the Virgin Mary — might not God give the child health and strength again?

She thought of Brother Edvin's word: that nowadays 'twas only marred and crippled children and those for whom good husbands could not be found that their fathers and mothers gave to God. She knew her father and mother were godly folks — yet had she never heard aught else but that she should wed — but when they understood that Ulvhild would be sickly all her days, they planned for her straightway that she should go to the cloister. . . .

And she had no mind to go herself — she strove against the thought that God would do a miracle for Ulvhild if she herself turned nun. She hung on Sira Eirik's word that in these days not many miracles come to pass. And yet she felt this evening it was as Brother Edvin said: had a man but faith enough, his faith might work miracles. But she had no mind to have that faith herself, she did not love God and His Mother, and the Saints *so* much, did not even wish to love them so — she loved the world and longed for the world.

Kristin pressed her lips down into Ulvhild's soft, silken hair. The child slept soundly, and the elder sister sat up restlessly, but lay down again. Her heart bled with sorrow and shame, but she knew she did not wish to believe in signs and wonders, for she would not give up her heritage of health and beauty and love.

So she tried to comfort herself with the thought, that her father and mother would not be willing she should do such a thing. Nor would they think it could avail. Then, too, she was promised already, and she was sure they would not give up Simon, of whom they were so fond. She felt it a betrayal of herself that they were so proud of this son-in-law; of a sudden she thought with dislike of Simon's round, red face and small laughing eyes — of his jaunty gait — he bounced like a ball, it came to her all at once; of his bantering talk, that made her feel awkward and foolish. 'Twas no such glory either to get him, and move with him just down to Formo. Still she would rather have him than be sent to a convent. But, ah! the world beyond the hills, the King's palace and the earls and knights Lady Aashild talked of — and a comely man with sorrowful eyes who would follow her in and out and never grow weary. She thought of Arne that summer day when he lay on his side and slept with his brown, glossy hair outspread among the heather — she had loved him then as though he were her brother. It was not well done of him to have spoken to her so, when he knew they could never belong to one another. . . .

Word came from Laugarbru that her mother would stay there overnight. Kristin got up to undress and go to rest. She began to unlace her dress — then she put her shoes on again, threw her cloak about her and went out.

The night sky stretched clear and green above the hill-crests. It was near time for the moon to rise, and where it was yet hid behind the fell, sailed some small clouds their lower edges shining like silver; the sky grew brighter and brighter, like metal under gathering drops of dew.

She ran up between the fences, over the road, and up the slope toward the church. It stood there, as though asleep, dark and shut, but she went up to the cross which stood near by to mark the place where St. Olav once rested as he fled before his enemies.

Kristin knelt down upon the stone and laid her

folded hands upon the base of the cross: "Holy Cross, strongest of masts, fairest of trees, bridge for the sick to the fair shores of health——"

At the words of the prayer, it was as if her longing widened out and faded little by little like rings on a pool. The single thoughts that troubled her smoothed themselves out one after the other, her mind grew calmer, more tender, and there came upon her a gentle, vague sadness in place of her distress.

She lay kneeling there and drank in all the sounds of the night. The wind sighed strangely, the rushing sound of the river came from beyond the wood by the church, the beck ran near by right across the road —— and all about, far and near, in the dark, she half saw and heard small rills of running and dripping water. The river gleamed white down below in the valley. The moon crept up in a little nick in the hills —— the dewy leaves and stones sparkled faintly, and the newly tarred timber of the belfry shone dull and dark by the churchyard gate. Then the moon was hid once more where the mountain ridge rose higher, and now many more white and shining clouds floated in the sky.

She heard a horse coming at a slow pace from higher up the road, and the sound of men's voices speaking low and even. She had no fear of folk here close at home where she knew every one —— so she felt quite safe.

Her father's dogs rushed at her, turned and dashed back into the wood, then turned back and leaped upon her again. Her father shouted a greeting as he came out from among the birches. He was leading Gulds-veinen by the bridle; a brace or two of birds hung dangling from the saddle, and Lavrans bore a hooded hawk upon his left wrist. He had with him a tall, bent man in a monk's frock, and even before Kristin had seen his face she knew it was Brother Edvin. She went to meet them, wondering no more than if it had been a dream —— she only smiled when Lavrans asked whether she knew their guest again.

Lavrans had chanced upon him up by the Rost bridge, and had coaxed him home with him to spend the night. But Brother Edvin would have it, they must let him lie in an outhouse: "For I'm grown so lousy," said he, "you cannot put me in the good beds."

And for all Lavrans talked and begged, the monk held out; nay, at first he would have it they should give him his food out in the courtyard. But at last they got him into the hall with them, and Kristin made up the fire in the fireplace in the corner and set candles on the board, while a serving-maid brought in meat and drink.

The monk seated himself on the beggars' bench by the door, and would have naught but cold porridge and water for his supper. Neither would he have aught of Lavrans' proffer to have a bath made ready for him, and have his clothes well washed.

Brother Edvin fidgeted and scratched himself, and laughed all over his lean, old face.

"Nay, nay," said he, "these things bite into my proud hide better than either whips or the Gardian's words. I have been sitting under a rock up here among the fells all summer — they gave me leave to go out into the wilderness to fast and pray, and there I sat and thought: now was I like a holy hermit indeed; and the poor folk away in Setnadal came up with food for me, and thought here they saw, in very truth, a godly and clean-living monk. Brother Edvin, they said, were there many such monks as you, we would be better men fast enough; but when we see priests and bishops and monks biting and fighting like young swine in a trough. . . . Ay, I told them it was unchristian-like to talk so — but I liked to hear it well enough, and I sang and I prayed till the mountain rang again. Now will it be wholesome for me to feel the lice biting and fighting upon my skin, and to hear the good house-wives, who would have all clean and seemly in their houses, cry out: 'That dirty pig of a monk can lie out in the barn well enough now 'tis summer.' I am for northwards now to Nidaros for St. Olav's vigil, and 'twill be well for me to mark that folk are none too fain to come nigh me—"

Ulvhild woke, and Lavrans went and lifted her up and wrapped her in his cloak:

"Here is the child I spoke of, dear Father. Lay your hands upon her and pray to God for her as you prayed for the boy away north in Meldal who we heard got his health again—"

The monk lifted Ulvhild's chin gently and looked into her face. And then he raised one of her hands and kissed it.

"Pray rather, you and your wife, Lavrans Björgulf-sön, that you be not tempted to try and bend God's will concerning this child. Our Lord Jesus Himself has set these small feet upon the path which will lead her most surely to the home of peace—I see it by your eyes, you blessed Ulvhild, you have your inter-cessors in our second home."

"The boy in Meldal got well, I have heard," said Lavrans, in a low voice.

"He was a poor widow's only child, and there was none but the parish to feed or clothe him when his mother should be gone. And yet the woman prayed only that God might give her a fearless heart so that she might have faith He would bring that to pass which would be best for the lad. Naught else did I do but join in that prayer of hers."

"'Tis hard for her mother and for me to rest con-tent with this," answered Lavrans heavily. "The more that she is so fair and so good."

"Have you seen the child at Lidstad, south in the Dale?" asked the monk. "Would you rather your daughter had been like that?"

Lavrans shuddered and pressed the child close to him.

"Think you not," said Brother Edvin again, "that in God's eyes we are all children He has cause to grieve

for, crippled as we are with sin? And yet we deem not
we are so badly off in this world."

He went to the picture of the Virgin Mary upon
the wall, and all knelt down while he said the evening
prayer. It seemed to them that Brother Edvin had
given them good comfort.

But, none the less, after he had gone from the room
to seek his place of rest, Astrid, the head serving-
wench, swept with care all parts of the floor where the
monk had stood, and cast the sweepings at once into
the fire.

Next morning Kristin rose early, took milk-porridge
and wheat-cakes in a goodly dish of flame-grained
birchwood — for she knew that the monk never
touched meat — and herself bore the food out to him.
But few of the folk were yet about in the houses.

Brother Edvin stood upon the bridge of the cow-
house, ready for the road with staff and scrip; with a
smile he thanked Kristin for her pains, and sat himself
down on the grass and ate, while Kristin sat at his feet.

Her little white dog came running up, the little bells
on his collar tinkling. She took him into her lap, and
Brother Edvin snapped his fingers at him, three small
bits of wheat-cake into his mouth, and praised him
mightily the while.

" 'Tis a breed Queen Euphemia brought to the country," said he. "You are passing fine here on Jörundgaard
now, both in great things and small."

Kristin flushed with pleasure. She knew already the
dog was of a fine breed, and she was proud of having
it; no one else in the parish had a lapdog. But she had
not known it was of the same kind as the Queen's pet
dogs.

"Simon Andressön sent him to me," said she, and
pressed it to her, while it licked her face. "His name
is Kortelin."

She had thought to speak to the monk about her
trouble, and to pray for his counsel. But she had no

longer any wish to let her mind dwell on the thoughts of the past evening. Brother Edvin was sure God would turn all things to the best for Ulvhild. And it was good of Simon to send her such a gift before even their betrothal was fixed. Arne she would not think of — he had not borne himself as he should towards her, she thought.

Brother Edvin took his staff and scrip, and bade Kristin greet those within the house — he would not stay till folk were up, but go while the day was yet cool. She went with him up past the church and a little way into the wood.

When they parted he wished her God's peace, and blessed her.

"Give me a word, like the word you gave to Ulvhild, dear Father," begged Kristin, as she stood with his hand in hers.

The monk rubbed his naked foot, knotted with gout, in the wet grass:

"Then would I bid you, daughter, that you lay to heart how God cares for folks' good here in the Dale. Little rain falls here, but He has given you water from the fells, and the dew freshens meadow and field each night. Thank God for the good gifts He has given you, and murmur not if you seem to miss aught you think might well be added to you. You have bonny yellow hair; see you fret not because it does not curl. Have you not heard of the old wife who sat and wept for that she had only a small bite of swine's flesh to give to her seven little ones for Christmas cheer? Pat at the moment St. Olav came riding by, and he stretched out his hand over the meat and prayed that God might give the poor little ravens their fill. But when the woman saw a whole pig's carcass lying upon the board, she wept that she had not pots and platters enow!"

Kristin ran homewards, with Kortelin dancing at her heels, snapping at the hem of her dress, and barking and ringing all his little silver bells.

6

ARNE stayed at home at Finsbrekken the last days before he was to set out for Hamar; his mother and sisters were making ready his clothes.

The day before he was to ride southward, he came to Jörundgaard to bid farewell. And he made a chance to whisper to Kristin: would she meet him on the road south of Laugarbru next evening?

"I would so fain we two should be alone the last time we are together," said he. "Does it seem such a great thing that I ask? — after all, we were brought up together like brother and sister," he said, when Kristin hung doubtful a little before making reply.

So she promised to come, if she could slip away from home.

It snowed next morning, but through the day it turned to rain, and soon roads and fields were a sea of grey mud. Wreaths of mist hung and drifted along the lower hillsides; now and then they sank yet lower and gathered into white rollers along the roots of the hills; and then the thick rain-clouds closed in again.

Sira Eirik came over to help Lavrans draw up some deeds. They went down to the hearth-room, for in such weather it was pleasanter there than in the great hall, where the fireplace filled the room with smoke. Ragnfrid was at Laugarbru, where Ramborg was now getting better of a fever she had caught early in the autumn.

Thus it was not hard for Kristin to slip away unseen, but she dared not take a horse, so she went on foot. The road was a quagmire of snow-slush and withered leaves; there was a saddening breath of death and decay in the raw, chill air, and now and again there came a gust of wind driving the rain into her face. She drew her hood well down over her head and, holding her cloak about her with both hands, went quickly forward. She was a little afraid — the roar of the river sounded so hollow in the heavy air, and the clouds drove dark and ragged over the hillcrests. Now and again she halted and listened for Arne's coming.

After a time she heard the splashing hoofs upon the slushy road behind her, and she stopped then where she was, for this was a somewhat lonely spot and she thought 'twas a good place for them to say their farewells in quiet. Almost at once, she saw the horseman coming, and Arne sprang from his horse and led it as he came to meet her.

" 'Twas kindly done of you to come," said he, "in this ugly weather."

" 'Tis worse for you who have so far to ride — and how is it you set out so late?" she asked.

"Jon has bidden me to lie the night at Loptsgaard," answered Arne. "I thought 'twas easier for you to meet me at this time of day."

They stood silent for a time. Kristin thought she had never seen before how fair a youth Arne was. He had on a smooth steel cap, and under that a brown woollen hood that sat tight about his face and spread out over his shoulders; under it, his narrow face showed bright and comely. His leather jerkin was old, spotted with rust and rubbed by the coat of mail which had been worn above it — Arne had taken it over from his father — but it fitted closely to his slim, lithe, and powerful body, and he had a sword at his side and in his hand a spear — his other weapons hung from his saddle. He was full-grown now and bore himself manfully.

She laid her hand upon his shoulder, and said:

"Mind you, Arne, you asked me once if I thought you as good a man as Simon Andressön? Now will I tell you one thing, before we part; 'tis that you seem to me as much above him in looks and bearing as he is reckoned above you in birth and riches by those who look most to such things."

"Why do you tell me this?" asked Arne breathlessly.

"Because Brother Edvin told me to lay to heart, that

we should thank God for His good gifts, and not be like the woman when St. Olav added to her meat, and she wept because she had not trenchers to put it in — so you should not grieve that He has not given you as much of riches as of bodily gifts — "

"Was it *that* you meant," said Arne. And then, as she was silent, he said:

"I wondered if you meant that you would rather be wedded to me than to the other — "

"That I would, truly," said she, in a low voice. ". . . I know you better — "

Arne threw his arms around her so that her feet were lifted from the ground. He kissed her face many times, and then set her down again:

"God help us, Kristin, what a child you are!"

She stood and hung her head, but left her hands upon his shoulders. He caught her wrists and held them tight:

"I see how 'tis with you, my sweeting: you little know how sore I am at heart to lose you. Kristin, you know we have grown up together like two apples on one branch: I loved you long before I began to understand that one day another would come and break you from me. As sure as God suffered death for us all — I know not how I can ever be happy in this world again after to-day — "

Kristin wept bitterly and lifted her face, so that he might kiss her.

"Do not talk so, my Arne," she begged, and patted him on the shoulder.

"Kristin," said Arne in a low voice, and took her into his arms again, "think you not that if you begged your father — Lavrans is so good a man, he would not force you against your will — if you begged them but to let you wait a few years — no one knows how fortune may turn for me — we are both of us so young — "

"Oh, I fear I must do as they wish at home," she wept.

And now weeping came upon Arne too.

"You know not, Kristin, how dear you are to me." He hid his face upon her shoulder. "If you did, and if you cared for me, for sure you would go to Lavrans and beg hard — "

"I cannot do it," she sobbed. "I could never come to love any man so much as to go against my father and mother for his sake." She groped with her hands for his face under the hood and the heavy steel cap. "Do not cry so, Arne, my dearest friend — "

"You must take this at least," said he after a time, giving her a little brooch; "and think of me sometimes, for I shall never forget you nor my grief — "

It was all but dark when Kristin and Arne had said their last farewell. She stood and looked after him when at length he rode away. A streak of yellow light shone through a rift in the clouds, and was reflected in the footprints, where they had walked and stood in the slush on the road — it all looked so cold and sorrowful, she thought. She drew up her linen neckerchief and dried her tear-stained face, then turned and went homeward.

She was wet and cold, and walked quickly. After a time she heard some one coming along the road behind her. She was a little frightened; even on such a night as this there might be strange folk journeying on the highway, and she had a lonely stretch before her. A great black scree rose right up on one side, and on the other the ground fell steeply and there was fir-forest all the way down to the leaden-hued river in the bottom of the Dale. So she was glad when the man behind her called to her by name; and she stood still and waited.

The newcomer was a tall, thin man in a dark surcoat with lighter sleeves; as he came nearer she saw he was dressed as a priest and carried an empty wallet on his back. And now she knew him to be Bentein Priestson, as they called him — Sira Eirik's daughter's son. She saw at once that he was far gone in drink.

"Ay, one goes and another comes," said he, laughing, when they had greeted one another. "I met Arne of Brekken even now — I see you are weeping. You might as well smile a little now I am come home — we have been friends, too, ever since we were children, have we not?"

" 'Tis an ill exchange, methinks, getting you into the parish in his stead," said Kristin bluntly. She had never like Bentein. "And so, I fear, will many think. Your grandfather here has been so glad you were in Oslo making such a fair beginning."

"Oh, ay," said Bentein, with a nickering laugh. "So 'twas a fair beginning I was making, you think? I was even like a pig in a wheatfield, Kristin — and the end was the same, I was hunted out with cudgels and the hue and cry. Ay, ay! ay, ay! 'Tis no great thing, the gladness my grandfather gets from his offspring. But what a mighty hurry you are in!"

"I am cold," said Kristin curtly.

"Not colder than I," said the priest. "I have no more clothes on me that you see here — my cloak I had to sell for food and beer in little Hamar. Now, you should still have some heat in your body from making your farewells with Arne — methinks you should let me get under your fur with you — " and he caught her cloak, pulled it over his shoulders and gripped her round the waist with his wet arm.

Kristin was so amazed with his boldness it was a moment before she could gather her wits — then she strove to tear herself away, but he had a hold of her cloak, and it was fastened together by a strong silver clasp, Bentein got his arms about her again, and made to kiss her, his mouth nearly touching her chin. She tried to strike, but he held her fast by the upper arm.

"I trow you have lost your wits," she hissed, as she struggled, "dare you to lay hands on me as I were a . . . dearly shall you rue this to-morrow, dastard that you are — "

"Nay, to-morrow you will not be so foolish," says

Bentein, putting his leg in front of her so that she half fell into the mud, and pressing one hand over her mouth.

Yet she had no thought of crying out. Now for the first time it flashed on her mind what he dared to want with her, but rage came upon her so wild and furious she had scarce a thought of fear: she snarled like an animal at grips with another, and fought furiously with the man as he tried to hold her down, while the ice-cold snow-water soaked through her clothes on to her burning skin.

"To-morrow you will have wit enough to hold your tongue," said Bentein, ". . . and if it cannot be hidden, you can put the blame on Arne — 'twill be believed the sooner — "

Just then one of his fingers got into her mouth, and at once she bit it with all her might, so that Bentein shrieked and let go his hold. Quick as lightning Kristin got one hand free, seized his face with it, and pressed her thumb with all her might against the ball of one of his eyes: he roared out and rose to his knees; like a cat she slipped from his grasp, threw herself upon him so that he fell upon his back, and, turning, rushed along the road with the mud splashing over her at every bound.

She ran and ran without looking back. She heard Bentein coming after, and she ran till her heart thumped in her throat, while she moaned softly and strained her eyes forward — should she never reach Laugarbru? At last she was out on the road where it passed through the fields; she saw the group of houses down on the hill-slope, and at the same moment she bethought her that she durst not run in there, where her mother was—in the state she was now in, plastered with clay and withered leaves from head to foot, and with her clothing torn to rags.

She marked that Bentein was gaining upon her; and on that she bent down and took up two great stones. She threw them when he came near enough;

one struck him with such force it felled him to the ground. Then she ran on again and stayed not before she stood upon the bridge.

All trembling, she stood and clutched the railing of the bridge; a darkness came before her eyes, and she feared she would drop down in a swoon — but then she thought of Bentein; what if he should come and find her. Shaken with rage and shame she went onwards, though her legs would scarce bear her, and now she felt her face smart where fingernails had scarred it, and felt too she had hurts upon both back and arms. Her tears came hot as fire.

She wished Bentein might have been killed by the stone she had thrown; she wished she had gone back and made an end of him; she felt for her knife, but found that she must have lost it.

Then again came the thought, she must not be seen at home as she was; and so it came into her mind that she would go to Romundgaard. She would complain to Sira Eirik.

But the priest had not come back yet from Jörundgaard. In the kitchen-house she found Gunhild, Bentein's mother; the woman was alone, and Kristin told her how her son had dealt with her. But that she had gone out to meet Arne she did not tell her. When she saw that Gunhild thought she had been at Laugarbru, she left her to think so.

Gunhild said little, but wept a great deal while she washed the mud off Kristin's clothes and sewed up the worst rents. And the girl was so shaken she paid no heed to the covert glances Gunhild cast on her now and then.

When Kristin went, Gunhild took her cloak and went out with her, but took the way to the stables. Kristin asked her whither she was going.

"Surely I may have leave to ride down and look after my son," answered the woman. "See whether you have killed him with that stone of yours, or how it fares with him."

There seemed to be naught Kristin could answer to this, so she said only that Gunhild should see to it Bentein got out of the parish as soon as might be, and kept out of her sight, ". . . or I will speak of this to Lavrans, and you can guess, I trow, what would happen then."

And indeed, Bentein went southward not more than a week later; he carried letters from Sira Eirik to the Bishop of Hamar, begging the Bishop to find work for him or otherwise to help him.

7

ONE day at Yuletide Simon Andressön came riding to Jörundgaard, a quite unlooked-for guest. He craved pardon for coming thus, unbidden and alone, without his kinsfolk. But Sir Andres was in Sweden on the King's business; he himself had been home at Dyfrin for a time, but only his young sisters and his mother, who lay ill abed, were there; so time had hung on his hands, and a great longing had taken him to look in upon them up here.

Ragnfrid and Lavrans thanked him much for having made this long journey in the depth of winter. The more they saw of Simon the more they liked him. He knew of all that had passed between Andres and Lavrans, and it was now fixed that his and Kristin's betrothal ale should be drunk before the beginning of Lent if Sir Andres could be home by that time, but, if not, then as soon as Easter was past.

Kristin was quiet and downcast when with her betrothed; she found not much to talk of with him. One evening when they had all been sitting drinking, he asked her to go out with him a little into the cool. Then, as they stood on the balcony in front of the upper hall, he put his arm round her waist and kissed her. After that he did the same often when they were alone. It gave her no gladness, but she suffered him to do it, since she knew the betrothal was a thing that must come. She thought of her wedding now only as something which she must go through with, not as something she wished for. None the less she liked Simon well enough — most, though, when he talked with others and did not touch or talk to her.

She had been so unhappy through this whole autumn. It was of no use, however often she told herself Bentein had been able to do her no harm; none the less she felt herself soiled and shamed.

Nothing could be the same as it had been before, since a man had dared try to wreak such a will on her. She lay awake of nights and burned with shame and could not stop thinking of it. She felt Bentein's body close against hers as when they fought, his hot, beery breath — she could not help thinking of what might have happened — and she thought, with a shudder through all her body, of what he had said: how Arne would get the blame if it could not be hidden. There rushed through her mind all that would have followed if such a calamity had befallen and then folk had heard of her meeting with Arne — what if her father and mother had believed such a thing of Arne — and Arne himself. . . . She saw him as she had seen him that last evening, and she felt as though she sank crushed before him at the very thought that she *might* have dragged him down with her into sorrow and disgrace. And then she had such ugly dreams. She had heard tell in church and in holy stories of fleshly lusts and the temptations of the body, but they had meant naught to her. Now it was become real to her that she herself and all mankind had a sinful, carnal body which enmeshed the soul and ate into it with hard bonds.

Then she would think out for herself how she might have killed or blinded Bentein. It was the only solace she could find — to sate herself with dreams of revenge upon the dark, hateful man who stood always in the way of her thoughts. But this did not help for long;

she lay by Ulvhild's side of nights and wept bitter tears at the thought of all this that had been brought upon her by brute force. Bentein had not failed altogether — he had wrought scathe to the maiden-hood of her spirit.

The first work-day after Christmas all the women on Jörundgaard were busy in the kitchen-house; Ragnfrid and Kristin had been there, too, for most of the day. Late in the evening, while some of the women were clearing up after the baking, and others making ready the supper, the dairymaid came rushing in, shrieking and wringing her hands:

"Jesus, Jesus — did ever any hear such a dreadful thing — they are bringing Arne Gyrdsön home dead on a sleigh — God help Gyrd and Inga in this misery — "

A man who dwelt in a cottage a little way down the road came in with Halvdan. It was these two who had met the bier.

The women crowded round them. Outside the circle stood Kristin, white and shaking. Halvdan, Lavrans' own body-servant, who had known Arne from his boyhood, wept aloud as he told the story:

It was Bentein Priestson who had killed Arne. On New Year's Eve the men of the Bishop's household were sitting and drinking in the men's hall, and Bentein had come in— he had been given a clerkship now with the Corpus Christi prebendary. The men did not want him amongst them at first, but he had put Arne in mind that they were both from the same parish, and Arne had let him sit by him, and they had drunk to-gether. But presently they had quarrelled and fought, and Arne had fallen on so fiercely that Bentein had snatched a knife from the table and stabbed him in the throat and then more than once in the breast. Arne had died almost at once.

The Bishop had taken this mischance much to heart; he himself had cared for the laying-out of the corpse, and had it brought all the long way home by his own folk. Bentein he had thrown into irons, cast him out from the church, and if he were not already hanged, he was going to be.

Halvdan had to tell all this over again many times as fresh people streamed in. Lavrans and Simon came over to the kitchen too, when they marked all the stir and commotion about the place. Lavrans was much moved; he bade them saddle his horse, he would ride over to Brekken at once. As he was about to go, his eyes fell on Kristin's white face.

"Maybe *you* would like to go with me?" he asked. Kristin faltered a little; she shuddered — but then she nodded, for she could not utter one word.

"Is't not too cold for her?" said Ragnfrid. "Doubtless they will have the wake to-morrow, and then 'tis like we shall all go together — "

Lavrans looked at his wife; he marked Simon's face too; and then he went and laid his arm round Kristin's shoulders.

"She is his foster-sister, you must bear in mind," said he. "Maybe, she would like to help Inga with the laying-out the body."

And though Kristin's heart was benumbed with despair and fear, she felt a glow of thankfulness to her father for his words.

Ragnfrid said then, that if Kristin was to go, they must eat their evening porridge before they started. She wished, too, to send gifts to Inga by them — a new linen sheet, wax-candles and fresh-baked bread; and she bade them say she would come up herself and help to prepare for the burial.

There was little eating, but much talking in the room while the food was on the table. One reminded the other of the trials that God had laid upon Gyrd and Inga. Their farm had been laid waste by stone-slips and floods; more than one of their elder children were dead, so that all Arne's brothers and sisters were still but little ones. They had had fortune with them now

for some years, since the Bishop placed Gyrd at Finsbrekken as his bailiff; and the children who were left
to them were fair and full of promise. But his mother
loved Arne more than all the rest. . . .

They pitied Sira Eirik too. The priest was beloved
and well respected, and the folk of the parish were
proud of him; he was learned and skilled in his office,
and in all the years he had had their church he had
never let a holy-day or a mass or a service pass that
he was in duty bound to hold. In his youth he had
been man-at-arms under Count Alv of Tornberg, but
he had had the misfortune to kill a man of very high
birth, and so had taken refuge with the Bishop of
Oslo; when the Bishop saw what a turn Eirik had for
book-learning, he had him trained for a priest. And
had it not been that he still had enemies by reason of
that slaying of long ago, it was like Sira Eirik would
not have have stayed here in this little charge. True
enough, he was very greedy of pence, both for his
own purse and for the church, but then, was not his
church richly fitted out with plate and vestments and
books? and he himself had these children — and he
had had naught but sorrow and trouble with his family.
In these far-away country parishes folk held it was not
reason that priests should live like monks, for they
must at the least have women to help on their farms,
and they might well need a woman to look after
things for them, seeing what long and toilsome journeys they must make round the parishes, and that too
in all kinds of weather; besides folk had not forgotten
that it was not so very long since priests in Norway
had been wedded men. Thus, no one had blamed Sira
Eirik overmuch that he had had three children by the
woman who tended his house, while he was yet young.
But this evening they said it looked, indeed, as though
'twas God's will to punish Eirik for his loose living,
so much evil had his children and his children's children
brought upon him. And some thought there was good
reason, too, that a priest should have neither wife nor

children — for after this it was much to be feared that bitterness and enmity would arise between the priest and the folk on Finsbrekken, who until now had been the best of friends.

Simon Andressön knew much of Bentein's doings in Oslo; and he told of them. Bentein had been clerk to the Dean of the Church of the Holy Virgin, and he had the name of being a quick-witted youth. There were many women, too, who liked him well — he had roving eyes, and a glib tongue. Some held him a comely man — these were for the most part such women as thought they had a bad bargain in their husbands. And then young maids, the sort that liked well that men should be somewhat free with them. Simon laughed — ay, they understood? Well, Bentein was so sly, he never went too far with that kind of woman; he was all talk with them, and so he got a name for clean-living. But the thing was that King Haakon, as they knew, was a good and pious man himself, and fain would keep order among his men, and hold them to a seemly walk and conversation — the young ones at least; the others were apt to be too much for him. And it came about that whatever pranks the youngsters managed to slip out and take part in — drinking bouts, gambling and beer-drinking and such-like — the priest of the King's household always got to hear of, and the madcaps had to confess and pay scot and suffer hard reproof; ay, two or three of the wildest youths of all were hunted away. But at last it came out, it was this fox, Bentein secretarius — unknown to any one he had been made free of all the beer-houses and worse places still; he confessed the serving-wenches and gave them absolution. . . .

Kristin sat at her mother's side; she tried to eat so that no one should mark how it was with her, though her hand shook so that she spilled the milk porridge at each spoonful, and her tongue felt so thick and dry in her mouth that she could not swallow the morsels of bread. But when Simon began to tell of Bentein, she

had to give up making believe to eat; she held on to
the bench beneath her — terror and loathing seized
her, so that she felt dizzy and sick. It was he who had
wanted to. . . . Bentein and Arne, Bentein and Arne.
. . . Beside herself with impatience, she waited for
them to be finished. She longed to see Arne, Arne's
comely face, to throw herself down beside him and
mourn and forget all else.

As her mother helped her with her outer wrappings,
she kissed her daughter on the cheek. Kristin was so
little used to endearments from her mother now, it
comforted her much — she laid her head upon
Ragnfrid's shoulder a moment, but she could not weep.

When they came out into the courtyard, she saw
that others were going with them — Halvdan, Jon
from Laugarbru, and Simon and his man. It gave her a
pang, she knew not why, that the two strangers should
be coming with them.

It was a bitter cold evening, and the snow crackled
underfoot; in the black sky the stars crowded thick,
glittering like rime. When they had ridden a little way,
they heard yells and howls and furious hoof-beats from
the flats to the south — a little farther up the road
a whole troop of horsemen came tearing up behind
and swept past them with a ringing of metal, leaving
behind a vapour of reeking, rime-covered horse-flesh,
which reached them even where they stood aside in
the deep snow. Halvdan hailed the wild crew — they
were youths from the farms in the south of the parish;
they were still keeping Yuletide and were out trying
their horses. Some, who were too drunk to understand,
thundered on at a gallop, roaring at the top of their
voices and hammering on their shields. But a few
grasped the tidings which Halvdan shouted to them;
they fell out of the troop, grew silent, joined Lavrans'
company and talked in whispers to those in the rear.

At last they came in sight of Finsbrekken, on the
hillside beyond the Sil river. There were lights about
the houses — in the middle of the courtyard pine-root

torches had been planted in a heap of snow, and their glare lay red over the white slopes, but the black houses looked as though smeared with clotted blood. One of Arne's little sisters stood outside and stamped her feet; she hugged her hands beneath her cloak. Kristin kissed the tear-stained, half-frozen child. Her heart was heavy as stone, and it seemed as though she had lead in her limbs, as she climbed the stairs to the loft-room where they had laid him.

The sound of singing and the glitter of many lighted candles met them in the doorway. In the middle of the room stood the coffin he had been brought home in, covered with a sheet; boards had been laid on trestles and the coffin placed upon them. At the head of the bier a young priest stood with a book in his hands, chanting; round about knelt the mourners with their faces hidden in their heavy cloaks.

Lavrans lit his candle at one of those already burning, set it firmly upon one of the boards of the bier and knelt down. Kristin tried to do the like, but could not get her candle to stand; so Simon took it and helped her. As long as the priest went on chanting, all stayed upon their knees and repeated his words in whispers, their breath hanging like steam about their mouths in the bitter cold air of the room.

When the priest shut his book and the folk rose — there were many gathered in the death-chamber already — Lavrans went forward to Inga. She stared at Kristin, and seemed scarce to hear what Lavrans said; she stood holding the gifts he had handed to her, as though she knew not she had aught in her hand.

"Are *you* come, too, Kristin," she said in a strange, choking voice. "Maybe you would see my son, so as he is come back to me?"

She pushed some of the candles aside, seized Kristin's arm with a shaking hand, and with the other swept the napkin from the face of the dead.

It was greyish-yellow like clay, and the lips had the

hue of lead; they had parted a little, so that the small, even, bone-white teeth showed through as in a mocking smile. Under the long eyelashes there was a gleam of the glassy eyes, and there were some livid stains below the temples, either marks of blows or the death-spots.

"Maybe you would kiss him?" asked Inga, as before; and Kristin bent forward at her bidding and pressed her lips upon the dead man's cheek. It was clammy as with dew, and she thought she could feel the least breath of decay; the body had begun to thaw perhaps with the heat from all the tapers round.

Kristin stayed still, lying with her hands on the bier, for she could not rise. Inga drew the shroud farther aside, so that the great gash above the collar-bone came to sight. Then she turned towards the people and said with a shaking voice:

"They lie, I see, who say a dead man's wounds will bleed when he is touched by him who wrought his death. He is colder now, my boy, and less comely, than when you met him last down there upon the road. You care not much to kiss him now, I see — but I have heard you scorned not his lips then."

"Inga," said Lavrans, coming forward, "have you lost your wits — are you raving — "

"Oh, ay, you are all so fine, down at Jörundgaard — you were far too rich a man, you Lavrans Björgulfson, for my son to dare think of courting your daughter with honour — and Kristin, too, she thought herself too good. But she was not too good to run after him on the highway at night and play with him in the thickets the night he left — ask her yourself and we will see if she dare deny it here, with Arne lying dead — and all through her lightness — "

Lavrans did not ask; he turned to Gyrd:

"Curb your wife, man — you see she has clean lost her wits — "

But Kristin lifted her white face and looked desperately about her:

"I went and met Arne the last evening because he begged me to. But naught of wrong passed between us." And then, as she seemed to come to herself and to understand all, she cried out: "I know not what you mean, Inga — would you slander Arne and he lying here — never did he tempt me nor lure me astray — "

But Inga laughed aloud:

"Nay, not Arne! but Bentein Priest — *he* did not let you play with him so — ask Gunhild, Lavrans, that washed the dirt off your daughter's back; and ask each man who was in the Bishop's henchmen's hall on New Year's Eve, when Bentein flouted Arne for that he had let her go, and leave him standing like a fool. She let Bentein walk homeward with her under her cloak, and would have played the same game with him — "

Lavrans took her by the shoulder and laid his hand over her mouth:

"Take her away, Gyrd. Shameful it is that you should speak such words by this good youth's body — but if all your children lay here dead, I would not stand and hear you lie about mine — you, Gyrd, must answer for what this mad-woman says — "

Gyrd took hold of his wife and tried to lead her away, but he said to Lavrans:

"'Tis true, though, 'twas of Kristin they talked, Arne and Bentein, when my son lost his life. Like enough you have not heard it, but there hath been talk in the parish here, too, this autumn — "

Simon struck a blow with his sword upon the clothes-chest beside him:

"Nay, good folk, now must you find somewhat else to talk of in this death-chamber than my betrothed. . . . Priest, can you not rule these folk and keep seemly order here — ?"

The priest — Kristin saw now he was the youngest son from Ulvsvolden, who had been at home for Yule — opened his book and stood up beside the bier. But Lavrans shouted that those who had talked about his

daughter, let them be who they might, should be made
to swallow their words; and Inga shrieked:

"Ay, take my life then, Lavrans, since she has taken
all my comfort and joy — and make her wedding with
this knight's son; but yet do all folk know that she
was wed with Bentein upon the highway. . . . Here
. . ." and she cast the sheet Lavrans had given her right
across the bier to Kristin, "I need not Ragnfrid's linen
to lay my Arne in the grave — make head-cloths of
it, you, or keep it to swaddle your roadside brat — and
go down and help Gunhild to moan for the man that's
hanged — "

Lavrans, Gyrd and the priest took hold of Inga.
Simon tried to lift Kristin, who was lying over the
bier. But she thrust his arm fiercely aside, drew herself
up straight upon her knees, and cried aloud:

"So God my Saviour help me, it is false!" and,
stretching out one hand, she held it over the nearest
candle on the bier.

It seemed as if the flame bent and waved aside —
Kristin felt all eyes fixed upon her — what seemed to
her a long time went by. And then all at once she grew
ware of a burning pain in her palm, and with a piercing cry she fell back upon the floor.

She thought herself she had swooned — but she
was aware that Simon and the priest raised her. Inga
shrieked out something; she saw her father's horror-
stricken face, and heard the priest shout that no one
must take account of this ordeal — not thus might one
call God to witness, — and then Simon bore her from
the room and down the stairs. Simon's man ran to the
stable, and soon after Kristin was sitting, still half
senseless, in front of Simon on his saddle, wrapped in
his cloak, and he was riding toward Jörundgaard as
fast as his horse could gallop.

They were nigh to Jörundgaard when Lavrans came
up with them. The rest of their company came thun-
dering along the road far behind.

"Say naught to your mother," said Simon, as he set

her down at the door of the house. "We have heard all too much wild talk to-night; 'tis no wonder you lost your wits yourself at the last."

Ragnfrid was lying awake when they came in, and she asked how things had been in the wake-chamber. Simon took it upon himself to answer for all. Ay, there had been many candles and many folk; ay, there had been a priest — Tormod from Ulvsvolden — Sira Eirik he heard had ridden off to Hamar this very evening, so there would be no trouble about the burial.

"We must have a mass said over the lad," said Ragnfrid. "God strengthen Inga; the good, worthy woman is sorely tried."

Lavrans sang the same tune as Simon, and in a little Simon said that now they must all go to rest, "for Kristin is both weary and sorrowful."

After a time, when Ragnfrid slept, Lavrans threw on a few clothes, and went and seated himself on the edge of his daughters' bed. He found Kristin's hand in the dark, and said very gently:

"Now must you tell me, child, what is true and what is false in all this talk Inga is spreading."

Sobbing, Kristin told him all that had befallen the evening Arne set out for Hamar. Lavrans said but little. Kristin crept toward him in her bed, threw her arms round his neck and wailed softly:

"It *is* my fault that Arne is dead — 'tis but too true, what Inga said — "

" 'Twas Arne himself that begged you to go and meet him," said Lavrans, pulling the coverlid up over his daughter's bare shoulders. "I trow it was heedless in me to let you two go about together, but I thought the lad would have known better. . . . I will not blame you two — I know these things are heavy for you to bear. Yet did I never think that daughter of mine would fall into ill-fame in this parish of ours — and 'twill go hard with your mother when she hears these

tidings. . . . But that you went to Gunhild with this
and not to me, 'twas so witless a thing — I understand
not how you could behave so foolishly — "

"I cannot bear to stay here in the Dale any more,"
sobbed Kristin. "Not a soul would I dare look in the
face — and all I have brought upon them — the folks
at Romundgaard and at Finsbrekken — "

"Ay, they will have to see to it, both Gyrd and Sira
Eirik," said Lavrans, "that these lies about you are
buried with Arne. For the rest, 'tis Simon Andressön
can best defend you in this business," said he, and patted
her in the dark. "Think you not he took the matter
well and wisely — "

"Father" — and Kristin clung close to him and
begged piteously and fervently — "send me to the
convent, father. Ay, listen to me — I have thought of
this for long; maybe Ulvhild will grow well if I go
in her stead. You know the shoes with beads upon
them that I sewed for her in the autumn — I pricked
my fingers sorely, and my hands bled from the sharp
gold-thread — yet I sat and sewed on them, for I
thought it was wicked of me not to love my sister so
that I would be a nun to help her — Arne once asked
if I would not. Had I but said 'Ay' then, all this would
not have befallen — "

Lavrans shook his head:

"Lie down now," he bade. "You know not yourself
what you say, poor child. Now you must try if you
can sleep — "

But Kristin lay and felt the smart in her burnt hand,
and despair and bitterness over her fate raged in her
heart. No worse could have befallen her had she been
the most sinful of women; every one would believe —
no, she could not, could not bear to stay on here in
the Dale. Horror after horror rose before her — when
her mother came to know of this — and now there
was blood between them and their parish priest, ill-will

betwixt all who had been friends around her the whole of her life. But the worst, the most crushing fear of all fell upon her when she thought of Simon and of how he had taken her and carried her away and stood forth for her at home, and borne himself as though she were his own possession — her father and mother had fallen aside before him as though she belonged already more to him than to them . . .

Then she thought of Arne's face in the coffin, cold and cruel. She remembered the last time she was at church, she had seen, as she left, an open grave that stood waiting for a dead man. The upthrown clods of earth lay upon the snow, hard and cold and grey like iron — to this had she brought Arne . . .

All at once the thought came to her of a summer evening many years before. She was standing on the balcony of the loft-room at Finsbrekken, the same room where she had been struck down that night. Arne was playing ball with some boys in the courtyard below, and the ball was hit up to her in the balcony. She had held it behind her back, and would not give it up when Arne came after it; then he had tried to wrest it from her by strength — and they had fought for it, in the balcony, in the room amid the chests, with the leather sacks, which hung there full of clothes, bumping their heads as they knocked against them in their frolic; they had laughed and struggled over that ball . . .

And then, at last, the truth seemed to come home to her: he was dead and gone, and she should never again see his comely, fearless face nor feel the touch of his warm, living hands. And she had been so childish and so heartless as never to give a thought to what it must be for him to lose her. . . . She wept bitter tears, and felt she had earned all her unhappiness. But then the thought came back of all that still awaited her, and she wept anew, for, after all, it seemed to her too hard a punishment . . .

* * *

It was Simon who told Ragnfrid of what had happened in the corpse-chamber at Brekken the night before. He did not make more of it than he needs must. But Kristin was so mazed with sorrow and night-waking that she felt a senseless anger against him because he talked as if it were not so dreadful a thing after all. Besides it vexed her sorely that her father and mother let Simon behave as though he were master in the house.

"And you, Simon — surely you believe not aught of this?" asked Ragnfrid fearfully.

"No," replied Simon. "Nor do I deem there is any one who believes it — they know you and her and this Bentein; but so little befalls for folk to talk of in these outparishes, 'tis but reason they should fall to on such a fat tidbit. 'Tis for us to teach them Kristin's good name is too fine fare for such clowns as they. But pity it was she let herself be so frighted by his grossness that she went not forthwith to you or to Sira Eirik with the tale — methinks this bordel-priest would but too gladly have avowed he meant naught worse than harmless jesting, had you, Lavrans, got a word with him."

Both Kristin's parents said that Simon was right in this. But she cried out, stamping her foot:

"But he threw me down on the ground, I say — I scarce know myself what he did or did not do — I was beside myself; I can remember naught — for all I know it may be as Inga says — I have not been well nor happy a single day since — "

Ragnfrid shrieked and clasped her hands together; Lavrans started up — even Simon's face fell. He looked at her sharply, then went up to her and took her by the chin. Then he laughed:

"God bless you, Kristin — you had remembered but too well if he had done you any harm. No marvel if she has been sad and ill since that unhappy evening she had such an ugly fright — she who had never known

aught but kindness and goodwill before," said he to
the others. "Any but the evil-minded, who would fain
think ill rather than good, can see by her eyes that she
is a maid, and no woman."

Kristin looked up into her betrothed's small, steady
eyes. She half lifted her hands — as if to throw them
round his neck — when he went on:

"You must not think, Kristin, that you will not forget this. 'Tis not in my mind that we should settle
down at Formo as soon as we are wed, so that you
would never leave the Dale. No one has the same hue
of hair or mind in both rain and sunshine, said old
King Sverre, when they blamed his Birch-legs * for
being over-bearing in good-fortune — "

Lavrans and Ragnfrid smiled — it was pleasant
enough to hear the young man discourse with the air
of a wise old bishop. Simon went on:

" 'Twould ill beseem me to seek to teach you, who
are to be my father-in-law; but so much, maybe, I may
make bold to say, that we, my brothers and sisters and
I, were brought up more strictly; we were not let run
about so freely with the house folk as I have seen that
Kristin is used to. My mother often said that if one
played with the cottar-carls' brats, 'twas like one
would get a louse or two in one's hair in the end —
and there's somewhat in that saying."

Lavrans and Ragnfrid held their peace; but Kristin
turned away, and the wish she had felt but a moment
before, to clasp Simon round the neck, had quite left
her.

Towards noon, Lavrans and Simon took their ski
and went out to see to some snares up on the mountain
ridges. The weather was fine outside — sunshine, and
the cold not so great. Both men were glad to slip away

---

* Birch-legs, see Note 10.

from all the sadness and weeping at home, and so they went far — right up among the bare hilltops.

They lay in the sun under a crag and drank and ate; Lavrans spoke a little of Arne — he had loved the boy well. Simon chimed in, praised the dead lad, and said he thought it not strange that Kristin grieved for her foster-brother. Then Lavrans said: maybe they should not press her much, but should give her a little time to get back her peace of mind before they drank the betrothal ale. She had said somewhat of wishing to go into a convent for a time.

Simon sat bolt upright and gave a long whistle.

"You like not the thought?" asked Lavrans.

"Nay, but I do, I do," said the other hastily. "Methinks it is the best way, dear father-in-law. Send her to the Sisters in Oslo for a year — there will she learn how folk talk one of the other out in the world. I know a little of some of the maidens who are there," he said, laughing. "*They* would not throw themselves down and die of grief if two mad yonkers tore each other to pieces for their sakes. Not that I would have such an one for wife — but methinks Kristin will be none the worse for meeting new folks."

Lavrans put the rest of the food into the wallet, and said, without looking at the youth:

"Methinks you love Kristin — ?"

Simon laughed a little and did not look at Lavrans.

"Be sure, I know her worth — and yours, too," he said quickly and shamefacedly, as he got up and took his ski. "None that I have ever met would I sooner wed with — "

A little before Easter, when there was still snow enough for sleighing down the Dale and the ice still bore on Mjösen, Kristin journeyed southward for the second time. Simon came up to bear her company — so now she journeyed driving in a sleigh, well wrapped in furs and with father and betrothed beside her; and after them followed her father's men, and sledges with her clothes and gifts of food and furs for the Abbess and the Sisters of Nonneseter.

THE BRIDAL WREATH

PART TWO

THE GARLAND

Aasmund Björgulfsön's church-boat stood in round the point of Hovedö * early one Sunday at the end of April, while the bells were ringing in the cloister-church and were answered from across the bay by the chime of bells from the town, now louder and now fainter as the breeze rose or fell.

Light, fluted clouds were floating over the high, pale-blue heavens, and the sun was glittering on the dancing ripples of the water. It was quite spring-like along the shores; the fields lay almost bare of snow, and over the leaf-tree thickets the light had a yellow shimmer and the shadows were blue. But in the pine-forests up on the high ridges, which framed in the settled lands of Akersbygd, there were glimpses of snow, and on the far blue fells to the westward, beyond the fjord, there still showed many flashes of white.

Kristin was standing in the bow of the boat with her father, and Gyrid, Aasmund's wife. She gazed at the town, with all the light-hued churches and stone buildings that rose above the swarm of grey-brown wooden houses and bare tree-tops. The wind ruffled the skirts of her cloak and snatched at her hair beneath her hood.

They had let the cattle out at Skog the day before, and a great longing had come on her to be at Jörundgaard. It would be a long time still before they could let the cattle out there — she longed with tender pity for the lean, winter-worn cows in the dark byres; they would have to wait and suffer a long while yet. Her mother, Ulvhild, who had slept in her arms each night all these years, little Ramborg — she yearned so

* Hovedö, see Note 11.

much for them; she longed for all the folk at home, and the horses and the dogs, for Kortelin, whom Ulvhild was to have while she was gone, and for her father's hawks as they sat there on their perches with their hoods over their heads. She saw the horse-hide gloves that hung beside them to wear when you took them on to your wrist, and the ivory staves to scratch them with.

It was as if all the woe of the last winter had gone far away from her, and she only saw her home as it used to be. They had told her, too, that none thought ill of her in the parish — Sira Eirik did not believe that story; he was angry and grieved at what Bentein had done. Bentein had fled from Hamar; 'twas said he had gone to Sweden. So things were not so bad between them and their neighbour as she had feared.

On the journey down to Oslo they had stayed as guests at Simon's home, and she had come to know his mother and sisters — Sir Andres was in Sweden still. She had not felt at ease there, and her dislike of the Dyfrin folk was all the stronger that she could think of no good ground for it. All the way thither, she had said to herself that they had no cause to be proud or to think themselves better than her kin — no man knew aught of Reidar Darre, the Birch-leg, before King Sverre got him the widow of the Dyfrin Baron * to wife. But lo! they were not proud at all; and when Simon himself spoke one night of his forefather: "I have found out now for sure — he was a comb-maker — so 'tis as though you were to come into a kingly stock — almost, Kristin," said he. "Take heed to your tongue, boy," said his mother, but they all laughed together. It vexed her strangely when she thought of her father; he laughed much, if Simon gave him the least cause — a thought came to her dimly that maybe her father would gladly have had more laughter in his

---

* Baron, see Note 12.

life. But 'twas not to her mind that he should like Simon so much.

They had all been at Skog over Easter. She had found that her uncle was a hard master to his farmers and serving-folk — she had met one and another who asked after her mother and spoke lovingly of Lavrans; they had better times when he lived here. Aasmund's mother, Lavrans' stepmother, lived on the manor in a house by herself; she was not so very old, but sickly and failing. Lavrans had but seldom spoken of her at home. Once when Kristin asked him if he had had a hard stepmother, her father answered: "She never did much to me of either good or ill."

Kristin felt for her father's hand, and he pressed hers:

"You will be happy soon enough, my daughter, with the good Sisters — you will have other things to think of besides longing to be home with us — "

They sailed so near by the town that the smell of tar and salt fish was borne out to them from the wharves. Gyrid named all the churches, the traders' quarters, and the open places which run up from the water's edge — Kristin remembered nothing from the time she was here before but the great heavy towers of St. Halvard's Church. They sailed westward past the whole town and laid to at the convent pier.

Kristin walked between her father and her uncle through a cluster of warehouses, and came out upon a road which led up through the fields. Simon came after, leading Gyrid by the hand. The serving-folk stayed behind to help some men from the convent load the baggage upon a cart.

Nonneseter and the whole Leiran quarter lay within the boundaries of the town grazing-grounds, but there were but a few clusters of houses here and there along the roadside. The larks were trilling over their heads in the pale-blue sky, and the small yellow flowers of the coltsfoot were thickly sprinkled over the wan clay slopes, but along by the fences the roots of the grass were green.

When they were through the gate and were come into the cloister, all the nuns came marching two by two towards them from the church, while song and music streamed out after them through the open door.

Ill at ease, Kristin watched the many black-robed women with white linen wimples about their faces. She curtsied low, and the men bowed with their hats held close to their breasts. After the nuns came a flock of young maidens — some of them but children — in gowns of undyed wadmal, their waists bound with belts of twined black and white, and their hair braided tightly back from their faces with cords of the same black and white. Without thinking, Kristin put on a bold and forward look as the young maids passed, for she felt bashful, and was afraid they must think she looked countrified and foolish.

The convent was so glorious that she was quite overcome. All the buildings round the inner court were of grey stone; on the north side the main wall of the church stood up high above the other houses; it had two tiers of roofs and towers at the west end. The court itself was laid with stone flags, and round the whole there ran a covered way, whose roof was borne on pillars fairly wrought. In the midst of the court stood a stone statue of the Mater Misericordiæ, spreading her cloak over some kneeling figures.

Then a lay-sister came and prayed them to go with her to the Abbess' parlour. The Lady Groa Guttormsdatter was a tall and stoutly made old woman — she would have been comely had she not had so many hairs about her mouth. Her voice was deep like a man's. But her bearing was gentle and kindly — she called to mind that she had known Lavrans' father and mother, and asked after his wife and his other children. Last she spoke to Kristin in friendly wise:

"I have heard good report of you, and you look to be wise and well nurtured — sure I am you will give us no cause for miscontent. I have heard that you are plighted to this good and well-born man, Simon Andressön, whom I see here — it seems to us that 'twas wise counsel of your father and your husband to be, to grant you leave to live here awhile in the Virgin Mary's house, that you may learn to obey and serve before you are called to rule and to command. Now would I have you lay to heart this counsel: that you learn to find joy in prayer and the worship of God, that you may use yourself in all your doings to remember your Creator, God's gentle Mother, and all the Saints who have given us the best patterns of strength, uprightness, faithfulness and all the virtues you must show forth in guiding your people and your goods and nurturing your children. And you will learn in this house, too, to take good heed of time, for here every hour has its use and its task also. Many young maids and women love all too well to lie abed late of a morning, and sit long at table of an evening in idle talk — yet look not you as you were one of these. Yet may you learn much in the year you are here that may profit you both here on earth and in our heavenly home."

Kristin curtsied and kissed her hand. After that Lady Groa bade Kristin go with a monstrously fat old nun, whom she called Sister Potentia, over to the nuns' refectory. The men and Gyrid she asked to dine with her in another house.

The refectory was a great and fair room with a stone floor and pointed windows with glass panes. There was a doorway into another room, where, Kristin could see, there must be glass windows too, for the sun shone in.

The Sisters were already seated at the table waiting for their food — the elder nuns upon a cushioned stone-bench along the wall under the windows; the younger Sisters and the bareheaded maidens in light-hued wadmal dresses sat upon a wooden bench on the outer side of the board. In the next room a board was laid too; this was for the commoners * and the lay-servants; there were a few old men among them. These folk did not wear the convent habit, but were none the less clad soberly in dark raiment.

Sister Potentia showed Kristin to a seat on the outer bench, but went and placed herself near to the Abbess' high-seat at the end of the board — the high-seat was empty to-day.

All rose, both in this room and in the side-room, while the Sisters said grace. After that a fair, young nun went and stood at a lectern placed in the doorway between the two chambers. And while the lay-sisters in the greater room, and two of the youngest nuns in the side-room, bore in food and drink, the nun read in a high and sweet voice, and without stopping or tripping at a single word, the story of St. Theodora and St. Didymus.

At first Kristin was thinking most of minding her table-manners, for she saw all the Sisters and the young maids bore them as seemly and ate as nicely as though they had been sitting at the finest feast. There was abundance of the best food and drink, but all helped themselves modestly, and dipped but the very tips of their fingers into the dishes; no one spilled the broth either upon the cloths or upon their garments, and all cut up the meat so small that they did not soil their mouths, and ate with so much care that not a sound was to be heard.

Kristin grew hot with fear that she might not seem as well behaved as the others; she was feeling ill at ease, too, in her bright dress in the midst of all these women in black and white — she fancied they were all looking at her. So when she had to eat a fat piece of breast of mutton, and was holding it by the bone with two fingers, while cutting morsels off with her right hand, and taking care to handle the knife lightly and neatly — suddenly the whole slipped from her

---

* Commoners, see Note 13.

fingers; her slice of bread and the meat flew on to the cloth, and the knife fell clattering on the stone flags.

The noise sounded fearfully in the quiet room. Kristin flushed red as fire and would have bent to pick up the knife, but a lay-sister came noiselessly in her sandals and gathered up the things.

But Kristin could eat no more. She found, too, that she had cut one of her fingers, and she was afraid of bleeding upon the cloth; so she sat with her hand wrapped in a corner of her skirt, and thought of how she was staining the goodly light blue dress she had gotten for the journey to Oslo, and she did not dare to raise her eyes from her lap.

Howbeit, in a little she began to listen more to what the nun was reading. When the ruler found he could not shake the steadfastness of the maid, Theodora — she would neither make offerings to the false gods nor let herself be given in marriage — he bade them lead her to a brothel. Yet while on the way thither he exhorted her to think of her freeborn kindred and her honoured father and mother, upon whom everlasting shame must now be brought, and gave his word she should be let live in peace and stay a maid, if she would but join the service of a heathen goddess, whom they called Diana.

Theodora answered fearlessly: "Chastity is like a lamp, but love of God is the flame; were I to serve the devil-woman whom you call Diana, my chastity were no more worth than a rusty lamp without flame or oil. Thou callest me freeborn, but we are all born bondsmen, since our first parents sold us to the devil; Christ has bought me free, and I am bound to serve Him, so that I cannot wed me with His foes. He will guard His dove; but should He even suffer you to break my body, that is the temple of His Holy Spirit, it shall not be counted to me for shame, if so be that I consent not to betray what is His into the hands of His enemies."

Kristin's heart began to throb, for this in some way

reminded her of her meeting with Bentein — she was smitten by the thought that this perhaps was her sin — she had not for a moment thought of God nor prayed for His help. And now Sister Cecilia read further of St. Didymus. He was a Christian knight, but heretofore he had kept his faith hidden from all save a few friends. He went now to the house where the maid was; he gave money to the woman who owned the house, and thus was the first to be let in to Theodora. She fled into a corner like a frightened hare, but Didymus hailed her as his sister and as his Lord's bride, and said he was come to save her. Then he spake with her awhile, saying: Was it not meet that a brother should wage his life for his sister's honour? And at last she did as he bade her, changed clothes with him, and let herself be clad in Didymus' coat of mail; he pulled the hat down over her eyes and drew the cape up about her chin, and bade her go out with her face hidden, like a youth who is abashed at having been in such a place.

Kristin thought of Arne, and was scarce able to hold back her tears. She gazed straight before her with wet eyes while the nun was reading to the end — how Didymus was led to the place of execution, and how Theodora came hastening down from the mountains, cast herself at the headsman's feet and begged that she might die in his stead. And now the holy man and maid strove together who should first win the crown; and both were beheaded on the one day. This was the eighth-and-twentieth day of April in the year 304 after the birth of Christ, in Antioch, as was written by St. Ambrosius.

When they rose from the table, Sister Potentia came and patted Kristin kindly on the cheek: "Ay, you are longing for your mother, I can well believe." And on that Kristin's tears began to fall. But the nun made as though she did not see them, and led Kristin to the hostel where she was to dwell.

It was in one of the stone houses by the cloisters, a

goodly room with glass windows and a big fireplace in
the short wall at the far end. Along one main wall
stood six bedsteads, and along the other all the maidens'
chests.

Kristin wished they would let her sleep with one of
the little girls, but Sister Potentia called a fat, fair-
haired, grown maiden: "Here is Ingebjörg Filippusdatter, who is to be your bed-fellow — you must see now
and learn to know each other." And with that she
went out.

Ingebjörg took Kristin at once by the hand and began
to talk. She was not very tall, and was much too fat,
above all in the face — her cheeks were so plump that
her eyes looked quite small. But her skin was clear,
red and white, and her hair was yellow as gold, and so
curly that her thick plaits twisted and twined together
like strands of rope, and small locks kept ever slipping
from under her snood.

She began straightway to question Kristin about
many things, but never waited for an answer; instead
she talked about herself, reckoned out the whole of
her kindred in all its branches — they were naught but
fine and exceeding rich folk. She was betrothed, too,
to a rich and mighty man, Einar Einarssön of Aganæs
— but he was far too old, and twice widowed; this was
her greatest sorrow, she said. Yet could Kristin not
mark that she took it much to heart. Then she talked
a little of Simon Darre — 'twas a marvel how closely
she had looked him over in the short moment when
they were passing in the cloisters. After that she had
a mind to look into Kristin's chest — but first she
opened her own and brought forth all her clothes.
While they were ransacking their chests, Sister Cecilia
came in — she rebuked them and said that this was no
seemly Sunday pastime. This made Kristin unhappy
again — she had never been taken to task by any but
her own mother, and that was not the same as being
chid by a stranger.

Ingebjörg was not abashed. After they were come

to bed in the evening, she lay chattering until Kristin
fell asleep. Two elder lay-sisters slept in a corner of
the room; they were to see that the maidens did not
take their shifts off at night — for it was against the
rules for the girls to undress entirely — and to see that
they were up in time for matins in the church. But
else they did not trouble themselves to keep order in
the hostel, and made as though they marked it not
when the maids were lying talking, or eating the
dainties which they had hidden in their chests.

When Kristin was awakened next morning, Ingebjörg was in the midst of a long tale already, so that
Kristin almost wondered whether the other had been
talking the whole night through.

2

THE FOREIGN merchants who lay in Oslo during the
summer and trafficked there, came to the town in the
spring about Holy Rood Day, which is ten days before
the Halvards-wake Fair.* To this folk streamed in
from all the parishes between Mjösen and the Swedish
marches, so that the town swarmed with people in
the first weeks of May. This was the best time to buy
from the strangers, before they had sold too many of
their wares.

Sister Potentia had the care of the marketing for
Nonneseter, and she had promised Ingebjörg and
Kristin that they should go with her down to the town
the day before the Halvards-wake. But about midday
some of Sister Potentia's kin came to the convent to
see her; and so she could not go that day. Then Ingebjörg begged and prayed till at last she let them go
alone — although it was against the rules. An old
peasant who was a commoner of the convent was sent
with them as escort — Haakon was his name.

* Saints' Days and Festivals, see Note 14.

Kristin had been three weeks now at Nonneseter, and in all that time she had not set foot outside the convent grounds and gardens. She wondered to see how spring-like it was outside. The little woods out in the fields were pale-green; the wood anemones grew thick as a carpet round the light-coloured tree stems; white fair-weather clouds came sailing up over the islands in the fjord, and the water lay fresh and blue, slightly ruffled here and there by the light flaws of wind.

Ingebjörg skipped about, plucked bunches of leaves from the trees and smelt them, and peeped round after the folk they met; till Haakon chid her — were these seemly goings-on for a wellborn maid, and in the convent habit too? The maidens were made to walk just behind him, hand in hand, quietly and seemly; but Ingebjörg used her eyes and her tongue all the same — Haakon was somewhat deaf. Kristin, too, was wearing the novices' garb now — an undyed, light-grey wadmal dress, woollen belt and head-band, and a plain, dark blue cloak over all, with a hood turned up so that the plaited hair was quite hid. Haakon strode in front with a stout brass-knobbed staff in his hand. He was dressed in a long black gown, had a leaden Agnus Dei hanging on his breast and an image of St. Christopher in his hat — his white hair and beard were so well brushed that they shone like silver in the sunshine.

The upper part of the town between the Nunsbeck and the bishop's palace was a quiet neighbourhood; there were here neither shops nor taverns; most of the dwelling-places belonged to great folk from the parishes around, and the houses turned dark, windowless, timber gables to the street. But on this day whole crowds of people were roaming about the roads even up here, and the serving-folk stood loitering about the courtyard gates gossiping with the passers-by.

When they were come out near the bishop's palace, there was a great crush upon the place in front of Halvard's Church and the Olav-cloister — booths had been set up on the grassy slopes, and there were show-men making trained dogs jump through barrelhoops. But Haakon would not have the maids stand and look at these things, and he would not let Kristin go into the church — he said 'twould be better worth her seeing on the great Feast-day itself.

As they came down over the open space by St. Clement's Church, Haakon took them by the hands, for here was the greatest press of folk coming from the wharves or out from the alleys between the traders' yards.* The maidens were bound for the Mickle Yard, where the shoemakers plied their trade. For Ingebjörg had found the clothes Kristin had brought from home very good and sightly, but she said the shoes she had with her from the Dale were not fit to wear for best. And when Kristin had seen the shoes from the outland Ingebjörg had in her chest — more pairs than one — she felt she could not rest until she too had bought some like them.

The Mickle Yard was one of the largest in Oslo; it stretched from the wharves up to the Souters' Alley, with more than forty houses round two great courts. And now they had set up booths with wadmal roofs in the courts as well. Above the roofs of these tents there rose a statue of St. Crispinus. Within the courts was a great throng of folk buying and selling, women running between the kitchens with pots and pails, children getting in the way of folks' feet, horses being led in and out of the stables, and serving-men carrying packages to and from the warehouses. From the bal-conies of the lofts above, where the finest wares were sold, shoemakers and their apprentices shouted to the two maids and dangled small gaily-coloured or gold-embroidered shoes before them.

But Ingebjörg made her way toward the loft where Didrek the shoemaker sat; he was a German, but had a Norse wife and owned a house in the Mickle Yard.

---

* Town Yards, see Note 15.

The old man was standing bargaining with an esquire wearing a traveller's cloak, and a sword at his belt; but Ingebjörg went forward unabashed, bowed, and said:

"Good sir, will you not suffer us of your courtesy to have speech with Didrek first? We must be home in our convent by vespers; you, perchance, have no such great haste?"

The esquire bowed and stepped aside. Didrek nudged Ingebjörg with his elbow and asked, laughing, whether they danced so much in the convent that she had worn out already all the shoon she had of him the year before. Ingebjörg nudged him again and said they were still unworn, thank Heaven, but here was this other maid — and she pulled Kristin forward. Then Didrek and his lad bore forth a box into the balcony; and out of it he brought forth shoes, each pair finer than the last. They had Kristin sit down upon a chest that he might try them on her — there were white shoes and brown and red and green and blue, shoes with painted wooden heels and shoes without heels, shoes with buckles and shoes with silken laces in them, shoes in leather of two or of three hues. Kristin felt she would fain have had them all. But they cost so dear she was quite dismayed — not one pair cost less than a cow at home. Her father had given her a purse with a mark of silver in counted money * when he left — that was for pocket money, and Kristin had deemed it great riches. But she soon saw that Ingebjörg thought it no great store to go a marketing with.

Ingebjörg, too, must try on some shoes for the jest of it; that cost no money, said Didrek laughing. She did buy one pair of leaf-green shoes with red heels — she said she must have them on trust, but then Didrek knew her and her folks.

Kristin thought, indeed, that Didrek liked this none too well, and that he was vexed too, that the tàll esquire

---

* Currency, see Note 16.

in the travelling cloak had left the loft — much time
had been taken up with the trying-on. So she chose for
herself a pair of heelless shoes of thin purple-blue
leather, broidered with silver and with rose-red stones.
But she liked not the green silk laces in them. Didrek
said he could change these, and took the maids with
him into a room at the back of the loft. Here he had
coffers full of silk ribbons and small silver buckles —
'twas against the law, strictly, for shoemakers to trade
in these things — and the ribbons, too; were many of
them too broad and the buckles too big for footgear.

They felt they had to buy one or two of the smaller
things, and when they had drunk a cup of sweet wine
with Didrek and he had packed the things they had
bought into a wadmal cloth, the hour was grown somewhat late, and Kristin's purse much lighter.

When they were come to the Ostre Stræte again
the sunlight was turned golden, and, by reason of the
traffic in the town, the dust hung over the street in a
bright haze. The evening was warm and fair, and folk
were coming down from Eikaberg with great armfuls
of young green branches wherewith to deck their
houses for the holy-day. And now the whim took
Ingebjörg that they should go out to the Gjeita bridge
— at fair-times there was wont to be so much merry-
making in the fields on the farther side of the river,
both jugglers and fiddlers — nay, Ingebjörg had heard
there was come a whole shipful of outlandish beasts
that were being shown in booths down by the
waterside.

Haakon had had a pot or two of German beer at
the Mickle Yard, and was now easy and mild of mood;
so when the maidens took him by the arm and begged
him sweetly, he gave way at last, and the three went
out towards Eikaberg.

Beyond the stream there were but a few small dwelling-places scattered about the green slopes between
the river and the steep hillside. They went past the
Minorite monastery, and Kristin's heart sank with

shame as she bethought her how she had meant to give most of her silver for the good of Arne's soul. But she had had no mind to speak of it to the priest at Nonneseter; she feared to be asked questions — she had thought that she could maybe come out to the barefoot friars and find if by chance Brother Edvin were in the cloister now. She was fain to meet him again — but she knew not, either, what would be the most seemly way to get speech with one of the monks and tell him her desire. And now she had so little money she knew not whether she could buy a mass — maybe she must be content to offer a thick wax-candle.

Of a sudden they heard a fearful yell from countless throats down by the shore — a storm seemed to sweep over the press of human beings down there — and now the whole mass rushed towards them, shrieking and shouting. All seemed wild with terror, and some of the runners-by cried out to Haakon and the maids that the pards were loose. . . .

They set out running back to the bridge, and heard folk shout to one another that a booth had fallen down and two pards had broken loose — some spoke of a serpent, too. The nearer they came to the bridge the worse became the crush. Just in front of them a woman dropped a little child out of her arms — Haakon stood astride the little one to shield it — soon after they caught sight of him far away with the child in his arms, and then they lost him.

At the narrow bridge the press of people was so great that the maids were pushed right out into a field. They saw folks run down to the river-bank; young men jumped in and swam, but elder folk sprang into boats that lay there, and these were overladen in a trice.

Kristin tried to make Ingebjörg hear — she cried out to her that they should run up to the Minorite cloister — they could see the Grey Friars come running out from it, striving to gather in the terrified people. Kristin was not so frightened as the other girl — they saw nothing, either, of the wild beasts — but Ingebjörg had quite lost her wits. And now, when there was a fresh uproar in the throng, and it was driven back by a whole troop of men from the nearest dwellings, who had armed themselves and forced their way back over the bridge, some riding and some running, and Ingebjörg was nigh coming under the feet of a horse — she gave a scream and set off running for the woods. Kristin had never thought the girl could have run so fast — it made her think of a hunted pig. She ran after her, so that they two, at least, should not be parted.

They were deep in the woods before Kristin could get Ingebjörg to stop — they were on a little path which seemed to lead down toward the road to Trælaborg. They stood still for a little to get their breath again; Ingebjörg was snivelling and weeping, and said she dared not go back alone through the town and all the way out to the convent.

Nor did Kristin deem that this would be well, with the streets in such commotion; she thought they must try to find a house where they might hire a lad to take them home. Ingebjörg thought there was a bridle-path to Trælaborg farther down by the short, and along it there lay some houses she knew. So they followed the path downward, away from the town.

Fearful and uneasy as they both were, it seemed to them they had gone far ere at last they came to a farmstead lying off in a field. In the courtyard there they found a band of men sitting drinking at a board under some ash trees, while a woman came and went, bearing out tankards to them. She looked wonderingly and sourly at the two maids in convent habit, and none of the men seemed to have a mind to go with them when Kristin told their need. At last, though, two young men stood up and said they would bring the girls to Nonneseter, if Kristin would give them a silver ducat.

She heard by their speech that they were not Norse, but she thought they seemed honest folk enough.

'Twas a shameless sum they asked, she thought, but Ingebjörg was beside herself with fright and she saw not how they could go home alone so late; and so she struck the bargain.

No sooner were they come to the forest-path than the men drew closer to them and began to talk. Kristin liked this but ill, but she would not show she was afraid; so she answered them quietly, told of the pards and asked the men where they were from. She spied about her, too, and made as though she looked each moment to meet the serving-men they had had with them — she talked as though there had been a whole band. As they went on the men spoke less and less — nor did she understand much of their speech.

After a while she became aware that they were not going the same way she had come with Ingebjörg — the course their path took was not the same; 'twas more northerly — and she deemed they had already gone much too far.

Deep within her there smouldered a fear she dared not let herself think upon — but it strengthened her strangely to have Ingebjörg with her, for the girl was so foolish that Kristin knew she must trust in herself alone to find a way out for them both. Under her cloak, she managed by stealth to pull out the cross with the holy relic she had had of her father; she clasped it in her hand, praying fervently in her heart that they might soon meet some one, and in all ways sought to gather all her courage and to make no sign.

Just after this she saw that the path came out on to a road and there was a clearing in the forest. The town and the bay lay far below. The men had led them astray, whether wilfully or because they knew not the paths — they were high up on the mountain-side and far north of Gjeita bridge, which she could see below; the road they had now met seemed to lead thither.

Thereupon she stopped, drew forth her purse and made to count out ten silver pennies into her hand.

"Now, good fellows," said she, "we need you not any more to guide us; for we know the way from here. We thank you for your pains, and here is the wage we bargained for. God be with you, good friends."

The men looked at one another so foolishly, that Kristin was near smiling. Then one said with an ugly grin that the road down to the bridge was exceeding lonely; 'twas not wise for them to go alone.

"None, surely, are such nithings or such fools that they would seek to stop two maids, and they in the convent habit," answered Kristin. "We would fain go our own way alone now —" and she held out the money.

The man caught her by the wrist, thrust his face close up to hers, and said somewhat of "kuss" and "beutel" — Kristin made out he was saying they might go in peace if she but gave him a kiss and her purse.

She remembered Bentein's face close to hers like this, and such a fear came on her for a moment that she grew faint and sick. But she pressed her lips together, and called in her heart upon God and the Virgin Mary — and in the same instant she thought she heard hoof-falls on the path from the north.

She struck the man in the face with her purse so that he staggered — and then she pushed him in the breast with all her strength so that he tumbled off the path and down into the wood. The other German gripped her from behind, tore the purse from her hand and her chain from her neck so that it broke — she was near falling, but clutched the man and tried to get her cross from him again. He struggled to get free — the robbers, too, had now heard folk coming — Ingebjörg screamed with all her might, and the riders on the path came galloping forward at full speed. They burst out of the thicket — three of them — and Ingebjörg ran shrieking to meet them as they sprang from their horses. Kristin knew one for the esquire of Didrek's loft; he drew his sword, seized the German she was struggling with by the back of the neck, and thrashed him with the flat of his blade. His men ran after the other, caught him and beat him to their heart's content.

Kristin leaned against the face of the rock; she was trembling now that all was over, but what she felt most was marvel that her prayer had brought such speedy help. Then she caught sight of Ingebjörg, who had thrown back her hood, hung her cape loosely over her shoulders and was in the act of bringing her heavy, shining plaits of hair forward into sight upon her breast. At this sight Kristin burst out a-laughing — her strength left her and she had to hold on to a tree to keep her feet, for 'twas as though the marrow of her bones was turned to water, she felt so weak; and so she trembled and laughed and cried.

The esquire came forward and laid a hand warily upon her shoulder:

"You were more frightened, I see, than you would show," said he, and his voice was kindly and gentle. "But now you must take a hold on yourself — you bore you so bravely while yet there was peril — "

Kristin could only look up at him and nod. He had fine, bright eyes set in a narrow, pale-brown face, and coal-black hair clipped somewhat short over the forehead and behind the ears.

Ingebjörg had her hair in order now; she came and thanked the stranger with many fair words. He stood there still with a hand on Kristin's shoulder while he anwered her comrade.

"We must take these birds along," said he to his men, who stood holding the two Germans — they were from a Rostock ship, they said — "we must have them along with us to the town that they may be sent to the black hole. But first must we take these two maids home to the convent. You can find some thongs, I trow, to bind them with — "

"Mean you the maids, Erlend?" asked one of the men. They were young, stout, well-appointed yeomen, and were in high feather from the tussle.

Their master frowned and seemed about to answer sharply, but Kristin laid her hand upon his sleeve:

"Let them go, dear sir!" She shuddered a little. "Loth would we be, in truth, both my sister and I, this matter should be talked of."

The stranger looked down at her — he bit his lip and nodded, as though he understood her. Then he gave each of the captives a blow on the nape with the flat of his sword which sent them sprawling forwards. "Run for it, then," he said, kicking them, and both scrambled up and took to their heels as fast as they could. Then he turned again to the maidens and asked if they would please to ride.

Ingebjörg let herself be lifted into Erlend's saddle, but it was soon plain that she could not keep her seat — she slid down again at once. He looked at Kristin doubtfully, and she said that she was used to ride on a man's saddle.

He took hold of her below the knees and lifted her up. A sweet and happy thrill ran through her to feel how carefully he held her from him, as though afraid to come near her — at home, no one ever minded how tight they held her when they helped her on to a horse. She felt marvellously honoured and uplifted.

The knight — as Ingebjörg called him, though he had but silver spurs — now offered that maiden his hand, and his men sprang to their saddles. Ingebjörg would have it that they should ride round the town to the northward below the Ryenberg and Martestokke, and not through the streets. First, she gave as a reason that Sir Erlend and his men were fully armed — were they not? The knight answered gravely that the ban on carrying arms was not over strict at any time — for travellers at least — and now every one in the town was out on a wild beast hunt. Then she said she was fearful of the pards. Kristin saw full well that Ingebjörg was fain to go by the longest and loneliest road, that she might have the more talk with Erlend.

"This is the second time this evening that we hinder you, good sir," said she, and Erlend answered soberly:

" 'Tis no matter, I am bound no farther than to Gerdarud to-night — and 'tis light the whole night long."

It liked Kristin well that he jested not, nor bantered them, but talked to her as though she were his like or even more than his like. She thought of Simon; she had not met other young men of courtly breeding. But 'twas true, this man seemed older than Simon.

They rode down into the valley below the Ryenberg hills and up along the beck. The path was narrow, and the young bushes swung wet, heavily scented branches against her — it was a little darker down here, and the air was cool and the leaves all dewy along the beck-path.

They went slowly, and the horses' hoofs sounded muffled on the damp, grass-grown path. She rocked gently in the saddle; behind her she heard Ingebjörg's chatter, and the stranger's deep, quiet voice. He said little, and answered as if his mind wandered — it sounded almost as if his mood were like her own, she thought — she felt strangely drowsy, yet safe and content now that all the day's chances were safely over.

It was like waking to come out of the woods on to the green slopes under the Martestokke hills. The sun was gone down, and the town and the bay lay below them in a clear, pale light — above the Aker ridges there was a light-yellow strip edging the pale-blue sky. In the evening hush, sounds were borne to them from far off, as they came out of the cool depths of the wood — a cart-wheel creaked somewhere upon a road, dogs on the farms bayed at each other across the valley. And from the woods behind them birds trilled and sang full-throated, now the sun was down.

Smoke was in the air from the fires on lands under clearance, and out in a field there was the red flare of a bonfire; against the great ruddy flame the clearness of the night seemed a kind of darkness.

They were riding between the fences of the convent-fields when the stranger spoke to her again. He asked her what she thought best; should he go with her to the gate and ask for speech of the Lady Groa, so that he might tell her how this thing had come about. But Ingebjörg would have it that they should steal in through the church; then maybe they might slip into the convent without any one knowing they had been away so much too long — it might be her kinsfolks' visit had made Sister Potentia forget them.

The open place before the west door of the church was empty and still, and it came not into Kristin's thoughts to wonder at this, though there was wont to be much life there of an evening, with folks from the neighbourhood who came to the nuns' church, and from the houses round about wherein lay-servants and commoners dwelt. They said farewell to Erlend here. Kristin stood and stroked his horse; it was black, and had a comely head and soft eyes — she thought it like Morvin, whom she had been wont to ride at home when she was a child.

"What is your horse's name, sir?" she asked, as it turned its head from her and snuffed at its master's breast.

"Bayard," said he, looking at her over the horse's neck. "You ask my horse's name, but not mine?"

"I would be fain to know your name, sir," she replied, and bent her head a little.

"I am called Erlend Nikulaussön," said he.

"Then, Erlend Nikulaussön, have thanks for your good service this night," said Kristin, and proffered him her hand.

Of a sudden she flushed red, and half withdrew her hand from his.

"Lady Aashild Gautesdatter of Dovre, is she your kinswoman?" she asked.

To her wonder she saw that he, too, blushed — he dropped her hand suddenly, and answered:

"She is my mother's sister. And I am Erlend Nikulaussön of Husaby." He looked at her so strangely that she became still more abashed, but she mastered herself, and said:

" 'Tis true I should have thanked you with better words, Erlend Nikulaussön; but I know not what I can say to you."

He bowed before her, and she felt that now she must bid him good-bye, though she would fain have spoken more with him. In the church door she turned, and as she saw that Erlend still stood beside his horse, she waved her hand to him in farewell.

The convent was in a hubbub, and all within in great dismay. Haakon had sent word home by a horseman, while he, himself, went seeking the maids in the town; and folks had been sent from the convent to help him. The nuns had heard the wild beasts had killed and eaten up two children down in the town. This, to be sure, was a lie, and the pard — there was only one — had been caught before vespers by some men from the King's palace.

Kristin stood with bent head and kept silence, while the Abbess and Sister Potentia poured out their wrath upon the two maidens. She felt as though something were asleep within her. Ingebjörg wept and began to make excuse — they had gone out with Sister Potentia's leave, with fitting attendance, and, sure, they were not to blame for what had happened after.

But Lady Groa said they might now stay in the church till the hour of midnight struck, that they might strive to turn their thoughts to the things of the spirit, and might thank God who had saved their lives and honour. "God hath now manifested clearly to you the truth about the world," said she; "wild beasts and the servants of the devil threaten his children there at every footstep, and there is no salvation except ye hold fast to Him with prayer and supplication."

She gave them each a lighted candle and bade them go with Sister Cecilia Baardsdatter, who was often alone in the church praying the whole night long.

Kristin put her candle upon St. Lawrence's altar and knelt on the praying-stool. She fixed her gaze on the flame while she said over the Paternoster and the Ave Maria softly. The sheen of the candle seemed little by little to enfold her and to shut out all that was outside her and the light. She felt her heart open and overflow with thankfulness and praise and love of God and His gentle Mother — they came so near to her. She had always known they saw her, but to-night she *felt* that it was so. She saw the world as in a vision; a great dark room whereinto fell a sunbeam; the motes were dancing in and out between the darkness and the light, and she felt that now she had at last slipped into the sunbeam.

She felt she would gladly have stayed for ever in this dark, still church — with the few small spots of light like golden stars in the night, the sweet stale scent of incense, and the warm smell of the burning wax. And she at rest within her own star.

It was as if some great joy were at an end, when Sister Cecilia came gliding to her and touched her shoulder. Bending before the altars, the three women went out of the little south door into the convent close.

Ingebjörg was so sleepy that she went to bed without a word. Kristin was glad — she had been loth to have her good thoughts broken in on. And she was glad, too, that they must keep on their shifts at night — Ingebjörg was so fat and had been so over-hot.

She lay awake long, but the deep flood of sweetness that she had felt lifting her up as she knelt in the church would not come again. Yet she felt the warmth of it within her still; she thanked God with all her heart, and thought she felt her spirit strengthened while she prayed for her father and mother and sisters, and for Arne Gyrdsön's soul.

Father, she thought — she longed so much for him, for all they had been to one another before Simon Darre came into their lives. There welled up in her a new tenderness for him — there was, as it were, a fore-taste of mother's love and care in her love for her father this night; dimly she felt that there was so much in life that he had missed. She called to mind the old, black wooden church at Gerdarud — she had seen there this last Easter the graves of her three little brothers and of her grandmother, her father's own mother, Kristin Sigurdsdatter, who died when she brought him into the world.

What could Erlend Nikulaussön have to do at Gerdarud — she could not think.

She had no knowledge that she had thought much of him that evening, but the whole time the thought of his dark, narrow face and his quiet voice had hung somewhere in the dusk outside the glow of light that enfolded her spirit.

When she awoke the next morning, the sun was shining into the dormitory, and Ingebjörg told her how Lady Groa herself had bidden the lay-sisters not to wake them for matins. She had said that when they woke, they might go over to the kitchen-house and get some food. Kristin grew warm with gladness at the Abbess' kindness — it seemed as if the whole world had been good to her.

3

THE FARMERS' guild * of Aker had St. Margaret for their patroness, and they began their festival each year on the twentieth of July, the day of St. Margaret's

---

* Farmers' Guilds, see Note 17.

Mass. On that day the guild brothers and sisters, with their children, their guests and their serving-folk, gathered at Aker's church and heard mass at St. Margaret's altar there; after that they wended their way to the hall of the guild, which lay near the Hofvin Hospital — there they were wont to hold a drinking-feast lasting five days.

But since both Aker's church and the Hofvin spital belonged to Nonneseter, and as, besides, many of the Aker farmers were tenants of the convent, it had come to be the custom that the Abbess and some of the elder Sisters should honour the guild by coming to the feasting on the first day. And those of the young maids who were at the convent only to learn, and were not to take the veil, had leave to go with them and to dance in the evening; therefore at this feast they wore their own clothes and not the convent habit.

And so there was great stir and bustle in the novices' sleeping rooms on the eve of St. Margaret's Mass; the maids who were to go to the guild feast ransacking their chests and making ready their finery, while the others, less fortunate, went about something moodily and looked on. Some had set small pots in the fireplace and were boiling water to make their skin white and soft; others were making a brew to be smeared on their hair — then they parted the hair into strands and twisted them tightly round strips of leather, and this gave them curling, wavy tresses.

Ingebjörg brought out all the finery she had, but could not think what she should wear — come what might, not her best, leaf-green velvet dress; that was too good and too costly for such a peasant rout. But a little, thin sister who was not to go with them — Helga was her name; she had been vowed to the convent by her father and mother while still a child — took Kristin aside and whispered: she was sure Ingebjörg would wear the green dress and her pink silk shift too.

"You have ever been kind to me, Kristin," said Helga. "It beseems me little to meddle in such doings

— but I will tell you none the less. The knight who brought you home that evening in the spring — I have seen and heard Ingebjörg talking with him since — they spoke together in the church, and he has tarried for her up in the hollow when she hath gone to Ingunn at the commoners' house. But 'tis you he asks for, and Ingebjörg has promised him to bring you there along with her. But I wager you have not heard aught of this before!"

"True it is that Ingebjörg has said naught of this," said Kristin. She pursed up her mouth that the other might not see the smile that would come out. So this was Ingebjörg's way. " 'Tis like she knows I am not of such as run to trysts with strange men round house-corners and behind fences," said she proudly.

"Then I might have spared myself the pains of bringing you tidings whereof 'twould have been but seemly I should say no word," said Helga, wounded, and they parted.

But the whole evening Kristin was put to it not to smile when any one was looking at her.

Next morning, Ingebjörg went dallying about in her shift, till Kristin saw she meant not to dress before she herself was ready.

Kristin said naught, but laughed as she went to her chest and took out her golden-yellow silken shift. She had never worn it before, and it felt so soft and cool as it slipped down over her body. It was broidered with goodly work, in silver and blue and brown silk, about the neck and down upon the breast, as much as should be seen above the low-cut gown. There were sleeves to match, too. She drew on her linen hose, and laced up the small, purple-blue shoes which Haakon, by good luck, had saved that day of commotion. Ingebjörg gazed at her — then Kristin said laughing:

"My father ever taught me never to show disdain of those beneath us — but 'tis like you are too grand to deck yourself in your best for poor tenants and peasant-folk —"

Red as a berry, Ingebjörg slipped her woollen smock down over her white hips and hurried on the pink silk shift. Kristin threw over her own head her best velvet gown — it was violet-blue, deeply cut out at the bosom, with long slashed sleeves flowing well-nigh to the ground. She fastened the gilt belt about her waist, and hung her grey squirrel cape over her shoulders. Then she spread her masses of yellow hair out over her shoulders and back, and fitted the golden fillet, chased with small roses, upon her brow.

She saw that Helga stood watching them. Then she took from her chest a great silver clasp. It was that she had on her cloak the night Bentein met her on the highway, and she had never cared to wear it since. She went to Helga, and said in a low voice:

"I know 'twas your wish to show me goodwill last night; think me not unthankful —" and with that she gave her the clasp.

Ingebjörg was a fine sight, too, when she stood fully decked in her green gown, with a red silk cloak over her shoulders and her fair, curly hair waving behind her. They had ended by striving to outdress each other, thought Kristin, and she laughed.

The morning was cool and fresh with dew as the procession went forth from Nonneseter and wound its way westward toward Frysja. The hay-making was near at an end here on the lowlands, but along the fences grew blue-bells and yellow crowsfoot in clumps; in the fields the barley was in ear, and bent its heads in pale silvery waves just tinged with pink. Here and there, where the path was narrow and led through the fields, the corn all but met about folks' knees.

Haakon walked at the head, bearing the convent's banner with the Virgin Mary's picture upon the blue silken cloth. After him walked the servants and the

commoners, and then came the Lady Groa and four
old Sisters on horseback, while behind these came the
young maidens on foot; their many-hued holiday attire
flaunted and shone in the sunlight. Some of the commoners' women-folk and a few armed serving-men
closed the train.

They sang as they went over the bright fields, and
the folk they met at the byways stood aside and gave
them reverent greeting. All round, out on the fields,
they could see small groups of men coming walking and riding, for folks were drawing toward the
church from every house and every farm. Soon they
heard behind them the sound of hymns chanted in
men's deep voices, and the banner of the Hovedö
monastery rose above a hillock — the red silk shone
in the sun, swaying and bending to the step of the
bearer.

The mighty, metal voice of the bells rang out above
the neighing and screaming of stallions as the procession climbed the last slope to the church. Kristin had
never seen so many horses at one time — a heaving,
restless sea of horses' backs round about the green
before the church door. Upon the sward stood and
sat lay folk dressed in all their best — but all rose in
reverence as the Virgin's flag from Nonneseter was
borne in amongst them, and all bowed deeply before
the Lady Groa.

It seemed as though more folk had come than the
church could hold, but for those from the convent
room had been kept in front near the altar. Straightway after them the Cistercian monks from Hovedö
marched in and went up into the choir — and forthwith song burst from the throats of men and boys and
filled the church.

Soon after the mass had begun, when the service
brought all to their feet, Kristin caught sight of Erlend
Nikulaussön. He was tall, and his head rose above those
about him — she saw his face from the side. He had
a high, steep, and narrow forehead, and a large, straight

nose — it jutted, triangle-like, from his face, and was strangely thin about the fine, quivering nostrils — something about it reminded Kristin of a restless, high-strung stallion. His face was not as comely as she had thought it — the long-drawn lines running down to his small, weak, yet well-formed mouth gave it as 'twere a touch of joylessness — ay, but yet he *was* comely.

He turned his head and saw her. She knew not how long they stood thus, looking into each other's eyes. From that time she thought of naught but the end of the mass; she waited, intent on what would then befall.

There was some pressing and thronging as the folks made their way out from the overcrowded church. Ingebjörg held Kristin back till they were at the rear of the throng; she gained her point — they were quite cut off from the nuns, who went out first — the two girls were among the last in coming to the offertory-box and out of the church.

Erlend stood without, just by the door, beside the priest from Gerdarud and a stoutish, red-faced man, splendid in blue velvet. Erlend himself was clad in silk, but of a sober hue — a long coat of brown, figured with black, and a black cloak with a pattern of small yellow hawks inwoven.

They greeted each other and crossed the green together to where the men's horses stood tethered. While they spoke of the fine weather, the goodly mass and the great crowd of folk that were mustered, the fat, ruddy knight — he bore golden spurs and was named Sir Munan Baardsön — took Ingebjörg by the hand; 'twas plain he was mightily taken with the maid. Erlend and Kristin fell behind — they were silent as they walked.

There was a great to-do upon the church-green as folk began to ride away — horses jostled one another, people shouted — some angry, others laughing. Many sat in pairs upon the horses; men had their wives behind them, or their children in front upon the saddle; youths swung themselves up beside a friend. They could see the church banners, the nuns and the priests far down the hill already.

Sir Munan rode by; Ingebjörg sat in front of him, his arm about her. Both of them called out and waved. Then Erlend said:

"My serving-men are both with me — they could ride one horse and you have Haftor's — if you would rather have it so?"

Kristin flushed as she replied: "We are so far behind the others already — I see not your serving-men here-abouts, and — " Then she broke into a laugh, and Erlend smiled.

He sprang to the saddle and helped her to a seat behind him. At home Kristin had often sat thus side-wise behind her father, after she had grown too big to ride astride the horse. Still, she felt a little bashful and none too safe as she laid a hand upon Erlend's shoulder; the other she put on the horse's back to steady herself. They rode slowly down towards the bridge.

In a while Kristin thought she must speak, since he was silent, so she said:

"We looked not, sir, to meet you here to-day."

"Looked you not to meet me?" asked Erlend, turn-ing his head. "Did not Ingebjörg Filippusdatter bear you my greeting, then?"

"No," said Kristin. "I heard naught of any greeting — she hath not named you once since you came to our help last May," said she guilefully. She was not sorry that Ingebjörg's falseness should come to light.

Erlend did not look back again, but she could hear by his voice that he was smiling when he asked again:

"But the little dark one — the novice — I mind not her name — her I even fee'd to bear you my greeting."

Kristin blushed, but she had to laugh too: "Ay, 'tis but Helga's due I should say that she earned her fee," she said.

Erlend moved his head a little — his neck almost touched her hand. Kristin shifted her hand at once farther out on his shoulder. Somewhat uneasily she thought, maybe she had been more bold than was fitting, seeing she had come to this feast after a man had, in a manner, made tryst with her there.

Soon after Erlend asked:

"Will you dance with me to-night, Kristin?"

"I know not, sir," answered the maid.

"You think, mayhap, 'tis not seemly?" he asked, and, as she did not answer, he said again: "It may well be it is not so. But I thought now maybe you might deem you would be none the worse if you took my hand in the dance to-night. But, indeed, 'tis eight years since I stood up to dance."

"How may that be, sir?" asked Kristin. "Mayhap you are wedded?" But then it came into her head that had he been a wedded man, to have made tryst with her thus would have been no fair deed of him. On that she tried to mend her speech, saying: "Maybe you have lost your betrothed maid or your wife?"

Erlend turned quickly and looked on her with strange eyes.

"Hath not Lady Aashild . . . ? Why grew you so red when you heard who I was that evening?" he asked a little after.

Kristin flushed red once more, but did not answer; then Erlend asked again:

"I would fain know what my mother's sister said to you of me."

"Naught else," said Kristin quickly, "but in your praise. She said you were so comely and so great of kin that — she said that beside such as you and her kin we were of no such great account — my folk and I —"

"Doth she still talk thus, living the life she lives," said Erlend, and laughed bitterly. "Ay, ay — if it comfort her. . . . Said she naught else of me?"

"What should she have said?" asked Kristin; she knew not why she was grown so strangely heavy-hearted.

"Oh, she might have said —" he spoke in a low tone, looking down, "she might have said that I had been under the Church's ban, and had to pay dear for peace and atonement —"

Kristin was silent a long time. Then she said softly:

"There is many a man who is not master of his own fortunes — so have I heard said. 'Tis little I have seen of the world — but I will never believe of you, Erlend, that 'twas for any — dishonourable — deed."

"May God reward you for those words, Kristin," said Erlend, and bent his head and kissed her wrist so vehemently that the horse gave a bound beneath them. When Erlend had it in hand again, he said earnestly: "Dance with me to-night then, Kristin. Afterward I will tell how things are with me — will tell you all — but to-night we will be happy together?"

Kristin answered: "Ay," and they rode a while in silence.

But ere long Erlend began to ask of Lady Aashild, and Kristin told all she knew of her; she praised her much.

"Then all doors are not barred against Björn and Aashild?" asked Erlend.

Kristin said they were thought much of, and that her father and many with him deemed that most of the tales about these two were untrue.

"How liked you my kinsman, Munan Baardsön?" asked Erlend, laughing slily.

"I looked not much upon him," said Kristin, "and methought, too, he was not much to look on."

"Knew you not," asked Erlend, "that he is her son?"

"Son to Lady Aashild!" said Kristin, in great wonder.

"Ay, her children could not take their mother's fair looks, though they took all else," said Erlend.

"I have never known her first husband's name," said Kristin.

"They were two brothers who wedded two sisters,"

said Erlend. "Baard and Nikulaus Munansön. My father
was the elder, my mother was his second wife, but he
had no children by his first. Baard, whom Aashild
wedded, was not young either, nor, I trow, did they
ever live happily together — ay, I was a little child
when all this befell, they hid from me as much as they
could. . . . But she fled the land with Sir Björn and
married him against the will of her kin — when Baard
was dead. Then folk would have had the wedding set
aside — they made out that Björn had sought her bed
while her first husband was still living, and that they
had plotted together to put away my father's brother.
'Tis clear they could not bring this home to them,
since they had to leave them together in wedlock.
But to make amends, they had to forfeit all their
estate — Björn had killed their sister's son, too — my
mother's and Aashild's, I mean — "

Kristin's heart beat hard. At home her father and
mother had kept strict watch that no unclean talk
should come to the ears of their children or of young
folk — but still, things had happened in their own
parish and Kristin had heard of them — a man had
lived in adultery with a wedded woman. That was
whoredom, one of the worst of sins; 'twas said they
plotted the husband's death, and that brought with it
outlawry and the Church's ban. Lavrans had said no
woman was bound to stay with her husband, if he had
had to do with another's wife; the state of a child
gotten in adultery could never be mended, not even
though its father and mother were free to wed afterward. A man might bring into his family and make his
heir his child by any wanton or strolling beggar-
woman, but not the child of his adultery — not if its
mother came to be a knight's lady. She thought of the
misliking she had ever felt for Sir Björn, with his
bleached face and fat, yet shrunken body. She could
not think how Lady Aashild could be so good and
yielding at all times to the man who had led her away

into such shame; how such a gracious woman could have let herself be beguiled by him. He was not even good to her; he let her toil and moil with all the farm-work; Björn did naught but drink beer. Yet Aashild was ever mild and gentle when she spoke with her husband. Kristin wondered if her father could know all this, since he had asked Sir Björn to their home. Now she came to think, too, it seemed strange Erlend should think fit to tell such tales of his near kin. But like enough he deemed she knew of it already.

"I would like well," said Erlend in a while, "to visit her, Moster * Aashild, some day — when I journey northwards. Is he comely still, Björn, my kinsman?"

"No," said Kristin. "He looks like hay that has lain the winter through upon the fields."

"Ay, ay, it tells upon a man, I trow," said Erlend, with the same bitter smile. "Never have I seen so fair a man — 'tis twenty years since, I was but a lad then — but his like have I never seen —"

A little after they came to the hospital. It was an exceeding great and fine place, with many houses both of stone and of wood — houses for the sick, alms-houses, hostels for travellers, a chapel and a house for the priest. There was great bustle in the courtyard, for food was being made ready in the kitchen of the hospital for the guild feast, and the poor and sick too, that were dwelling in the place, were to be feasted on the best this day.

The hall of the guild was beyond the garden of the hospital, and folks took their way thither through the herb-garden, for this was of great renown. Lady Groa had had brought hither plants that no one had heard of in Norway before, and, moreover, all plants that else folks were used to grow in gardens, throve better in her herbaries, both flowers and pot-herbs and heal-ing herbs. She was a most learned woman in all such matters, and had herself put into the Norse tongue the

---

* Moster = mother's sister.

herbals of the Salernitan school. . . . Lady Groa had
been more than ever kind to Kristin since she had
marked that the maid knew somewhat of herb-lore,
and was fain to know yet more of it.

So Kristin named for Erlend what grew in the beds
on either side the grassy path they walked on. In the
midday sun there was a warm and spicy scent of dill
and celery, garlic and roses, southernwood and wall-
flower. Beyond the shadeless, baking herb-garden, the
fruit orchards looked cool and enticing — red cherries
gleamed amid the dark leafy tops, and the apple trees
drooped their branches heavy with green fruit.

About the garden was a hedge of sweet briar. There
were some flowers on it still — they looked the same
as other briar roses, but in the sun the leaves smelt of
wine and apples. Folk plucked sprays to' deck themselves as they went past. Kristin, too, took some roses
and hung them on her temples, fixed under her golden
fillet. One she kept in her hand. . . . After a time
Erlend took it, saying no word. A while he bore it in
his hand as they walked, then fastened it with the
brooch upon his breast — he looked awkward and
bashful as he did it, and was so clumsy that he pricked
his fingers till they bled.

Broad tables were spread in the loft-room of the
guild's hall — two by the main walls, for the men and
the women; and two smaller boards out on the floor,
where children and young folk sat side by side.

At the women's board Lady Groa was in the high-
seat, the nuns and the chief of the married women sat
on the inner bench along the wall, and the unwedded
women on the outer benches, the maids from Nonneseter at the upper end. Kristin knew that Erlend
was watching her, but she durst not turn her head
even once, either when they rose or when they sat
down. Only when they got up at last to hear the priest
read the names of the dead guild-brothers and sisters,
she stole a hasty glance at the men's table — she caught
a glimpse of him where he stood by the wall, behind

the candles burning on the board. He was looking at her.

The meal lasted long, with all the toasts in honour of God, the Virgin Mary, and St. Margaret and St. Olav and St. Halvard, and prayers and song between.

Kristin saw through the open door that the sun was gone; sounds of fiddling and song came in from the green without, and all the young folks had left the tables already when Lady Groa said to the convent maidens that they might go now and play themselves for a time if they listed.

Three red bonfires were burning upon the green; around them moved the many-coloured chains of dancers. The fiddlers sat aloft on heaped-up chests and scraped their fiddles — they played and sang a different tune in every ring; there were too many folk for *one* dance. It was nearly dark already — northward the wooded ridge stood out coal-black against the yellow-green sky.

Under the loft-balcony folk were sitting drinking. Some men sprang forward, as soon as the six maids from Nonneseter came down the steps. Munan Baardsön flew to meet Ingebjörg and went off with her, and Kristin was caught by the wrist — Erlend, she knew his hand already. He pressed her hand in his so that their rings grated on one another and bruised the flesh.

. He drew her with him to the outermost bonfire. Many children were dancing there; Kristin gave her other hand to a twelve-year-old lad, and Erlend had a little, half-grown maid on his other side.

No one was singing in the ring just then — they were swaying in and out to the tune of the fiddle as they moved round. Then some one shouted that Sivord the Dane should sing them a new dance. A tall, fair-haired man with huge fists stepped out in front of the chain and struck up his ballad:

Fair goes the dance at Monkolm
  On silver sand.
There danceth Ivar Sir Alfsön —
  Holds the Queen's own hand.
    Know ye not Ivar Sir Alfsön?

The fiddlers knew not the tune, they thrummed their strings a little, and the Dane sang alone — he had a strong, tuneful voice:

" Mind you, Queen of the Danemen,
    That summer fair,
  They led you out of Sweden,
    To Denmark here?

  They led you out of Sweden,
    To Denmark here,
  All with a crown of the red gold
    And many a tear.

  All with a crown of the red gold
    And tear-filled eyne —
  — Mind you, Queen of the Danemen
    You first were mine?"

The fiddles struck in again, the dancers hummed the new-learned tune and joined in the burden:

"And are you, Ivar Sir Alfsön,
    Sworn man to me,
  Then shall you hang to-morrow
    On the gallows tree! "

  But 'twas Ivar Sir Alfsön,
    All unafraid
  He leaped into the gold-bark
    In harness clad.

"God send you, oh Dane-Queen,
    So many a good night,
  As in the high heavens
    Are stars alight.

  God send you, oh Dane-King,
    So many ill years
  As be leaves on the linden —
    Or the hind hath hairs."
    Know ye not Ivar Sir Alfsön?

It was far on in the night, and the fires were but heaps of embers growing more and more black. Kristin and Erlend stood hand in hand under the trees by the garden fence. Behind them the noise of the revellers was hushed — a few young lads were hopping round the glowing mounds singing softly, but the fiddlers had sought their resting-places, and most of the people were gone. One or two wives went round seeking their husbands, who were lying somewhere out of doors overcome by the beer.

"Where think you I can have laid my cloak?" whispered Kristin. Erlend put his arm about her waist and drew his mantle round them both. Close pressed to one another they went into the herb-garden.

A lingering breath of the day's warm spicy scents, deadened and damp with the chill of the dew, met them in there. The night was very dark, the sky overcast, with murky grey clouds close down upon the tree-tops. But they could tell that there were other folks in the garden. Once Erlend pressed the maiden close to him and asked in a whisper:

"Are you not afraid, Kristin?"

In her mind she caught a faint glimpse of the world outside this night — and knew that this was madness. But a blessed strengthlessness was upon her. She only leaned closer to the man and whispered softly — she herself knew not what.

They came to the end of the path; a stone wall divided them from the woods. Erlend helped her up. As she jumped down on the other side, he caught her and held her lifted in his arms a moment before he set her on the grass.

She stood with upturned face to take his kiss. He held her head between his hands — it was so sweet to her to feel his fingers sink into her hair — she felt she must repay him, and so she clasped his head and sought to kiss him, as he had kissed her.

When he put his hands upon her breast, she felt as

though he drew her heart from out her bosom; he parted the folds of silk ever so little and laid a kiss betwixt them — it sent a glow into her inmost soul.

"You I could never harm," whispered Erlend. "You should never shed a tear through fault of mine. Never had I dreamed a maid might be so good as you, my Kristin — "

He drew her down into the grass beneath the bushes; they sat with their backs against the wall. Kristin said naught, but when he ceased from caressing her, she put up her hand and touched his face.

In a while Erlend asked: "Are you not weary, my dear one?" And when Kristin nestled in to his breast, he folded his arms around her, and whispered: "Sleep, sleep, Kristin, here in my arms — "

She slipped deeper and deeper into darkness and warmth and happiness upon his breast.

When she came to herself again, she was lying outstretched in the grass with her cheek upon the soft brown silk above his knees. Erlend was sitting as before with his back to the stone wall, his face looked grey in the grey twilight, but his wide opened eyes were marvellously clear and fair. She saw he had wrapped his cloak all about her — her feet were so warm and snug with the fur lining around them.

"Now have you slept in my lap," said he, smiling faintly. "May God bless you, Kristin — you slept as safe as a child in its mother's arms — "

"Have *you* not slept, Sir Erlend?" asked Kristin; and he smiled down into her fresh opened eyes:

"Maybe the night will come when you and I may lie down to sleep together — I know not what you will think when you have weighed all things. I have watched by you to-night — there is still so much betwixt us two that 'tis more than if there had lain a naked sword between you and me. Tell me if you will hold me dear, when this night is past?"

"I will hold you dear, Sir Erlend," said Kristin. "I will hold you dear, so long as you will — and thereafter I will love none other."

"Then," said Erlend slowly, "may God forsake me if any maid or woman come to my arms ere I may make you mine in law and honour. Say you this, too," he prayed. Kristin said:

"May God forsake me if I take any other man to my arms so long as I live on earth."

"We must go now," said Erlend, a little after, "before folk waken."

They passed along without the wall among the bushes.

"Have you bethought you," asked Erlend, "what further must be done in this?"

" 'Tis for you to say what we must do, Erlend," answered Kristin.

"Your father," he asked in a little, "they say at Gerdarud he is a mild and a righteous man. Think you he will be so exceeding loth to go back from what he hath agreed with Andres Darre?"

"Father has said so often, he would never force us, his daughters," said Kristin. "The chief thing is that our lands and Simon's lie so fitly together. But I trow father would not that I should miss all my gladness in this world for the sake of that." A fear stirred within her that so simple as this perhaps it might not prove to be — but she fought it down.

"Then maybe 'twill be less hard than I deemed in the night," said Erlend. "God help me, Kristin — methinks I *cannot* lose you now — unless I win you now, never can I be glad again."

They parted among the trees, and in the dawning light Kristin found her way to the guest-chamber where the women from Nonneseter were to lie. All the beds were full, but she threw a cloak upon some straw on the floor and laid her down in all her clothes.

When she awoke, it was far on in the day. Ingebjörg

Filippusdatter was sitting on a bench near by, stitching down an edge of fur that had been torn loose on her cloak. She was full of talk as ever.

"Were you with Erlend Nikulaussön the whole night?" she asked. "'Twere well you went warily with that lad, Kristin — how think you Simon Andressön would like it if you came to be dear friends with him?"

Kristin found a hand-basin and began to wash herself.

"And your betrothed — think you he would like that you danced with Dumpy Munan last night? Surely we must dance with him who chooses us out on such a night of merry-making — and Lady Groa had given us leave."

Ingebjörg pshawed.

"Einar Einarssön and Sir Munan are friends — and, besides, he is wedded and old. Ugly he is to boot for that matter — but likeable and hath becoming ways — see what he gave me for a remembrance of last night," and she held forth a gold clasp which Kristin had seen in Sir Munan's hat the day before. "But this Erlend — 'tis true he was freed of the ban at Easter last year, but they say Eline Ormsdatter has been with him at Husaby since — Sir Munan says Erlend hath fled to Sira Jon at Gerdarud, and he deems 'tis because he cannot trust himself not to fall back into sin, if he meet her again —"

Kristin crossed over to the other — her face was white.

"Knew you not this?" said Ingebjörg. "That he lured a woman from her husband somewhere in Haalogaland in the North — and held her with him at his manor in despite of the King's command and the Archbishop's ban — they had two children together — and he was driven to fly to Sweden, and hath been forced to pay in forfeit so much of his lands and goods, Sir Munan says he will be a poor man in the end unless he mend his ways the sooner."

"Think not but that I know all this," said Kristin, with a set face. "But 'tis known the matter is ended now."

"Ay, but as to that Sir Munan said there had been an end between them so many times before," said Ingebjörg pensively. "But all these things can be nothing to you — you that are to wed Simon Darre. But a comely man is Erlend Nikulaussön, sure enough."

The company from Nonneseter was to set out for home that same day after nones. Kristin had promised Erlend to meet him by the wall where they had sat the night before, if she could but find a way to come.

He was lying face downwards in the grass with his head upon his hands. As soon as he saw her, he sprang to his feet and held out both his hands, as she was about jumping from the wall.

Kristin took them, and the two stood a little, hand in hand. Then said Kristin:

"Why told you me that of Sir Björn and Lady Aashild yesterday?"

"I can see you know it all," said Erlend, and let go her hands suddenly. "What think you of me now, Kristin?"

"I was eighteen then," he went on vehemently, " 'tis ten years since that the King, my kinsman, sent me with the mission to Vargöyhus,* and we stayed the winter at Steigen. . . . She was wife to the Lagmand, Sigurd Saksulvsön. . . . I thought pity of her, for he was old and ugly beyond belief. I know not how it came to pass — ay, but I loved her too. I bade Sigurd crave what amends he would; I would fain have done right by him — he is a good and doughty man in many ways — but he would have it that all must go by law; he took the matter to the Thing — I was to be branded for whoredom with the wife of him whose guest I had been, you understand . . .

---

* Mission to Vargöyhus, see Note 18.

"Then it came to my father's ears, and then to King Haakon's . . . he — he drove me from his court. And if you must know the whole — there is naught more now betwixt Eline and me save the children, and she cares not much for them. They are in Österdal, upon a farm I owned there; I have given it to Orm, the boy — but she will not stay with them. Doubtless she reckons that Sigurd cannot live for ever — but I know not what she would be at.

"Sigurd took her back again — but she says she fared like a dog and a bondwoman in his house — so she set a tryst with me at Nidaros. 'Twas little better for me at Husaby with my father. I sold all I could lay hands on, and fled with her to Holland — Count Jacob stood my friend. Could I do aught else? — she was great with my child. I knew many a man had lived even so with another's wife and had got off cheap enough — if he were rich, that is. But so it is with King Haakon, he is hardest upon his own kin. We were away from one another for a year, but then my father died and then she came back. Then there were other troubles. My tenants denied me rent and would have no speech with my bailiffs because I lay under ban — I, on my side, dealt harshly with them, and so they brought suit against me for robbery; but I had not the money to pay my household withal; and you can see I was too young to meet these troubles wisely, and my kinsfolk would not help me — save Munan — he did all his wife would let him. . . .

"Ay, now you know it, Kristin: I have lost much both of lands and goods and of honour. True it is; you would be better served if you held fast to Simon Andressön."

Kristin put her arms about his neck.

"We will abide by what we swore to each other yesternight, Erlend — if so be you think as I do."

Erlend drew her close to him, kissed her and said:

"You will see too, trust me, that all things will be changed with me now — for none in the world has power on me now but you. Oh, my thoughts were many last night, as you slept upon my lap, my fairest one. So much power the devil cannot have over a man that I should ever work you care and woe — you, my dearest life. . . ."

4

At the time he dwelt at Skog, Lavrans Björgulfsön had made gifts of land to Gerdarud church, that masses for the souls of his father and mother might be said on their death-days. Björgulf Ketilsön's day was the thirteenth of August, and Lavrans had settled with his brother that this year Aasmund should bring Kristin out to Skog that she might be at the mass.

She went in fear that something should come in the way, so that her uncle would not keep his promise — she thought she had marked that Aasmund did not care overmuch about her. But the day before the mass was to be, Aasmund Björgulfsön came to the convent to fetch his brother's daughter. Kristin was told to clothe herself in lay garb, but simply and in dark garments. There had been some carping at the Sisters of Non-neseter for going about too much without the convent walls; therefore the Bishop had given order that the maidens who were not to take the veil must wear naught like to the habit of the order when they went visiting their kinsfolk — so that laymen could not mistake them for novices or nuns.

Kristin's heart was full of gladness as she rode along the highway with her uncle, and Aasmund grew more friendly and merry with her when he saw the maid was not so tongue-tied after all with folk. Otherwise Aasmund was somewhat moody and downcast; he said it looked as though there would be a call to arms in the autumn, and that the King would lead an army into Sweden to avenge the slaying of his son-in-law

and the husband of his niece. Kristin had heard of the
murder of the Swedish Dukes, and thought it a most
foul deed — yet all these questions of state seemed
far away from her. No one spoke much of such things
at home in the Dale; she remembered, too, that her
father had been to the war against Duke Eirik at
Ragnhildarholm and Konungahella. Then Aasmund
told her of all that had come and gone between the
King and the Dukes. Kristin understood but little of
this, but she gave careful heed to all her uncle told of
the making and breaking of the betrothals of the
King's daughters. It gave her comfort to think 'twas
not everywhere as it was at home in her countryside,
that a betrothal once fixed by word of mouth was
held to bind nigh as fast as a wedding. Then she took
courage to tell of her adventure on the evening before
Halvard-wake, and asked her uncle if he knew Erlend
of Husaby. Aasmund spoke well of Erlend — said he
had guided his affairs unwisely, but his father and the
King were most to blame; they had borne themselves
as though the young lad were a very limb of the devil
only because he had fallen into this misfortune. The
King was over-pious in such matters, and Sir Nikulaus
was angry because Erlend had lost much good land,
so they had thundered about whoredom and hell fire
— "and there must be a bit of the dare-devil in every
likely lad," said Aasmund Björgulfsön. "And the
woman was most fair. But you have no call now to
look Erlend's way, so trouble yourself no more about
his doings."

Erlend came not to the mass, as he had promised
Kristin he would, and she thought about this more
than of God's word. She felt no sorrow that this was
so — she had only that strange new feeling that she
was cut off from all the ties that she had felt binding
on her before.

She tried to take comfort — like enough Erlend

deemed it wisest that no one in whose charge she was should come to know of their friendship at this time. She could understand herself that 'twas wise. But her heart had longed so for him, and she wept when she had gone to rest in the loft-room where she was to sleep with Aasmund's little daughters.

The day after, she went up into the wood with the youngest of her uncle's children, a little maid of six years. When they were come to the pastures among the woods a little way off, Erlend came running after them. Kristin knew it was he before she had seen who was coming.

"I have sat up here in the hill spying down into the courtyard the whole day," said he. "I thought surely you would find a chance to come out —"

"Think you I came out to meet you then?" said Kristin, laughing. "And are you not afraid to beat about my uncle's woods with dogs and bow?"

"Your uncle gave me leave to take my pastime hunting here," said Erlend. "And the dogs are Aasmund's — they found me out this morning." He patted them and lifted the little girl up in his arms.

"*You* know me, Ragndid? But say not you have spoken with me, and you can have this" — and he took out a bunch of raisins and gave them to the child. "I had brought them for you," he said to Kristin. "Think you this child can hold her tongue?"

They talked fast and laughed together. Erlend was dressed in a short close-fitting brown jacket and had a small red silk cap pulled down over his black hair — he looked so young; he laughed and played with the child; but sometimes he would take Kristin's hand, and press it till it hurt her.

He spoke of the rumours of war and was glad: " 'Twill be easier for me to win back the King's friendship," said he, "and then will all things be easy," he said vehemently.

At last they sat down in a meadow up among the woods. Erlend had the child on his lap; Kristin sat by his side; under cover of the grass he played with her fingers. He pressed into her hand three gold rings bound together by a cord:

"By and by," he whispered, "you shall have as many as will go on your fingers. . . .

"I shall wait for you here on this field each day about this time, as long as you are at Skog," he said, as they parted. "And you must come if you can."

The next day Aasmund Björgulfsön set out with his wife and children to the manor of Gyrid's kin in Hadeland. They had been scared by the talk of war; the folk about Oslo still went in terror since Duke Eirik's harrying of that countryside some years before. Aasmund's old mother was so fearful, she was minded to seek shelter in Nonneseter — besides, she was too weak to travel with the others. So Kristin was to stay at Skog with the old woman — she called her grand-mother — till Aasmund came back from Hadeland.

About the midday hour, when the folk on the farm were resting, Kristin went to the loft-room where she slept. She had brought some clothes with her in a sheepskin bag, and now she changed her garments, humming to herself the while.

Her father had given her a dress of thick cotton stuff from the East, sky-blue with a close pattern of red flowers; this she put on. She brushed and combed out her hair and bound it back from her face with a red silk ribbon, wound a red silk belt tightly about her waist, and put Erlend's rings upon her fingers; all the time she wondered if he would think her fair.

The two dogs that had been with Erlend in the forest had slept in the loft-room over-night — she called them to go with her now. She stole out round the houses and took the same path as the day before up through the hill-pastures.

The field amid the forest lay lonely and silent in the burning midday sun; the pine woods that shut it in on all sides gave out a hot, strong scent. The sun stung, and the blue sky seemed strangely near and close down upon the tree-tops.

Kristin sat down in the shade in the borders of the wood. She was not vexed that Erlend was not there; she was sure he would come, and it gave her an odd gladness to sit there alone a little and to be the first.

She listened to the low hum of tiny life above the yellow, scorched grass, pulled a few dry, spicy-scented flowers that she could reach without moving more than her hand, and rolled them between her fingers and smelt them — she sat with wide-open eyes sunk in a kind of drowse.

She did not move when she heard a horse in the woods. The dogs growled, and the hair on their necks bristled — then they bounded up over the meadow, barking and wagging their tails. Erlend sprang from his horse at the edge of the forest, let it go with a clap on its flank, and ran down towards her with the dogs jumping about him. He caught their muzzles in his hands and came to her leading the two elk-grey, wolf-like beasts. Kristin smiled and held out her hand without getting up.

Once, while she was looking at the dark head that lay in her lap, between her hands, something bygone flashed on her mind. It stood out, clear yet distant, as a homestead far away on a mountain slope may start to sight of a sudden, from out dark clouds, when a sunbeam strikes it on a stormy day. And it was as though there welled up in her heart all the tenderness Arne Gyrdsön had once begged for, while, as yet, she did not understand his words. With timid passion, she drew the man up to her and laid his head upon her breast, kissing him as if afraid he should be taken from her. And when she saw his head upon her arm, she felt as though she clasped a child — she hid his eyes with one of her hands, and showered little kisses upon his mouth and cheek.

The sunshine had gone from the meadow — the leaden colour above the tree-tops had thickened to dark-blue, and spread over the whole sky; little, coppery flashes like fire-tinged smoke flickered within the clouds. Bayard came down to them, neighed loudly once, and then stood stock-still, staring before him. Soon after came the first flash of lightning, and the thunder followed close, not far away.

Erlend got up and took hold of the horse. An old barn stood at the lowest end of the meadow; they went thither, and he tied Bayard to some woodwork just inside the door. At the back of the barn lay some hay; Erlend spread his cloak out, and they seated themselves with the dogs at their feet.

And now the rain came down like a sheet before the doorway. It hissed in the trees and lashed the ground — soon they had to move farther in, away from the drips from the roof. Each time it lightened and thundered, Erlend whispered:

"Are you not afraid, Kristin — ?"

"A little — " she whispered back, and drew closer to him.

They knew not how long they had sat — the storm had soon passed over — it thundered far away, but the sun shone on the wet grass outside the door, and the sparkling drops fell more and more rarely from the roof. The sweet smell of the hay in the barn grew stronger.

"Now must I go," said Kristin; and Erlend answered: "Ay, 'tis like you must." He took her foot in his hand: "You will be wet — you must ride and I must walk — out of the woods . . ." and he looked at her so strangely.

Kristin shook — it must be because her heart beat so, she thought — her hands were cold and clammy. As he kissed her vehemently she weakly tried to push him from her. Erlend lifted his face a moment — she thought of a man who had been given food at the convent one day — he had kissed the bread they gave him. She sank back upon the hay. . . .

She sat upright when Erlend lifted his head from her arms. He raised himself suddenly upon his elbow:

"Look not so — Kristin!"

His voice sent a new, wild pang into Kristin's soul — he was not glad — *he* was unhappy too — !

"Kristin, Kristin! Think you I lured you out here to me in the woods meaning this — to make you mine by force — ?" he asked in a little.

She stroked his hair and did not look at him.

" 'Twas not force, I trow — you had let me go as I came, had I begged you — " said she, in a low voice.

"I know not," he answered, and his face in her lap. . . .

"Think you that I would betray you?" asked he vehemently. "Kristin — I swear to you by my Christian faith — may God forsake me in my last hour, if I keep not faith with you till the day of my death — "

She could say naught, she only stroked his hair again and again.

" 'Tis time I went home, is it not?" she asked at length, and she seemed to wait in deadly terror for his answer.

"Maybe so," he answered dully. He got up quickly, went to the horse, and began to loosen the reins.

Then she, too, got up. Slowly, wearily, and with crushing pain it came home to her — she knew not what she had hoped he might do — set her upon his horse, maybe, and carry her off with him so she might be spared from going back amongst other people. It was as though her whole body ached with wonder — that this ill thing was what was sung in all the songs. And since Erlend had wrought her this, she felt herself grown so wholly his, she knew not how she should live away from him any more. She was to go from him now, but she could not understand that it should be so.

Down through the woods he went on foot, leading the horse. He held her hand in his, but they found no words to say.

When they were come so far that they could see the houses at Skog, he bade her farewell.

"Kristin — be not so sorrowful — the day will come or ever you know it, when you will be my wedded wife — "

But her heart sank as he spoke.

"Must you go away, then?" she asked, dismayed.

"As soon as you are gone from Skog," said he, and his voice already rang more bright. "If there be no war, I will speak to Munan — he has long urged me that I should wed — he will go with me and speak for me to your father."

Kristin bent her head — at each word he said, she felt the time that lay before grow longer and more hard to think of — the convent, Jörundgaard — she seemed to float upon a stream which bore her far from it all.

"Sleep you alone in the loft-room, now your kinsfolk are gone?" asked Erlend. "Then will I come and speak with you to-night — will you let me in?"

"Ay," said Kristin low. And so they parted.

The rest of the day she sat with her father's mother, and after supper she took the old lady to her bed: Then she went up to the loft-room, where she was to lie. There was a little window in the room; Kristin sate herself down on the chest that stood below it — she had no mind to go to bed.

She had long to wait. It was quite dark without when she heard the soft steps upon the balcony. He knocked upon the door with his cloak about his knuckles, and Kristin got up, drew the bolt, and let Erlend in.

She marked how glad he was, when she flung her
arms about his neck and clung to him.

"I have been fearing you would be angry with me,"
he said.

"You must not grieve for our sin," he said, sometime
after. " 'Tis not a deadly sin. God's law is not like to
the law of the land in this. . . . Gunnulv, my brother,
once made this matter plain to me — if two vow to
have and hold each other fast for all time, and thereafter lie together, then they are wedded before God
and may not break their troths without great sin. I
can give you the words in Latin when they come to
my mind — I knew them once. . . ."

Kristin wondered a little why Erlend's brother
should have said this — but she thrust from her the
hateful fear that it might have been said of Erlend and
another — and sought to find comfort in his words.

They sat together on the chest, he with his arm
about her, and now Kristin felt that 'twas well with
her once more and she was safe — beside him was the
only spot now where she could feel safe and sheltered.

At times Erlend spoke much and cheerfully — then
he would be silent for long, while he sat caressing her.
Without knowing it, Kristin gathered up out of all he
said each little thing that could make him fairer and
dearer to her, and lessen his blame in all she knew of
him that was not good.

Erlend's father, Sir Nikulaus, had been so old before
he had children, he had not patience enough nor
strength enough left to rear them up himself; both the
sons had grown up in the house of Sir Baard Petersön
at Hestnæs. Erlend had no sisters and no brother save
Gunnulv; he was one year younger and was a priest at
Christ's Church in Nidaros. "He is dearest to me of all
mankind, save only you."

Kristin asked if Gunnulv were like him, but Erlend
laughed and said they were much unlike, both in mind
and body. Now Gunnulv was in foreign lands study-
ing — he had been away these three years, but had

sent letters home twice, the last a year ago, when he thought to go from St. Geneviève's in Paris and make his way to Rome. "He will be glad, Gunnulv, when he comes home and finds me wed," said Erlend.

Then he spoke of the great heritage he had had from his father and mother — Kristin saw he scarce knew himself how things stood with him now. She knew somewhat of her father's dealings in lands. . . . Erlend had dealt in his the other way about, sold and scattered and wasted and pawned, worst of all in the last years, when he had been striving to free him of his paramour, thinking that, this done, his sinful life might in time be forgotten and his kin stand by him once more; he had thought he might some day come to be Warden * of half the Orkdöla country, as his father had been before him.

"But now do I scarce know what the end will be," said he. "Maybe I shall sit at last on a mountain croft like Björn Gunnarsön, and bear out the dung on my back as did the thralls of old, because I have no horse."

"God help you," said Kristin, laughing. "Then I must come to you for sure — I trow I know more of farm-work and country ways than you."

"I can scarce think you have borne out the dung-basket," said he, laughing too.

"No; but I have seen how they spread the dung out — and sown corn have I, well-nigh every year at home. 'Twas my father's wont to plough himself the fields nearest the farm, and he let me sow the first piece that I might bring good fortune." The thought sent a pang through her heart, so she said quickly: "And a woman you must have to bake, and brew the small beer, and wash your one shirt, and milk — and you must hire a cow or two from the rich farmer near by — "

"Oh, God be thanked that I hear you laugh a little

---

* Wardens, see Note 19.

once more!" said Erlend and caught her up so that she
lay on his arms like a child.

Each of the six nights which passed ere Aasmund
Björgulfsön came home, Erlend was in the loft-room
with Kristin.

The last night he seemed as unhappy as she; he said
many times they must not be parted from one another
a day longer than needful. At last he said very low:

"Now should things go so ill that I cannot come
back hither to Oslo before winter — and if it so falls
out you need help of friends — fear not to turn to
Sira Jon here at Gerdarud; we are friends from childhood up; and Munan Baardsön, too, you may safely
trust."

Kristin could only nod. She knew he spoke of what
she had thought on each single day; but Erlend said
no more of it. So she, too, said naught, and would not
show how heavy of heart she was.

On the other nights he had gone from her when
the night grew late, but this last evening he begged
hard that he might lie and sleep by her an hour. Kristin
was fearful, but Erlend said haughtily, "Be sure that
were I found here in your bower, I am well able to
answer for myself." She herself, too, was fain to keep
him by her yet a little while, and she had not strength
enough to deny him aught.

But she feared that they might sleep too long. So
most of the night she sat leaning against the head of
the bed, dozing a little at times, and scarce knowing
herself when he caressed her and when she only
dreamed it. Her one hand she held upon his breast,
where she could feel the beating of his heart beneath,
and her face was turned to the window that she might
see the dawn without.

At length she had to wake him. She threw on some
clothes and went out with him upon the balcony. He
clambered over the railing on the side that faced on to
another house near by. Now he was gone from her

sight — the corner hid him. Kristin went in again and crept into her bed; and now she quite gave way and fell to weeping for the first time since Erlend had made her all his own.

5

AT Nonneseter the days went by as before. Kristin's time was passed between the dormitory and the church, the weaving-room, the book-hall and the refectory. The nuns and the convent-folk gathered in the pot-herbs and the fruits from the herb-garden and the orchard; Holycross Day came in the autumn with its procession, then there was the fast before Michaelmas. Kristin wondered — none seemed to mark any change in her. But she had ever been quiet when amongst strangers, and Ingebjörg Filippusdatter, who was by her night and day, was well able to chatter for them both.

Thus no one marked that her thoughts were far away from all around her. Erlend's paramour — she said to herself, she was Erlend's paramour now. It seemed now as though she had dreamed it all — the eve of St. Margaret's Mass, that hour in the barn, the nights in her bower at Skog — either she had dreamed it, or else all about her now was a dream. But one day she must waken, one day it must all come out. Not for a moment did she think aught else than that she bore Erlend's child within her.

But what would happen to her when this came to light, she could not well think. Would she be put into the black hole, or be sent home? She saw dim pictures of her father and mother far away. Then she shut her eyes, dizzy and sick, bowed in fancy beneath the coming storm and tried to harden herself to bear it, since she thought it must end by sweeping her for ever into Erlend's arms — the only place where now she felt she had a home.

Thus was there in this strained waiting as much of
hope as terror, as much of sweetness as of torment.
She was unhappy — but she felt her love for Erlend
as it were a flower planted within her — and, in spite
of her unhappiness, it put forth fresher and richer
blooms each day. That last night when he had slept by
her side she had felt, as a faint and fleeting bliss, that
there awaited her a joy and happiness in his arms such
as she had not yet known — she thrilled now at the
thought of it; it came to her like warm, spicy breaths
from sun-heated gardens. Wayside brat — Inga had
flung the word at her — she opened her arms to it and
pressed it to her bosom. Wayside brat was the name
they gave to the child begotten in secret in woods or
fields. She felt the sunshine, and the smell of the pines
in the forest pasture. Each new, creeping tremor, each
sudden pulse-beat in her body she took as a reminder
from the unborn babe that now she was come out
into new paths — and were they never so hard to
follow to the end, she was sure they must lead to
Erlend at the last.

She sat betwixt Ingebjörg and Sister Astrid and
sewed at the great tapestry of knights and birds amidst
leafy tendrils. And as she sewed she thought of how
she should fly when the time was come, and it could
no longer be hidden. She saw herself walking along
the highways, clothed like a poor woman; all she
owned of gold and silver she bore within a bundle in
her hand. She bought herself shelter on a farm somewhere in a far-away countryside — she went as a serv-
ing-wench, bore the water-carrier's yoke upon her
neck, worked in the byres, baked and washed, and
was cursed because she would not tell who was the
child's father. Then Erlend came and found her.

Sometimes she dreamed that he came too late. She
lay snow-white and fair in the poor peasant's bed.
Erlend stooped as he came in at the door; he had on
the long black cloak he had used to wear when he

came to her by night at Skog. The woman led him forward to where she lay, he sank down and took her cold hands, his eyes were sad as death — Dost thou lie here, my one delight . . . ? Bent with sorrow he went out with his tender son clasped to his breast, in the folds of his cloak — nay, she thought not in good sooth that it would so fall out; she had no mind to die, Erlend should have no such sorrow. . . . But her heart was so heavy it did her good to dream these dreams. . . .

Then for a moment it stood out cold and clear as ice before her — the child, that was no dream, that must be faced; she must answer one day for what she had done — and it seemed as if her heart stood still with terror.

But after a little time had gone by, she came to think 'twas not so sure after all she was with child. She understood not herself why she was not glad — it was as though she had lain and wept beneath a warm covering, and now must get up in the cold. A month went by — then two; now she was sure that she had been spared this ill-hap — and, empty and chill of soul, she felt yet unhappier than before. In her heart there dawned a little bitterness toward Erlend. Advent drew near, and she had heard neither from or of him; she knew not where he was.

And now she felt she could not bear this fear and doubt — it was as though a bond betwixt them had snapped; now she was afraid indeed — might it not so befall that she should never see him more? All she had been safely linked to once, she was parted from now — and the new tie that bound her to her lover was such such a frail one. She never thought that he would mean to play her false — but there was so much that might happen. . . . She knew not how she could go on any longer day after day, suffering the tormenting doubt of this time of waiting.

Now and then she thought of her father and mother and sisters — she longed for them, but as for something she had lost for ever.

And sometimes in church, and elsewhere too, she would feel a great yearning to take part in all that this meant, the communion of mankind with God. It had ever been a part of her life; now she stood outside with her unconfessed sin.

She told herself that this cutting adrift from home and kin and Church was but for a time. Erlend must take her by the hand and lead her back into it all. When her father had given consent to their love, she could go to him as of yore; when she and Erlend were wed, they could confess and do penance for their transgression.

She began to seek for tokens that other folk were not without sin any more than they. She hearkened more to tale-bearing, and marked all the little things about her which showed that not even the Sisters in the convent here were altogether godly and unworldly. These were only little things — under Lady Groa's rule Nonneseter to the world was a pattern of what a godly sisterhood should be. Zealous in their devotions, diligent, full of care for the poor and sick, were the nuns. Their aloofness from the world was not so strict but that the Sisters both had visits from their friends and kin in the parlour, and themselves were given leave to visit these in the town when aught was afoot; but no nun had brought shame upon the house by her life all the years of Lady Groa's rule.

But Kristin had now an ear alive to all the little jars within the convent walls — little wranglings and spites and vanities. Save in the nursing of the sick, none of the Sisters would help with the rough housework — all were minded to be women of learning or skilled in some craft; the one strove to outdo the other, and the Sisters who had no turn for learning or the nobler crafts, lost heart and mooned through the hours as though but half awake.

Lady Groa herself was wise as well as learned; she kept a wakeful eye on her spiritual daughters' way of life and their diligence, but she troubled herself little about their souls' health. She had been kind and friendly to Kristin at all times — she seemed to like her better than the other young girls, but that was because Kristin was apt at books and needlework, diligent and sparing of words. Lady Groa never looked for an answer from any of the Sisters; but, on the other hand, she was ever glad to speak with men. They came and went in her parlour — tenant farmers and bailiffs of the convent. Preaching Friars from the Bishop, stewards of estates on Hovedö with whom she was at law. She had her hands full with the oversight of the convent's great estates, with the keeping of accounts, sending out church vestments, and taking in books to be copied and sending them away again. Not the most evil-minded of men could find aught unseemly in Lady Groa's way of life. But she liked only to talk of such things as women seldom know about.

The prior, who dwelt in a house by himself, northward of the church, seemed to have no more will of his own than the Abbess's writing-reed or her scourge. Sister Potentia looked after most things within the house; and she thought most of keeping such order as she had seen in the far-famed German convent where she had passed her noviciate. She had been called Sigrid Ragnvaldsdatter before, but had taken a new name when she took the habit of the order, for this was much the use in other lands; it was she, too, who had thought of making the maidens, who were at Nonneseter as pupils, and for a time only, wear novice's dress.

Sister Cecilia Baardsdatter was not as the other nuns. She went about quietly, with downcast eyes, answered always gently and humbly, was serving-maid to all, did for choice all the roughest work, fasted much more than she need — as much as Lady Groa would let her — and knelt by the hour in the church after even-song or went thither before matins.

But one evening, after she had been all day at the beck with two lay-sisters washing clothes, she suddenly burst into a loud sobbing at the supper-table. She cast herself upon the stone floor, crept among the Sisters on hands and knees, beat her breast, and with burning cheeks and streaming tears begged them all to forgive her. She was the worst sinner of them all — she had been hard as stone with pride all her days; pride, and not meekness or thankfulness for Jesus's redeeming death, had held her up, when she had been tempted in the world; she had fled thither not because she loved a man's soul, but because she loved her own vainglory. She had served her sisters out of pride, vanity had she drunken from her water-cup, self-righteousness had she spread thick upon her dry bread, while the other Sisters were drinking their beer and eating their bread-slices with butter.

Of all this Kristin understood no more than that not even Cecilia Baardsdatter was truly godly at heart. An unlit tallow candle that has hung from the roof and grown foul with soot and cobweb — to this she herself likened her unloving chastity.

Lady Groa went herself and lifted up the sobbing woman. Sternly she said, that for this disorder Cecilia should as a punishment move from the Sisters' dormitory into the Abbess's own bed, and lie there till she was free of this fever.

"And thereafter, Sister Cecilia, shall you sit in my seat for the space of a week; we will seek counsel of you in spiritual things and give you such honour for your godly life, that you may have your fill of the homage of sinful mankind. Thus may you judge if it be worth so much striving, and thereafter choose whether you will live by the rules, as do we others, or keep on in exercises that no one demands of you. Then can you ponder whether you will do for the love of God, that He may look down upon you in His mercy, all those things which you say you have done that we should look up to you."

And so it was done. Sister Cecilia lay in the Abbess's room for fourteen days; she had a high fever, and Lady Groa herself tended her. When she got up again, she had to sit for a week at the side of the Abbess in the high-seat, both in the church and in the convent, and all waited on her — she wept all the time as though she were being beaten with whips. But afterwards she was much calmer and happier. She lived much as before, but she blushed like a bride if anyone looked at her, whether she was sweeping the floor or going alone to the church.

None the less did this matter of Sister Cecilia awake in Kristin a great longing for peace and atonement with all wherefrom she had come to feel herself cast out. She thought of Brother Edvin, and one day she took courage and begged leave of Lady Groa to go out to the barefoot friars and visit a friend she knew there.

She marked that Lady Groa misliked this — there was scant friendship between the Minorites and the other cloisters in the bishopric. And the Abbess was no better pleased when she heard who was Kristin's friend. She said this Brother Edvin was an unstable man of God — he was ever wandering about the country and seeking leave to pay begging visits to strange bishoprics. The common folk in many places held him to be a holy man, but he did not seem to understand that a Franciscan's first duty was obedience to those set over him. He had shriven freebooters and outlaws, baptized their children and chanted them to their graves, without asking leave — yet, doubtless, he had sinned as much through ignorance as in despite, and he had borne meekly the penances laid upon him on account of these things. He was borne with, too, because he was skilled in his handicraft — but even in working at this, he had fallen out with his craft-fellows; the master-limners of the Bishop of Bergen

would not suffer him to come and work in the
bishopric there.

Kristin made bold to ask where he had come from,
this monk with the un-Norse name. Lady Groa was in
the mood for talking; she told how he had been born
here in Oslo; but his father was an Englishman,
Rikard Platemaster, who had wedded a farmer's
daughter from the Skogheim Hundred, and had taken
up his abode in the town — two of Edvin's brothers
were armourers of good repute in Oslo. But this eldest
of the Platemaster's sons had been a restless spirit all
his days. 'Twas true he had felt a call to the life of
the cloister from childhood up; he had joined the
Cistercians at Hovedö as soon as he was old enough.
They sent him to a monastery in France to be trained
— for his gifts were good; while still there he had
managed to get leave to pass from the Cistercian into
the Minorite Order. And at the time the unruly friars
began building their church eastward in the fields in
despite of the Bishop's command, Brother Edvin had
been one of the worst and most stiffnecked of them
all — nay, he had half killed with his hammer one of
the men the Bishop sent to stop the work.

It was a long time now since any one had spoken
so much with Kristin at one time, so when Lady
Groa said that now she might go, the young girl bent
and kissed the Abbess's hand, fervently and reverently;
and as she did so, tears came into her eyes. And Lady
Groa, who saw she was weeping, thought it was from
sorrow — and so she said: maybe she might, after all,
let her go out one day to see Brother Edvin.

And a few days later she was told some of the
convent folk had an errand to the King's palace, and
they could take her out along with them to the
Brothers in the fields.

Brother Edvin was at home. Kristin had not thought
she could have been so glad to see any one, except it
had been Erlend. The old man sat and stroked her
hand while they talked together, in thanks for her

coming. No, he had not been in her part of the country since the night he lay at Jörundgaard, but he had heard she was to wed, and he wished her all good fortune. Then Kristin begged that he would go over to the church with her.

They had to go out of the monastery and round to the main door; Brother Edvin durst not take her through the courtyard. He seemed altogether exceeding downcast, and fearful of doing aught that might offend. He had grown very old, thought Kristin.

And when she had laid upon the altar her offering for the officiant monk who was in the church, and afterward asked Edvin if he would confess her, he grew very frightened. He dared not, he said; he had been strictly forbidden to hear confession.

"Ay, maybe you have heard of it," said he. "So it was that I felt I could not deny to those poor unfortunates the gifts which God had given me of His free grace. But, 'tis true, I should have enjoined on them to seek forgiveness in the right place — ay, ay. ... And you, Kristin, you are in duty bound to confess to your own prior."

"Nay, but this is a thing I cannot confess to the prior of the convent," said Kristin.

"Think you it can profit you aught to confess to me what you would hide from your true father confessor?" said the monk more severely.

"If so be you cannot confess me," said Kristin, "at least you can let me speak with you and ask your counsel about what lies upon my soul."

The monk looked about him. The church was empty at the moment. Then he sate himself down on a chest which stood in a corner: "You must remember that I cannot absolve you, but I will counsel you, and keep silence as though you had told me in confession."

Kristin stood up before him, and said:

"It is this: I cannot be Simon Darre's wife."

"Therein you know well that I can counsel no otherwise than would your own prior," said Brother Edvin.

"To undutiful children God gives no happiness, and your father has looked only to your welfare — that you know full well."

"I know not what your counsel will be, when you have heard me to the end," answered Kristin. "Thus stands it now with us: Simon is too good to gnaw the bare branch from which another man has broken the blossom."

She looked the monk straight in the face. But when she met his eyes and marked how the dry, wrinkled old face changed, grew full of sorrow and dismay — something seemed to snap within her, tears started to her eyes, and she would have cast herself upon her knees. But Edvin stopped her hurriedly:

"Nay, nay, sit here upon the chest by me — confess you I cannot." He drew aside and made room for her.

She went on weeping; he stroked her hand, and said gently:

"Mind you that morning, Kristin, I first saw you there on the stairway in the Hamar church . . . ? I heard a tale once, when I was in foreign lands, of a monk who could not believe that God loved all us wretched sinners. . . . Then came an angel and touched his eyes and he beheld a stone in the bottom of the sea, and under the stone there lived a blind, white, naked creature; and he gazed at it until he came to love it, for it was so frail and weak. When I saw you sitting there, so little and so frail, within the great stone house, methought it was but reason that God should love such as you. Fair and pure you were, and yet did you need a helper and a protector. Methought I saw the whole church, with you in it, lying in the hollow of God's hand."

Kristin said low:

"We have bound ourselves one to the other with the dearest oaths — and I have heard that, in the eyes of God, such a pact hallows our coming together as much as if our fathers and mothers had given us one to the other."

The monk answered sadly:

"I see well, Kristin, some one who knew it not to the full has spoken to you of the canonical law. You could not bind yourself by oath to this man without sinning against your father and mother: them had God set over you before you met him. And is not a sorrow and a shame for his kin, too, if they learn that he has lured astray the daughter of a man who has borne his shield with honour at all seasons — betrothed, too, to another? I hear by your words, you deem you have not sinned so greatly — yet dare you not confess this thing to your appointed priest. And if so be you think you are as good as wed to this man, wherefore set you not on your head the linen coif of wedlock, but go still with flowing hair amidst the young maids with whom you can have no great fellowship any more — for now must the chief of your thoughts be with other things than they have in mind?"

"I know not what they have in their minds," said Kristin wearily. "True it is that all my thoughts are with the man I long for. Were it not for my father and mother, I would gladly bind up my hair this day — little would I care if I were called wanton, if only I might be called his."

"Know you if this man means so to deal toward you, that you may be called his with honour some day?" asked Brother Edvin.

Then Kristin told of all that had passed between Erlend Nikulaussön and herself. And while she spoke, she seemed not even to call to mind that she had ever doubted the outcome of it all.

"See you not, Brother Edvin," she began again, "we could not help ourselves. God help me, if I were to meet him without here, when I go from you, and should he pray me to go with him, I would go. I wot well, too, I have seen now there be other folk who have sinned as well as we. . . . When I was a girl at home 'twas past my understanding how aught could win such power over the souls of men that they could forget the fear of sin; but so much have I learnt now: if the wrongs men do through lust and anger cannot be atoned for, then must heaven be an empty place. They tell of you, even, that you, too, once struck a man in wrath — ”

“ ’Tis true,” said the monk. “God’s mercy alone have I to thank that I am not called manslayer. ’Tis many years agone — I was a young man then, and methought I could not endure the wrong the Bishop would have put upon us poor friars. King Haakon — he was Duke then — had given us the ground for our house, but we were so poor we had to work upon our church ourselves — with some few workmen who gave their help more for heavenly reward than for what we could pay them. Maybe ’twas sinful pride in us beggar-monks to wish to build our church so fair and goodly — but we were happy as children in the fields, and sang songs of praise while we hewed and built and toiled. Brother Ranulv — God rest his soul — was master-builder — he was a right skilful stonecutter; nay, I trow the man had been granted skill in all knowledge and all arts by God Himself. I was a carver of stone panels in those days; I had but just finished one of St. Clara, whom the angels were bearing to the church of St. Francis in the dawn of Christmas Day — a most fair panel it had proved, and all of us joyed in it greatly — then the hellish miscreants tore down the walls, and a stone fell and crushed my panels — I struck at a man with my hammer, I could not contain me. . . .

“Ay, now you smile, my Kristin. But see you not that ’tis not well with you now, since you would rather hear such tales of other folks’ frailties than of the life and deeds of good men, who might serve you as a pattern . . . ?

“ ’Tis no easy matter to give you counsel,” he said, when it was time for her to go. “For were you to do what were most right, you would bring sorrow to your father and mother and shame to all your kin. But you must see to it that you free yourself from the troth you plighted to Simon Andressön — and then must you wait in patience for the lot God may send you, make in your heart what amends you can — and let not this Erlend tempt you to sin again, but pray him lovingly to seek atonement with your kin and with God.

"From your sin I cannot free you," said Brother Edvin, as they parted, "but pray for you I will with all my might . . ."

He laid his thin, old hands upon her head and prayed, in farewell, that God might bless her and give her peace.

6

AFTERWARD, there was much in what Brother Edvin had said to her that Kristin could not call to mind. But she left him with a mind strangely clear and peaceful.

Hitherto she had striven with a dull, secret fear and tried to brave it out; telling herself she had not sinned so deeply. Now she felt Edvin had shown her plainly and clearly that she had sinned indeed; such and such was her sin, and she must take it upon her and try to bear it meekly and well. She strove to think of Erlend without impatience — either because he did not send word of himself, or because she must want his caresses. She would only be faithful and full of love for him.

She thought of her father and mother, and vowed to herself that she would requite them for all their love, once they had got over the sorrow she must bring upon them by breaking with the Dyfrin folk. And well-nigh most of all, she thought of Brother Edvin's words of how she must not seek comfort in looking on others' faults; she felt she grew humble and kind, and now she saw at once how easy it was for her to win folks' friendship. Then was she comforted by the thought that after all 'twas not so hard

to come to a good understanding with people — and
so it seemed to her it surely could not be so hard for
her and Erlend either.

Until the day she gave her word to Erlend, she had
always striven earnestly to do what was right and good
— but she had done all at the bidding of others. Now
she felt she had grown from maid to woman. 'Twas
not only by reason of the fervent secret caresses she
had taken and given, not only that she had passed
from her father's ward and was now under Erlend's
will. For Edvin had laid upon her the burden of
answering for her own life, ay, and for Erlend's too.
And she was willing to bear it well and bravely. Thus
she went about among the nuns at Yuletide; and
throughout the goodly rites and the joy and peace of
the holy time, though she felt herself unworthy, yet
she took comfort in thinking that the time would soon
come when she could set herself right again.

But the second day of the new year, Sir Andres
Darre with his wife and all five children came, all
unlooked for, to the convent. They were come to
keep the last days of Yuletide with their friends and
kindred in the town, and they asked that Kristin might
have leave to be with them in their lodging for a short
space.

"For methought, my daughter," said Lady Angerd,
"you would scarce be loth to see a few new faces for
a time."

The Dyfrin folk dwelt in a goodly house that stood
in a dwelling-place * near the Bishop's palace — Sir
Andres' cousin owned it. There was a great hall where
the serving-folk slept, and a fine loft-room with a fireplace of masonry and three good beds; in the one
Sir Andres and Lady Angerd slept with their youngest
son, Gudmund, who was yet a child; in another slept

---

* Town dwelling-places, see Note 15.

Kristin and their two daughters, Astrid and Sigrid, and in the third Simon and his eldest brother Gyrd Andressön.

All Sir Andres' children were comely; Simon the least so, yet he too was reckoned to be well-favoured. And Kristin marked still more than when she was at Dyfrin the year before, that both his father and mother and his four brothers and sisters hearkened most to Simon, and did all he would have them. They all loved each other dearly, but all agreed, without grudging or envy, in setting Simon foremost amongst them.

Here these good folk lived a merry, care-free life. They visited the churches and made their offerings every day, came together with their friends and drank in their company each evening, while the young folk had full leave to play and dance. All showed Kristin the greatest kindness, and none seemed to mark how little glad she was.

Of an evening, when the light had been put out in the loft-room, and all had sought their beds, Simon was wont to get up and go to where the maidens lay. He would sit a while on the edge of the bed; his talk was mostly to his sisters, but in the dark he would let his hand rest on Kristin's bosom — while she lay there hot with wrath.

Now that her sense of such things was keener, she understood well that there were many things Simon was both too proud and too shy to say to her, since he saw she had no mind to such talk from him. And she felt strangely bitter and angry with him, for it seemed to her as though he would fain be a better man than he who had made her his own — even though Simon knew not there was such a one.

But one night, when they had been dancing at another house, Astrid and Sigrid were left behind there to sleep with a playmate. When, late at night, the Dyfrin folk had gone to rest in their loft-room, Simon came to Kristin's bed and climbed up into it; he laid himself down above the fur cover.

Kristin pulled the coverlid up to her chin and crossed her arms firmly upon her breast. In a little Simon tried to put his hand upon her bosom. She felt the silken broidery on his wristband, and knew he had not taken off any of his clothes.

"You are just as bashful in the dark as in the light, Kristin," said Simon, laughing a little. "Surely you can at least let me have one hand to hold," he said, and Kristin gave him the tips of her fingers.

"Think you not we should have somewhat to talk of, when it so falls out that we can be alone a little while?" said he; and Kristin thought, now was the time for her to speak. So she answered "Yes." But after that she could not utter a word.

"May I come under the fur?" he begged again. " 'Tis cold in the room now — " And he slipped in between the fur coverlid and the woollen blanket she had next her. He bent one arm round the bed head, but so that he did not touch her. Thus they lay awhile.

"You are not over-easy to woo, i' faith," said Simon soon after, with a resigned laugh. "Now I pledge you my word, I will not so much as kiss you, if you would not I should. But surely you can speak to me at least?"

Kristin wet her lips with the tip of her tongue, but still she was silent.

"Nay, if you are not lying there trembling!" went on Simon. "Surely it cannot be that you have aught against me, Kristin?"

She felt she could not lie to Simon, so she said "No," — but nothing more.

Simon lay a while longer; he tried to get her into talk with him. But at last he laughed again, and said:

"I see well you think I should be content with hearing that you have naught against me — for to-night — and be glad to boot. 'Tis a parlous thing, so proud as you are — yet one kiss must you give me; then will I go my way and not plague you any more — "

He took the kiss, then sat up and put his feet to the floor. Kristin thought, now must she say to him what she had to say — but he was away already by his own bed, and she heard him undress.

The day after Lady Angerd was not so friendly to Kristin as was her wont. The girl saw that the lady must have heard somewhat the night before, and that she deemed her son's betrothed had not borne her toward him as she held was fitting.

Late that afternoon Simon spoke of a friend's horse he was minded to take in barter for one of his own. He asked Kristin if she would go with him to look at it. She was nothing loth; and they went out into the town together.

The weather was fresh and fair. It had snowed a little overnight, but now the sun was shining, and it was freezing so that the snow crackled under their feet. Kristin felt 'twas good to be out and walk in the cold air, and when Simon brought out the horse to show her, she talked of it with him gaily enough; she knew something of horses, she had been so much with her father. And this was a comely beast — a mouse-grey stallion with a black stripe down the back and a clipped mane, well-shapen and lively, but something small and slightly built.

"He would scarce hold out under a full-armed man for long," said Kristin.

"Indeed, no; nor did I mean him for such a rider," said Simon.

He led the horse out into the home-field behind the house, made it trot and walk, mounted to try its paces, and would have Kristin ride it too. Thus they stayed together a good while out on the snowy field.

At last, as Kristin stood giving the horse bread out of her hand, while Simon leant with his arm over its back, he said all at once:

"Methinks, Kristin, you and my mother are none too loving one with another."

"I have not meant to be unloving to your mother," said she, "but I find not much to say to Lady Angerd."

"Nor seems it you find much to say to me either," said Simon. "I would not force myself upon you, Kristin, before the time comes — but things cannot go on as now, when I can never come to speech with you."

"I have never been one for much speaking," said Kristin. "I know it myself; and I look not you should think it so great a loss, if what is betwixt us two should come to naught."

"You know well what my thoughts are in that matter," said Simon, looking at her.

Kristin flushed red as blood. And it gave her a pang that she could not mislike the fashion of Simon Darre's wooing. After a while he said:

"Is it Arne Gyrdsön, Kristin, you feel you cannot forget?" Kristin but gazed at him; Simon went on, and his voice was gentle and kind: "Never would I blame you for that — you had grown up like brother and sister, and scarce a year is gone by. But be well assured, for your comfort, that I have your good at heart — "

Kristin's face had grown deathly white. Neither of them spoke again as they went back through the town in the twilight. At the end of the street, in the blue-green sky, rode the new moon's sickle with a bright star within its horn.

A year, thought Kristin; and she could not think when she had last given a thought to Arne. She grew afraid — maybe she was a wanton, wicked woman — but one year since she had seen him on his bier in the wake-room, and had thought she should never be glad again in this life — she moaned within herself for terror of her own heart's inconstancy, and of the fleeting changefulness of all things. Erlend! Erlend! — could he forget her — and yet it seemed to her 'twould be worse, if at any time she should forget him.

Sir Andres went with his children to the great Yule-tide feast at the King's palace. Kristin saw all the pomp and show of the festival — they came, too, into the hall where sat King Haakon and the Lady Isabel Bruce, King Eirik's widow. Sir Andres went forward and did homage to the King, while his children and Kristin stood somewhat behind. She thought of all Lady Aashild had told her; she called to mind that the King was near of kin to Erlend, their fathers' mothers were sisters — and she was Erlend's light-o'-love, she had no right to stand here, least of all amid these good and worthy folk, Sir Andres' children.

Then all at once she saw Erlend Nikulaussön — he had stepped forward in front of Queen Isabel, and stood with bowed head, and with his hand upon his breast, while she spoke a few words to him; he had on the brown silk clothes that he had worn at the guild feast. Kristin stepped behind Sir Andres' daughters.

When some time after, Lady Angerd led her daughters up before the Queen, Kristin could not see him anywhere, but indeed she dared not lift her eyes from the floor. She wondered whether he was standing somewhere in the hall, she thought she could feel his eyes upon her — but she thought, too, that all folks looked at her as though they must know she was a liar, standing there with the golden garland on her outspread hair.

He was not in the hall where the young folk were feasted, and where they danced when the tables had been taken away; this evening it was Simon with whom Kristin must dance.

Along one of the longer walls stood a fixed table, and thither the King's men bore ale and mead and wine the whole night long. Once when Simon drew her thither and drank to her, she saw Erlend standing near, behind Simon's back. He looked at her, and Kristin's hand shook when she took the beaker from Simon's hand and set it to her lips. Erlend whispered vehemently to the man who was with him — a tall, comely man, well on in years and somewhat stout, who shook his head impatiently and looked as he were vexed. Soon after Simon led her back to the dance.

She knew not how long this dancing lasted — the music seemed as though 'twould never end, and each moment was long and evil to her with longing and unrest. At last it was over, and Simon drew her to the drinking-board again.

A friend came forward to speak to him, and led him away a few steps, to a group of young men. And Erlend stood before her.

"I have so much I would fain say to you," he whispered. "I know not what to say first — in Jesus' name, Kristin, what ails you?" he asked quickly, for he saw her face grow white as chalk.

She could not see him clearly; it seemed as though there were running water between their two faces. He took a goblet from the table, drank from it and handed it to her. Kristin felt as though 'twas all too heavy for her, or as though her arm had been cut off at the shoulder; do as she would, she could not lift the cup to her mouth.

"Is it so, then, that you will drink with your betrothed, but not with me?" asked Erlend softly; but Kristin dropped the goblet from her hand and sank forward into his arms.

When she awoke she was lying on a bench with her head in a strange maiden's lap — some one was standing by her side, striking the palms of her hands, and she had water on her face.

She sat up. Somewhere in the ring about her she saw Erlend's face, white and drawn. Her own body felt weak, as though all her bones had melted away, and her head seemed as it were large and hollow; but somewhere within it shone one clear, desperate thought — she must speak with Erlend.

She said to Simon Darre — he stood near by:

"'Twas too hot for me, I trow — so many tapers are burning here — and I am little used to drink so much wine —"

"Are you well again now?" asked Simon. "You frightened folks. Mayhap you would have me take you home now?"

"We must wait, surely, till your father and mother go," said Kristin calmly. "But sit down here — I can dance no more." She touched the cushion at her side — then she held out her other hand to Erlend:

"Sit you here, Erlend Nikulaussön; I had no time to speak my greetings to an end. 'Twas but of late Ingebjörg said she deemed you had clean forgotten her."

She saw it was far harder for him to keep calm than for her — and it was all she could do to keep back the little tender smile, which would gather round her lips.

"You must bear the maid my thanks for thinking of me still," he stammered. "Almost I was afraid she had forgotten me."

Kristin paused a little. She knew not what she should say, which might seem to come from the flighty Ingebjörg and yet might tell Erlend her meaning. Then there welled up in her the bitterness of all these months of helpless waiting, and she said:

"Dear Erlend, can you think that we maidens could forget the man who defended our honour so gallantly — "

She saw his face change as though she had struck him — and at once she was sorry; then Simon asked what this was they spoke of. Kristin told him of Ingebjörg's and her adventure in the Eikaberg woods. She marked that Simon liked the tale but little. Then she begged him to go and ask of Lady Angerd, whether they should not soon go home; 'twas true that she was weary. When he was gone, she looked at Erlend.

" 'Tis strange," said he in a low voice, "you are so quick-witted — I had scarce believed it of you."

"Think you not I have had to learn to hide and be secret?" said she gloomily.

Erlend's breath came heavily; he was still very pale.

" 'Tis so then?" he whispered. "Yet did you promise

me to turn to my friends if this should come to pass.
God knows, I have thought of you each day, in dread
that the worst might have befallen — "

"I know well what you mean by the worst," said
Kristin shortly. "*That* you have no need to fear. To
me what seemed the worst was that you would not
send me one word of greeting — can you not understand that I am living there amongst the nuns — like
a stranger bird — ?" She stopped — for she felt that
the tears were coming.

"Is it therefore you are with the Dyfrin folk now?"
he asked. Then such grief came upon her that she
could make no answer.

She saw Lady Angerd and Simon come through the
doorway. Erlend's hand lay upon his knee, near her,
and she could not take it.

"I must have speech with you," said he eagerly, "we
have not said a word to one another we should have
said — "

"Come to mass in the Maria Church at Epiphany,"
said Kristin quickly, as she rose and went to meet the
others.

Lady Angerd showed herself most loving and careful of Kristin on the way home, and herself helped her
to bed. With Simon she had no talk until the day
after. Then he said:

"How comes it that you bear messages betwixt this
Erlend and Ingebjörg Filippusdatter? 'Tis not fit you
should meddle in the matter, if there be hidden dealings between them!"

"Most like there is naught in it," said Kristin. "She
is but a chatterer."

"Methinks too," said Simon, "you should have taken
warning by what's past, and not trusted yourself out
in the wild-wood paths alone with that magpie." But
Kristin reminded him hotly, that it was not their fault
they had strayed and lost themselves. Simon said no
more.

The next day the Dyfrin folks took her back to the convent, before they themselves left for home.

Erlend came to evensong in the convent church every evening for a week without Kristin getting a chance to change a word with him. She felt as she thought a hawk must feel sitting chained to its perch with its hood over its eyes. Every word that had passed between them at their last meeting made her unhappy too — it should never have been like that. It was of no use to say to herself: it had come upon them so suddenly, they had hardly known what they said.

But one afternoon in the twilight there came to the parlour a comely woman, who looked like a townsman's wife. She asked for Kristin Lavransdatter, and said she was the wife of a mercer and her husband had come from Denmark of late with some fine cloaks; Aasmund Bjorgulfsön had a mind to give one to his brother's daughter, and the maid was to go with her and choose for herself.

Kristin was given leave to go with the woman. She thought it was unlike her uncle to wish to give her a costly gift, and strange that he should send an unknown woman to fetch her. The woman was sparing of her words at first, and said little in answer to Kristin's questions, but when they were come down to the town, she said of a sudden:

"I will not play you false, fair child that you are — I will tell you all this thing as it is, and you must do as you deem best. 'Twas not your uncle who sent me, but a man — maybe you can guess his name, and if you cannot, then you shall not come with me. I have no husband — I make a living for myself and mine by keeping a house of call and selling beer; for such a one it boots not to be too much afraid either of sin or of the watchmen — but I will not lend my house for you to be betrayed inside my doors."

Kristin stood still, flushing red. She was strangely sore and ashamed for Erlend's sake. The woman said:

"I will go back with you to the convent, Kristin; but you must give me somewhat for my trouble — the knight promised me a great reward; but I, too, was fair once, and I, too, was betrayed. And 'twould not be amiss if you should name me in your prayers to-night — they call me Brynhild Fluga."

Kristin drew a ring off her finger and gave it to the woman:

" 'Tis fairly done of you, Brynhild — but if the man be my kinsman Erlend Nikulaussön, then have I naught to fear; he would have me make peace betwixt him and my uncle. You may set your mind at ease; but I thank you none the less that you would have warned me."

Brynhild Fluga turned away to hide a smile.

She led Kristin by the alleys behind St. Clement's Church, northward towards the river. Here a few small dwelling-places stood by themselves along the river-bank. They went towards one of them, along a path between fences, and here Erlend came to meet them. He looked about him on all sides, then took off his cloak, wrapped it about Kristin, and pulled the hood over her face.

"What think you of this device?" he asked, quickly and low. "Think you 'tis a great wrong I do? — yet needs must I speak with you."

"It boots but little now, I trow, to think what is right and what is wrong," said Kristin.

"Speak not so," begged Erlend. "I bear the blame. . . . Kristin, every day and every night have I longed for you," he whispered close to her.

A shudder passed through her as she met his eyes for a moment. She felt it as guilt in her, when he looked so at her, that she had thought of anything but her love for him.

Brynhild Fluga had gone on before. Erlend asked, when they were come into the courtyard:

"Would you that we should go into the living-room, or shall we talk up in the loft-room?"

"As you will," answered Kristin; and they mounted to the loft-room.

The moment he had barred the door behind them she was in his arms. . . .

She knew not how long she had lain folded thus in his arms, when Erlend said:

"Now must we say what has to be said, my Kristin — I scarce dare let you stay here longer."

"I dare stay here all night long if you would have me stay," whispered she.

Erlend pressed his cheeks to hers.

"Then were I not your friend. 'Tis bad enough as it is, but you shall not lose your good name for my sake."

Kristin did not answer — but a soreness stirred within her; how could he speak thus — he who had lured her here to Brynhild Fluga's house; she knew not why, but she felt it was no honest place. And he had looked that all should go as it had gone, of that she was sure.

"I have thought at times," said Erlend again, "that if there be no other way, I must bear you off by force — into Sweden. Lady Ingebjörg welcomed me kindly in the autumn and was mindful of our kinship. But now do I suffer for my sins — I have fled the land before, as you know — and I would not they should name you as the like of that other."

"Take me home with you to Husaby," said Kristin low. "I cannot bear to be parted from you, and to live on among the maids at the convent. Both your kin and mine would surely hearken to reason, and let us come together and be reconciled with them —"

Erlend clasped her to him, and groaned:

"I cannot bring you to Husaby, Kristin."

"Why can you not?" she asked softly.

"Eline came thither in the autumn," said he after a moment. "I cannot move her to leave the place," he went on hotly, "not unless I bear her to the sledge by force and drive away with her. And that methought I could not do — she has brought both our children home with her."

Kristin felt herself sinking, sinking. In a voice breaking with fear, she said:

"I deemed you were parted from her."

"So deemed I, too," answered Erlend shortly. "But she must have heard in Österdal, where she was, that I had thoughts of marriage. You saw the man with me at the Yuletide feast — 'twas my foster-father, Baard Petersön of Hestnæs. I went to him when I came from Sweden; I went to my kinsman, Heming Alvsön in Saltviken, too; I talked with both about my wish to wed, and begged their help. Eline must have come to hear of it. . . .

"I bade her ask what she would for herself and the children — but Sigurd, her husband — they look not that he should live the winter out — and then none could deny us if we would live together. . . .

"I lay in the stable with Haftor and Ulv, and Eline lay in the hall in my bed. I trow my men had a rare jest to laugh at behind my back."

Kristin could not say a word. A little after, Erlend spoke again:

"See you, the day we pledge each other at our espousals, she must understand that all is over between her and me — she has no power over me any more. . . .

"But 'tis hard for the children. I had not seen them for a year — they are fair children — and little can I do to give them a happy lot. 'Twould not have helped them greatly had I been able to wed their mother."

Tears began to roll down over Kristin's cheeks. Then Erlend said:

"Heard you what I said but now, that I had talked with my kinsfolk? Ay, they were glad enough that I was minded to wed. Then I said 'twas you I would have and none other."

"And they liked not that?" asked Kristin at length, forlornly.

"See you not," said Erlend gloomily, "they could say but one thing — they cannot and they will not ride with me to your father, until this bargain 'twixt you and Simon Andressön is undone again. It has made it none the easier for us, Kristin, that you have spent your Yuletide with the Dyfrin folk."

Kristin gave way altogether and wept noiselessly. She had felt ever that there was something of wrong and dishonour in her love, and now she knew the fault was hers.

She shook with the cold when she got up soon after, and Erlend wrapped her in both the cloaks. It was quite dark now without, and Erlend went with her as far as St. Clement's Church; then Brynhild brought her the rest of the way to Nonneseter.

7

A WEEK later Brynhild Fluga came with word that the cloak was ready, and Kristin went with her and met Erlend in the loft-room as before.

When they parted, he gave her a cloak: "So that you may have something to show in the convent," said he. It was of blue velvet with red silk inwoven, and Erlend bade her mark that 'twas of the sames hues as the dress she had worn that day in the woods. Kristin wondered it should make her so glad that he said this — she thought he had never given her greater happiness than when he said these words.

But now they could no longer make use of this way of meeting, and it was not easy to find a new one. But Erlend came often to vespers at the convent church, and sometimes Kristin would make herself an errand after the service, up to the commoners' houses; and then they would snatch a few words together by stealth up by the fences in the murk of the winter evening.

Then Kristin thought of asking leave of Sister Potentia to visit some old, crippled women, alms-folk of the convent, who dwelt in a cottage standing in one of the fields. Behind the cottage was an outhouse where the women kept a cow; Kristin offered to tend it for them; and while she was there Erlend would join her and she would let him in.

She wondered a little to mark that, glad as Erlend was to be with her, it seemed to rankle in his mind that she could devise such a plan.

" 'Twas no good day for you when you came to know me," said he one evening. "Now have you learnt to follow the ways of deceit."

"*You* ought not to blame me," answered Kristin sadly.

" 'Tis not you I blame," said Erlend quickly, with a shamed look.

"I had not thought myself," went on Kristin, "that 'twould come so easy to me to lie. But one *can* do what one *must* do."

"Nay, 'tis not so at all times," said Erlend as before. "Mind you not last winter, when you could not bring yourself to tell your betrothed that you would not have him?"

To this Kristin answered naught, but only stroked his face.

She never felt so strongly how dear Erlend was to her, as when he said things like this, that made her grieve or wonder. She was glad when she could take upon herself the blame for all that was shameful and wrong in their love. Had she found courage to speak to Simon as she should have done, they might have been a long way now on the road to have all put in order. Erlend had done all he could when he had spoken of their wedding to his kinsmen. She said this

to herself, when the days in the convent grew long
and evil — Erlend had wished to make all things right
and good again. With little tender smiles she thought
of him as he drew a picture of their wedding for her
— she should ride to church in silks and velvet, she
should be led to the bridal-bed with the high golden
crown on her flowing hair — your lovely, lovely hair,
he said, drawing her plaits through his hand.

"Yet can it not be the same to you as though I had
never been yours," said Kristin musingly, once when
he talked thus.

Then he clasped her to him wildly:

"Can I call to mind the first time I drank in Yuletide,
think you, or the first time I saw the hills at home turn
green when winter was gone? Ay, well do I mind the
first time you were mine, and each time since — but
to have you for my own is like keeping Yule and
hunting birds on green hillsides for ever — "

Happily she nestled to him. Not that she ever
thought for a moment it would turn out as Erlend was
so sure it would — Kristin felt that before long a
day of judgment must come upon them. It could not
be that things should go well for them in the end. . . .
But she was not so much afraid — she was much more
afraid Erlend might have to go northward before it all
came to light, and she be left behind, parted from him.
He was over at the castle at Akersnes now; Munan
Baardsön was posted there while the bodyguard was
at Tunsberg, where the King lay grievously sick. But
sometime Erlend must go home and see to his possessions. That she was afraid of his going home to Husaby
because Eline sat there waiting for him, she would not
own even to herself; and neither would she own that
she was less afraid to be taken in sin along with Erlend,
than of standing forth alone and telling Simon and her
father what was in her heart.

Almost she could have wished for punishment to
come upon her, and that soon. For now she had no
other thought than of Erlend; she longed for him in

the day and dreamed of him at night; she could not feel remorse, but she took comfort in thinking the day would come when she would have to pay dear for all they had snatched by stealth. And in the short evening hours she could be with Erlend in the almswomen's cowshed, she threw herself into his arms with as much passion as if she knew she had paid with her soul already that she might be his.

But time went on, and it seemed as though Erlend might have the good fortune he had counted on. Kristin never marked that any in the convent mistrusted her. Ingebjörg, indeed, had found out that she met Erlend, but Kristin saw the other never dreamed 'twas aught else than a little passing sport. That a maid of good kindred, promised in marriage, should dare wish to break the bargain her kinsfolk had made, such a thought would never come to Ingebjörg, Kristin saw. And once more a pang of terror shot through her — it might be 'twas a quite unheard-of thing, this she had taken in hand. And at this thought she wished again that discovery might come, and all be at an end.

Easter came. Kristin knew not how the winter had gone; every day she had not seen Erlend had been long as an evil year, and the long evil days had linked themselves together into weeks without end; but now it was spring and Easter was come, she felt 'twas no time since the Yuletide feast. She begged Erlend not to seek her till the Holy Week was gone by; and he yielded to her in this, as he did to all her wishes, thought Kristin. It was as much her own blame as his that they had sinned together in not keeping the Lenten fast. But Easter she was resolved they should keep. Yet it was misery not to see him. Maybe he would have to go soon; he had said naught of it, but she knew that now the King lay dying, and mayhap this might bring some turn in Erlend's fortunes, she thought.

* * *

Thus things stood with her, when one of the first days after Easter word was brought her to go down to the parlour to her betrothed.

As soon as he came toward her and held out his hand, she felt there was somewhat amiss — his face was not as it was wont to be; his small, grey eyes did not laugh, they did not smile when he smiled. And Kristin could not help seeing it became him well to be a little less merry. He looked well, too, in a kind of travelling dress — a long blue, close-fitting outer-garment men called *kothardi*, and a brown shoulder-cape with a hood, which was thrown back now; the cold air had given his light-brown hair a yet stronger curl.

They sat and talked for a while. Simon had been at Formo through Lent, and had gone over to Jörungaard almost daily. They were well there; Ulvhild as well as they dared look that she should be; Ramborg was at home now, she was a fair child and lively.

" 'Twill be over one of these days — the year you were to be here at Nonneseter," said Simon. "By this the folks at your home will have begun to make ready for our betrothal-feast — yours and mine."

Kristin said naught, and Simon went on:

"I said to Lavrans, I would ride hither to Oslo and speak to you of this."

Kristin looked down and said low:

"I, too, would fain speak with you of that matter, Simon — alone."

"I saw well myself that we must speak of it alone," answered Simon; "and I was about to ask even now that you would pray Lady Groa to let us go together into the garden for a little."

Kristin rose quickly and slipped from the room without a sound. Soon after she came back followed by one of the nuns with a key.

There was a door leading from the parlour out into an herb-garden that lay behind the most westerly of the convent buildings. The nun unlocked the door and they stepped out into a mist so thick they could see but a few paces in among the trees. The nearest stems were coal-black; the moisture stood in beads on every twig and bough. A little fresh snow lay melting upon the wet mould, but under the bushes some white and yellow lily plants were blooming already, and a fresh, cool smell rose from the violet leaves.

Simon led her to the nearest bench. He sat a little bent forward, with his elbows resting upon his knees. Then he looked up at her with a strange little smile:

"Almost I think I know what you would say to me," said he. "There is another man, who is more to you than I — "

"It is so," answered Kristin faintly.

"Methinks I know his name, too," said Simon, in a harder tone. "It is Erlend Nikulaussön of Husaby?"

After a while Kristin asked in a low voice:

"It has come to your ears, then?"

Simon was a little slow in answering:

"You can scarce think I could be so dull as not to see somewhat when we were together at Yule? I could say naught then, for my father and mother were with us. But this it is that has brought me hither alone this time. I know not whether it be wise of me to touch upon it — but methought we must talk of these things before we are given to one another.

". . . But so it is now, that when I came hither yesterday — I met my kinsman, Master Öistein. And he spoke of you. He said you two had passed across the churchyard of St. Clement's one evening, and with you was a woman they call Brynhild Fluga. I swore a great oath that he must have been amiss! And if you say it is untrue, I shall believe your word."

"The priest saw aright," answered Kristin defiantly. "You forswore yourself, Simon."

He sat still a little ere he asked:

"Know you who this Brynhild Fluga is, Kristin?" As she shook her head, he said: "Munan Baardsön set her up in a house here in the town, when he wedded —

she carries on unlawful dealings in wine — and other things — "

"You know her?" asked Kristin mockingly.

"I was never meant to be a monk or a priest," said Simon, reddening. "But I can say at least that I have wronged no maid and no man's wedded wife. See you not yourself that 'tis no honourable man's deed to bring you out to go about at night in such company — ?"

"Erlend did not draw me on," said Kristin, red with anger, "nor has he promised me aught. I set my heart on him without his doing aught to tempt me — from the first time I saw him, he was dearer to me than all other men."

Simon sat playing with his dagger, throwing it from one hand to the other.

"These are strange words to hear from a man's betrothed maiden," said he. "Things promise well for us two now, Kristin."

Kristin drew a deep breath:

"You would be ill served should you take me for your wife now, Simon."

"Ay, God Almighty knows that so it seems indeed," said Simon Andressön.

"Then I dare hope," said Kristin meekly and timidly, "that you will uphold me, so that Sir Andres and my father may let this bargain about us be undone."

"Do you so?" said Simon. He was silent for a little. "God knows whether you rightly understand what you say."

"That do I," said Kristin. "I know the law is such that none may force a maid to marriage against her will; else can she take her plea before the Thing — "

"I trow 'tis before the Bishop," said Simon, with something of a grim smile. "True it is, I have had no cause to search out how the law stands in such things. And I wot well you believe not either that 'twill come to that pass. You know well enough that I will not hold you to your word, if your heart is too much set against it. But can you not understand — 'tis two years now since our marriage was agreed, and you have said no word against it till now, when all is ready for the betrothal and the wedding. Have you thought what it will mean, if you come forth now and seek to break the bond, Kristin?"

"But you want not me either," said Kristin.

"Ay, but I do," answered Simon curtly. "If you think otherwise, you must even think better of it — "

"Erlend Nikulaussön and I have vowed to each other by our Christian faith," said she, trembling, "that if we cannot come together in wedlock, then neither of us will have wife or husband all our days — "

Simon was silent a good while. Then he said with effort:

"Then I know not, Kristin, what you meant when you said Erlend had neither drawn you on nor promised you aught — he has lured you to set yourself against the counsel of all your kin. Have you thought what kind of husband you will get, if you wed a man who took another's wife to be his paramour — and now would take for wife another man's betrothed maiden — ?"

Kristin gulped down her tears; she whispered thickly:

"This you say but to hurt me."

"Think you I would wish to hurt you?" asked Simon, in a low voice.

" 'Tis not as it would have been, had you . . ." said Kristin falteringly. "You were not asked either, Simon — 'twas your father and my father who made the pact. It had been otherwise had you chosen me yourself — "

Simon struck his dagger into the bench so that it stood upright. A little after he drew it out again, and tried to slip it back into its sheath, but it would not go down, the point was bent. Then he sat passing it from hand to hand as before.

"You know yourself," said he, in a low tone and with a shaking voice, "you know that you lie, if you

would have it that I did not —. You know well
enough what I would have spoken of with you —
many times — when you met me so that I had not
been a man, had I been able to say it — after that —
not if they had tried to drag it out of me with red-hot
pincers. . . .

"First I thought 'twas yonder dead lad. I thought I
must leave you in peace awhile — you knew me not
— I deemed 'twould have been a wrong to trouble you
so soon after. Now I see you did not need so long a
time to forget — now — now — now —"

"No," said Kristin quietly. "I know it, Simon. Now
I cannot look that you should be my friend any
longer."

"*Friend . . . !*" Simon gave a short strange laugh.
"Do you need my friendship now, then?"

Kristin grew red.

"You are a man," said she softly. "And old enough
now — you can choose yourself whom you will wed."

Simon looked at her sharply. Then he laughed as
before.

"I understand. You would have me say 'tis I who —.
I am to take the blame for the breaking of our bond?

"If so be that your mind is fixed — if you have the
will and the boldness to try to carry through your
purpose — then I will do it," he said low. "At home,
with all my own folks, and before all your kin — save
one. To your father you must tell the truth, even as
it is. If you would have it so, I will bear your message
to him, and spare you, in giving it, in so far as I can —
but Lavrans Björgulfsön shall know that never, with
my will, would I go back from one word that I have
spoken to him."

Kristin clutched the edge of the bench with both
hands; this was harder for her to bear than all else that
Simon Darre had said. Pale and fearful, she stole a
glance at him.

Simon rose.

"Now must we go in," said he. "Methinks we are

nigh frozen, both of us, and the sister is sitting waiting
with the key. I will give you a week to think upon the
matter — I have business in the town here. I shall come
hither and speak with you when I am ready to go, but
you will scarce care to see aught of me meanwhile."

8

KRISTIN said to herself: now that, at least, is over. But
she felt broken with weariness and sick for Erlend's
arms.

She lay awake most of the night, and she resolved
to do what she had never dared think of before —
send word to Erlend. It was not easy to find any one
who could go such an errand for her. The lay-sisters
never went out alone, nor did she know of any of
them she thought would be willing; the men who did
the farm-work were elder folk and but seldom came
near the dwellings of the nuns, save to speak with the
Abbess herself. There was only Olav. He was a half-
grown lad who worked in the gardens; he had been
Lady Groa's foster-son from the time when he was
found, a newborn babe, upon the church steps one
morning. Folk said one of the lay-sisters was his
mother; she was to have been a nun; but after she had
been kept in the dark cell for six months — for grave
disobedience, as 'twas said — and it was about that
time the child was found — she had been given the
lay-sisters' habit and had worked in the farmyard ever
since. Kristin had often thought of Sister Ingrid's fate
throughout these months, but she had had few chances
to speak with her. It was venturesome to trust to Olav
— he was but a child, and Lady Groa and all the nuns
were wont to chat and jest with him, when they saw
the boy. But Kristin deemed it mattered little what
risks she took now. And a day or two later, when
Olav was for the town one morning, Kristin sent word

by him to Akersnes, that Erlend must find some way whereby they might meet alone.

That same afternoon Erlend's own man, Ulf, came to the grille. He said he was Aasmund Björgulfsön's man, and was to pray, on his master's behalf, that his brother's daughter might go down to the town for a little, for Aasmund had not time to come to Nonneseter. Kristin thought this device must surely fail — but when Sister Potentia asked if she knew the bearer of the message, she said, "Yes." So she went with Ulf to Brynhild Fluga's house.

Erlend awaited her in the loft-room — he was uneasy and anxious, and she knew at once, 'twas that he was afraid again of what he seemed to fear the most.

Always it cut her to the soul he should feel such a haunting dread that she might be with child — when yet they could not keep apart. Harassed as she was this evening, she said this to him — hotly enough. Erlend's face flushed darkly, and he laid his head down upon her shoulder.

"You are right," said he. "I must try to let you be, Kristin — not to put your happiness in such jeopardy. If you will — "

She threw her arms around him and laughed, but he caught her round the waist, forced her down upon a bench, and seated himself on the farther side of the board. When she stretched her hand over to him, he covered the palm with vehement kisses.

"I have tried more than you," said he with passion. "You know not how much I deem it means for both of us, that we should be wed with all honour."

"Then you should not have made me yours," said Kristin.

Erlend hid his face in his hands.

"Ay, would to God I had not done you that wrong," he said.

"Neither you nor I wish that," said Kristin, laughing boldly. "And if I may but be forgiven and make my

peace at last with my kindred and with God, then shall
I not sorrow overmuch though I must wear the
woman's hood when I am wed. Ay, and often it seems
to me, I could do without peace even, if only I may be
with you."

"You shall bring honour with you into my house
once more," said Erlend, "not I drag *you* down into
dishonour."

Kristin shook her head. Then she said:

" 'Tis like you will be glad then, when you hear
that I have talked with Simon Andressön — and he
will not hold me to the pact that was made for us by
our fathers before I met you."

At once Erlend was wild with joy, and Kristin was
made to tell him all. Yet she told not of the scornful
words Simon had spoken of Erlend, though she said
that before Lavrans he would not take the blame upon
himself.

" 'Tis but reason," said Erlend shortly. "They like
each other well, your father and he? Ay, me he will
like less, I trow — Lavrans."

Kristin took these words as a sign that Erlend felt
with her she had still a hard road to travel ere yet they
reached their journey's end; and she was thankful to
him for it. But he did not come back to this matter;
he was glad above measure, saying he had feared so
that she would not have courage to speak with Simon.

"You like him after a fashion, I mark well," said he.

"Can it be aught to you," asked Kristin, ". . . after
all that has come and gone between you and me, that
I can see that Simon is an honest man and a stout?"

"Had you never met me," said Erlend, "you might
well have had good days with him, Kristin. Why
laugh you?"

"Oh, I did but call to mind somewhat Lady Aashild
said once," answered Kristin. "I was but a child then
— but 'twas somewhat about good days falling to wise
folk, but the best days of all to those who dare be
unwise."

"God bless my kinswoman, if she taught you that," said Erlend, and took her upon his knee. " 'Tis strange, Kristin, never have I marked that you were afraid."

"Have you never marked it?" she asked, as she nestled close to him.

He seated her on the bedside and drew off her shoes, but then drew her back again to the table.

"Oh, my Kristin — now at last it looks as if bright days might come for us two. Methinks I had never dealt with you as I have done," he said, stroking and stroking her hair, "had it not been that each time I saw you, I thought ever 'twas not reason that they should give so fine and fair a wife to *me*. . . . Sit you down here and drink to me," he begged.

A moment after came a knock on the door — it sounded like the stroke of a sword hilt.

"Open, Erlend Nikulaussön, if you are within!"

" 'Tis Simon Darre," said Kristin, in a low voice.

"Open, man, in the devil's name — if you be a man!" shouted Simon, and beat on the door again.

Erlend went to the bed and took his sword down from the peg in the wall. He looked round, at a loss what to do: "There is nowhere here you can hide — "

" 'Twould scarce make things better if I hid," said Kristin. She had risen to her feet; she spoke very quietly, but Erlend saw that she was trembling. "You must open," she said, in the same tone. Simon hammered on the door again.

Erlend went and drew the bolt. Simon stepped in; he had a drawn sword in his hand, but he thrust it back into its sheath at once.

For a while the three stood in silence. Kristin trembled; but yet, in this first moment, she felt a strange, sweet thrill — from deep within her something rose, scenting the combat between two men — she drew a deep breath; here was an end to these endless months of dumb waiting and longing and dread. She looked from one to the other, pale and with shin-

ing eyes — then the strain within her broke in a chill,
unfathomable despair. There was more of cold scorn
than of rage or jealousy in Simon Darre's eyes, and
she saw that Erlend, behind his defiant bearing, burned
with shame. It dawned upon her, how other men
would think of him, who had let her come to him in
such a place, and she saw 'twas as though he had had
to suffer a blow in the face; she knew he burned to
draw his sword and fall upon Simon.

"Why have you come hither, Simon?" she cried
aloud in dread.

Both men turned towards her.

"To fetch you home," said Simon. "Here you
cannot be — "

" 'Tis not for you, any more, to lay commands on
Kristin Lavransdatter," said Erlend fiercely, "she is
mine now — "

"I doubt not she is," said Simon savagely, "and a
fair bridal bower have you brought her to — " He
stood a little, panting; then he mastered his voice and
spoke quietly: "But so it is that I am her betrothed
still — till her father can come for her. And for so
long I mean to guard with edge and point so much of
her honour as can be saved — in others' eyes —"

"What need of *you* to guard her; I can — " he
flushed red as blood under Simon's eyes. Then, flying
out: "Think you I will suffer threats from a boy like
you," he cried, laying his hand on his sword-hilt.

Simon clapped both hands behind him.

"I am not such a coward as to be afraid you should
deem me afraid," said he as before. "I will fight you,
Erlend Nikulaussön, you may stake your soul upon
that, if, within due time, you have not made suit for
Kristin to her father — "

"That will I never do at your bidding, Simon
Andressön," said Erlend angrily; the blood rushed into
his face again.

"Nay — do you it to set right the wrong you have

done so young a maid," answered Simon, unmoved,
" 'twill be better so for Kristin."

Kristin gave a loud cry, in pain at Erlend's pain.
She stamped upon the floor:

"Go, then, Simon, go — what have you to do with
our affairs?"

"I told you but now," said Simon. "You must bear
with me till your father has loosed you and me from
each other."

Kristin broke down utterly.

"Go, go, I will follow straightway. . . . Jesus! why
do you torture me so, Simon? . . . you know you deem
not yourself I am worthy that you should trouble
about me — "

" 'Tis not for your sake I do it," answered Simon.
"Erlend — will you not tell her to go with me?"

Erlend's face quivered. He touched her on the
shoulder:

"You must go, Kristin. Simon Darre and I will speak
of this at another time — "

Kristin got up obediently, and fastened her cloak
about her. Her shoes stood by the bedside. . . . She
remembered them, but she could not put them on
under Simon's eyes.

Outside, the fog had come down again. Kristin flew
along, with head bent and hands clutched tight in the
folds of her cloak. Her throat was bursting with tears
— wildly she longed for some place where she could
be alone, and sob and sob. The worst, the worst was
still before her; but she had proved a new thing this
evening, and she writhed under it — she had proved
how it felt to see the man to whom she had given
herself humbled.

Simon was at her elbow as she hurried through the
lanes, over the common lands and across the open
places, where the houses had vanished and there was
naught but fog to be seen. Once when she stumbed

over something, he caught her arm and kept her from falling.

"No need to run so fast," said he. "Folk are staring after us. . . . How you are trembling!" he said more gently. Kristin held her peace and walked on.

She slipped in the mud of the street, her feet were wet through and icy cold — the hose she had on were of leather, but they were thin; she felt they were giving way, and the mud was oozing through to her naked feet.

They came to the bridge over the convent beck, and went more slowly up the slopes on the other side.

"Kristin," said Simon of a sudden, "your father must never come to know of this."

"How knew you that I was — there?" asked Kristin.

"I came to speak with you," answered Simon shortly. "Then they told me of this man of your uncle's coming. I knew Aasmund was in Hadeland. You two are not over cunning at making up tales. — Heard you what I said but now?"

"Ay," said Kristin. "It was I who sent word to Erlend that we should meet at Fluga's house; I knew the woman — "

"Then shame upon you! But, oh, you could not know what she is — and he. . . . Do you hear," said Simon harshly, "if so be it *can* be hidden, you must hide from Lavrans what you have thrown away. And if you cannot hide it, then you must strive to spare him the worst of the shame."

"You are ever so marvellous careful for my father," said Kristin, trembling. She strove to speak defiantly, but her voice was ready to break with sobs.

Simon walked on a little. Then he stopped — she caught a glimpse of his face, as they stood there alone together in the midst of the fog. He had never looked like this before.

"I have seen it well, each time I was at your home," said he, "how little you understood, you his women-folk, what a man Lavrans is. Knows not how to rule you, says yonder Trond Gjesling — and 'twere like he should trouble himself with such work — he who was born to rule over *men*. He was made for a leader, ay, and one whom men would have followed — gladly. These are no times for such men as he — my father knew him at Baaghaus. . . . But, as things are, he has lived his life up there in the Dale, as he were little else but a farmer. . . . He was married off all too young — and your mother, with her heavy mood, was not the one to make it lighter for him to live that life. So it is that he has many friends — but think you there is *one* who is his fellow? His sons were taken from him — 'twas you, his daughters, who were to build up his race after him — must he live now to see the day when one is without health and the other without honour — ?"

Kristin pressed her hands tightly over her heart — she felt she must hold it in to make herself as hard as she had need to be.

"Why say you this?" she whispered after a time. "It cannot be that you would ever wish to wed me now — "

"That — would I — not," said Simon unsteadily. "God help me, Kristin — I think of you that evening in the loft-room at Finnsbrekken. — But may the foul fiend fly away with me living the day I trust a maiden's eyes again!

" . . . Promise me, that you will not see Erlend before your father comes," said he, when they stood at the gate.

"That will I not promise," answered Kristin.

"Then *he* shall promise," said Simon.

"I will not see him," said Kristin quickly.

"The little dog I sent you once," said Simon before they parted, "him you can let your sisters have — they are grown so fond of him — if you mislike not too much to see him in the house.

". . . I ride north to-morrow early," said he, and then he took her hand in farewell, while the sister who kept the door looked on.

Simon Darre walked downward towards the town. He flung out a clenched fist as he strode along, talked half aloud, and swore out into the fog. He swore to himself that he grieved not over *her*. Kristin — 'twas as though he had deemed a thing pure gold — and when he saw it close at hand, it was naught but brass and tin. White as a snowflake had she knelt and thrust her hand into the flame — that was last year; this year she was drinking wine with an outcast ribald in Fluga's loft-room. The devil, no! 'Twas for Lavrans Björgulf-sön he grieved, sitting up there on Jörundgaard believing — full surely never had it come into Lavrans' mind that he could be so betrayed by his own. And now he himself was to bear the tidings, and help to lie to *that* man — it was for this that his heart burned with sorrow and wrath.

Kristin had not meant to keep her promise to Simon Darre, but, as it befell, she spoke but a few words with Erlend — one evening up on the road.

She stood and held his hand, strangely meek, while he spoke of what had befallen in Brynhilds loft-room at their last meeting. With Simon Andressön he would talk another time. "Had we fought there, 'twould have been all over the town," said Erlend hotly. "And that he too knew full well — this Simon."

Kristin saw how this thing had galled him. She, too, had thought of it unceasingly ever since — there was no hiding the truth, Erlend came out of this business with even less honour than she herself. And she felt that now indeed they were one flesh — that she must answer for all he did, even though she might mislike his deeds, and that she would feel it in her own flesh when so much as Erlend's skin was scratched.

* * *

Three weeks later Lavrans Björgulfsön came to Oslo to fetch his daughter.

Kristin was afraid, and she was sore of heart as she went to the parlour to meet her father. What first struck her, when she saw him standing there speaking to Sister Potentia, was that he did not look as she remembered him. Maybe he was but little changed since they parted a year ago — but she had seen him all her years at home as the young, lusty, comely man she had been so proud to have for father when she was little. Each winter, and each summer that passed over their heads up there at home, had doubtless marked him with the marks of growing age, as they had unfolded her into a full-grown young woman — but she had not seen it. She had not seen that his hair was fading here and there and had taken on a tinge of rusty red near the temples — as yellow hair does when 'tis turning grey. His cheeks had shrunken and grown longer so that the muscles ran in harder lines down to the mouth; his youthful white and red had faded to one weather-beaten shade. His back was not bowed — but yet his shoulder-blades had an unaccustomed curve beneath his cloak. His step was light and firm, as he came toward her with outstretched hand, but yet 'twas not the old brisk and supple motion. Doubtless, all these things had been there last year, only she had not seen them. Perhaps there had been added a little touch — of sadness — which made her see them now. She burst into weeping.

Lavrans put his arm about her shoulder and laid his hand against her cheek.

"Come, come, be still now, child," he said gently.

"Are you angry with me, father?" she asked low.

"Surely you must know that I am," he answered — but he went on stroking her cheek. "Yet so much, too, you sure must know, that you have no need to be afraid of me," said he sadly. "Nay, now must you be still, Kristin; are you not ashamed to bear you in such childish wise." For she was weeping so that she had to seat herself upon the bench. "We will not speak of these things here, where folk go out and in," said he, and he sat himself down by her side and took her hand. "Will you not ask after your mother then — and your sisters . . . ?"

"What does my mother say of this?" asked his daughter.

"Oh, that you can have no need to ask — but we will not talk of it now," he said again. "Else she is well — " and he set to telling this and that of the happenings at home on the farm, till Kristin grew quieter little by little.

But it seemed to her that the strain did but grow worse because her father said naught of her breach of troth. He gave her money to deal out among the poor of the convent and to make gifts to her fellow-pupils. He himself gave rich gifts to the cloister and the Sisters; and no one in Nonneseter knew aught else than that Kristin was now to go home for her betrothal and her wedding. They both ate the last meal at Lady Groa's board in the Abbess's room, and the Lady spoke of Kristin with high praise.

But all this came to an end at last. She had said her last farewell to the Sisters and her friends at the convent gate; Lavrans led her to her horse and lifted her into the saddle. 'Twas so strange to ride with her father and the men from Jörundgaard down to the bridge, along this road, down which she had stolen in the dark; wonderful, too, it seemed to ride through the streets of Oslo freely and in honour. She thought of their splendid wedding train, that Erlend had talked of so often — her heart grew heavy; 'twould have been easier had he carried her away with him. There was yet such a long time before her in which she must live one life in secret and another openly before folks. But then her eye fell on her father's grave, ageing face, and she tried to think that, after all, Erlend was right.

* * *

There were a few other travellers in the inn. At eventide they all supped together in a little hearth-room, where there were two beds only; Lavrans and Kristin were to sleep there, for they were the first in rank among the guests. Therefore, when the night drew on a little, the others bade them a friendly good-night as they broke up and went to seek their sleeping-places. Kristin thought how it was she who had stolen to Brynhild Fluga's loft-room to Erlend's arms — sick with sorrow and with fear that she might never more be his, she thought, no, there was no place for her any more amongst these others.

Her father was sitting on the farther bench looking at her.

"We are not to go to Skog this time?" asked Kristin, to break the silence.

"No," answered Lavrans. "I have had enough for some time with what your mother's brother made me listen to — because I would not constrain you," he added, as she looked up at him questioningly.

"And, truly, I would have made you keep your word," said he a little after, "had it not been that Simon said he would not have an unwilling wife."

"*I* have never given my word to Simon," said Kristin quickly. "You have ever said before, that you would never force me into wedlock — "

" 'Twould not have been force if I had held you to a bargain that had been published long since and was known to all men," answered Lavrans. "These two winters past you two have borne the name of hand-fasted folk, and you have said naught against it, nor shown yourself unwilling, till now your wedding-day was fixed. If you would plead that the business was put off last year, so that you have not yet given Simon your troth, then that I call not upright dealing."

Kristin stood gazing down into the fire.

"I know not which will seem the worse," went on her father, "that it be said that you have cast off Simon, or that he has cast off you. Sir Andres sent me a word," Lavrans flushed red as he said it, "he was wroth with the lad, and bade me crave such amends as I should think fit. I had to say what was true — I know not if aught else had been better — that, should there be amends to make, 'twas rather for us to make them. We are shamed either way."

"I cannot think there is such great shame," said Kristin low. "Since Simon and I are of one mind."

"Of one mind?" repeated Lavrans. "He did not hide from me that he was unhappy, but he said, after you had spoken together, he deemed naught but misfortune could come of it if he held you to the pact. . . . But now must you tell me how this has come over you."

"Has Simon said naught?" asked Kristin.

"It seemed as though he thought," said her father, "that you have given your love to another man. Now must you tell me how this is, Kristin."

Kristin thought for a little.

"God knows," said she, in a low voice, "I see well, Simon might be good enough for me, and maybe too good. But 'tis true that I came to know another man; and then I knew I would never have one happy hour more in all my life were I to live it out with Simon — not if all the gold in England were his to give — I would rather have the other if he owned no more than a single cow."

"You look not that I should give you to a serving-man, I trow?" said her father.

"He is as well born as I, and better," answered Kristin. "I meant but this — he has enough both of lands and goods, but I would rather sleep with him on the bare straw than with another man in a silken bed — "

Her father was silent a while.

" 'Tis one thing, Kristin, that I will not force you to take a man that likes you not — though God and St. Olav alone know what you can have against the man I had promised you to. But 'tis another thing whether the man you have set your heart upon is such as I can wed you to. You are young yet, and not over-wise — and to cast his eyes upon a maid who is promised to another — 'tis not the wont of an upright man — "

"No man can rule himself in that matter," broke in Kristin.

"Ay, but he can. But so much you can understand, I trow: I will not do such offence to the Dyfrin folk as to betroth you to another the moment you have turned your back on Simon — and least of all to a man who might be more high in rank or richer.— You must say who this man is," he said after a little.

Kristin pressed her hands together and breathed deeply. Then she said very slowly:

"I cannot, father. Thus it stands, that should I not get this man, then you can take me back to the convent and never take me from it again. . . . I shall not live long there, I trow. But 'twould not be seemly that I should name his name, ere yet I know he bears as good a will toward me as I have to him. You — you must not force me to say who he is, before — before 'tis seen whether — whether he is minded to make suit for me through his kin."

Lavrans was a long time silent. He could not but be pleased that his daughter took the matter thus; he said at length:

"So be it, then. 'Tis but reason that you would fain keep back his name, if you know not more of his purposes."

"Now must you to bed, Kristin," he said a little after. He came and kissed her.

"You have wrought sorrow and pain to many by this waywardness of yours, my daughter — but this you know, that your good lies next my heart. . . . God help me, 'twould be so, I fear me, whatever you might do — He and his Gentle Mother will surely help us, so that this may be turned to the best. . . . Go now, and see that you sleep well."

After he had lain down, Lavrans thought he heard

a little sound of weeping from the bed by the other wall, where his daughter lay. But he made as though he slept. He had not the heart to say to her that he feared the old talk about her and Arne and Bentein would be brought up again now, but it weighed heavily upon him that 'twas but little he could do to save the child's good name from being besmirched behind his back. And the worst was that he must deem much of the mischief had been wrought by her own thoughtlessness.

THE BRIDAL WREATH

PART THREE

LAVRANS BJÖRGULFSÖN

KRISTIN came home when the spring was at fairest. The Laagen rushed headlong round its bend, past the farmstead and the fields; through the tender leaves of the alder-thickets its current glittered and sparkled with flashes of silver. 'Twas as though the gleams of light had a voice of their own, and joined in the river's song, for when the evening twilight fell, the waters seemed to go by with a duller roar. But day and night the air above Jörundgaard was filled with the rushing sound, till Kristin thought she could feel the very timbers of the houses quivering like the sound-box of a cithern.

Small threads of water shone high up on the fellsides, that stood wrapped in blue haze day after day. The heat brooded and quivered over the fields; the brown earth of the plough-lands was nigh hidden by the spears of corn; the meadows grew deep with grass, and shimmered like silk where the breaths of wind passed over. Groves and hillsward smelt sweet; and as soon as the sun was down, there streamed out all around the strong, cool, sourish breath of sap and growing things — it was as though the earth gave out a long, lightened sigh. Kristin thought, trembling, of the moment when Erlend's arms released her. Each evening she lay down, sick with longing, and in the mornings she awoke, damp with sweat and tired out with her dreams.

'Twas more than she could understand how the folks at home could forbear to speak ever a word of the one thing that was in her thoughts. But week went by after week, and naught was said of Simon and her broken faith, and none asked what was in her heart. Her father lay much out in the woods, now he had the spring ploughing and sowing off his hands — he went to see to his tar-burners' work, and he took hawks and hounds with him, and was away many days together. When he was at home, he spoke to his daughter kindly as ever — but it was as though he had little to say to her, and never did he ask her to go with him when he rode out.

Kristin had dreaded to go home to her mother's chidings; but Ragnfrid said never a word — and this seemed even worse.

Every year when he feasted his friends at St. John's Mass, it was Lavrans Björgulfsön's wont to give out among the poor folks of the parish the meat and all sorts of food that had been saved in his household in the last week of the Fast. Those who lived nighest to Jörundgaard would come themselves to fetch away the alms; these poor folks were ever welcomed and feasted, and Lavrans and his guests, and all the house-servants, would gather round them; for some of them were old men who had by heart many sagas and lays. They sat in the hearth-room and whiled the time away with the ale-cup and friendly talk; and in the evening they danced in the courtyard.

This year the Eve of St. John was cloudy and cold; but none was sorry that it was so, for by now the farmers of the Dale had begun to fear a drought. No rain had fallen since St. Halvard's Wake, and there had been little snow in the mountains; not for thirteen years could folk remember to have seen the river so low at midsummer.

So Lavrans and his guests were of good cheer when they went down to greet the almsmen in the hearth-room. The poor folks sat round the board eating milk-porridge and washing it down with strong ale; and Kristin stood by the table, and waited on the old folk and the sick.

Lavrans greeted his poor guests, and asked if they were content with their fare. Then he went about the

board to bid welcome to an old bedesman, who had
been brought thither that day for his term at Jörundgaard. The man's name was Haakon; he had fought
under King Haakon the Old, and had been with the
King when he took the field for the last time in Scot-
land. He was the poorest of the poor now, and was all
but blind; the farmers of the Dale had offered to set
him up in a cottage of his own, but he chose rather to
be handed on as bedesman from farm to farm, for
everywhere folk welcomed him more like an honoured
guest, since he had seen much of the world, and had
laid up great store of knowledge.

Lavrans stood by with a hand on his brother's
shoulder; for Aasmund Björgulfsön had come to Jörundgaard on a visit. He asked Haakon, too, how the
food liked him.

"The ale is good, Lavrans Björgulfsön," said Haakon.
"But methinks a jade has cooked our porridge for us
to-day. 'While the cook cuddles, the porridge burns,'
says the byword; and this porridge is singed."

"An ill thing indeed," said Lavrans, "that I should
give you singed porridge. But I wot well the old
byword doth not always say true, for 'tis my daughter, herself, who cooked the porridge for you." He
laughed, and bade Kristin and Tordis make haste to
bring in the trenchers of meat.

Kristin slipped quickly out and made across to the
kitchen. Her heart was beating hard — she had caught
a glimpse of Aasmund's face when Haakon was
speaking.

That evening she saw her father and his brother
walking and talking together in the courtyard, long
and late. She was dizzy with fear; and it was no better
with her the next day, when she marked that her father
was silent and joyless. But he said no word.

Nor did he say aught after his brother was gone.
But Kristin marked well that he spoke less with Haakon
than was his wont, and, when their turn for harbour-
ing the old warrior was over, Lavrans made no sign

towards keeping him a while longer, but let him move on to the next farm.

For the rest, Lavrans Björgulfsön had reason enough this summer to be moody and downcast, for now all tokens showed that the year would be an exceeding bad one in all the country round; and the farmers were coming together time and again to take counsel how they should meet the coming winter. As the late summer drew on, it was plain to most, that they must slaughter great part of their cattle or drive them south for sale, and buy corn to feed their people through the winter. The year before had been no good corn year, so that the stocks of old corn were but scanty.

One morning in early autumn Ragnfrid went out with all her three daughters to see to some linen she had lying out on the bleachfield. Kristin praised much her mother's weaving. Then the mother stroked little Ramborg's hair, and said:

"We must save this for your bride-chest, little one."

"Then, mother," said Ulvhild, "shall I not have any bride-chest when I go to the nunnery?"

"You know well," said Ragnfrid, "your dowry will be nowise less than your sisters'. But 'twill not be such things as they need that you will need. And then you know full well, too, that you are to bide with your father and me as long as we live — if so be you will."

"And when you come to the nunnery," said Kristin unsteadily, "it may be, Ulvhild, that I shall have been a nun there for many years."

She looked across at her mother, but Ragnfrid held her peace.

"Had I been such an one that I could marry," said Ulvhild, "never would I have turned away from Simon — he was so kind, and he was so sorrowful when he said farewell to us all."

"You know your father bade us not speak of this," said Ragnfrid; but Kristin broke in defiantly:

"Ay; well I know that 'twas far more sorrow for him parting from you than from me."

Her mother spoke in anger:

"And little must his pride have been, I wot, had he shown his sorrow before you — you dealt not well and fairly by Simon Andressön, my daughter. Yet did he beg us to use neither threats nor curses with you —"

"Nay," said Kristin as before, "he thought, maybe, he had cursed me himself so much, there was no need for any other to tell me how vile I was. But I marked not ever that Simon had much care for me, till he saw that I loved another more than him."

"Go home, children," said Ragnfrid to the two little ones. She sat herself down on a log that lay by the green, and drew Kristin down beside her.

"You know, surely," said she then, "that it has ever been held seemly and honourable, that a man should not talk overmuch of love to his betrothed maiden — nor sit with her much alone, nor woo too hotly —"

"Oh!" said Kristin, "much I wonder whether young folk that love one another bear ever in mind what old folk count for seemly, and forget not one time or another all such things."

"Be you ware, Kristin," said her mother, "that you forget them not." She sat a little while in silence: "What I see but too well now is that your father goes in fear that you have set your heart on a man he can never gladly give you to."

"What did my uncle say?" asked Kristin in a little while.

"Naught said he," answered her mother, "but that Erlend of Husaby is better of name than of fame. Ay, for he spoke to Aasmund, it seems, to say a good word for him to Lavrans. Small joy was it to your father when he heard this."

But Kristin sat beaming with gladness. Erlend had spoken to her father's brother. And she had been vexing her heart because he made no sign!

Then her mother spoke again:

"Yet another thing is: that Aasmund said somewhat of a waif word that went about in Oslo, that folk had seen this Erlend hang about in the byways near by the convent, and that you had gone out and spoken with him by the fences there."

"What then?" asked Kristin.

"Aasmund counselled us, you understand, to take this proffer," said Ragnfrid. "But at that Lavrans grew more wroth than I can call to mind I saw him ever before. He said that a wooer who tried to come to his daughter by that road should find him in his path sword in hand. 'Twas little honour enough to us to have dealt as we had with the Dyfrin folk; but were it so that Erlend had lured you out to gad about the ways in the darkness with him, and that while you were dwelling in a cloister of holy nuns, 'twas a full good token you would be better served by far by missing such a husband."

Kristin crushed her hands together in her lap — the colour came and went in her face. Her mother put an arm about her waist — but the girl shrank away from her, beside herself with the passion of her mood, and cried:

"Let me be, mother! Would you feel, maybe, if my waist hath grown — "

The next moment she was standing up, holding her hand to her cheek — she looked down bewildered at her mother's flashing eyes. None had ever struck her before since she was a little child.

"Sit down," said Ragnfrid. "Sit down," she said again, and the girl was fain to obey. The mother sat awhile silent; when she spoke, her voice was shaking:

"I have seen it full well, Kristin — much have you never loved me. I told myself, maybe 'twas that you thought I loved not you so much — not as your father loves you. I bided my time — I thought when the time came that you had borne a child yourself, you would surely understand. . . .

"While yet I was suckling you, even then was it so, that when Lavrans came near us two, you would let go my breast and stretch out towards him, and laugh so that my milk ran out over your lips. Lavrans thought 'twas good sport — and God knows I was well content for his sake. I was well content, too, for your sake, that your father laughed and was merry each time he laid eyes on you. I thought my own self 'twas pity of you, you little being, that I could not have done with all that much weeping. I was ever thinking more whether I was to lose you too, than joying that I had you. But God and His holy Mother know that I loved you no whit less than Lavrans loved."

The tears were running down over Ragnfrid's cheeks, but her face was quite calm now, and so too was her voice:

"God knows I never bore him or you a grudge for the love that was between you. Methought 'twas little enough joy I had brought him in the years we had lived together; I was glad that he had joy in you. I thought, too, that had my father, Ivar, been such a father to me . . .

"There are many things, Kristin, that a mother should have taught her daughter to beware of. But methought there was little need of this with you, who have followed about with your father all these years — you should know, if any know, what right and honour are. That word you spoke but now — think you I could believe you would have the heart to bring on Lavrans such a sorrow . . . ?

"I would say but this to you — my wish is that you may win for husband a man you can love well. But that this may be, you must bear you wisely — let not Lavrans have cause to think that he you have chosen is a breeder of trouble, and one that regards not the peace of women, nor their honour. For to such an one he will never give you — not if it were to save you

from open shame. Rather would Lavrans let the steel
do judgment between him and the man who had
marred your life. . . ."

And with this the mother rose and went from her.

2

At the Haugathing held on the day of Bartholomew's
Mass, the 24th of August, the daughter's son of King
Haakon of happy memory was hailed as King. Among
the men sent thither from Northern Gudbrandsdal was
Lavrans Björgulfsön. He had had the name of kings-
man since his youth, but in all these years he had but
seldom gone nigh the Household, and the good name
he had won in the war against Duke Eirik he had
never sought to turn to account. Nor had he now
much mind to this journey to the homaging, but he
could not deny himself to the call. Besides, he and the
other Thing-men from the upper valley were charged
to try and buy corn in the south and send it round by
ship to Romsdal.

The folk of the parishes round about were heartless
now, and went in dread of the winter that was at hand.
An ill thing, too, the farmers deemed it that once
again a child would be King in Norway. Old folks
called to mind the time when King Magnus was dead
and his sons were little children, and Sira Eirik said:
"*Væ terræ, ubi puer rex est*. Which in the Norse
tongue is: 'No resting o' nights for rats in the house
where the cat's a kitten.'"

Ragnfrid Ivarsdatter managed all things on the manor
while her husband was gone, and it was good both for
Kristin and for her that they had their heads and
hands full of household cares and work. All over the
parish the folks were busy gathering in moss from the
hills and stripping bark from the trees, for the hay-
crop had been but light, and of straw there was next

to none; and even the leaves gathered after St. John's Eve were yellow and sapless. On Holy Cross Day, when Sira Eirik bore the crucifix about the fields, there were many in the procession who wept and prayed aloud to God to have mercy on the people and the dumb beasts.

A week after Holy Cross, Lavrans Björgulfsön came home from the Thing.

It was long past the house-folks' bedtime, but Ragnfrid still sat in the weaving-house. She had so much to see to in the daytime now, that she often worked on late into the night at weaving and sewing. Ragnfrid liked the house well, too. It had the name of being the oldest on the farm; it was called the Mound-house, and folk said it had stood there ever since the old heathen ages. Kristin and the girl called Astrid were with Ragnfrid; they were sitting spinning by the hearth.

They had been sitting for a while sleepy and silent, when they heard the hoof-beats of a single horse — a man came riding at a gallop into the wet farm-place. Astrid went to the outer room to look out — in a moment she came in again, followed by Lavrans Björgulfsön.

Both his wife and his daughter saw at once that he had been drinking more than a little. He reeled in his walk, and held to the pole of the smoke-vent while Ragnfrid took from him his dripping wet cloak and hat and unbuckled his sword-belt.

"What have you done with Halvdan and Kolbein?" she said, in some fear; "have you left them behind on the road?"

"No, I left them behind at Loptsgaard," he said, with a little laugh. "I had such a mind to come home again — there was no rest for me till I did — the men went to bed down at Loptsgaard, but I took Gulds-veinen and galloped home. . . .

"You must find me a little food, Astrid," he said to the servant. "Bring it in here, girl; then you need not go so far in the rain. But be quick, for I have eaten no food since early morning —"

"Had you no food at Loptsgaard, then?" asked his wife in wonder.

Lavrans sat rocking from side to side on the bench, laughing a little.

"Food there was, be sure — but I had no stomach to it when I was there. I drank a while with Sigurd — but — methought then 'twas as well I should come home at once as wait till to-morrow —"

Astrid came back bearing food and ale; she brought with her, too, a pair of dry shoes for her master.

Lavrans fumbled with his spur-buckles to unloose them; but came near to falling on his face.

"Come hither, Kristin, my girl," he said, "and help your father. I know you will do it from a loving heart — ay, a loving heart — to-day."

Kristin kneeled down to obey. Then he took her head between his two hands and turned her face up:

"One thing I trow you know, my daughter — I wish for naught but your good. Never would I give you sorrow, except I see that thereby I save you from many sorrows to come. You are full young yet, Kristin — 'twas but seventeen years old you were this year — three days after Halvard's Mass — but seventeen years old —"

Kristin had done with her service now. She was a little pale as she rose from her knees and sat down again on her stool by the hearth.

Lavrans' head seemed to grow somewhat clearer as he ate and was filled. He answered his wife's questions and the servant-maid's about the Haugathing. . . . Ay, 'twas a fair gathering. They had managed to buy corn, and some flour and malt, part at Oslo and part at Tunsberg; the wares were from abroad — they might have been better, but they might have been worse, too. Ay, he had met many, both kinsfolk and friends, and they had sent their greetings home with him. . . . But the answers dropped from him, one by one, as he sat there.

"I spoke with Sir Andres Gudmundsön," he said, when Astrid was gone out. "Simon marries the young widow at Manvik; he has held his betrothal feast. The wedding will be at Dyfrin at St. Andrew's Mass. He has chosen for himself this time, has the boy. I held aloof from Sir Andres at Tunsberg, but he sought me out — 'twas to tell me he knew for sure that Simon saw Lady Halfrid for the first time this midsummer. He feared that I should think Simon had this rich marriage in mind when he broke with us." Lavrans paused a little and laughed joylessly. "You understand — that good and worthy man feared much that we should believe such a thing of his son."

Kristin breathed more freely. She thought it must be this that had troubled her father so sorely. Maybe he had been hoping all this time that it might come to pass after all, her marriage with Simon Andressön. At first she had been in dread lest he had heard some tidings of her doings in the south at Oslo.

She rose up and said good-night; but her father bade her stay yet a little.

"I have one more thing to tell," said Lavrans. "I might have held my peace about it before you — but 'tis better you should know it. This it is, Kristin — the man you have set your heart on, him must you strive to forget."

Kristin had been standing with arms hanging down and bent head. She looked up now into her father's face. She moved her lips, but no sound came forth that could be heard.

Lavrans looked away from his daughter's eyes; he struck out sideways with his hand:

"I wot well you know that never would I set myself against it, could I anyways believe 'twould be for your good."

"What are the tidings that have been told you on this journey, father?" said Kristin, in a clear voice.

"Erlend Nikulaussön and his kinsman, Sir Munan Baardsön, came to me at Tunsberg," answered Lavrans. "Sir Munan asked for you for Erlend, and I answered him: No."

Kristin stood awhile, breathing heavily.

"Why will you not give me to Erlend Nikulaussön?" she asked.

"I know not how much you know of the man you would have for husband," said Lavrans. "If you cannot guess the reason for yourself, 'twill be no pleasing thing for you to hear from my lips."

"Is it because he has been outlawed, and banned by the Church?" asked Kristin as before.

"Know you what was the cause that King Haakon banished his near kinsman from his Court — and how at last he fell under the Church's ban for defying the Archbishop's bidding — and that when he fled the land 'twas not alone?"

"Ay," said Kristin. Her voice grew unsteady: "I know, too, that he was but eighteen years old when he first knew her — his paramour."

"No older was I when I was wed," answered Lavrans. "We reckoned, when I was young, that at eighteen years a man was of age to answer for himself, and care for others' welfare and his own."

Kristin stood silent.

"You called her his paramour, the woman he has lived with for ten years, and who has borne him children," said Lavrans after awhile. "Little joy would be mine the day I sent my daughter from her home with a husband who had lived openly with a paramour year out, year in, before ever he was wed. But you know that 'twas not loose life only, 'twas life in adultery."

Kristin spoke low:

"You judged not so hardly of Lady Aashild and Sir Björn."

"Yet can I not say I would be fain we should wed into their kindred," answered Lavrans.

"Father," said Kristin, "have you been so free from sin all your life, that you can judge Erlend so hardly — ?"

"God knows," said Lavrans sternly, "I judge no man to be a greater sinner before Him than I am myself. But 'tis not just reckoning that I should give away my daughter to any man that pleases to ask for her, only because we all need God's forgiveness."

"You know I meant it not so," said Kristin hotly. "Father — mother — you have been young yourselves — have you not your youth *so* much in mind that you know 'tis hard to keep oneself from the sin that comes of love — ?"

Lavrans grew red as blood:

"No," he said curtly.

"Then you know not what you do," cried Kristin wildly, "if you part Erlend Nikaulaussön and me."

Lavrans sate himself down again on the bench.

"You are but seventeen, Kristin," he began again. "It may be so that you and he — that you have come to be more dear to each other than I thought could be. But he is not so young a man but he should have known — had he been a good man, he had never come near a young, unripe child like you, with words of love. . . . That you were promised to another seemed to him, mayhap, but a small thing.

"But I wed not my daughter to a man who has two children by another's wedded wife. You know that he has children?

"You are too young to understand that such a wrong breeds enmity in a kindred — and hatred without end. The man cannot desert his own offspring, and he cannot do them right — hardly will he find a way to bring his son forth among good folk, or to get his daughter married with any but a serving-man or a cottar. They were not flesh and blood, those children, if they hated not you and your children with a deadly hate. . . .

"See you not, Kristin — such sins as these — it may be that God may forgive such sins more easily than many others — but they lay waste a kindred in such wise that it can never be made whole again. I thought of Björn and Lady Aashild too — there stood this Munan, her son; he was blazing with gold; he sits in the Council of the King's Counsellors; they hold their mother's heritage, he and his brothers; and he hath not come once to greet his mother in her poverty in all these years. Ay, and 'twas this man your lover had chosen to be his spokesman.

"No, I say — no! Into that kindred you shall never come, while my head is above the ground."

Kristin buried her face in her hands and broke into weeping:

"Then will I pray God night and day, night and day, that if you change not your will, He may take me away from this earth."

"It boots not to speak more of this to-night," said her father; with anguish in his voice. "You believe it not now, maybe; but I must needs guide your life so as I may hope to answer it hereafter. Go now, child, and rest."

He held out his hand toward her; but she would not see it, and went sobbing from the room.

The father and mother sat on a while. Then Lavrans said to his wife:

"Would you fetch me in a draught of ale? — no, bring in a little wine," he asked. "I am weary — "

Ragnfrid did as he asked. When she came back with the tall wine stoup, her husband was sitting with his face hidden in his hands. He looked up, and passed his hand over her headdress and her sleeves:

"Poor wife, now you are wet. . . . Come, drink to me, Ragnfrid."

She barely touched the cup with her lips.

"Nay, now drink with me," said Lavrans vehemently, and tried to draw her down on his knees. Unwillingly the woman did as he bade. Lavrans said: "You will stand by me in this thing, wife of mine, will you not? Surely 'twill be best for Kristin herself that she understand from the very outset she must drive this man from her thoughts."

" 'Twill be hard for the child," said the mother.

"Ay; well do I see it will," said Lavrans.

They sat silent awhile, then Ragnfrid asked:

"How looks he, this Erlend of Husaby?"

"Oh," said Lavrans slowly, "a proper fellow enough — after a fashion. But he looks not a man that is fit for much but to beguile women."

They were silent again for awhile; then Lavrans said: "The great heritage that came to him from Sir Nikulaus — with that I trow he has dealt so that it is much dwindled. 'Tis not for such a son-in-law that I have toiled and striven to make my children's lives sure."

The mother wandered restlessly up and down the room. Lavrans went on:

"Least of all did it like me that he sought to tempt Kolbein with silver — to bear a secret letter to Kristin."

"Looked you what was in the letter?" asked Ragnfrid.

"No, I did not choose," said Lavrans curtly. "I handed it back to Sir Munan, and told him what I thought of such doings. Erlend had hung his seal to it too — I know not what a man should say of such child's tricks. Sir Munan would have me see the device of the seal; that 'twas King Skule's privy seal, come to Erlend through his father. His thought was, I trow, that I might bethink me how great an honour they did me to sue for my daughter. But 'tis in my mind that Sir Munan had scarce pressed on this matter for Erlend so warmly, were it not that in this man's hands 'tis downhill with the might and honour of the Husaby kindred, that it won in Sir Nikulaus' and Sir Baard's days. . . . No longer can Erlend look to make such a match as befitted his birth."

Ragnfrid stopped before her husband:

"Now I know not, husband, if you are right in this matter. First must it be said that, as times are now, many men round about us on the great estates have had to be content with less of power and honour than their fathers had before them. And you, yourself, best know that 'tis less easy now for a man to win riches either from land or from merchantry than it was in the old world — "

"I know, I know," broke in Lavrans impatiently. "All the more does it behove a man to guide warily the goods that have come down to him — "

But his wife went on:

"And this, too, is to be said: I see not that Kristin can be an uneven match for Erlend. In Sweden your kin sit among the best, and your father, and his father before him, bore the name of knights in this land of Norway. My forefathers were Barons * of shires, son after father, many hundred years, down to Ivar the Old; my father and my father's father were Wardens.* True it is, neither you nor Trond have held titles or lands under the Crown. But, as for that, methinks it may be said that 'tis no otherwise with Erlend Nikulaussön than with you."

"'Tis not the same," said Lavrans hotly. "Power and the knightly name lay ready to Erlend's hand, and he turned his back on them to go a-whoring. But I see, now, you are against me, too. Maybe you think, like Aasmund and Trond, 'tis an honour for me that these great folks would have my daughter for one of their kinsmen — "

Ragnfrid spoke in some heat: "I have told you, I see not that you need be so over-nice as to fear that Erlend's kinsmen should think they stoop in these

---

* Barons and Wardens, see Note 19.

dealings. But see you not what all things betoken — a gentle and a biddable child to find courage to set herself up against us and turn away Simon Darre — have you not seen that Kristin is nowise herself since she came back from Oslo — see you not she goes around like one bewitched. . . . Will you not understand, she loves this man so sorely, that, if you yield not, a great misfortune may befall?"

"What mean you by that?" asked the father, looking up sharply.

"Many a man greets his son-in-law and knows not of it," said Ragnfrid.

The man seemed to stiffen where he sat; his face grew slowly white:

"You that are her mother!" he said hoarsely. "Have you — have you seen — such sure tokens — that you dare charge your own daughter — "

"No, no," said Ragnfrid quickly. "I meant it not as you think. But when things are thus, who can tell what has befallen, or what may befall? I have seen her heart; not one thought hath she left but her love for this man — 'twere no marvel if one day she showed us that he is dearer to her than her honour — or her life."

Lavrans sprang up:

"Oh, you are mad! Can you think such things of our fair, good child? No harm, surely, can have come to her where she was — with the holy nuns. I wot well she is no byre-wench to go clipping behind walls and fences. Think but of it: 'tis not possible she can have seen this man or talked with him so many times — be sure it will pass away; it cannot be aught but a young maid's fancy. God knows, 'tis a heavy sight enough for me to see her sorrow so; but be sure it must pass by in time.

"Life, you say, and honour. . . . At home here by my own hearthstone 'twill go hard if I cannot guard my own maiden. Nor do I deem that any maid come of good people and bred up Christianly in shamefast-

ness will be so quick to throw away her honour — nor
yet her life. Ay, such things are told of in songs and
ballads, sure enough — but methinks 'tis so that when
a man or a maid is tempted to do such a deed, they
make up a song about it, and ease their hearts thereby
— but the deed itself they forbear to do —.

"You yourself," he said, stopping before his wife:
"there was another man you would fain have wed, in
those days when we were brought together. How
think you it would have gone with you, had your
father let you have your will on that score?"

It was Ragnfrid now that was grown deadly pale:
"Jesus, Maria! Who hath told — "

"Sigurd of Loptsgaard said somewhat . . . 'twas when
we were just come hither to the Dale," said Lavrans.
"But answer me what I asked. . . . Think you your
life had been gladder had Ivar given you to that
man?"

His wife stood with head bowed low:

"That man," she said — he could scarce hear the
words: " 'twas *he* would not have *me*." A throb
seemed to pass through her body — she struck out
before her with her clenched hand.

The husband laid his hands softly on her shoulders:
"Is it *that*," he asked as if overcome, and a deep and
sorrowful wonder sounded in his voice; ". . . is it *that*
— through all these years — have you been sorrowing
for *him* — Ragnfrid?"

She trembled much, but she said nothing.

"Ragnfrid?" he asked again. "Ay, but afterward —
when Björgulf was dead — and afterward — when
you — when you would have had me be to you as —
as I could not be. Were you thinking then of that
other?" He spoke low, in fear and bewilderment and
pain.

"How can you have such thoughts?" she whispered,
on the verge of weeping.

Lavrans pressed his forehead against hers and moved
his head gently from side to side.

"I know not. You are so strange — and all you have said tonight. I was afraid, Ragnfrid. Like enough I understand not the hearts of women — "

Ragnfrid smiled palely and laid her arms about his neck.

"God knows, Lavrans — I was a beggar to you, because I loved you more than 'tis good that a human soul should love. . . . And I hated that other so that I felt the devil joyed in my hate."

"I have held you dear, my wife," said Lavrans, kissing her, "ay, with all my heart have I held you dear. You know that, surely? Methought always that we two were happy together — Ragnfrid?"

"You were the best husband to me," said she with a little sob, and clung close to him.

He pressed her to him strongly:

"To-night I would fain sleep with you, Ragnfrid. And if you would be to me as you were in old days, I should not be — such a fool — "

The woman seemed to stiffen in his arms — she drew away a little:

"'Tis Fast-time." She spoke low — in a strange, hard voice.

"It is so." He laughed a little. "You and I, Ragnfrid — we have kept all the fasts, and striven to do God's bidding in all things. And now almost I could think — maybe we had been happier had we more to repent — "

"Oh, speak not so — *you*," she begged wildly, pressing her thin hands to his temples. "You know well I would not you should do aught but what you feel yourself is the right."

He drew her to him closely once more — and groaned aloud: "God help her! God help us all, my Ragnfrid — "

Then: "I am weary," he said, and let her go. "And 'tis time, too, for you to go to rest."

He stood by the door waiting, while she quenched the embers on the hearth, blew out the little iron

lamp by the loom, and pinched out the glowing wick.
Together they went across through the rain to the
hall.

Lavrans had set foot already on the loft-room stair,
when he turned to his wife, who was still standing in
the entry-door.

He crushed her in his arms again, for the last time,
and kissed her in the dark. Then he made the sign of
the cross over his wife's face, and went up the stair.

Ragnfrid flung off her clothes and crept into bed.
Awhile she lay and listened to her husband's steps in
the loft-room above; then she heard the bed creak,
and all was still. Ragnfrid crossed her thin arms over
her withered breasts.

Ay, God help her! What kind of woman was she,
what kind of mother? She would soon be old now.
Yet was she the same; though she no longer begged
stormily for love, as when they were young and her
passion had made this man shrink and grow cold when
she would have had him be lover and not only husband.
So had it been — and so, time after time, when she was
with child, had she been humbled, beside herself with
shame, that she had not been content with his lukewarm husband-love. And then, when things were so
with her, and she needed goodness and tenderness —
then he had so much to give; the man's tireless, gentle
thought for her, when she was sick and tormented, had
fallen on her soul like dew. Gladly did he take up all
she laid on him and bear it — but there was ever something of his own he would not give. She had loved her
children, so that each time she lost one, 'twas as
though the heart was torn from her. God! God! what
woman was she then, that even then, in the midst of
her torments, she could feel it as a drop of sweetness
that he took her sorrow into his heart and laid it close
beside his own.

Kristin — gladly would she have passed through the
fire for her daughter; they believed it not, neither

Lavrans nor the child — but 'twas so. Yet did she feel toward her now an anger that was near to hate — 'twas to forget his sorrow for the child's sorrow that he had wished to-night that he could give himself up to his wife. . . .

Ragnfrid dared not rise, for she knew not but that Kristin might be lying awake in the other bed. But she raised herself noiselessly to her knees, and with forehead bent against the footboard of the bed she strove to pray. For her daughter, for her husband and for herself. While her body, little by little, grew stiff with the cold, she set out once more on one of the night-wanderings she knew so well, striving to break her way through to a home of peace for her heart.

3

HAUGEN lay high up in the hills on the west side of the valley. This moonlight night the whole world was white. Billow after billow, the white fells lay domed under the pale blue heavens with their thin-strewn stars. Even the shadows that peaks and domes stretched forth over the snow-slopes seemed strangely thin and light, the moon was sailing so high.

Downward, toward the valley, the woods stood fleecy-white with snow and rime, round the white fields of crofts scrolled over with tiny huts and fences. But far down in the valley-bottom the shadows thickened into darkness.

Lady Aashild came out of the byre, shut the door after her, and stood awhile in the snow. White — the whole world; yet was it more than three weeks still to Advent. Clementsmass cold — 'twas like winter had come in earnest already. Ay, ay; in bad years it was often so.

The old woman sighed heavily in the desolate air. Winter again, and cold and loneliness. . . . Then she took up the milk-pail and went towards the dwelling-house. She looked once again down over the valley.

Four black dots come out of the woods half-way up the hillside. Four men on horseback — and the moon-light glanced from a spearhead. They were ploughing heavily upward — none had come that way since the snowfall. Were they coming hither?

Four armed men. . . . 'Twas not like that any who had a lawful errand here would come so many in company. She thought of the chest with her goods and Björn's in it. Should she hide in the outhouse?

She looked out again over the wintry waste about her. Then she went into the living-house. The two old hounds that lay before the smoky fireplace smote the floor-boards with their tails. The young dogs Björn had with him in the hills.

Aashild blew the embers of the fire into flame, and laid more wood on them; filled the iron pot with snow and set it on the fire; then poured the milk into a wooden bowl and bore it to the closet beside the outer room.

Then she doffed her dirty, undyed, wadmal gown, that smelt of the byre and of sweat, put on a dark-blue garment, and changed her tow-linen hood for a coif of fine white linen, which she smoothed down fairly round her head and neck. Her shaggy boots of skin she drew off, and put on silver-buckled shoes. Then she fell to setting her room in order — smoothed the pillows and the skin in the bed where Björn had lain that day, wiped the long-board clean, and laid the bench-cushions straight.

When the dogs set up their warning barking, she was standing by the fireplace, stirring the supper-porridge. She heard horses in the yard, and the tread of men in the outer room; some one knocked on the door with a spear-butt. Lady Aashild lifted the pot from the fire, settled her dress about her, and, with the dogs at her side, went forward to the door and opened.

"Moster * Aashild! come you yourself to open to us? Nay, then must I say *Ben trouvè!*"

"Sister's son, is it you indeed? Then the same say I to you! Go into the room, while I show your men the stable."

"Are you all alone on the farm?" asked Erlend. He followed her while she showed the men where to go.

"Ay; Sir Björn and our man are gone into the hills with the sleigh — they are to see and bring home some fodder we have stacked up there," said Lady Aashild. "And serving-woman I have none," she said, laughing.

A little while after, the four young men were sitting on the outer bench with their backs to the board, looking at the old lady, as, busily but quietly, she went about making ready their supper. She laid a cloth on the board, and set on it a lighted candle; then brought forth butter, cheese, a bear-ham and a high pile of thin slices of fine bread. She fetched ale and mead up from the cellar below the room, and then poured out the porridge into a dish of fine wood, and bade them sit in to the board and fall to.

" 'Tis but little for you young folk," she said, laughing. "I must boil another pot of porridge. To-morrow you shall fare better — but I shut up the kitchen-house in the winter, save when I bake or brew. We are few folks on the farm, and I begin to grow old, kinsman."

Erlend laughed and shook his head. He had marked that his men behaved before the old woman seemly and modestly as he had scarce ever seen them bear themselves before.

"You are a strange woman, Moster. Mother was ten years younger than you, and she looked older when last we were in your house than you look to-day."

"Ay, Magnhild's youth left her full early," said Lady Aashild softly. "Where are you come from, now?" she asked after a while.

"I have been for a season at a farmstead up north in

---

* Moster = mother's sister.

Lesja," said Erlend. "I had hired me lodging there. I know not if you can guess what errand has brought me to this countryside?"

"You would ask: know I that you have had suit made to Lavrans Björgulfsön of Jörundgaard for his daughter?"

"Ay," said Erlend. "I made suit for her in seemly and honourable wise, and Lavrans Björgulfsön answered with a churlish: No. Now I see no better way, since Kristin and I will not be forced apart, than that I bear her off by the strong hand. I have — I have had a spy in this countryside, and I know that her mother was to be at Sundbu at Clementsmass and for a while after, and Lavrans is gone to Romsdal with the other men to fetch across the winter stores to Sil."

Lady Aashild sat silent awhile.

"The counsel, Erlend, you had best let be," said she. "I deem not either that the maid will go with you willingly; and I trow you would not use force?"

"Ay, but she will. We have spoken of it many times — she has prayed me herself many times to bear her away."

"Kristin has — ?" said Lady Aashild. Then she laughed. "None the less I would not have you make too sure that the maid will follow when you come to take her at her word."

"Ay, but she will," said Erlend. "And, Moster, my thought was this: that you send word to Jörundgaard and bid Kristin come and be your guest — a week or so, while her father and mother are from home. Then could we be at Hamar before any knew she was gone," he added.

Lady Aashild answered, still smiling:

"And had you thought as well what we should answer, Sir Björn and I, when Lavrans comes and calls us to account for his daughter?"

"Ay," said Erlend. "We were four well-armed men, and the maid was willing."

"I will not help you in this," said the lady hotly.

"Lavrans has been a trusty man to us for many a year — he and his wife are honourable folk, and I will not be art or part in deceiving them or beshaming their child. Leave the maid in peace, Erlend. 'Twill soon be high time, too, that your kin should hear of other deeds of yours than running in and out of the land with stolen women."

"I must speak with you alone, lady," said Erlend shortly.

Lady Aashild took a candle, led him to the closet, and shut the door behind them. She sate herself down on a corn-bin; Erlend stood with his hands thrust into his belt, looking down at her.

"You may say this, too, to Lavrans Björgulfsön: that Sira John of Gerdarud joined us in wedlock ere we went on our way to Lady Ingebjörg Haakonsdatter in Sweden."

"Say you so?" said Lady Aashild. "Are you well assured that Lady Ingebjörg will welcome you, when you are come thither?"

"I spoke with her at Tunsberg," said Erland. "She greeted me as her dear kinsman, and thanked me when I proffered her my service either here or in Sweden. And Munan hath promised me letters to her."

"And know you not," said Aashild, "that even should you find a priest that will wed you, yet will Kristin have cast away all right to the heritage of her father's lands and goods? Nor can her children be your lawful heirs. Much I doubt if she will be counted as your lawfully wedded wife."

"Not in this land, maybe. 'Tis therefore we fly to Sweden. Her forefather, Laurentius Lagmand, was never wed to the Lady Bengta in any other sort — they could never win her brother's consent. Yet was she counted as a wedded lady — "

"There were no children," said Lady Aashild. "Think you my sons will hold their hands from your heritage if Kristin be left a widow with children and their lawful birth can be cast in dispute?"

"You do Munan wrong," said Erlend. "I know but little of your other children — I know indeed that you have little cause to judge them kindly. But Munan has ever been my trusty kinsman. He is fain to have me wed; 'twas he went to Lavrans with my wooing. . . . Besides, afterwards, by course of law, I can assure our children their heritage and rights."

"Ay, and thereby mark their mother as your concubine," said Lady Aashild. "But 'tis past my understanding how that meek and holy man, Jon Helgesön, will dare to brave his Bishop by wedding you against the law."

"I confessed — *all* — to him last summer," said Erlend, in a low voice. "He promised then to wed us, if all other ways should fail."

"Is it even so?" said Lady Aashild slowly. . . . "A heavy sin have you laid upon your soul, Erlend Nikulaussön. 'Twas well with Kristin at home with her father and mother — a good marriage was agreed for her with a comely and honourable man of good kindred — "

"Kristin hath told me herself how you said once that she and I would match well together. And that Simon Andressön was no husband for her — "

"Oh — I have said, and I have said!" Aashild broke in. "I have said so many things in my time. . . . Neither can I understand at all that you can have gained your will with Kristin so lightly. So many times you cannot have met together. And never could I have thought that maid had been so light to win — "

"We met at Oslo," said Erlend. "Afterwards she was dwelling out at Gerdarud with her father's brother. She came out and met me in the woods." He looked down and spoke very low: "I had her alone to myself out there — "

Lady Aashild started up. Erlend bent his head yet lower.

"And after that . . . she still was friends with you?" she asked unbelievingly.

"Ay." Erlend smiled a weak, wavering smile. "We were friends still. And 'twas not so bitterly against her — but no blame lies on her. 'Twas then she would have had me take her away — she was loth to go back to her kin — "

"But you would not?"

"No. I was minded to try to win her for my wife with her father's will."

"Is it long since?" asked Lady Aashild.

"'Twas a year last Lawrence-mass," answered Erlend.

"You have not hasted overmuch with your wooing," said the other.

"She was not free before from her first betrothal."

"And since then you have not come nigh her?" asked Aashild.

"We managed so that we met once and again." Once more the wavering smile flitted over the man's face. "In a house in the town."

"In God's name!" said Lady Aashild. "I will help you and her as best I may. I can see it well: not long could Kristin bear to live there with her father and mother, hiding such a thing as this. . . . Is there yet more?" she asked of a sudden.

"Not that I have heard," said Erlend shortly.

"Have you bethought you," asked the lady in a while, "that Kristin has friends and kinsmen dwelling all down the Dale?"

"We must journey as secretly as we can," said Erlend. "And therefore it behoves us to make no delay in setting out, that we may be well on the way before her father comes home. You must lend us your sleigh, Moster."

Aashild shrugged her shoulders.

"Then is there her uncle at Skog — what if he hear that you are holding your wedding with his brother's daughter at Gerdarud?"

"Aasmund has spoken for me to Lavrans," said Erlend. "He would not be privy to our counsels, but

'tis like he will wink an eye — we must come to the
priest by night, and journey onward by night. And
afterward, I trow well Aasmund will put it to Lavrans
that it befits not a God-fearing man like him to part
them that a priest has wedded — and that 'twill be best
for him to give his consent, that we may be lawful
wedded man and wife. And you must say the like to
the man, Moster. He may set what terms he will for
atonement between us, and ask all such amends as he
deems just."

"I trow Lavrans Björgulfsön will be no easy man to
guide in this matter," said Lady Aashild. "And God
and St. Olav know, sister's son, I like this business but
ill. But I see well 'tis the last way left you to make
good the harm you have wrought Kristin. To-morrow
will I ride myself to Jörundgaard, if so be you will
lend me one of your men, and I get Ingrid of the croft
above us here to see to my cattle."

Lady Aashild came to Jörundgaard next evening
just as the moonlight was struggling with the last
gleams of day. She saw how pale and hollow-cheeked
Kristin was, when the girl came out into the courtyard
to meet her guest.

The lady sat by the fireplace playing with the two
children. Now and then she stole keen glances at
Kristin, as she went about and set the supper-board.
Thin she was truly, and still in her bearing. She had
ever been still, but it was a stillness of another kind
that was on the girl now. Lady Aashild guessed at all
the straining and the stubborn defiance that lay behind.

" 'Tis like you have heard," said Kristin, coming over
to her, "what befell here this last autumn."

"Ay — that my sister's son has made suit for you."

"Mind you," asked Kristin, "how you said once
he and I would match well together? Only that he was
too rich and great of kin for me?"

"I hear that Lavrans is of another mind," said the
lady drily.

There was a gleam in Kristin's eyes, and she smiled a little. She will do, no question, thought Lady Aashild. Little as she liked it, she must hearken to Erlend, and give the helping hand he had asked.

Kristin made ready her parents' bed for the guest, and Lady Aashild asked that the girl should sleep with her. After they had lain down and the house was silent, Lady Aashild brought forth her errand.

She grew strangely heavy at heart as she saw that this child seemed to think not at all on the sorrow she would bring on her father and mother. Yet *I* lived with Baard for more than twenty years in sorrow and torment, she thought. Well, maybe 'tis so with all of us. It seemed Kristin had not even seen how Ulvhild had fallen away this autumn — 'tis little like, thought Aashild, that she will see her little sister any more. But she said naught of this — the longer Kristin could hold to this mood of wild and reckless gladness, the better would it be, no doubt.

Kristin rose up in the dark, and gathered together her ornaments in a little box which she took with her into the bed. Then Lady Aashild could not keep herself from saying:

"Yet methinks, Kristin, the best way of all would be that Erlend ride hither, when your father comes home — that he confess openly he hath done you a great wrong — and put himself in Lavrans' hands."

"I trow that, then, father would kill Erlend," said Kristin.

"That would not Lavrans, if Erlend refuse to draw steel against his love's father."

"I have no mind that Erlend should be humbled in such wise," said Kristin. "And I would not father should know that Erlend had touched me before he asked for me in seemliness and honour."

"Think you Lavrans will be less wroth," asked Aashild, "when he hears that you have fled from his house with Erlend; and think you 'twill be a lighter

sorrow for him to bear? So long as you live with
Erlend, and your father has not given you to him, you
can be naught but his paramour before the law."

" 'Tis another thing," said Kristin, "if I be Erlend's
paramour after he has tried in vain to win me for his
lawful wife."

Lady Aashild was silent. She thought of her meeting
with Lavrans Björgulfsön when he came home and
learnt that his daughter had been stolen away.

Then Kristin said:

"I see well, Lady Aashild, I seem to you an evil,
thankless child. But so has it been in this house ever
since father came from the Haugathing, that every day
has been a torment to him and to me. 'Tis best for all
that there be an end of this matter."

They rode from Jörundgaard betimes the next day,
and came to Haugen a little after nones. Erlend met
them in the courtyard, and Kristin threw herself into
his arms, paying no heed to the man who was with
her and Lady Aashild.

In the house she greeted Björn Gunnarsön; and then
greeted Erlend's two men, as though she knew them
well already. Lady Aashild could see no sign in her
of bashfulness or fear. And after, when they sat at the
board, and Erlend set forth his plan, Kristin put her
word in with the others and gave counsel about the
journey: that they should ride forth from Haugen
next evening so late that they should come to the
gorge when the moon was setting, and should pass in
the dark through Sil to beyond Loptsgaard, thence
up along the Otta stream to the bridge, and from
thence along the west side of the Otta and the Laagen
over by-paths through the waste as far as the horses
could bear them. They must lie resting through the
day at one of the empty spring sæters on the hillside
there; "for till we are out of the Holledis country
there is ever fear that we may come upon folk that
know me."

"Have you thought of fodder for the horses?" said Aashild. "You cannot rob folk's sæters in a year like this — even if so be there is fodder there — and you know none in all the Dale has fodder to sell this year."

"I have thought of that," answered Kristin. "You must lend us three days' food and fodder. 'Tis a reason the more why we must not journey in so strong a troop. Erlend must send Jon back to Husaby. The year has been better on the Trondheim side, and surely some loads can be got across the hills before the Yule-tide snows. There are some poor folk dwelling south-ward in the parish, Lady Aashild, that I would fain you should help with a gift of fodder from Erlend and me."

Björn set up an uncanny, mirthless horse-laugh. Lady Aashild shook her head. But Erlend's man Ulf lifted his keen, swarthy visage and looked at Kristin with his bold smile:

"At Husaby there is never abundance, Kristin Lavransdatter, neither in good years nor in bad. But maybe things will be changed when you come to be mistress there. By your speech a man would deem you are the housewife that Erlend needs."

Kristin nodded to the man calmly, and went on. They must keep clear of the high-road as far as might be. And she deemed it not wise to take the way that led through Hamar. But, Erlend put in, Munan was there — and the letter to the Duchess they must have.

"Then Ulf must part from us at Fagaberg and ride to Sir Munan, while we hold on west of Mjösen and make our way by land and the byroads through Hade-land down to Håkedal. Thence there goes a waste way south to Margretadal, I have heard my uncle say. 'Twere not wise for us to pass through Raumarike in these days, when a great wedding-feast is toward at Dyfrin," she said with a smile.

Erlend went round and laid his arm about her shoulders, and she leaned back to him, paying no heed to the others who sat by looking on. Lady Aashild said angrily:

"None would believe aught else than that you are well-used to running away"; and Sir Björn broke again into his horse-laugh.

In a little while Lady Aashild stood up to go to the kitchen-house and see to the food. She had made up the kitchen fire so that Erlend's men could sleep there at night. She bade Kristin go with her: "For I must be able to swear to Lavrans Björgulfsön that you were never a moment alone together in my house," she said wrathfully.

Kristin laughed and went with the lady. Soon after, Erlend came strolling in after them, drew a stool forward to the hearth, and sat there, hindering the women in their work. He caught hold of Kristin every time she came nigh him, as she hurried about her work. At last he drew her down on his knee:

"'Tis even as Ulf said, I trow; you are the house-wife I need."

"Ay, ay," said Aashild, with a vexed laugh. "She will serve your turn well enough. 'Tis she that stakes all in this adventure — you hazard not much."

"You speak truth," said Erlend. "But I wot well I have shown I had the will to come to her by the right road. Be not so angry, Moster Aashild."

"I do well to be angry," said the lady. "Scarce have you set your house in order, but you must needs guide things so that you have to run from it all again with a woman."

"You must bear in mind, kinswoman — so hath it ever been, that 'twas not the worst men who fell into trouble for a woman's sake — all sagas tell us that."

"Oh, God help us all!" said Aashild. Her face grew young and soft. "That tale have I heard before, Erlend." She laid her hand on his head and gave his hair a little tug.

At that moment Ulf Haldorsön tore open the door, and shut it quickly behind him:

"Here is come yet another guest, Erlend — the one you are least fain to see, I trow."

"Is it Lavrans Björgulfsön?" said Erlend, starting up.

"Well if it were," said the man. " 'Tis Eline Ormsdatter."

The door was opened from without; the woman who came in thrust Ulf aside and came forward into the light. Kristin looked at Erlend; at first he seemed to shrivel and shrink together; then he drew himself up, with a dark flush on his face:

"In the devil's name, where come you from — what would you here?"

Lady Aashild stepped forward and spoke:

"You must come with us to the hall, Eline Ormsdatter. So much manners at least we have in this house, that we welcome not our guests in the kitchen."

"I look not, Lady Aashild," said the other, "to be welcomed as a guest by Erlend's kinsfolk. — Asked you from whence I came? — I come from Husaby, as you might know. I bear you greetings from Orm and Margret; they are well."

Erlend made no answer.

"When I heard that you had had Gissur Arnfinsön raise money for you, and that you were for the south again," she went on, "I thought 'twas like you would bide awhile this time with your kinsfolk in Gudbrandsdal. I knew that you had made suit for the daughter of a neighbour of theirs."

She looked across at Kristin for the first time, and met the girl's eyes. Kristin was very pale, but she looked calmly and keenly at the other.

She was stony-calm. She had known it from the moment she heard who was come — this was the thought she had been fleeing from always; this thought it was she had tried to smother under impatience, restlessness and defiance; the whole time she had been striving not to think whether Erlend had freed himself wholly and fully from his former paramour. Now she was overtaken — useless to struggle any more. But she begged not nor beseeched for herself.

She saw that Eline Ormsdatter was fair. She was young no longer; but she was fair — once she must have been exceeding fair. She had thrown back her hood; her head was round as a ball, and hard; the cheek-bones stood out — but none the less it was plain to see, once she had been very fair. Her coif covered but the back part of her head; while she was speaking, her hands kept smoothing the waving, bright-gold front-hair beneath the linen. Kristin had never seen a woman with such great eyes; they were dark brown, round and hard; but under the narrow coal-black eye-brows and the long lashes they were strangely beauti-ful against her golden hair. The skin of her cheeks and lips was chafed and raw from her ride in the cold, but it could not spoil her much; she was too fair for that. The heavy riding-dress covered up her form, but she bore herself in it as does only a woman most proud and secure in the glory of a fair body. She was scarce as tall as Kristin; but she held herself so well that she seemed yet taller than the slender, spare-limbed girl.

"Hath she been with you at Husaby the whole time?" asked Kristin, in a low voice.

"I have not been at Husaby," said Erlend curtly, flushing red again. "I have dwelt at Hestnæs the most of the summer."

"Here now are the tidings I came to bring you, Erlend," said Eline. "You need not any longer take shelter with your kinsfolk and try their hospitality for that I am keeping your house. Since this autumn I have been a widow."

Erlend stood motionless.

"It was not I that bade you come to Husaby last year, to keep my house," said he with effort.

"I heard that all things were going to waste there," said Eline. "I had so much kindness left for you from old days, Erlend, that methought I should lend a hand to help you — although God knows you have not dealt well with our children or with me."

"For the children I have done what I could," said Erlend. "And well you know, 'twas for their sake I suffered you to live on at Husaby. That you profited them or me by it you scarce can think yourself, I trow," he added, smiling scornfully. "Gissur could guide things well enough without your help."

"Ay, you have ever had such mighty trust in Gissur," said Eline, laughing softly. "But now the thing is this, Erlend — now I am free. And if so be you will, you can keep the promise now you made me once."

Erlend stood silent.

"Mind you," asked Eline, "the night I bore your son? You promised then that you would wed me when Sigurd died."

Erlend passed his hand up under his hair, that hung damp with sweat.

"Ay, — I remember," he said.

"Will you keep that promise now?" asked Eline.

"No," said Erlend.

Eline Ormsdatter looked across at Kristin — then smiled a little and nodded. The she looked again at Erlend.

"It is ten years since, Eline," said the man. "And since that time you and I have lived together year in year out like two damned souls in hell."

"But not only so, I trow!" said she, with the same smile.

"It is years and years since aught else has been," said Erlend dully. "The children would be none the better off. And you know — you know I can scarce bear to be in a room with you any more!" he almost screamed.

"I marked naught of that when you were at home in the summer," said Eline, with a meaning smile. "Then we were not unfriends — always."

"If you deem that we were friends, have it as you will, for me," said Erlend wearily.

"Will you stand here without end?" broke in Lady Aashild. She poured the porridge from the pot into two great wooden dishes and gave one to Kristin. The girl took it. "Bear it to the hall — and you, Ulf, take the other — and set them on the board; supper we must have, whether it be so, or so."

Kristin and the man went out with the dishes. Lady Aashild said to the two others:

"Come now, you two; what boots it that you stand here barking at each other?"

" 'Tis best that Eline and I have our talk out together now," said Erlend.

Lady Aashild said no more, but went out and left them.

In the hall Kristin had laid the table and fetched ale from the cellar. She sat on the outer bench, straight as a wand and calm of face, but she ate nothing. Nor had the others much stomach to their food, neither Björn nor Erlend's men. Only the man that had come with Eline and Björn's hired man ate greedily. Lady Aashild sate herself down and ate a little of the porridge. No one spoke a word.

At length Eline Ormsdatter came in alone. Lady Aashild bade her sit between Kristin and herself; Eline sat down and ate a little. Now and again a gleam as of a hidden smile flitted across her face, and she stole a glance at Kristin.

Awhile after, Lady Aashild went out to the kitchenhouse.

The fire on the hearth was almost burnt out. Erlend sat by it on his stool, crouched together, his head down between his arms.

Lady Aashild went to him and laid her hand on his shoulder.

"God forgive you, Erlend, that you have brought things to this pass."

Erlend turned up to her a face besmeared with wretchedness.

"She is with child," he said, and shut his eyes.

Lady Aashild's face flamed up, she gripped his shoulder hard.

"Which of them?" she asked, roughly and scornfully.

"My child it is not," said Erlend, in the same dead voice. "But like enough you will not believe me — none will believe me — " He sank together again.

Lady Aashild sat down in front of him on the edge of the hearth.

"Now must you try to play the man, Erlend. 'Tis not so easy to believe you in this matter. Do you swear it is not yours?"

Erlend lifted his ravaged face.

"As surely as I need God's mercy — as surely as I hope — that God in heaven has comforted mother for all she suffered here — I have not touched Eline since first I saw Kristin!" He cried out the words, so that Lady Aashild had to hush him.

"Then I see not that this is so great a misfortune. You must find out who the father is, and make it worth his while to wed her."

" 'Tis in my mind that it is Gissur Arnfinsön — my steward at Husaby," said Erlend wearily. "We talked together last year — and since then too — Sigurd's death has been looked for this long time past. He was willing to wed her, when she was a widow, if I would give her a fitting portion — "

"Well?" said Lady Aashild. Erlend went on:

"She swears with great oaths she will have none of him. She will name me as the father. And if I swear I am not — think you any will believe aught but that I am forsworn?"

"You must sure be able to turn her purpose," said Lady Aashild. "There is no other way now but that

you go home with her to Husaby no later than
to-morrow. And there must you harden your heart
and stand firm till you have this marriage fixed between
your steward and Eline."

"Aye," said Erlend. Then he threw himself forward
again and groaned aloud:

"Can you not see — Moster — what think you
Kristin will believe — ?"

At night Erlend lay in the kitchen-house with the
men. In the hall Kristin slept with Lady Aashild in
the lady's bed, and Eline Ormsdatter in the other bed
that was there. Björn went out and lay down in the
stable.

The next morning Kristin went out with Lady
Aashild to the byre. While the lady went to the
kitchen to make ready the breakfast, Kristin bore the
milk up to the hall.

A candle stood burning on the table. Eline was sitting dressed on the edge of her bed. Kristin greeted
her silently, then fetched a milkpan and poured the
milk into it.

"Will you give me a drink of milk?" asked Eline.
Kristin took a wooden ladle, filled it and handed it to
the other; she drank eagerly, looking at Kristin over
the rim of the cup.

"So you are that Kristin Lavransdatter, that hath
stolen from me Erlend's love," she said, as she gave back
the ladle.

"You should know best if there was any love to
steal," said the girl.

Eline bit her lip.

"What will *you* do," she said, "if Erlend one day
grow weary of you, and offer to wed you to his
serving-man? Will you do his will in that as well?"

Kristin made no answer. Then the other laughed,
and said:

"You do his will in all things now, I well believe.
What think you, Kristin — shall we throw dice for

our man, we two paramours of Erlend Nikulaussön?"
When no answer came, she laughed again and said:
"Are you so simple, that you deny not you are his
paramour?"

"To you I care not to lie," said Kristin.

" 'Twould profit you but little if you did," answered
Eline, still laughing. "I know the boy too well. He
flew at you like a blackcock, I trow, the second time
you were together. 'Tis pity of you too, fair child that
you are."

Kristin's cheeks grew white. Sick with loathing, she
said low:

"I will not speak with you —"

"Think you he is like to deal with you better than
with me?" went on Eline. Then Kristin answered
sharply:

"No blame will I ever cast on Erlend, whatever he
may do. I went astray of my own will — I shall not
whimper or wail if the path lead out on to the
rocks —"

Eline was silent for a while. Then she said unsteadily,
flushing red:

"*I* was a maid too, when he came to me, Kristin —
even though I had been wife in name to the old man
for seven years. But like enough you could never
understand what the misery of that life was."

Kristin began to tremble violently. Eline looked at
her. Then from her travelling-case that stood by her
on the step of the bed she took a little horn. She broke
the seal that was on its mouth and said softly:

"You are young and I am old, Kristin. I know well
it boots not for me to strive against you — your time
is now. Will you drink with me, Kristin?"

Kristin did not move. Then the other raised the
horn to her own lips; but Kristin marked that she did
not drink. Eline said:

"So much honour you sure can do me, to drink to
me — and promise you will not be a hard stepmother
to my children?"

Kristin took the horn. At that moment Erlend opened the door. He stood a moment, looking from one to the other of the women.

"What is this?" he asked.

Kristin answered, and her voice was wild and piercing:

"We are drinking to each other — we — your paramours — "

He gripped her wrist and took the horn from her.

"Be still," he said harshly. "You shall not drink with her."

"Why not?" cried Kristin as before. "She was pure as I was, when you tempted her— "

"That hath she said so often, that I trow she is come to believe it herself," said Erlend. "Mind you, Eline, when you made me go to Sigurd with that tale, and he brought forth witness that he had caught you before with another man?"

White with loathing, Kristin turned away. Eline had flushed darkly — now she said defiantly:

"Yet will it scarce bring leprosy on the girl, if she drink with me!"

Erlend turned on Eline in wrath — then of a sudden his face seemed to grow long and hard as stone, and he gasped with horror:

"Jesus!" he said below his breath. He gripped Eline by the arm.

"Drink to *her*, then," he said, in a harsh and quivering voice. "Drink you first; then she shall drink to you."

Eline wrenched herself away with a groan. She fled backwards through the room, the man after her. "Drink," he said. He snatched the dagger from his belt and held it as he followed. "Drink out the drink you have brewed for Kristin!" He seized Eline's arm again and dragged her to the table, then forced her head forward toward the horn.

Eline shrieked once and buried her face on her arm. Erlend released her and stood trembling.

"A hell was mine with Sigurd," shrieked Eline. "You — you promised — but you have been worst to me of all, Erlend!"

Then came Kristin forward and grasped the horn:

"One of us two must drink — both of us you cannot keep — "

Erlend wrenched the horn away and flung her from him so that she reeled and fell near by Lady Aashild's bed. Again he pushed the horn against Eline Ormsdatter's mouth — with one knee on the bench he stood by her side, and with a hand round her head tried to force the drink between her teeth.

She reached out under his arm, snatched his dagger from the table, and struck hard at the man. The blow did but scratch his flesh through the clothes. Then she turned the point against her own breast, and the instant after sank sidelong down into his arms.

Kristin rose and came to them. Erlend was holding Eline, her head hanging back over his arm. The rattle came in her throat almost at once — blood welled up and ran out of her mouth. She spat some of it out and said:

" 'Twas for you I meant — that drink — for all the times — you deceived me — "

"Bring Lady Aashild hither," said Erlend, in a low voice. Kristin stood immovable.

"She is dying," said Erlend as before.

"Then is she better served than we," said Kristin. Erlend looked at her — the despair in his eyes softened her. She left the room.

"What is it?" asked Lady Aashild, when Kristin called her out from the kitchen.

"We have killed Eline Ormsdatter," said Kristin. "She is dying — "

Lady Aashild set off running to the hall. But Eline breathed her last as the lady crossed the threshold.

Lady Aashild had laid out the dead woman on the bench, wiped the blood from her face and covered it with the linen of her coif. Erlend stood leaning against the wall, behind the body.

"Know you," said Aashild, "that this was the worst thing that could befall?"

She had filled the fireplace with twigs and firewood; now she thrust the horn into the midst of them and blew them into a blaze.

"Can you trust your men?" asked the lady again.

"Ulf and Haftor are trusty, methinks — of Jon and the man with Eline I know but little."

"You know, belike," said the lady, "should it come out that Kristin and you were together here, and that you two were alone with her when she died, 'twere as well for Kristin you had let her drink of Eline's brew. . . . And should there be talk of poison, all men will call to mind what once was laid to *my* charge. . . . Had she any kindred or friends?"

"No," said Erlend, in a low voice. "She had none but me."

"Yet," said Lady Aashild again, "it may well be a hard matter to cover up this thing and hide the body away, without the ugliest of misthought falling on you."

"She shall rest in hallowed ground," said Erlend, "if it cost me Husaby. What say you, Kristin?"

Kristin nodded.

Lady Aashild sat silent. The more she thought, the more hopeless it seemed to her to find any way out. In the kitchen-house were four men — even if Erlend could bribe them all to keep silence, even if some of them, if Eline's man, could be bribed to leave the country — still, sure they could never be. And 'twas known at Jörundgaard that Kristin had been here — if Lavrans heard of this, she feared to think what he would do. And how to bear the dead woman hence. The mountain-path to the west was not to be thought of now — there was the road to Romsdal, or over the hills to Trondheim, or south down the Dale. And should the truth come out, it would never be believed — even if folk let it pass for true.

"I must take counsel with Björn in this matter," she said, and rose and went out to call him.

Björn Gunnarsön listened to his wife's story without moving a muscle and without withdrawing his eyes from Erlend's face.

"Björn," said Aashild desperately. "There is naught for it but that one must swear he saw her lay hands upon herself."

Björn's dead eyes grew slowly dark, as life came into them; he looked at his wife, and his mouth drew aside into a crooked smile:

"And you mean that I should be the one?"

Lady Aashild crushed her hands together and lifted them towards him:

"Björn, you know well what it means for these two — "

"And you think that, whether or no, 'tis all over with me?" he said slowly. "Or think you there is so much left of the man I once was that I dare be forsworn to save that boy there from going down to ruin? I that was dragged down myself — all those years ago. Dragged down, I say," he repeated.

"You say it because I am old now," whispered Aashild.

Kristin burst out into such weeping that the piercing sound filled the room. She had sat in the corner by Aashild's bed, stark and silent. Now she began weeping wildly and loud. It was as though Lady Aashild's voice had torn her heart open. The voice had been heavy with the memories of the sweetness of love; it was as though its sound had made her understand for the first time what her love and Erlend's had been. The memory of hot and passionate happiness swept over all else — swept away the hard despair and hatred of last night. All she knew of now was her love and her will to hold out.

They looked at her — all three. Then Sir Björn

went across and lifted her chin with his hand and looked at her:

"Say *you*, Kristin, she did it herself?"

"Every word you have heard is true," said Kristin firmly. "We threatened her till she did it."

"She had meant Kristin should suffer a worse fate," said Aashild.

Sir Björn let go the girl. He went over to the body, lifted it up into the bed where Eline had lain the night before, and laid it close to the wall, drawing up the coverings well over it:

"Jon and the man you do not know you must send home to Husaby, with word that Eline is journeying south with you. Let them ride at midday. Say that the women are asleep in the hall; they must take their food in the kitchen. Afterward you must speak with Ulf and Haftor. Hath she threatened before to do this? So that you can bring witness to it, if such question should be asked?"

"Every soul that was at Husaby the last years we lived together there," said Erlend wearily, "can witness that she threatened to take her own life — and mine too sometimes — when I spoke of parting from her."

Bjorn laughed harshly:

"I thought as much. To-night we must clothe her in her riding-coats and set her in the sleigh. You must sit beside her — "

Erlend swayed on his feet where he stood:

"I cannot!"

"God knows how much manhood will be left in *you* when you have gone your own gait twenty years more," said Björn. "Think you, then, you can drive the sleigh? For then will I sit beside her. We must travel by night and by lonely paths, till we are come down to Fron. In this cold none can know how long she has been dead. We will drive into the monks' hospice at Roaldstad. There will you and I bear witness that you two were together in the sleigh, and it came to bitter words betwixt you. There is witness enough that you would not live with her since the ban was taken off you, and that you have made suit for a maiden of birth that fits your own. Ulf and Haftor must hold themselves aloof the whole way, so they can swear, if need be, she was alive when last they saw her. You can bring them to do so much, I trow? At the monastery you can have the monks lay her in her coffin — and afterward you must bargain with the priests for grave-peace for her and soul's peace for yourself. . . .

". . . Ay, a fair deed it is not. But so as you have guided things, no fairer can it be. Stand not there like a breeding woman ready to swoon away. God help you, boy, a man can see *you* have not proved before what 'tis to feel the knife-edge at your throat."

A biting blast came rushing down from the mountains, driving a fine silvery smoke from the snow-wreaths up into the moon-blue air, as the men made ready to drive away.

Two horses were harnessed, one in front of the other. Erlend sat in the front of the sleigh. Kristin went up to him:

"This time, Erlend, you must try to send me word how this journey goes, and what becomes of you after."

He crushed her hand till she thought the blood must be driven out from under the nails.

"Dare you still hold fast to me, Kristin?"

"Ay, still," she said; and after a moment: "Of this deed we are both guilty — I egged you on — for I willed her death."

Lady Aashild and Kristin stood and looked after the sleigh, as it rose and dipped over the snow-drifts. It went down from sight into a hollow — then came forth again farther down on a snowslope. And then the men passed into the shadow of a fell, and were gone from sight for good.

* * *

The two women sat by the fireplace, their backs to the empty bed, from which Aashild had borne away all the bedding and straw. Both could feel it standing there empty and gaping behind them.

"Would you rather that we should sleep in the kitchen-house to-night?" asked Lady Aashild at length.

" 'Tis like it will be the same where we lie," said Kristin.

Lady Aashild went out to look at the weather.

"Ay, should the wind get up or a thaw come on, they will not journey far before it comes out," said Kristin.

"Here at Haugen it blows ever," answered Lady Aashild. " 'Tis no sign of a change of weather."

They sat on as before.

"You should not forget," said the lady at last, "what fate she had meant for you two."

Kristin answered low:

"I was thinking, maybe in her place I had willed the same."

"Never would you have willed that another should be a leper," said Aashild vehemently.

"Mind you, Moster, you said to me once that 'tis well when we dare not do a thing we think is not good and fair, but not so well when we think a thing not good and fair because we dare not do it?"

"You had not dared to do it, because 'twas sin," said Lady Aashild.

"No, I believe not so," said Kristin. "Much have I done already that I deemed once I dared not do because 'twas sin. But I saw not till now what sin brings with it — that we must tread others underfoot."

"Erlend would fain have made an end of his ill life long before he met you," said Aashild eagerly. "All was over between those two."

"I know it," said Kristin. "But I trow she had never cause to deem Erlend's purposes so firm that she could not shake them."

"Kristin," begged the lady fearfully, "surely you would not give up Erlend now? You cannot be saved now except you save each other."

"So would a priest scarce counsel," said Kristin, smiling coldly. "But well I know that never can I give up Erlend now — not if I should tread my own father underfoot."

Lady Aashild rose:

"We had as well put our hands to some work as sit here thus," she said. "Like enough 'twould be vain for us to try to sleep."

She fetched the butter-churn from the closet, then bore in some pans of milk, filled the churn and made ready to begin churning.

"Let me do it," Kristin asked. "My back is younger."

They worked without speaking; Kristin stood by the closet-door churning, while Aashild carded wool by the hearth. At last, when Kristin had emptied the churn and was kneading the butter, the girl asked of a sudden:

"Moster Aashild — are you never afraid of the day when you must stand before God's judgment?"

Lady Aashild rose, and came and stood before Kristin in the light:

"It may be I shall find courage to ask Him that hath made me as I am, if He will have mercy on me in His own good time. For I have never begged for His mercy when I broke His commands. And never have I begged God or man to forgive me a farthing of the price I have paid here in this mountain hut."

A little while after she said softly:

"Munan, my eldest son, was twenty years old. He was not such an one then, as I know he is now. They were not such ones then, my children — "

Kristin answered low:

"But yet have you had Sir Björn by your side each day and each night in all these years."

"Ay — that too have I had," said Aashild.

In a little while after, Kristin was done with the

butter-making. Lady Aashild said then that they must lie down and try to sleep a little.

Inside, in the dark bed, she laid her arm round Kristin's shoulders, and drew the young head in to her breast. And it was not long before she heard by her even and gentle breathing that Kristin was fallen asleep.

4

THE FROST held on. In every byre in the parish the half-starved beasts bellowed dolefully with hunger and cold. Already the farmers were skimping and saving on their fodder, every straw they could.

There was little visiting round at Yule this year; folks stayed quiet in their own homes.

During Yuletide the cold grew greater — it was as though each day was colder than the last. Scarce any one could call to mind so hard a winter — there came no more snow, not even up in the mountains; but the snow that had fallen at Clementsmass froze hard as a stone. The sun shone from a clear sky, now the days began to grow lighter. At night the northern lights flickered and flamed above the range to the north — they flamed over half the heaven, but they brought no change of weather; now and again would come a cloudy day, and a little dry snow would sprinkle down — and then came clear weather again and biting cold. The Laagen muttered and gurgled sluggishly under its ice-bridges.

Kristin thought each morning that she could bear no more, that she could never hold out to the day's end. For each day she felt was as a duel between her and her father. And *could* they be against each other so, when every living being in the parish, man and beast, was suffering under one common trial? . . . But still, when the evening came, she had held out one day more.

It was not that her father was unfriendly. They spoke no word of what was between them, but she felt, behind all that he did not say, his firm unbending will to hold fast to his denial.

And her heart ached within her for the lack of his friendship. The ache was so dreadful in its keenness, because she knew how much else her father had on his shoulders — and had things been as before, he would have talked with her of it all. . . . It was indeed so, that at Jörundgaard they were in better case than most other places; but here, too, they felt the pinch of the year each day and each hour. Other years it had been Lavrans' wont in the winters to handle and break in his young colts; but this year he had sent them all south in the autumn and sold them. And his daughter missed the sound of his voice out in the courtyard, and the sight of him struggling with the slender, ragged two-year-olds in the game he loved so well. Storehouses and barns and bins at Jörundgaard were not bare yet — there was store left from the harvest of the year before — but many folk came to ask for help — to buy, or to beg for gifts — and none ever asked in vain.

Late one evening came a huge old skin-clad man on ski. Lavrans talked with him out in the courtyard, and Halvdan bore food across to the hearth-room for him. None on the place who had seen him knew who he was — he might well be one of those wild folk who lived far in among the fells; like enough Lavrans had came upon him there. But Lavrans said naught of the visitor, nor Halvdan either.

But one evening came a man whom Lavrans Björgulfsön had been at odds with for many years. Lavrans went to the storeroom with him. When he came back to the hall again he said:

"They come to me for help, every man of them. But here in my own house you are all against me. You, too, wife," he said hotly.

The mother flamed up at Kristin:

"Hear you what your father says to me! No, I am not against you, Lavrans. I know — and I wot well you know it too, Kristin — what befell away south at Roaldstad late in the autumn, when he journeyed down the Dale with that other adulterer, his kinsman of Haugen — she took her own life, the unhappy woman he had lured away from all her kin."

Kristin stood with a hard, frozen face:

"I see that 'tis all one — you blame him as much for the years he has striven to free himself from sin, as for the years he lived in it."

"Jesus, Maria!" cried Ragnfrid, clasping her hands together: "What is come to you! Has even this not availed to change your heart?"

"No," said Kristin. "I have not changed."

Then Lavrans looked up from the bench where he sat by Ulvhild:

"Neither have I changed, Kristin," he said, in a low voice.

But Kristin felt within her that in a manner she was changed, in thoughts if not in heart. She had had tidings of how it had fared with them on that dreadful journey. As things fell out it had gone off more easily than they looked it should. Whether the cold had got into the hurt or whatever the cause might be, the knife-wound in Erlend's breast had festered, and constrained him to lie sick some while in the hospice at Roaldstad, Sir Björn tending him. But that Erlend was wounded made it easier to win belief for their tale of how that other things had befallen.

When he was fit to journey on, he had taken the dead woman with him in a coffin all the way to Oslo. There, by Sira Jon's help, he had won for her Christian burial in the churchyard of the old church of St. Nikolaus that had been pulled down. Then had he made confession to the Bishop of Oslo himself, and the Bishop had laid on him as penance to go on pilgrimage to the Holy Blood at Schwerin.* Now was he gone out of the land.

She could not make pilgrimage to any place on earth, and find absolution. For her there was naught but to sit here and wait and think, and strive to hold out in the struggle with her father and mother. A strange wintry-cold light fell on all her memories of meetings with Erlend. She thought of his vehemency — in love and in grief — and it was borne in on her that had she been able, like him, to take up all things of a sudden, and straightway rush forward with them headlong, afterwards maybe they might have seemed less fearful and heavy to bear. At times, too, she would think: maybe Erlend will give me up. It seemed to her she must always have had a little lurking fear that if things grew too hard for them he would fail her. But she would never give *him* up, unless he himself loosed her from all vows.

So the winter dragged on toward its end. And Kristin could not cheat herself any more; she had to see that the hardest trial of all lay before them — that Ulvhild had not long to live. And in the midst of her bitter sorrow for her sister she saw with horror that truly her own soul was wildered and eaten away with sin. For, with the dying child and the parents' unspeakable sorrow before her eyes, she was still brooding on this one thing — if Ulvhild dies, how can I bear to look at my father and not throw myself at his feet and confess all and beseech him to forgive me — and command me . . .

They were come far on in the long fast. Folks had begun slaughtering the small stock they had hoped to save alive, for fear they should die of themselves. And the people themselves sickened and pined from living

---

* The Holy Blood at Schwerin, see Note 20.

on fish, with naught besides but a little wretched meal and flour. Sira Eirik gave leave to the whole parish to eat milk food if they would. But few of the folk could come by a drop of milk.

Ulvhild lay in bed. She lay alone in the sisters' bed, and some one watched by her each night. It chanced sometimes that both Kristin and her father would be sitting by her. On such a night Lavrans said to his daughter:

"Mind you what Brother Edvin said that time about Ulvhild's lot. Even then the thought came to me that maybe he meant this. But I thrust it from me then."

Sometimes in these nights he would speak of this thing and that from the time when the children were small. Kristin sat there, white and desperate — she knew that behind the words her father was beseeching her.

One day Lavrans had gone with Kolbein to hunt out a bear's winter lair in the wooded hills to the north. They came home with a she-bear on a sledge, and Lavrans brought with him a living bear-cub in the bosom of his coat. Ulvhild brightened a little when he showed it to her. But Ragnfrid said that was surely no time to rear up such a beast — what would he do with it at a time like this?

"I will rear it up and bind it before my daughters' bower," said Lavrans, laughing harshly.

But they could not get for the cub the rich milk it needed, and Lavrans had to kill it a few days after.

The sun had gained so much strength now that sometimes, at midday, the roofs would drip a little. The titmice clambered about, clinging on the sunny side of the timber walls, and pecked till the wood rang, digging for the flies sleeping in the cracks. Over the rolling fields around, the snow shone hard and bright as silver.

At last one evening clouds began to draw together

over the moon. And the next morning the folk at
Jörundgaard woke in the midst of a whirling world of
snow that shut in their sight on every hand.

That day they knew that Ulvhild was dying.

All the house-folk were indoors, and Sira Eirik came
over to them. Many candles were burning in the hall.
Early in the evening Ulvhild passed away quietly and
peacefully, in her mother's arms.

Ragnfrid bore it better than any had thought possible. The father and mother sat together; both were
weeping very quietly. All in the room were weeping.
When Kristin went across to her father, he laid his
arm round her shoulders. He felt how she shook and
trembled, and he drew her close in to him. But to her
it seemed that he must feel as if she were farther from
him far than the dead child in the bed.

She understood not how it was that she still held
out. She scarce remembered herself what it was she
held out for; but, dulled and dumb with grief as she
was, she held herself up and did not yield. . . .

. . . A few planks were torn up from the church
floor in front of St. Thomas's shrine, and a grave was
hewn in the stone-hard ground beneath for Ulvhild
Lavransdatter.

It was snowing thick and silently all through those
days, while the child lay in the dead-straw; it was
snowing still when she was borne to the grave; and it
went on snowing, almost without cease, till a whole
month was out.

To the folk of the Dale, waiting and waiting for
the spring to deliver them, it seemed as though it
would never come. The days grew long and light, and
the steam-cloud from the melting snow lay on all the
valley as long as the sun shone. But the cold still held
the air, and there was no strength in the heat to overcome it. By night it froze hard — there was loud crack-
ing from the ice, there were booming sounds from

the distant fells; and the wolves howled and the fox barked down among the farms as at midwinter. Men stripped the bark from the trees for their cattle, but they dropped down dead in their stalls by scores. None could tell how all this was to end.

Kristin went out on such a day, when water was trickling in the ruts, and the snow on the fields around glistened like silver. The snow-wreaths had been eaten away hollow on the side toward the sun, so that the fine ice-trellis of the snow-crust edges broke with a silver tinkle when her foot touched them. But everywhere, where the smallest shadow fell, the sharp cold held the air and the snow was hard.

She went upward towards the church — she knew not herself what she went to do, but something drew her there. Her father was there — some of the free-holders, guild-brothers, were to meet in the cloister-way, she knew.

Half-way up the hill she met the troop of farmers, coming down. Sira Eirik was with them. The men were all on foot; they walked stoopingly in a dark, shaggy knot, and spoke no word together. They gave back her greeting sullenly as she went by them.

Kristin thought how far away the time was when every soul in the parish had been her friend. Like enough all men knew now that she was a bad daughter. Perhaps they knew yet more about her. It might well be that all believed now there had been some truth in the old talk about her and Arne and Bentein. It might be that she had fallen into the worst ill-fame. She held her head high and passed on toward the church.

The door stood ajar. It was cold in the church, yet was it as though a mild warmth streamed into her heart from the brown dusky hall with the high, up-springing pillars holding up the darkness under the roof-beams. There was no light on the altars, but a ray of sun shone in through the chink of the door and gleamed faintly back from the pictures and the holy vessels.

Far in before the altar of St. Thomas she saw her father kneeling with head bent forward on his folded hands, which held his cap crushed to his breast.

Shrinking back in fear and sadness, Kristin stole out and stood in the cloister-way, with her hands about two of its small pillars. Framed in the arch between them she saw Jörundgaard lying below, and behind her home the pale blue haze that filled the valley. Where the river lay stretched through the country-side its ice and water sent out white sparkles in the sunshine. But the alder thickets along its bed were yellow-brown with blossom, even the pinewood up by the church was tinged with spring green, and there was a piping and twittering and whistling of little birds in the grove near by. Ay, there had been bird-song like this each evening after the sun was down.

And she felt that the longing she thought must have been racked out of her long since, the longing in her body and her blood, was stirring now again, faintly and feebly, as about to waken from a winter sleep.

Lavrans Björgulfsön came out and locked the church door behind him. He came and stood by his daughter, looking out through the arch next to her. She saw how the winter gone by had harrowed her father's face. She understood not herself how she could touch now on what was between them, but the words seemed to rush out of themselves:

"Is it true what mother told me the other day — that you said to her: had it been Arne Gyrdsön you would have given me my will?"

"Ay," said Lavrans, not looking at her.

"You said not so while yet Arne lived," said Kristin.

"It never came in question. I saw well enough that the boy held you dear — but he said nothing — and he was young — and I marked not ever that you had such thoughts towards him. You could scarce think I would *proffer* my daughter to a man of no estate?" He smiled slightly. "But I loved the boy," he said, in a low voice; "and had I seen you pining for love of him — "

They stood still, gazing. Kristin felt that her father was looking at her — she strove hard to be calm of face, but she felt herself grow deadly white. Then her father came towards her, put both his arms around her and pressed her strongly to him. He bent her head backwards, looked down into his daughter's face, and then hid it again on his shoulder.

"Jesus Kristus, little Kristin, are you *so* unhappy — ?"

"I think I shall die of it, father," she said, her face pressed to him.

She burst into weeping. But she wept because she had felt in his caress and seen in his eyes that now he was so worn out with pain that he could not hold out against her any more. She had overcome him.

Far on in the night she was wakened in the dark by her father's touch on her shoulder.

"Get up," he said softly. "Do you hear — ?"

She heard the singing of the wind round the house-corners — the deep, full note of the south wind, heavy with wetness. Streams were pouring from the roof; there was the whisper of rain falling on soft, melting snow.

Kristin flung her dress on her back and went after her father to the outer door. They stood together looking out into the twilight of the May night. Warm wind and rain smote against them; the heavens were a welter of tangled drifting rain-clouds, the woods roared, the wind whistled between the houses, and from far up in the fells they heard the dull boom of snow-masses falling.

Kristin felt for her father's hand and held it. He had called her that he might show her this. So had it been between them before, that he would have done this; and so it was now again.

When they went in to go to bed again, Lavrans said:

"The stranger serving-man that came last week brought me letters from Sir Munan Baardsön. He is minded to come up the Dale to our parts next summer to see his mother; and he asked if he might meet me and have speech with me."

"What will you answer him, my father?" she whispered.

"That can I not tell you now," said Lavrans. "But I will speak with him; and then must I order this matter so as I may deem I can answer it to God, my daughter."

Kristin crept in again beside Ramborg, and Lavrans went and lay down by the side of his sleeping wife. He lay thinking that if the flood came over-sudden and strong there were few places in the parish that lay so much in its path as Jörundgaard. Folk said there was a prophecy that some day the river would carry it away.

5

SPRING came at a single bound. Only a few days after the sudden thaw the whole parish lay dark brown under the flooding rain. The waters rushed foaming down the hillsides, the river swelled up and lay in the valley-bottom, like a great leaden-grey lake, with lines of tree-tops floating on its waters and a treacherous bubbling furrow where the current ran. At Jörundgaard the water stood far up over the fields, but everywhere the mischief done was less than folks had feared.

Of necessity the spring work was thrown late, and the people sowed their scanty corn with prayers to God that He would save it from the night-frosts in autumn. And it looked as though He would hearken to them and a little ease their burdens. June came in with mild, growing weather, the summer was good, and folk set their faces forward in hope that the marks of the evil year might be wiped out in time.

* * *

The hay harvest had been got in, when one evening four men rode up to Jörundgaard. First came two knights, and behind them their serving-men; and the knights were Sir Munan Baardsön and Sir Baard Peterssön of Hestnæs.

Ragnfrid and Lavrans had the board spread in the upper hall, and beds made ready in the guest-room over the store-house. But Lavrans begged the knights to tarry with their errand till the next day, when they should be rested from their journey.

Sir Munan led the talk throughout the meal; he turned much to Kristin in talking, and spoke as if he and she were well acquainted. She saw that this was not to her father's liking. Sir Munan was square built, red-faced, ugly, talkative, and something of a buffoon in his bearing. People called him Dumpy Munan or Dance Munan. But for all his flighty bearing, Lady Aashild's son was a man of understanding and parts, who had been used by the Crown more than once in matters of trust, and was known to have a word in the counsels of them that guided the affairs of the kingdom. He held his mother's heritage in the Skog-heim Hundred; was exceeding rich, and had made a rich marriage. Lady Katrin, his wife, was hard-featured beyond the common, and seldom opened her mouth; but her husband ever spoke of her as if she were the wisest of dames, so that she was known in jest as Lady Katrin the Ready-witted, or the Silver-tongued. They seemed to live with each other well and lovingly, though Sir Munan was known all too well for the looseness of his life both before and after his marriage.

Sir Baard Peterssön was a comely and a stately old man, even though now somewhat ample of girth and heavy-limbed. His hair and beard were faded now, but their hue was still as much yellow as 'twas white. Since King Magnus Haakonsön's death he had lived retired, managing his great possessions in Nordmöre. He was a widower for the second time, and had many children, who, it was said, were all comely, well-nurtured and well-to-do.

The next day Lavrans and his guests went up to the upper hall for their parley. Lavrans would have had his wife be present with them, but she would not.

"This matter must be in your hands wholly. You know well 'twill be the heaviest of sorrows for our daughter if it should come to naught; but I see well that there are but too many things that may make against this marriage."

Sir Munan brought forth a letter from Erlend Nikulaussön. Erlend's proffer was that Lavrans should fix, himself, each and all of the conditions,* if he would betroth his daughter Kristin to him. Erlend was willing to have all his possessions valued and his incomings appraised by impartial men, and to grant to Kristin such extra-gift and morning-gift, that she would possess a third of all his estate besides her own dowry and all such heritage as might come to her from her kin, should she be left a widow without living children. Further, his proffer was to grant Kristin full power to deal at her pleasure with her share of the common estate, both what she had of her own kindred and what came to her from her husband. But if Lavrans wished for other terms of settlement, Erlend was most willing to hear his wishes and to follow them in all things. To one thing only he asked that Kristin's kindred, on their side, should bind themselves: that, should the guardianship of his children and Kristin's ever come to them, they would never try to set aside the gifts he had made to his children by Eline Ormsdatter, but would let all such gifts hold good, as having passed from his estate before his entry into wedlock with Kristin Lavransdatter. At the end of all Erlend made proffer to hold the wedding in all seemly state at Husaby.

* Marriage Settlements, see Note 21.

Lavrans spoke in reply:

"This is a fair proffer. I see by it that your kinsman has it much at heart to come to terms with me. All the more is this plain to me by reason that he has moved you, Sir Munan, to come for the second time on such an errand to a man like me, who am of little weight beyond my own countryside; and that a knight like you, Sir Baard, hath been at the pains of making such a journey to further his cause. But concerning Erlend's proffer I would say this: my daughter has not been bred up to deal herself with the ordering of goods and gear, but I have ever hoped to give her to such a man as that I could lay the maid's welfare in his hands with an easy mind. I know not, indeed, whether Kristin be fit to be set in such authority, but I can scarce believe that 'twould be for her good. She is mild of mood and biddable — and 'twas one of the reasons I have had in mind in setting myself against this marriage, that 'tis known Erlend has shown want of understanding in more matters than one. Had she been a power-loving, bold and headstrong woman, then indeed the matter had taken on another face."

Sir Munan burst out laughing:

"Dear Lavrans, lament you that the maid is not headstrong enough?" and Sir Baard said with a little smile:

"Methinks your daughter has shown that she lacks not a will of her own — for two years now she has held to Erlend clean against your will."

Lavrans said:

"I have not forgotten it; yet do I know well what I say. She has suffered sorely herself all this time she has stood against me; nor will she long be glad with a husband who cannot rule her."

"Nay, then the devil's in it!" said Sir Munan. "Then must your daughter be far unlike all the women I have known; for I have never seen *one* that was not fain to rule herself — and her man to boot!"

Lavrans shrugged his shoulders and made no answer.

Then said Baard Peterssön:

"I can well believe, Lavrans Björgulfsön, that you have found this marriage between your daughter and my foster-son no more to your liking, since the woman who had lived with him came to the end we know of last year. But you must know it has come out now that the unhappy woman had let herself be led astray by another man, Erlend's steward at Husaby. Erlend knew of this when he went with her down the Dale; he had proffered to portion her fittingly, if the man would wed her."

"Are you well assured that this is so?" asked Lavrans. "And yet I know not," he said again, "if the thing is anyway bettered thereby. Hard must it be for a woman come of good kindred to go into a house hand and hand with the master, and be led out by the serving-man."

Munan Baardsön took the word:

"'Tis plain to me, Lavrans Björgulfsön, that what goes against my cousin most with you, is that he has had these hapless dealings with Sigurd Saksulvsön's wife. And true it is that 'twas not well done of him. But in God's name, man, you must remember this — here was this young boy dwelling in one house with a young and fair woman, and she had an old, cold, strengthless husband — and the night is a half-year long up there: methinks a man could scarce look for aught else to happen, unless Erlend had been a very saint. There is no denying it: Erlend had made at all time but a sorry monk; but methinks your young, fair daughter would give you little thanks, should you give her a monkish husband. True it is that Erlend bore himself like a fool then, and a yet greater fool since. . . . But the thing should not stand against him for ever — we his kinsmen have striven to help the boy to his feet again; the woman is dead; and Erlend has done all in his power to care for her body and her soul; the Bishop of Oslo himself hath absolved him of his sin, and now is he come home again made clean by the Holy Blood at Schwerin — would you be stricter than

the Bishop of Oslo, and the Archbishop at Schwerin —
or whoever it may be that hath charge of that precious
blood . . . ?

"Dear Lavrans, true it is that chastity is a fair thing
indeed; but 'tis verily hard for a grown man to attain
to it without a special gift of grace from God. By St.
Olav . . . Ay, and you should remember too that the
holy King himself was not granted that gift till his life
here below was drawing to an end — very like 'twas
God's will that he should first beget that doughty
youth King Magnus, who smote down the heathen
when they raged against the Nordlands. I wot well
King Olav had that son by another than his Queen
— yet doth he sit amidst the highest saints in the host
of heaven. Ay, I can see in your face that you deem
this unseemly talk — "

Sir Baard broke in:

"Lavrans Björgulfsön, I liked this matter no better
than you, when first Erlend came to me and said he
had set his heart on a maid that was handfast to
another. But since then I have come to know that there
is so great kindness between these two young folk,
that 'twould be great pity to part their loves. Erlend
was with me at the last Yuletide feasting King Haakon
held for his men — they met together there, and scarce
had they seen each other when your daughter swooned
away and lay a long while as one dead — and I saw in
my foster-son's face that he would rather lose his life
than lose her."

Lavrans sat still awhile before answering:

"Ay; all such things sound fair and fine when a man
hears them told in a knightly saga of the southlands.
But we are not in Bretland here, and 'tis like you too
would ask more in the man you would choose for
son-in-law than that he had brought your daughter to
swoon away for love in all folks' sight — "

The two others were silent, and Lavrans went on:

" 'Tis in my mind, good sirs, that had Erlend
Nikulaussön not made great waste both of his goods

and of his fame, you would scarce be sitting here
pleading so strongly with a man of my estate that I
should give my daughter to him. But I would be loth
it should be said of Kristin that 'twas an honour for
her to wed a great estate and a man from amongst the
highest in the land — after the man had so beshamed
himself, that he could not look to make a better match,
or keep undiminished the honour of his house."

He rose in heat, and began walking to and fro.

But Sir Munan started up:

"Now, before God, Lavrans, if the talk is of shame,
I would have you know you are over-proud in — "

Sir Baard broke in quickly, going up to Lavrans:

"Proud you are, Lavrans — you are like those udal
farmers we have heard of in olden times, who would
have naught to do with the titles the Kings would have
given them, because their pride could not brook that
folk should say they owed thanks to any but themselves. I tell you, that were Erlend still master of all
the honour and riches the boy was born to, yet would
I never deem that I demeaned him or myself in asking
a well-born and wealthy man to give his daughter to
my foster-son, if I knew that the two young creatures
might break their hearts if they were parted. And the
rather," he said in a low voice, laying his hand on
Lavrans' shoulder, "if so it were that 'twould be best
for the souls of both they should wed each other."

Lavrans drew away from the other's hand; his face
grew set and cold:

"I scarce believe I understand your meaning, Sir
Knight?"

The two men looked at each other for a space; then
Sir Baard said:

"I mean that Erlend has told me, they two have
sworn troth to each other with the dearest oaths.
Maybe you would say that you have power to loose
your child from her oath, since she swore without
your will. But Erlend you cannot loose. . . . And for
aught I can see what most stands in the road is your

pride — and the hate you bear to sin. But in that 'tis to me as though you were minded to be stricter than God Himself, Lavrans Björgulfsön."

Lavrans answered somewhat uncertainly:

"It may be there is truth in this that you say to me, Sir Baard. But what most has set me against this match is that I have deemed Erlend to be so unsure a man that I could not trust my daughter to his hands."

"Methinks I can answer for my foster-son now," said Baard quietly. "Kristin is so dear to him that I know, if you will give her to him, he will prove in the event such a son-in-law that you shall have no cause of grief."

Lavrans did not answer at once. Then Sir Baard said earnestly, holding out his hand:

"In God's name, Lavrans Björgulfsön, give your consent!"

Lavrans laid his hand in Sir Baard's:

"In God's name!"

Ragnfrid and Kristin were called to the upper hall, and Lavrans told them his will. Sir Baard greeted the two women in fair and courtly fashion; Sir Munan took Ragnfrid by the hand and spoke to her in seemly wise, but Kristin he greeted in the foreign fashion with a kiss, and he took time over his greeting. Kristin felt that her father looked at her while this was doing.

"How like you your new kinsman, Sir Munan?" he asked jestingly, when he was alone with her for a moment late that evening.

Kristin looked beseechingly at him. Then he stroked her face a little and said no more.

When Sir Baard and Sir Munan went to their room, Munan broke out:

"Not a little would I give to see this Lavrans Björgulfsön's face, should he come to know the truth about this precious daughter of his. Here have you and I had to beg on our knees to win for Erlend a woman he has had with him in Brynhild's house many times — "

"Hold your peace — no word of that," answered Sir Baard in wrath. " 'Twas the worst deed Erlend ever did, to lure that child to such places — and see that Lavrans never hear aught of it; the best that can happen now for all, is that those two should be friends."

The feast for the drinking of the betrothal ale was appointed to be held that same autumn. Lavrans said he could not make the feast very great, the year before had been such a bad one in the Dale; but to make up he would bear the cost of the wedding himself, and hold it at Jörundgaard in all seemly state. He named the bad year again as the cause why he required that the time of betrothal should last a year.

6

FOR more reasons than one the betrothal feast was put off; it was not held till the New Year; but Lavrans agreed that the bridal need not therefore be delayed; it was to be just after Michaelmas, as was fixed at first.

So Kristin sat now at Jörundgaard as Erlend's betrothed in all men's sight. Along with her mother she looked over all the goods and gear that had been gathered and saved up for her portion, and strove to add still more to the great piles of bedding and clothes; for when once Lavrans had given his daughter to the master of Husaby, it was his will that naught should be spared.

Kristin wondered herself at times that she did not feel more glad. But, in spite of all the busyness, there was no true gladness at Jörundgaard.

Her father and mother missed Ulvhild sorely, that she saw. But she understood too that 'twas not that alone which made them so silent and so joyless. They were kind to her, but when they talked with her of her betrothed, she saw that they did but force themselves to it to please her and show her kindness; 'twas not that they themselves had a mind to speak of Erlend. They had not learned to take more joy in the marriage she was making, now they had come to know the man. Erlend, too, had kept himself quiet and withdrawn the short time he had been at Jörundgaard for the betrothal — and like enough this could not have been otherwise, thought Kristin; for he knew it was with no goodwill her father had given his consent.

She herself and Erlend had scarce had the chance to speak ten words alone together. And it had brought a strange unwonted feeling, to sit together thus in all folks' sight; at such times they had little to say, by reason of the many things between them that could not be said. There arose in her a doubtful fear, vague and dim, but always present — perhaps 'twould make it hard for them in some way after they were wedded, that they had come all too near to each other at the first, and after had lived so long quite parted.

But she tried to thrust the fear away. It was meant that Erlend should visit them at Whitsuntide; he had asked Lavrans and Ragnfrid if they had aught against his coming, and Lavrans had laughed a little, and answered that Erlend might be sure his daughter's bridegroom would be welcome.

At Whitsuntide they would be able to go out together; they would have a chance to speak together as in the old days, and then surely it would fade away, the shadow that had come between them in this long time apart, when each had gone about alone bearing a burden the other could not share.

At Easter Simon Andressön and his wife came to Formo. Kristin saw them in the church. Simon's wife was standing not far off from her.

She must be much older than he, thought Kristin —

nigh thirty years old. Lady Halfrid was little and
slender and thin, but she had an exceeding gracious
visage. The very hue of her pale brown hair as it
flowed in waves from under her linen coif, seemed, as
it were, so gentle, and her eyes too were full of gentle-
ness; they were great grey eyes flecked with tiny
golden specks. Every feature of her face was fine and
pure — but her skin was something dull and grey,
and when she opened her mouth one saw that her
teeth were not good. She looked not as though she
were strong, folks said indeed that she was sickly —
she had miscarried more than once already, Kristin had
heard. She wondered how it would fare with Simon
with this wife.

The Jörundgaard folk and they of Formo had
greeted each other across the church-green more than
once, but had not spoken. But on Easter-day Simon
was in the church without his wife. He went across
to Lavrans, and they spoke together awhile. Kristin
heard Ulvhild's name spoken. Afterward he spoke
with Ragnfrid. Ramborg, who was standing by her
mother, called out aloud: "I mind you quite well — *I*
know who you are." Simon lifted the child up a little
and twirled her round: " 'Tis well done of you,
Ramborg, not to have forgotten me." Kristin he only
greeted from some way off; and her father and mother
said no word afterward of the meeting.

But Kristin pondered much upon it. For all that had
come and gone, it had been strange to see Simon Darre
again as a wedded man. So much that was past came
to life again at the sight; she remembered her own
blind and all-yielding love for Erlend in those days.
Now, she felt, there was some change in it. The
thought came to her: how if Simon had told his wife
how they had come to part, he and she — but she
knew he had kept silence — "for my father's sake,"
she thought scoffingly. 'Twas a poor showing, and
strange, that she should be still living here unwed, in

her parents' house. But at least they were betrothed; Simon could see that they had had their way in spite of all. Whatever else Erlend might have done, to *her* he had held faithfully, and she had not been loose or wanton.

One evening in early spring Ragnfrid had to send down the valley to old Gunhild, the widow who sewed furs. The evening was so fair that Kristin asked if she might not go; at last they gave her leave, since all the men were busy.

It was after sunset, and a fine white frost-haze was rising toward the gold-green sky. Kristin heard at each hoof-stroke the brittle sound of the evening's ice as it broke and flew outwards in tinkling splinters. But from all the roadside brakes there was a happy noise of birds singing, softly but full-throated with spring, into the twilight.

Kristin rode sharply downwards; she thought not much of anything, but felt only it was good to be abroad alone once more. She rode with her eyes fixed on the new moon sinking down toward the mountain ridge on the far side of the Dale; and she had near fallen from her horse when he suddenly swerved aside and reared.

She saw a dark body lying huddled together at the roadside — and at first she was afraid. The hateful fear that had passed into her blood — the fear of meeting people alone by the way — she could never quite be rid of. But she thought 'twas maybe a wayfaring man who had fallen sick; so when she had mastered her horse again, she turned and rode back, calling out to know who it was.

The bundle stirred a little, and a voice said:

"Methinks 'tis you yourself, Kristin Lavrans-datter — "

"Brother Edvin?" she asked softly. She came near to thinking this was some phantom or some deviltry sent to trick her. But she went nigh to him; it was the old monk himself, and he could not raise himself from the ground without help.

"Dear my Father — are you out wandering at this time of the year?" she said in wonder.

"Praise be to God, who sent you this way to-night," said the monk. Kristin saw that his whole body was shaking. "I was coming north to you folks, but my legs would carry me no farther this night. Almost I deemed 'twas God's will that I should lie down and die on the roads I have been wandering about on all my life. But I was fain to see you once again, my daughter — "

Kristin helped the monk up on her horse; then led it homeward by the bridle, holding him on. And all the time he was lamenting that now she would get her feet wet in the icy slush, she could hear him moaning softly with pain.

He told her that he had been at Eyabu since Yule. Some rich farmers of the parish had vowed in the bad year to beautify their church with new adornments. But the work had gone slowly; he had been sick the last of the winter — the evil was in his stomach — it could bear no food, and he vomited blood. He believed himself he had not long to live, and he longed now to be home in his cloister, for he was fain to die there among his own brethren. But he had a mind first to come north up the Dale one last time, and so he had set out, along with the monk who came from Hamar to be the new prior of the pilgrim hospice at Roaldstad. From Fron he had come on alone.

"I heard that you were betrothed," he said, "to that man — and then such a longing came on me to see you. It seemed to me a sore thing that that should be our last meeting, that time in our church at Oslo. It has been a heavy burden on my heart, Kristin, that you had strayed away into the path where is no peace — "

Kristin kissed the monk's hand.

"Truly I know not, Father, what I have done, or how deserved, that you show me such great love."

The monk answered in a low voice:

"I have thought many a time, Kristin, that had it so befallen we had met more often, then might you have come to be as my daughter in the spirit."

"Mean you that you would have brought me to turn my heart to the holy life of the cloister?" asked Kristin. Then, a little after, she said: "Sira Eirik laid a command on me that, should I not win my father's consent and be wed with Erlend, then must I join with a godly sisterhood and make atonement for my sins — "

"I have prayed many a time that the longing for the holy life might come to you," said Brother Edvin. "But not since you told me that you wot of — I would have had you come to God, wearing your garland, Kristin — "

When they came to Jörundgaard Brother Edvin had to be lifted down and borne in to his bed. They laid him in the old winter-house, in the hearth-room, and cared for him most tenderly. He was very sick, and Sira Eirik came and tended him with medicines for the body and the soul. But the priest said the old man's sickness was cancer, and it could not be that he had long to live. Brother Edvin himself said that when he had gained a little strength he would journey south again and try to come home to his own cloister. But Sira Eirik told the others he could not believe this was to be thought of.

It seemed to all at Jörundgaard that a great peace and gladness had come to them with the monk. Folks came and went in the hearth-room all day long, and there was never any lack of watchers to sit at nights by the sick man. As many as had time flocked in to listen, when Sira Eirik came over and read to the dying man from godly books, and they talked much with Brother Edvin of spiritual things. And though much of what he said was dark and veiled, even as his speech was wont to be, it seemed to these folks that he strengthened and comforted their souls, because each and all could see that Brother Edvin was wholly filled with the love of God.

But the monk was fain to hear, too, of all kind of other things — asked the news of the parishes round, and had Lavrans tell him all the story of the evil year of drought. There were some folk who had betaken them to evil courses in that tribulation, turning to such helpers as Christian men should most abhor. Some way in over the ridges west of the Dale was a place in the mountains where were certain great white stones, of obscene shapes, and some men had fallen so low as to sacrifice boars and gib-cats before these abominations. So Sira Eirik moved some of the boldest, most God-fearing farmers to come with him one night and break the stones in pieces. Lavrans had been with them, and could bear witness that the stones were all besmeared with blood, and there lay bones and other refuse all around them. 'Twas said that up in Heidal the people had had an old crone sit out on a great earthfest rock three Thursday nights, chanting ancient spells.

One night Kristin sat alone by Brother Edvin. At midnight he woke up, and seemed to be suffering great pain. Then he bade Kristin take the book of the Miracles of the Virgin Mary, which Sira Eirik had lent to Brother Edvin, and read to him.

Kristin was little used to read aloud, but she set herself down on the step of the bed and placed the candle by her side; she laid the book on her lap and read as well as she could.

In a little while she saw that the sick man was lying with teeth set tight, clenching his wasted hands as the fits of agony took him.

"You are suffering much, dear Father," said Kristin sorrowfully.

"It seems so to me now. But I know 'tis but that God has made me a little child again, and is tossing me about, up and down. . . .

"I mind me one time when I was little — four winters old I was then — I had run away from home into the woods. I lost myself, and wandered about many days and nights. My mother was with the folks that found me, and when she caught me up in her arms, I mind me well, she bit me in my neck. I thought it was that she was angry with me — but afterward I knew better. . . .

"I long, myself, now, to be home out of this forest. It is written: 'Forsake ye all things and follow Me' — but there has been all too much in this world that I had no mind to forsake — "

"*You*, Father?" said Kristin. "Ever have I heard all men say that you have been a pattern for pure life and poverty and humbleness — "

The monk laughed slily.

"Ay, a young child like you thinks, maybe, there are no other lures in the world than pleasure and riches and power. But I say to you, these are small things men find by the wayside; and I — I have loved the ways themselves — not the small things of the world did I love, but the *whole* world. God gave me grace to love Lady Poverty and Lady Chastity from my youth up, and thus methought with these playfellows it was safe to wander, and so I have roved and wandered, and would have been fain to roam over all the ways of the earth. And my heart and my thoughts have roamed and wandered too — I fear me I have often gone astray in my thoughts on the most hidden things. But now 'tis all over, little Kristin; I will home now to my house and lay aside all my own thoughts, and hearken to the clear words of the Gardian telling what I should believe and think concerning my sin and the mercy of God — "

A little while after, he dropped asleep. Kristin went and sat by the hearth, tending the fire. But well on in the morning, when she was nigh dozing off herself, of a sudden Brother Edvin spoke from the bed:

"Glad am I, Kristin, that this matter of you and Erlend Nikulaussön is brought to a good end."

Kristin burst out weeping:

"We have done so much wrong before we came so far. And what gnaws at my heart most is that I have brought my father so much sorrow. He has no joy in this wedding either. And even so he knows not; did he know all, I trow he would take his kindness quite from me."

"Kristin," said Brother Edvin gently, "see you not, child, that 'tis therefore you must keep it from him, and 'tis therefore you must give him no more cause of sorrow — because he never will call on you to pay the penalty. Nothing you could do could turn your father's heart from you."

A few days later Brother Edvin was grown so much better that he would fain set out on his journey southward. Since his heart was set on this, Lavrans had a kind of litter made, to be slung between two horses, and on this he brought the sick man as far south as to Lidstad; there they gave him fresh horses and men to tend him on his way, and in this wise was he brought as far as Hamar. There he died in the cloister of the Preaching Friars, and was buried in their church. Afterward the Barefoot Friars claimed that his body should be delivered to them; for that many folks all about in the parishes held him to be a holy man, and spoke of him by the name of Saint Evan. The peasants of the Uplands and the Dales, all the way north to Trondheim, prayed to him as a saint. So it came about that there was a long dispute between the two Orders about his body.

Kristin heard naught of this till long after. But she grieved sorely at parting from the monk. It seemed to her that he alone knew all her life — he had known the innocent child as she was in her father's keeping, and he had known her secret life with Erlend; so that he was, as it were, a link binding together all that

had first been dear to her with all that now filled her
heart and mind. Now was she quite cut off from
herself as she had been in the time when she was yet
a maid.

7

"Ay," said Ragnfrid, feeling with her hand the lukewarm brew in the vats, "methinks 'tis cool enough now
to mix in the barm."

Kristin had been sitting in the brew-house doorway
spinning, while she waited for the brew to cool. She
laid down the spindle on the threshold, unwrapped the
rug from the pail of risen yeast, and began measuring
out.

"Shut the door first," bade her mother, "so the
draught may not come in — you seem walking in your
sleep, Kristin," she said testily.

Kristin poured the yeast into the vats, while Ragnfrid stirred.

. . . Geirhild Drivsdatter called on Hatt,* but he was
Odin. So he came and helped her with the brewing;
and he craved for his wage that which was between
the vat and her. . . . 'Twas a saga that Lavrans had
once told when she was little.

. . . That which was between the vat and her. . . .

Kristin felt dizzy and sick with the heat and the
sweet, spicy-smelling steam that filled the dark close-
shut brew-house.

Out in the farm-place Ramborg and a band of
children were dancing in a ring, singing:

> "The eagle sits on the topmost hill-crag
>   Crooking his golden claws — "

Kristin followed her mother through the little outer
room where lay empty ale-kegs and all kinds of brew-

---

* Hatt, see Note 22.

ing gear. A door led from it out to a strip of ground
between the back wall of the brew-house and the
fence round the barley-field. A herd of pigs jostled
each other, and bit and squealed as they fought over
the lukewarm grains thrown out to them.

Kristin shaded her eyes against the blinding midday
sunlight. The mother looked at the pigs, and said:

"With less than eighteen reindeer we shall never
win through."

"Think you we shall need so many?" said her
daughter absently.

"Ay, for we must have game to serve up with the
pork each day," answered Ragnfrid. "And of wild-
fowl and hare we shall scarce have more than will
serve for the table in the upper hall. Remember, 'twill
be well on toward two hundred people we shall have
on the place — counting serving-folk and children —
and the poor that have to be fed. And even should you
and Erlend set forth on the fifth day, some of the
guests, I trow, will stay out the week — at least."

"You must stay here and look to the ale, Kristin,"
she went on. " 'Tis time for me to get dinner for your
father and the reapers."

Kristin fetched her spinning gear and sat herself
down there in the back doorway. She put the distaff
with the bunch of wool up under her arm-pit, but her
hands, with the spindle in them, sank into her lap.

Beyond the fence the ears of barley gleamed silvery
and silken in the sunshine. Above the song of the river
she heard now and again from the meadows on the
river-island the ring of a scythe — sometimes the iron
would strike upon a stone. Her father and the house-
folk were hard at work on the hay-making, to get it
off their hands. For there was much to get through
and to make ready against her wedding.

The scent of the lukewarm grains, and the rank
smell of the swine — she grew qualmish again. And the
midday heat made her so dizzy and faint. White and

stiffly upright she sat and waited for it to pass over —
she *would* not be sick again. . . .

Never before had she felt what now she felt. 'Twas
of no avail to try to tell herself for comfort; it was not
certain yet — she might be wrong. . . . That which was
between the vat and her. . . .

Eighteen reindeer. Well on toward two hundred
wedding guests. . . . Folk would have a rare jest to
laugh at when 'twas known that all this hubbub had
but been about a breeding woman they had to see and
get married before . . .

Oh no! She threw her spinning from her and started
up as the sickness overcame her again. . . . Oh no! it
was sure enough! . . .

They were to be wedded the second Sunday after
Michaelmas, and the bridal was to last for five days.
There were more than two months still to wait; they
would be sure to see it on her — her mother and the
other housewives of the parish. They were ever so wise
in such things — knew them months before Kristin
could understand how they saw them. "Poor thing, she
grows so pale. . . ." Impatiently Kristin rubbed her
hands against her cheeks; she felt that they were white
and bloodless.

Before, she had so often thought: this must happen
soon or late. And she had not feared it so terribly. But
'twould not have been the same then, when they could
not — were forbidden to come together in lawful wise.
It was counted — ay, a shame in a manner, and a sin
too — but if 'twere two young things who *would not*
let themselves be forced apart, folk remembered that
'twas so, and spoke of them with forbearance. *She*
would not have been ashamed. But when such things
happened between a betrothed pair — there was naught
for them but laughter and gross jesting. She saw it
herself — one could not but laugh: here was brewing
and mixing of wine, slaughtering and baking and cooking for a wedding that should be noised far abroad
in the land — and she, the bride, grew qualmish if she

but smelt food, and crept in a cold sweat behind the outhouses to be sick.

Erlend! She set her teeth hard in anger. He should have spared her this. For she had not been willing. He should have remembered that before, when all had been so unsure for her, when she had had naught to trust to but his love, she had ever, ever gladly been his. He should have let her be now, when she tried to deny him because she thought 'twas not well of them to take aught by stealth, after her father had joined their hands together in the sight of Erlend's kinsmen and hers. But he had taken her to him, half by force, with laughter and caresses; so that she had not had strength enough to show him she was in earnest in her denial.

She went in and saw to the beer in the vats, then came back again and stood leaning on the fence. The standing grain moved gently in shining ripples before a breath of wind. She could not remember any year when she had seen the corn-fields bear such thick and abundant growth. . . . The river glittered far off, and she heard her father's voice shouting — she could not catch the words, but she could hear the reapers on the island laughing.

. . . Should she go to her father and tell him: 'Twould be best to let be all this weary bustle and let Erlend and her come together quietly without church-wedding or splendid feasts — now that the one thing needful was that she should bear the name of wife before 'twas plain to all men that she bore Erlend's child under her heart already?

He would be a laughing-stock, Erlend too, as much as she — or even more, for he was no green boy any longer. But it was he who would have this wedding; he had set his heart on seeing her stand as his bride in silk and velvets and tall golden crown — *that* was his will, and it had been his will, too, to possess her in those sweet secret hours of last spring. She had yielded to him in that. And she must do his will too in this other thing.

But in the end 'twas like he would be forced to see — no one could have it both ways in such things. He had talked so much of the great Yuletide feast he would hold at Husaby the first year she sat there as mistress of his house — how he would show forth to all his kinsmen and friends and all the folks from far around the fair wife he had won. Kristin smiled scornfully. A seemly thing 'twould be this Yuletide, such a home-coming feast!

Her time would be at St. Gregory's Mass or thereabout. Thoughts seemed to swarm and jostle in her mind when she said to herself that at Gregory's Mass she was to bear a child. There was some fear among the thoughts — she remembered how her mother's cries had rung all round the farm-place for two whole days, the time that Ulvhild was born. At Ulvsvold two young wives had died in childbirth, one after the other — and Sigurd of Loptsgaard's first wives too. And her own father's mother, whose name she bore. . . .

But fear was not uppermost in her mind. She had often thought, when after that first time she saw no sign that she was with child — maybe this was to be their punishment — hers and Erlend's. She would always be barren. They would wait and wait in vain for what they had feared before, would hope as vainly as of old they had feared needlessly — till at last they would know that one day they should be borne forth from the home of his fathers, and be as though they had never been — for his brother was a priest, and the children he had could inherit naught from him. Dumpy Munan and his sons would come in and sit in their seats, and Erlend would be blotted out from the line of his kindred.

She pressed her hand hard to her body. It was there — between the fence and her — between the vat and her. 'Twas between her and all the world — Erlend's own son. She had made the trial already that she had once heard Lady Aashild speak of; with blood from her right arm and her left. 'Twas a son that was coming to her — whatever fate he was to bring. . . . She remembered her dead little brothers, her parents' sorrowful faces when they spoke of them; she remembered all the times she had seen them both in despair for Ulvhild's sake — and the night when Ulvhild died. And she thought of all the sorrow she herself had brought them, of her father's grief-worn face — and the end was not yet of the sorrows she was to bring on her father and mother.

And yet — and yet, Kristin laid her head on the arm that rested on the fence; the other hand she still held to her body. Even if it brought her new sorrows, even if it led her feet down to death — she would rather die in bearing Erlend a son than that they should both die one day, and leave their houses standing empty, and the corn on their lands should wave for strangers. . . .

She heard a footstep in the room behind her. The ale! thought Kristin — I should have seen to it long ago. She stood up and turned — and Erlend came stooping through the doorway and stepped out into the sunlight — his face shining with gladness.

"Is this where you are?" he asked. "And not a step will you come to meet me, even?" he said; and came and threw his arms about her.

"Dearest; are you come hither?" she said in wonder.

It was plain he was just alighted from his horse — his cloak still hung from his shoulder, and his sword at his side — he was unshaven, travel-soiled and covered with dust. He was clad in a red surcoat that hung in folds from its collar and was open up the sides almost to the arm-pits. As they passed through the brew-house and across the courtyard, the coat swung and flapped about him so that his thighs showed right up to the waist. His legs bent a little outwards when he walked — it was strange she had never marked it before — she had only seen that he had long slender legs, with fine ankles and small well-shaped feet.

Erlend had come well attended — with five men and four led horses. He told Ragnfrid that he was come to fetch Kristin's goods — 'twould be more homely for her, he thought, to find the things awaiting her at Husaby when she came thither. And so late in the autumn as the wedding was to be, it might be harder then to have the goods brought across the hills — besides they might easily be spoiled by the sea-water on shipboard. Now the Abbott of Nidarholm had proffered to give him leave to send them by the Laurentius galleass — 'twas meant she should sail from Veöy about Assumption Day. So he was come to have the goods carted over to Romsdal and down to Næs.

He sat in the doorway of the kitchen-house, drinking ale and talking while Ragnfrid and Kristin plucked the wild-duck Lavrans had brought home the day before. Mother and daughter were alone on the place; all the women were busy raking in the meadows. He looked so glad and happy — he was pleased with himself for coming on such a wise and prudent errand.

Ragnfrid went out, and Kristin stayed minding the spit with the roasting birds. Through the open door she could catch a glimpse of Erlend's men lying in the shadow on the other side of the courtyard, with the ale-bowl circling among them. Erlend himself sat on the threshold, chatting and laughing — the sun shone right down on his uncovered coal-black hair; she spied some white threads in it. Ay, he must be near thirty-two years old — but he bore himself like a mischievous boy. She knew she would not be able to tell him of her trouble — time enough when he saw it for himself. Laughing tenderness streamed through her heart, over the hard little spot of anger at its core, like a glittering river flowing over stones.

She loved him above all on earth — her soul was filled with her love, though all the time she saw and remembered all those other things. How ill this gallant in the fine red surcoat, with silver spurs on heel and belt adorned with gold, suited with the busy harvest-time at Jörundgaard. . . . She marked well, too, that her father came not up to the farm, though her mother had sent Ramborg down to the river to bear him word of the guest that was come.

Erlend stood beside her and passed his arm around her shoulders:

"Can you believe it!" he said joyfully. "Seems it not marvellous to you — that 'tis for our wedding, all this toil and bustle?"

Kristin gave him a kiss and thrust him aside — then turned to basting the birds and bade him stand out of the way. No, she would not say it. . . .

It was not till supper-time that Lavrans came back to the farm — along with the other harvesters. He was clad much like his workmen in an undyed wadmal coat cut off at the knees and loose breeches reaching to the ankles; he walked barefoot, with his scythe over his shoulder. There was naught in his dress to mark him off from the serving-men, save the leathern shoulder-piece that made a perch for the hawk he bore on his left shoulder. He led Ramborg by the hand.

He greeted his son-in-law heartily enough, begging him to forgive that he had not come before — 'twas that they must push on with the farmwork as hard as they could, for he himself had a journey to make to the market-town between the hay and the corn harvests. But when Erlend told the errand he had come on, as they sat at the supper-board, Lavrans grew something out of humour.

'Twas impossible he should spare carts and horses for such work at this time. Erlend answered: he had brought four pack-horses with him. But Lavrans said there would be three cartloads at the least. Besides, the maid must have her wearing apparel with her here. And the bed-furniture that Kristin was to have with

her they would need here too for the wedding, so
many guests as they would have in the house.

Well, well, said Erlend. Doubtless some way could
be found to have the goods sent through in the
autumn. But he had been glad, and had thought it
seemed a wise counsel, when the Abbot had proffered
to have the goods brought in the church galleass. The
Abbot had reminded him of their kinship. "They are
all ready now to remember that," said Erlend, smiling.
His father-in-law's displeasure seemed not to trouble
him in the least.

But in the end it was agreed that Erlend should be
given the loan of a cart, and should take away a cart-
load of the things Kristin would need most when first
she came to her new home.

The day after they were busy with the packing. The
big and the little loom the mother thought might go
at once — Kristin would scarce have time for weaving
much more before the wedding. Ragnfrid and her
daughter cut off the web that was on the loom. It was
undyed wadmal, but of the finest, softest wool, with
inwoven tufts of black sheep's wool that made a
pattern of spots. Kristin and her mother rolled up the
stuff and laid it in the leather sack. Kristin thought:
'twould make good warm swaddling cloths — and
right fair ones, too, with blue or red bands wrapped
round them.

The sewing-chair, too, that Arne had once made
her, was to be sent. Kristin took out of the box-seat
all the things Erlend had given her from time to time.
She showed her mother the blue velvet cloak patterned
in red that she was to wear at the bridal, on the ride
to church. The mother turned it about and about, and
felt the stuff and the fur lining.

"A costly cloak, indeed," said Ragnfrid. "When was
it Erlend gave you this?"

"He gave it me when I was at Nonneseter," said her
daughter.

Kristin's bride-chest, that held all the goods her mother had gathered together and saved up for her since she was a little child, was emptied and packed anew. Its sides and cover were all carved in squares, with a leaping beast or a bird amidst leaves in each square. The wedding-dress Ragnfrid laid away in one of her own chests. It was not quite ready yet, though they had sewed on it all winter. It was of scarlet silk, cut to sit very close to the body. Kristin thought, 'twould be all too tight across the breast now.

Toward evening the whole load stood ready, firmly bound under the wagon-tilt. Erlend was to set forth early the next morning.

He stood with Kristin leaning over the courtyard gate, looking northward to where a blue-black storm-cloud filled the Dale. Thunder was rolling far off in the mountains — but southward the green fields and the river lay in yellow, burning sunshine.

"Mind you the storm that day in the woods at Gerdarud?" he asked softly, playing with her fingers.

Kristin nodded and tried to smile. The air was so heavy and close — her head ached, and at every breath she took her skin grew damp with sweat.

Lavrans came across to the two as they stood by the gate, and spoke of the storm. 'Twas but rarely it did much harm down here in the parish — but God knew if they should not hear of cattle and horses killed up in the mountains.

It was black as night above the church up on the hillside. A lightning-flash showed them a troop of horses standing uneasily huddled together on the green-sward outside the church gate. Lavrans thought they could scarce belong here in the parish — rather must they be horses from Dovre that had been running loose up on the hills below Jetta; but yet he had a mind to go up and look at them, he shouted through a peal of thunder — there might be some of his among them. . . .

A fearful lightning-flash tore the darkness above the church — the thunder crashed and bellowed so as to deafen them to all other sounds. The cluster of horses burst asunder, scattering over the hill-slopes beneath the mountain-ridge. All three of them crossed themselves. . . .

Then came another flash; it was as though the heavens split asunder right above them, a mighty snow-white flame swooped down upon them — the three were thrown against each other, and stood with shut, blinded eyes, and a smell in their nostrils as of burning stone — while the crashing thunder rent their ears.

"Saint Olav, help us!" said Lavrans, in a low voice.

"Look! the birch — the birch!" shouted Erlend; the great birch-tree in the field near by seemed to totter, and a huge bough parted from the tree and sank to the ground, leaving a great gash in the trunk.

"Think you 'twill catch fire — Jesus Kristus! The church-roof is alight!" shouted Lavrans.

They stood and gazed — no — yes! Red flames were darting out among the shingles beneath the ridge-turret.

Both men rushed back across the courtyard. Lavrans tore open the doors of all the houses he came to, and shouted to those inside; the house-folk came swarming out.

"Bring axes, bring axes — timber axes," he cried, "and bill-hooks." He ran on to the stables. In a moment he came out leading Guldsveinen by the mane; he sprang on the horses's bare back and dashed off up the hill, with the great broad-axe in his hand. Erlend rode close behind him — all the men followed; some were a-horseback, but some could not master the terrified beasts, and, giving up, ran off afoot. Last came Ragnfrid and all the women on the place with pails and buckets.

None seemed to heed the storm any longer. By the light of the flashes they could see folk streaming out

of the houses farther down the valley. Sira Eirik was
far up the hill already, running with his house-folk
behind him. There was a thunder of horses' hoofs on
the bridge below — some men galloped past, turning
white, appalled faces toward their burning church.*

It was blowing a little from the south-east. The fire
had a strong hold on the north wall; on the west the
entrance door was blocked already. But it had not
caught yet on the south side nor on the apse.

Kristin and the women from Jörundgaard came into
the graveyard south of the church at a place where
the fence was broken.

The huge red glare lighted up the grove of trees
north of the church, and the green by it where there
were bars to tie the horses to. None could come thither
for the glowing heat — the great cross stood alone out
there, bathed in the light of the flames. It looked as
though it lived and moved.

Through the hissing and roar of the flames sounded
the thudding of axes against the staves of the south
wall. There were men in the cloister-way hewing and
hammering at the wall, while others tried to tear down
the cloister itself. Some one called out to the Jörundgaard women that Lavrans and a few other men had
followed Sira Eirik into the church, and now 'twas
high time to cut a passage through the south wall —
small tongues of flame were peeping out among the
shingles here too; and should the wind go round or
die down, the fire would take hold on the whole
church.

To think of putting out the fire was vain; there was
no time to make a chain down to the river; but at
Ragnfrid's bidding the women made a line and passed
water along from the little beck that ran by the roadside — it was but little to throw on the south wall and
over the men working there. Many of the women
sobbed and wept the while, in terror for the men who

---

* Stave churches, see Note 23.

had made their way into the burning building, and in sorrow for their church.

Kristin stood foremost in the line of women handing along the pails. She gazed breathless at the burning church; they were both there, inside — her father, and surely Erlend too.

The torn-down pillars of the cloister-way lay in a tangled mass of timber and shingles from its roof. The men were attacking the inner wall of staves now with all their might — a group of them had lifted up a great log and were battering the wall with it.

Erlend and one of his men came out of the little door in the south wall of the choir, carrying between them the great chest from the sacristy — the chest Eirik was used to sit on when he heard confession. Erlend and the man flung the chest out into the churchyard.

He shouted out something, but Kristin could not hear; he dashed on at once into the cloister-way. Nimble as a cat he seemed as he ran — he had thrown off his outer garments and had naught on him but shirt, breeches and hose.

The others took up his shout — the choir and the sacristy were burning; none could pass from the nave to the south door any longer — the fire had blocked both ways of escape. Some of the staves in the wall had been splintered by the ram. Erlend had seized a fire-hook, and with it he tugged and wrenched at the wreckage of the staves; he and those with him tore a hole in the side of the church, while other folks cried to take care, for the roof might fall and shut in the men inside; the shingle roof on this side too was burning hard now, and the heat had grown till 'twas scarce to be borne.

Erlend burst through the hole and helped out Sira Eirik. The priest came bearing the holy vessels from the altars in the skirt of his gown.

A young boy followed, with one hand over his face and the other holding the tall processional cross lance-wise in front of him. Lavrans came next. He kept his eyes shut against the smoke — he staggered under the weight of the great crucifix, which he bore in his arms; it was much taller than the man himself.

Folk ran forward and helped them out and into the churchyard. Sira Eirik stumbled and fell on his knees, and the altar vessels rolled out down the slope. The silver dove flew open and the Host fell out; the priest took it up, brushed the soil off it and kissed it, sobbing aloud; he kissed the gilded head, too, that had stood on the altar with shreds of the nails and hair of St. Olav in it.

Lavrans Björgulfsön still stood holding up the Holy Rood. His arm lay along the arms of the cross; his head was bowed against the shoulder of the Christ-figure; it seemed as though the Redeemer bent His fair, sorrowful face over the man to pity and to comfort.

The roof on the north side of the church had begun to fall in by bits — a burning piece from a falling beam was hurled outwards and struck the great bell in the belfry by the churchyard gate. The bell gave out a deep sobbing note, which died in a long wail that was drowned in the roaring of the flames.

None had paid heed to the weather all this time — the whole had lasted indeed no long time, but whether short or long scarce any could have told. The thunder and lightning had passed now far down the Dale; the rain, that had begun some time back, fell ever the more heavily, and the wind had died down.

But of a sudden it was as though a sheet of flame shot up from the groundsill of the building — a moment, and with a mounting roar the fire had swallowed up the church from end to end.

The people scattered, rushing away to escape the devouring heat. Erlend was at Kristin's side on the instant, dragging her away down the hill. The whole man smelt of burning — when she stroked his head and face her hand came away full of burnt hair.

They could not hear each other's voices for the

roaring of the fire. But she saw that his eyebrows were burnt off to the roots; he had burns on his face, and great holes were burnt in his shirt. He laughed as he dragged her along with him after the others.

All the folk followed the old priest as he went weeping, with Lavrans Björgulfsön bearing the crucifix.

At the foot of the churchyard Lavrans set the Rood from him up against a tree, and sank down to a seat on the wreckage of the fence. Sira Eirik was sitting there already; he stretched out his arms toward the burning church:

"Farewell, farewell, thou Olav's Church; God bless thee, thou my Olav's Church; God bless thee for every hour I have chanted in thee and said mass in thee — thou Olav's Church, good-night, good-night — "

The church-folk wept aloud with their priest. The rain streamed down on the groups of people, but none thought of seeking shelter. Nor did it seem to check the fierce burning of the tarred woodwork — brands and glowing shingles were tossed out on every side. Then, suddenly, the ridge-turret crashed down into the fiery furnace, sending a great shower of sparks high into the air.

Lavrans sat with one hand over his face; the other arm lay in his lap, and Kristin saw that the sleeve was all bloody from the shoulder down, and blood ran down over his fingers. She went to him and touched his arm.

"Not much is amiss, methinks — there fell somewhat on my shoulder," he said, looking up. He was white to the lips. "Ulvhild," he murmured in anguish, gazing into the burning pile.

Sira Eirik heard the word, and laid a hand on his shoulder.

" 'Twill not wake your child, Lavrans — she will sleep none the less sound for the burning above her bed. *She* hath not lost her soul's home, as we others have lost ours this night."

Kristin hid her face on Erlend's breast, and stood

there feeling the grasp of his arm round her shoulders. Then she heard her father asking for his wife.

Some one answered that a woman had fallen in labour from the fright; they had borne her down to the parsonage, and Ragnfrid had gone with her there.

Then Kristin called to mind again that she had clean forgotten ever since they saw that the church was afire. She should not have looked on this. There lived a man in the south of the parish who had a red stain over half his face; 'twas said he was thus because his mother had looked at a burning house while she was big with him. "Dear, holy Virgin Mother," she prayed in her heart, "let not my child have been marred by this!"

The day after, the whole parish was called to meet on the church-green to take counsel how best to build up the church anew.

Kristin sought out Sira Eirik at Romundgaard before the time set for the meeting. She asked the priest if he deemed she should take this as a sign. Maybe 'twas God's will that she should say to her father she was unworthy to wear the bridal crown; that it were more seemly she should be given in marriage to Erlend Nikulaussön without feasting or bridal honours.

But Sira Eirik flew up at her with eyes glistening with wrath:

"Think you that God cares so much how you sluts may fly about and cast yourselves away, that He would burn up a fair, venerable church for your sake? Leave you your sinful pride, and bring not on your mother and Lavrans such a sorrow as they would scarce win through for many a day. If you wear not the crown with honour on your honourable day — the worse for you; but the more need have you and Erlend of all the rites of the Church when ye are brought together. Each and all of us have sins to answer for; 'tis therefore, I trow, that this visitation is come upon us all. See you to it that you mend your

life, and that you help to build up our church a
both you and Erlend."

It was in Kristin's mind that he knew not all, for
that yet she had not told him of this last thing that was
come upon her — but she rested content and said no
more.

She went with the men to the meeting. Lavrans
came with his arm in a sling, and Erlend had many
burns on his face; he was ill to look upon, but he
laughed it off. None of the wounds were large, and
he said he hoped they would not spoil his face too
much when he came to be a bridegroom. He stood up
after Lavrans and promised four marks of silver as an
offering to the church, and, for his betrothed, with
Lavrans' assent, land * worth sixty cows from her
holdings in the parish.

It was found needful for Erlend to stay a week at
Jörundgaard by reason of his burns. Kristin saw that
'twas as though Lavrans had come to like his son-in-law
better since the night of the fire: the men seemed now
to be good friends enough. She thought, maybe her
father might grow to like Erlend Nikulaussön so well
that he would not judge them too strictly, and would
not take the matter so hardly as she had feared when
the time came when he must know that they had
transgressed against him.

8

THE YEAR proved a rarely good one over all the north
part of the Dale. The hay crop was heavy, and it was
got in dry; the folk came home from the sæters in
autumn with great store of dairy stuff and full and
fat flocks and herds — they had been mercifully spared
from wild beasts, too, this year. The corn stood tall
and thick as few folks could call to mind having seen

* Land measurement, see Note 24.

it before — it grew full-eared and ripened well, and the weather was fair as heart could wish. Between St. Bartholomew's and the Virgin's Birthfeast, the time when night frosts were most to be feared, it rained a little and was mild and cloudy, but thereafter the time of harvest went by with sun and wind and mild, misty nights. The week after Michaelmas most of the corn had been garnered all over the parish.

At Jörundgaard all folks were toiling and moiling, making ready for the great wedding. The last two months Kristin had been so busy from morning to night that she had but little time to trouble over aught but her work. She saw that her bosom had filled out; the small pink nipples were grown brown, and they were tender as smarting hurts when she had to get out of bed in the cold — but it passed over when she had worked herself warm, and after that she had no thought but of all she must get done before evening. When now and again she was forced to straighten up her back and stand and rest a little, she felt that the burden she bore was growing heavy — but to look on she was still slim and slender as she had ever been. She passed her hands down her long, shapely thighs. No, she would not grieve over it now. Sometimes a faint creeping longing would come over her with the thought: like enough in a month or so she might feel the child quick within her. . . . By that time she would be at Husaby. . . . Maybe Erlend would be glad. . . . She shut her eyes and fixed her teeth on her betrothal ring — then she saw before her Erlend's face, pale and moved, as he stood in the hall here in the winter and said the words of espousal with a loud clear voice:

"So be God my witness and these men standing here, that I Erlend Nikulaussön do espouse Kristin Lavransdatter according to the laws of God and men, on such conditions as here have been spoken before these witnesses standing hereby. That I shall have thee to my wife and thou shalt have me to thy husband, so long as we two do live, to dwell together in wedlock, with all such fellowship as God's law and the law of the land do appoint."

As she ran on errands from house to house across the farm-place, she stayed a moment — the rowan trees were so thick with berries this year — 'twould be a snowy winter. The sun shone over the pale stubble-fields where the corn sheaves stood piled on their stakes. If this weather might only hold over the wedding!

Lavrans stood firmly to it that his daughter should be wedded in church. It was fixed, therefore, that the wedding should be in the chapel at Sundbu. On the Saturday the bridal train was to ride over the hills to Vaage; they were to lie for the night at Sundbu and the neighbouring farms, and ride back on Sunday after the wedding mass. The same evening after vespers, when the holy-day was ended, the wedding feast was to be held, and Lavrans was to give his daughter away to Erlend. And after midnight the bride and bridegroom were to be put to bed.

On Friday afternoon, Kristin stood in the upper hall balcony, watching the bridal train come riding from the north, past the charred ruins of the church on the hillside. It was Erlend coming with all his groomsmen; she strained her eyes to pick him out among the others. They must not see each other — no man must see her now before she was led forth to-morrow in her bridal dress.

Where the ways divided, a few women left the throng and took the road to Jörundgaard. The men rode on toward Laugarbru; they were to sleep there that night.

Kristin went down to meet the comers. She felt wearied after the bath, and the skin of her head was sore from the strong lye her mother had used to wash her hair, that it might shine fair and bright on the morrow.

Lady Aashild slipped down from her saddle into Lavrans' arms. How can she keep so light and young? thought Kristin. Her son Sir Munan's wife, Lady Katrin, might have passed for older than she; a big, plump dame, with dull and hueless skin and eyes. Strange, thought Kristin; she is ill-favoured and he is unfaithful, and yet folks say they live well and kindly together. Then there were two daughters of Sir Baard Peterssön, one married and one unmarried. They were neither comely nor ill-favoured; they looked honest and kind, but held themselves something stiffly in the strange company. Lavrans thanked them courteously that they had been pleased to honour this wedding at the cost of so far a journey so late in the year.

"Erlend was bred up in our father's house, when he was a boy," said the elder, moving forward to greet Kristin.

But now two youths came riding into the farm-place at a sharp trot — they leaped from their horses and rushed laughing after Kristin, who ran indoors and hid herself. They were Trond Gjesling's two young sons, fair and likely lads. They had brought the bridal crown with them from Sundbu in a casket. Trond and his wife were not to come till Sunday, when they would join the bridal train after the mass.

Kristin fled into the hearth-room; and Lady Aashild, coming after, laid her hands on the girl's shoulders, and drew down her face to hers to kiss it.

"Glad am I that I live to see this day," said Lady Aashild.

She saw how thin they were grown, Kristin's hands, that she held in hers. She saw that all else about her was grown thin, but that her bosom was high and full. All the features of the face were grown smaller and finer than before; the temples seemed as though sunken in the shadow of the heavy damp hair. The girl's cheeks were round no longer, and her fresh hue was faded. But her eyes were grown much larger and darker.

Lady Aashild kissed her again:

"I see well you have had much to strive against, Kristin," she said. "To-night will I give you a sleepy drink, that you may be rested and fresh to-morrow."

Kristin's lips began to quiver.

"Hush," said Lady Aashild, patting her hand. "I joy already that I shall deck you out to-morrow — none hath seen a fairer bride, I trow, than you shall be to-morrow."

Lavrans rode over to Laugarbru to feast with his guests who were housed there.

The men could not praise the food enough — better Friday food than this a man could scarce find in the richest monastery. There was rye-meal porridge, boiled beans and white bread — for fish they had only trout, salted and fresh, and fat dried halibut.

As time went on and the men drank deeper, they grew ever more wanton of mood, and the jests broken on the bridegroom's head ever more gross. All Erlend's groomsmen were much younger than he — his equals in age and his friends were all long since wedded men. The darling jest among the groomsmen now was that he was so aged a man and yet was to mount the bridal-bed for the first time. Some of Erlend's older kinsmen, who kept their wits, sat in dread, at each new sally, that the talk would come in upon matters it were best not to touch. Sir Baard of Hestnæs kept an eye on Lavrans. The host drank deep, but it seemed not that the ale made him more joyful — he sat in the high-seat, his face growing more and more strained, even as his eyes grew more fixed. But Erlend, who sat on his father-in-law's right hand, answered in kind the wanton jest flung at him, and laughed much; his face was flushed red and his eyes sparkled.

Of a sudden Lavrans flew out:

"That cart, son-in-law — while I remember — what have you done with the cart you had of me on loan in the summer?"

"Cart — ?" said Erlend.

"Have you forgot already that you had a cart on loan from me in the summer. . . . God knows 'twas so good a cart I look not ever to see a better, for I saw to it myself when 'twas making in my own smithy on the farm. You promised and you swore — I take God to witness, and my house-folk know it besides — you gave your word to bring it back to me — but that word you have not kept — "

Some of the guests called out that this was no matter to talk of now, but Lavrans smote the board with his fist and swore that he would know what Erlend had done with his cart.

"Oh, like enough it lies still at the farm at Næs, where we took boat out to Veöy," said Erlend lightly. "I thought not 'twas meant so nicely. See you, father-in-law, thus it was — 'twas a long and a toilsome journey with a heavy-laden cart over the hills, and when we were come down to the fjord, none of my men had a mind to bring the cart all the way back here, and then journey north again over the hills to Trondheim. So we thought we might let it be there for a time — "

"Now, may the devil fly off with me from where I sit this very hour, if I have ever heard of your like," Lavrans burst out. "Is this how things are ordered in your house — doth the word lie with you or with your men, where they are to go or not to go — ?"

Erlend shrugged his shoulders:

"True it is, much hath been as it should not have been in my household. . . . But now will I have the cart sent south to you again, when Kristin and I are come thither. . . . Dear my father-in-law," said he, smiling and holding out his hand, "be assured, 'twill be changed times with all things, and with me too, when once I have brought Kristin home to be mistress of my house.

'Twas an ill thing, this of the cart. But I promise you, this shall be the last time you have cause of grief against me."

"Dear Lavrans," said Baard Peterssön, "forgive him in this small matter — "

"Small matter or great — " began Lavrans, but checked himself, and took Erlend's hand.

Soon after he made the sign for the feast to break up, and the guests sought their sleeping-places.

On the Saturday before noon all the women and girls were busy in the old storehouse loft-room, some making ready the bridal bed, some dressing and adorning the bride.

Ragnfrid had chosen this house for the bride-house, in part for its having the smallest loft-room — they could make room for many more guests in the new storehouse loft, the one they had used themselves in summer-time to sleep in when Kristin was a little child, before Lavrans had set up the great new dwelling-house, where they lived now both summer and winter. But besides this, there was no fairer house on the farm than the old storehouse, since Lavrans had had it mended and set in order — it had been nigh falling to the ground when they moved in to Jörundgaard. It was adorned with the finest wood-carving both outside and in, and if the loft-room were not great, 'twas the easier to hang it richly with rugs and tapestries and skins.

The bridal bed stood ready made, with silk-covered pillows; fine hangings made as it were a tent about it; over the skins and rugs on the bed was spread a broidered silken coverlid. Ragnfrid and some other women were busy now hanging tapestries on the timber walls and laying cushions in order on the benches.

Kristin sat in a great arm-chair that had been brought up thither. She was clad in her scarlet bridal robe. Great silver brooches held it together over her bosom, and fastened the yellow silk shift showing in the neck-opening; golden armlets glittered on the yellow silken sleeves. A silver-gilt belt was passed thrice around her waist, and on her neck and bosom lay neck-chain over neck-chain, the uppermost her father's old gold chain with the great reliquary cross. Her hands, lying in her lap, were heavy with rings.

Lady Aashild stood behind her chair, brushing her heavy, gold-brown hair out to all sides.

"To-morrow shall you spread it loose for the last time," she said, smiling, as she wound the red and green silk cords that were to hold up the crown, around Kristin's head. Then the women came thronging round the bride.

Ragnfrid and Gyrid of Skog took the great bridal crown of the Gjesling kin from the board. It was gilt all over, the points ended in alternate crosses and clover-leaves, and the circlet was set with great rock-crystals.

They pressed it down on the bride's head. Ragnfrid was pale, and her hands were shaking, as she did it.

Kristin rose slowly to her feet. Jesus! how heavy 'twas to bear up all this gold and silver. . . . Then Lady Aashild took her by the hand and led her forward to a great tub of water — while the bridesmaids flung open the door to the outer sunlight, so that the light in the room should be bright.

"Look now at yourself in the water, Kristin," said Lady Aashild, and Kristin bent over the tub. She caught a glimpse of her own face rising up white through the water; it came so near that she saw the golden crown above it. Round about, many shadows, bright and dark, were stirring in the mirror — there was somewhat she was on the brink of remembering — then 'twas as though she was swooning away — she caught at the rim of the tub before her. At that moment Lady Aashild laid her hand on hers, and drove her nails so hard into the flesh, that Kristin came to herself with the pain.

Blasts of a great horn were heard from down by the

bridge. Folk shouted up from the courtyard that the bridegroom was coming with his train. The women led Kristin out on to the balcony.

In the courtyard was a tossing mass of horses in state trappings and people in festive apparel, all shining and glittering in the sun. Kristin looked out beyond it all, far out into the Dale. The valley of her home lay bright and still beneath a thin misty-blue haze; up above the haze rose the mountains, grey with screes and black with forest, and the sun poured down its light into the great bowl of the valley from a cloudless sky.

She had not marked it before, but the trees had shed all their leaves — the groves around shone naked and silver-grey. Only the alder-thickets along the river had a little faded green on their topmost branches, and here and there a birch had a few yellow-white leaves clinging to its outermost twigs. But, for the most, the trees were almost bare — all but the rowans; they were still bright with red-brown leaves around the clusters of their blood-red berries. In the still, warm day a faint mouldering smell of autumn rose from the ashen covering of fallen leaves that strewed the ground all about.

Had it not been for the rowans, it might have been early spring. And the stillness too — but this was an autumn stillness, deathly still. When the horn-blasts died away, no other sound was heard in all the valley but the tinkling of bells from the stubble fields and fallows where the beasts wandered, grazing.

The river was shrunken small, its roar sunk to a murmur; it was but a few strands of water running amidst banks of sand and great stretches of white round boulders. No noise of becks from the hillsides — the autumn had been so dry. The fields all around still gleamed wet — but 'twas but the wetness that oozes up from the earth in autumn, howsoever warm the days may be, and however clear the air.

* * *

The crowd that filled the farm-place fell apart to make way for the bridegroom's train. Straightway the young groomsmen came riding forward — there went a stir among the women in the balcony.

Lady Aashild was standing by the bride.

"Bear you well now, Kristin," said she, " 'twill not be long now till you are safe under the linen coif." *

Kristin nodded helplessly. She felt how deathly white her face must be.

"Methinks I am all too pale a bride," she said, in a low voice.

"You are the fairest bride," said Lady Aashild; "and there comes Erlend, riding — fairer pair than you twain would be far to seek."

Now Erlend himself rode forward under the balcony. He sprang lightly from his horse, unhindered by his heavy, flowing garments. He seemed to Kristin so fair that 'twas pain to look on him.

He was in dark raiment, clad in a slashed silken coat falling to the feet, leaf-brown of hue and inwoven with black and white. About his waist he had a gold-bossed belt, and at his left thigh hung a sword with gold on hilt and sheath. Back over his shoulders fell a heavy dark-blue velvet cloak, and pressed down on his coal-black hair he wore a black French cap of silk that stood out at both sides in puckered wings and ended in two long streamers, whereof one was thrown from his left shoulder right across his breast and out behind over the other arm.

Erlend bowed low before his bride as she stood about; then went up to her horse and stood by it with his hand on the saddle-bow, while Lavrans went up the stairs. A strange dizzy feeling came over Kristin at the sight of all this splendour — in this solemn garment of green velvet, falling to his feet, her father might have been some stranger. And her mother's face, under the linen coif, showed ashy-grey against the red

---

* Linen coif, see Note 25.

of her silken dress. Ragnfrid came forward and laid the cloak about her daughter's shoulders.

Then Lavrans took the bride's hand and led her down to Erlend. The bridegroom lifted her to the saddle, and himself mounted. They stayed their horses, side by side, these two, beneath the bridal balcony, while the train began to form and ride out through the courtyard gate. First the priests: Sira Eirik, Sira Tormod from Ulvsvolden, and a Brother of the Holy Cross from Hamar, a friend of Lavrans. Then came the groomsmen and the bridesmaids, pair by pair. And now 'twas for Erlend and her to ride forth. After them came the bride's parents, the kinsmen, friends and guests, in a long line down betwixt the fences to the highway. Their road for a long way onward was strewn with clusters of rowan-berries, branchlets of pine, and the last white dog-fennel of autumn, and folk stood thick along the waysides where the train passed by, greeting them with a great shouting.

On the Sunday, just after sunset, the bridal train rode back to Jörundgaard. Through the first falling folds of darkness the bonfires shone out red from the courtyard of the bridal house. Minstrels and fiddlers were singing and making drums and fiddles speak as the crowd of riders drew near to the warm red glare of fires.

Kristin came near to falling her length on the ground when Erlend lifted her from her horse beneath the balcony of the upper hall.

" 'Twas so cold upon the hills," she whispered. "I am so weary — " She stood for a moment, and when she climbed the stairs to the loft-room, she swayed and tottered at each step.

Up in the hall the half-frozen wedding guests were soon warmed up again. The many candles burning in the room gave out heat; smoking hot dishes of food were borne around, and wine, mead and strong ale circled about. The loud hum of voices and the noise of many eating sounded like a far-off roaring in Kristin's ears.

It seemed as she sat there she would never be warm through again. In a while her checks began to burn, but her feet were still unthawed, and shudders of cold ran down her back. All the heavy gold that was on her head and body forced her to lean forward as she sat in the high-seat by Erlend's side.

Every time her bridegroom drank to her, she could not keep her eyes from the red stains and patches that stood out on his face so sharply as he began to grow warm after his ride in the cold. They were the marks left by the burns of last summer.

The horror had come upon her last evening, when they sat over the supper-board at Sundbu, and she met Björn Gunnarsön's lightless eyes fixed on her and Erlend — unwinking, unwavering eyes. They had dressed up Sir Björn in knightly raiment — he looked like a dead man brought to life by an evil spell.

At night she had lain with Lady Aashild, the bridegroom's nearest kinswoman in the wedding company.

"What is amiss with you, Kristin?" said Lady Aashild, a little sharply. "Now is the time for you to bear up stiffly to the end — not give way thus."

"I am thinking," said Kristin, cold with dread, "on all them we have brought to sorrow that we might see this day."

" 'Tis not joy alone, I trow, that you two have had," said Lady Aashild. "Not Erlend at the least. And methinks it has been worse still for you."

"I am thinking on his helpless children," said the bride again. "I am wondering if they know their father is drinking to-day at his wedding-feast — "

"Think on your own child," said the lady. "Be glad that you are drinking at your wedding with him who is its father."

Kristin lay awhile, weak and giddy. 'Twas so strange to hear that name that had filled her heart and mind each day for three months and more, and whereof yet she had not dared speak a word to a living soul. It was but for a little, though, that this helped her.

"I am thinking on her who had to pay with her life, because she held Erlend dear," she whispered, shivering.

"Well if you come not to pay with your life yourself, ere you are half a year older," said Lady Aashild harshly. "Be glad while you may —

"What shall I say to you, Kristin?" said the old woman in a while, despairingly. "Have you clean lost courage this day of all days? Soon enough will it be required of you twain that you shall pay for all you have done amiss — have no fear that it will not be so."

But Kristin felt as though all things in her soul were slipping, slipping — as though all were toppling down that she had built up since that day of horror at Haugen, in that first time when, wild and blind with fear, she had thought but of holding out one day more, and one day more. And she had held out till her load grew lighter — and at last grew even light, when she had thrown off all thought but this one thought: that now their wedding-day was coming at last, Erlend's wedding-day at last.

But when she and Erlend knelt together in the wedding-mass, all around her seemed but some trickery of the sight — the tapers, the pictures, the glittering vessels, the priests in their copes and white gowns. All those who had known her where she had lived before — they seemed like visions of a dream, standing there, close-packed in the church in their unwonted garments. But Sir Björn stood against a pillar, looking at those two with his dead eyes, and it seemed to her that that other who was dead must needs have come back with him, on his arm.

She tried to look up at Saint Olav's picture — he stood there red and white and comely, leaning on his axe, treading his own sinful human nature underfoot

— but her glance would ever go back to Sir Björn; and nigh to him she saw Eline Ormsdatter's dead face, looking unmoved upon her and Erlend. They had trampled her underfoot that they might come hither — and she grudged it not to them.

The dead woman had arisen and flung off her all the great stones that Kristin had striven to heap up above her: Erlend's wasted youth, his honour and his welfare, his friends' good graces, his soul's health. The dead woman had shaken herself free of them all. He would have me and I would have him; you would have him and he would have you, said Eline. I have paid — and he must pay and you must pay when your time comes. When the time of sin is fulfilled it brings forth death. . . .

It seemed to her she was kneeling with Erlend on a cold stone. He knelt there with the red, burnt patches on his pale face; she knelt under the heavy bridal crown, and felt the dull, crushing weight within her — the burden of sin that she bore. She had played and wantoned with her sin, had measured it as in a childish game. Holy Virgin — now the time was nigh when it should lie full-born before her, look at her with living eyes; show her on itself the brands of sin, the hideous deformity of sin; strike in hate with misshapen hands at its mother's breast. When she had borne her child, when she saw the marks of her sin upon it and yet loved it as she had loved her sin, then would the game be played to an end.

Kristin thought: what if she shrieked aloud now, a shriek that would cut through the song and the deep voices intoning the mass, and echo out over the people's heads? Would she be rid then of Eline's face — would there come life into the dead man's eyes? But she clenched her teeth together.

. . . Holy King Olav, I cry upon thee. Above all in heaven I pray for help to thee, for I know thou didst love God's justice above all things. I call upon thee, that thou hold thy hand over the innocent that is in my womb. Turn away God's wrath from the innocent; turn it upon me. Amen, in the precious name of the Lord. . . .

My children, said Eline's voice, are *they* not guiltless? Yet is there no place for them in the lands where Christians dwell. Your child is begotten outside the law, even as were my children. No rights can you claim for it in the land you have strayed away from, any more than I for mine. . . .

Holy Olav! Yet do I pray for grace. Pray thou for mercy for my son; take him beneath thy guard; so shall I bear him to thy church on my naked feet, so shall I bear my golden garland of maidenhood in to thee and lay it down upon thy altar, if thou wilt but help me. Amen.

Her face was set hard as stone in her struggle to be still and calm; but her whole body throbbed and quivered as she knelt there through the holy mass that wedded her to Erlend.

And now, as she sat beside him in the high-seat at home, all things around her were but as shadows in a fevered dream.

There were minstrels playing on harps and fiddles in the loft-room; and the sound of music and song rose from the hall below and the courtyard outside. There was a red glare of fire from without, when the door was opened for the dishes and tankards to be borne in and out.

Those around the board were standing now; she was standing up between her father and Erlend. Her father made known with a loud voice that he had given Erlend Nikulaussön his daughter Kristin to wife. Erlend thanked his father-in-law, and he thanked all good folk who had come together there to honour him and his wife.

She was to sit down, they said — and now Erlend laid his bridal gifts in her lap. Sira Eirik and Sir Munan Baardsön unrolled deeds and read aloud from them

concerning the jointures and settlements of the wedded
pair; while the groomsmen stood around, with spears
in their hands, and now and again during the reading,
or when gifts and bags of money were laid on the
table, smote with the butts upon the floor.

The tables were cleared away; Erlend led her forth
upon the floor, and they danced together. Kristin
thought: our groomsmen and our bridesmaids — they
are all too young for us — all they that were young
with us are gone from these places; how is it we are
come back hither?

"You are so strange, Kristin," whispered Erlend, as
they danced. "I am afraid of you, Kristin — are you
not happy — ?"

They went from house to house and greeted their
guests. There were many lights in all the rooms, and
everywhere crowds of people drinking and singing
and dancing. It seemed to Kristin she scarce knew her
home again — and she had lost all knowledge of time
— hours and the pictures of her brain seemed strangely
to float about loosely, mingled with each other.

The autumn night was mild; there were minstrels in
the courtyard too, and people dancing round the bonfire. They cried out that the bride and bridegroom
must honour them too — and then she was dancing
with Erlend on the cold, dewy sward. She seemed to
wake a little then, and her head grew more clear.

Far out in the darkness a band of white mist floated
above the murmur of the river. The mountains stood
around coal-black against the star-sprinkled sky.

Erlend led her out of the ring of dancers, and
crushed her to him in the darkness under the balcony.

"Not once have I had the chance to tell you —
you are so fair — so fair and so sweet. Your cheeks
are red as flames — " He pressed his cheek to hers as
he spoke. "Kristin, what is it ails you?"

"I am so weary, so weary," she whispered back.

"Soon now will we go and sleep," answered her

bridegroom, looking up at the sky. The Milky Way had wheeled, and now lay all but north and south. "Mind you that we have not once slept together since that one only night I was with you in your bower at Skog?"

Soon after, Sira Eirik shouted with a loud voice out over the farmstead that now it was Monday. The women came to lead the bride to bed. Kristin was so weary that she was scarce able to struggle and hold back as 'twas fit and seemly she should do. She let herself be seized and led out of the loft-room by Lady Aashild and Gyrid of Skog. The groomsmen stood at the foot of the stair with burning torches and naked swords; they formed a ring round the troop of women and attended Kristin across the farm-place, and up into the old loft-room.

The women took off her bridal finery, piece by piece, and laid it away. Kristin saw that over the bed-foot hung the violet velvet robe she was to wear on the morrow, and upon it lay a long, snow-white, finely-pleated linen cloth. It was the wife's linen coif. Erlend had brought it for her; to-morrow she was to bind up her hair in a knot and fasten the head-linen over it. It looked to her so fresh and cool and restful.

At last she was standing before the bridal bed, on her naked feet, bare-armed, clad only in the long golden-yellow silken shift. They had set the crown on her head again; the bridegroom was to take it off, when they two were left alone.

Ragnfrid laid her hands on her daughter's shoulders, and kissed her on the cheek — the mother's face and hands were strangely cold, but it was as though sobs were struggling deep in her breast. Then she drew back the coverings of the bed, and bade the bride seat herself in it. Kristin obeyed, and leaned back on the pillows heaped up against the bed-head — she had to bend her head a little forward to keep on the crown. Lady Aashild drew the coverings up to the bride's waist, and laid her hands before her on the silken coverlid; then took her shining hair and drew it forward over her bosom and the slender bare upper arms.

Next the men led the bridegroom into the loft-room. Munan Baardsön unclasped the golden belt and sword from Erlend's waist; when he leaned over to hang it on the wall above the bed, he whispered something to the bride — Kristin knew not what he said, but she did her best to smile.

The groomsmen unlaced Erlend's silken robe and lifted off the long heavy garment over his head. He sate him down in the great chair and they helped him off with his spurs and boots.

Once, and once only, the bride found courage to look up and meet his eyes.

Then began the good-nights. Before long all the wedding-guests were gone from the loft. Last of all, Lavrans Björgulfsön went out and shut the door of the bride-house.

Erlend stood up, stripped off his underclothing, and flung it on the benches. He stood by the bed, took the crown and the silken cords from off her hair, and laid them away on the table. Then he came back and mounted into the bed. Kneeling by her side he clasped her round the head, and pressed it in against his hot, naked breast, while he kissed her forehead all along the red streak the crown had left on it.

She threw her arms about his shoulders and sobbed aloud — she had a sweet, wild feeling that now the horror, the phantom visions, were fading into air — now, now once again naught was left but he and she. He lifted up her face a moment, looked down into it, and drew his hand down over her face and body, with a strange haste and roughness, as though he tore away a covering.

"Forget," he begged, in a fiery whisper, "forget all, my Kristin — all but this, that you are my own wife, and I am your own husband. . . ."

With his hand he quenched the flame of the last candle, then threw himself down beside her in the dark — he too was sobbing now:

"Never have I believed it, never in all these years, that we should see this day. . . ."

Without, in the courtyard, the noise died down little by little. Wearied with the long day's ride, and dizzy with much strong drink, the guests made a decent show of merry-making a little while yet, but more and ever more of them stole away and sought out the places where they were to sleep.

Ragnfrid showed all the guests of honour to their places, and bade them good-night. Her husband, who should have helped her in this, was nowhere to be seen.

The dark courtyard was empty, save for a few small groups of young folks — servants most of them — when at last she stole out to find her husband and bring him with her to his bed. She had seen as the night wore on that he had grown very drunken.

She stumbled over him at last, as she crept along in her search outside the cattle-yard — he was lying in the grass behind the bath-house on his face.

Groping in the darkness, she touched him with her hand — ay, it was he. She thought he was asleep, and took him by the shoulder — she must get him up off the icy-cold ground. But he was not asleep, at least not wholly.

"What would you?" he asked, in a thick voice.

"You cannot lie here," said his wife. She held him up, as he stood swaying. With one hand she brushed the soil off his velvet robe. " 'Tis time we too went to rest, husband." She took him by the arm, and drew him, reeling, up towards the farmyard buildings.

"*You* looked not up, Ragnfrid, when you sat in the bridal bed beneath the crown," he said in the same voice. "Our daughter — *she* was not so shamefast —

her eyes were not shamefast when she looked upon her bridegroom."

"She has waited for him seven half-years," said the mother in a low voice. "No marvel if she found courage to look up — "

"Nay, devil damn me if they have waited!" screamed the man, as his wife strove fearfully to hush him.

They were in the narrow passage between the back of the privy and a fence. Lavrans smote with his clenched fist on the beam across the cess-pit.

"I set thee here for a scorn and for a mockery, thou beam. I set thee here that filth might eat thee up. I set thee here in punishment for striking down that tender little maid of mine. — I should have set thee high above my hall-room door, and honoured thee and thanked thee with fairest carven ornament; because thou didst save her from shame and from sorrow — because 'twas thy work that my Ulvhild died a sinless child. . . ."

He turned about, reeled toward the fence and fell forward upon it, and with his head between his arms fell into an unquenchable passion of weeping, broken by long, deep groans.

His wife took him by the shoulder.

"Lavrans, Lavrans!" But she could not stay his weeping. "Husband!"

"Oh, never, never, never should I have given her to that man! God help me — I must have known it all the time — he had broken down her youth and her fairest honour. I believed it not — nay, could I believe the like of Kristin? — but still I knew it. And yet is she too good for this weakling boy, that hath made waste of himself and her — had he lured her astray ten times over, I should never have given her to him, that he may spill yet more of her life and her happiness — "

"But what other way was there?" said the mother despairingly. "You know now, as well as I — she was his already — "

"Ay, small need was there for me to make such a

mighty to-do in giving Erlend what he had taken for himself already," said Lavrans. " 'Tis a gallant husband she has won — my Kristin — " He tore at the fence; then fell again a-weeping. He had seemed to Ragnfrid as though sobered a little, but now the fit overcame him again.

She deemed she could not bring him, drunken and beside himself with despair as he was, to the bed in the hearth-room where they should have slept — for the room was full of guests. She looked about her — close by stood a little barn where they kept the best hay to feed to the horses at the spring ploughing. She went and peered in — no one was there; she took her husband's hand, led him inside the barn, and shut the door behind them.

She piled up hay over herself and him and laid their cloaks above it to keep them warm. Lavrans fell a-weeping now and again, and said somewhat — but his speech was so broken she could find no meaning in it. In a little while she lifted up his head on to her lap.

"Dear my husband — since now so great a love is between them, maybe 'twill all go better than we think — "

Lavrans spoke by fits and starts — his mind seemed growing clearer:

"See you not — he has her now wholly in his power — he that has never been man enough to rule himself. . . . 'Twill go hard with her before she finds courage to set herself against aught her husband wills — and should she one day be forced to it, 'twill be bitter grief to her — my own gentle child —

". . . Now am I come so far I scarce can understand why God hath laid so many and such heavy sorrows upon me — for I have striven faithfully to do His will. Why hath He taken our children from us, Ragnfrid, one by one — first our sons — then little Ulvhild — and now have I given her that I loved dearest, honour-less, to an untrusty and a witless man. Now is there none left to us but the little one — and unwise must I deem it to take joy in her, before I see how it will go with her — with Ramborg."

Ragnfrid shook like a leaf. Then the man laid his arm about her shoulders:

"Lie down," he said, "and let us sleep —" He lay for a while with his head against his wife's arm, sighing now and then, but at last he fell asleep.

It was still pitch dark in the barn when Ragnfrid stirred — she wondered to find that she had slept. She felt about with her hand; Lavrans was sitting up, with knees updrawn and his arms around them.

"Are *you* awake already?" she asked in wonder. "Are you cold?"

"No," said he, in a hoarse voice; "but I cannot go to sleep again."

"Is it Kristin you are thinking on?" asked the mother. "Like enough 'twill go better than we think, Lavrans," she said again.

"Ay, 'tis of that I was thinking," said the man. "Ay, ay — maid or woman, at least she is come to the bride-bed with the man she loves. And 'twas not so with either you or me, my poor Ragnfrid."

His wife gave a deep, dull moan, and threw herself down on her side amongst the hay. Lavrans put out a hand and laid it on her shoulder.

"But 'twas that I *could* not," said he, with passion and pain. "No, I *could* not — be as you would have had me — when we were young. I am not such a one —"

In a while Ragnfrid said softly through her weeping:

"Yet 'twas well with us in our life together, Lavrans — was it not? — all these years?"

"So thought I myself," answered he gloomily.

Thoughts crowded and tossed to and fro within him. That single unveiled glance in which the hearts of bridegroom and bride had leapt together — the two young faces flushing up redly — to him it seemed a very shamelessness. It had been agony, a scorching pain to him, that this was his daughter. But the sight of those eyes would not leave him; and wildly and blindly he strove against the tearing away of the veil from something in his own heart, something that he had never owned was there, that he had guarded against his own wife when she sought for it.

'Twas that he *could* not, he said again stubbornly, to himself. In the devil's name — he had been married off as a boy; he had not chosen for himself; she was older than he — he had not desired her; he had had no will to learn this of her — to love. He grew hot with shame even now when he thought of it — that she would have had him love her, when he had no will to have such love from her. That she had proffered him all this that he had never prayed for.

He had been a good husband to her — so he had ever thought. He had shown her all the honour he could, given her full power in her own affairs, and asked her counsel in all things; he had been true to her — and they had had six children together. All he had asked had been that he might live with her, without her for ever grasping at this thing in his heart that he would not lay bare. . . .

To none had he ever borne love. . . . Ingunn, Karl Steinsön's wife, at Bru? Lavrans flushed red in the pitch darkness. He had been their guest ever, as often as he journeyed down the Dale. He could not call to mind that he had spoken with the housewife *once* alone. But when he saw her — if he but thought of her, a sense came over him as of the first breath of the plough-lands in spring, when the snows are but now melted and gone. He knew it now — it might have befallen him too — he, too, could have loved.

But he had been wedded so young, and he had grown shy of love. And so it had come about that he throve best in the wild woods — or out on the waste uplands — where all things that live must have wide spaces around them — room to flee through — fearfully they look on any stranger that would steal upon them. . . .

One time in the year there was, when all the beasts in the woods and on the mountains forgot their shyness — when they rushed to their mates. But his had been given him unsought. And she had proffered him all he had not wooed her for.

But the young ones in the nest — they had been the little warm green spot in the wilderness — the inmost, sweetest joy of his life. Those little girl-heads under his hand. . . .

Marriage — they had wedded him, almost unasked. Friends — he had many, and he had none. War — it had brought him gladness, but there had been no more war — his armour hung there in the loft-room, little used. He had turned farmer. . . . But he had had his daughters — all his living and striving had grown dear to him, because by it he cherished them and made them safe, those soft, tender little beings he had held in his hands. He remembered Kristin's little two-year-old body on his shoulder, her flaxen, silky hair against his cheek; her small hands holding to his belt, while she butted her round, hard child's forehead against his shoulder-blades, when he rode out with her behind him on his horse.

And now had she that same glow in her eyes — and she had won what was hers. She sat there in the half-shadow against the silken pillows of the bed. In the candle-light she was all golden — golden crown and golden shift and golden hair spread over the naked golden arms. Her eyes were shy no longer —

Her father winced with shame.

And yet it was as though his heart was bleeding within him, for what he himself had never won; and for his wife, there by his side, whom he had never given what should have been hers.

Weak with pity, he felt in the darkness for Ragnfrids hand:

"Ay, methought it was well with us in our life together," he said. "Methought 'twas but that you sorrowed for our children — ay, and that you were born heavy of mood. Never did it come to my mind, it might be that I was no good husband to you — "

Ragnfrid trembled fitfully:

"You were ever a good husband, Lavrans."

"H'm!" Lavrans sat with his chin resting on his knees. "Yet had it mayhap been better with you, if you had been wedded even as our daughter was to-day — "

Ragnfrid started up with a low, piercing cry:

"You know! How did you know it — how long have you known — ?"

"I know not what 'tis you speak of," said Lavrans after a while, in a strange, deadened voice.

"This do I speak of — that I was no maid, when I came to be your wife," said Ragnfrid, and her voice rang clear in her despair.

In a little while Lavrans answered, as before:

"That have I never known, till now."

Ragnfrid laid her down among the hay, shaken with weeping. When the fit was over she lifted her head a little. A faint grey light was beginning to creep in through the window-hole in the wall. She could dimly see her husband, sitting with his arms thrown round his knees, motionless as stone.

"Lavrans — speak to me — " she wailed.

"What would you I should say?" asked he, without stirring.

"Oh — I know not — curse me — strike me — "

" 'Twould be something late now," answered the man; there seemed to be the shade of a scornful smile in his voice.

Ragnfrid wept again: "Ay — I heeded not then that I was betraying you. So betrayed and so dishonoured, methought, had I been myself. There was none had spared me. They came and brought you — you know yourself, I saw you but three times before we were wed. . . . Methought you were but a boy, white and red — so young and childish — "

"I was so," said Lavrans, and a faint ring of life came to his voice. "And therefore a man might deem that you, who were a woman — you might have been more afraid to — to deceive one who was so young that he knew naught — "

"So did *I* think after," said Ragnfrid, weeping. "When I had come to know you. Soon came the time, when I would have given my soul twenty times over, to be guiltless of sin against you."

Lavrans sat silent and motionless; then said his wife: "You ask not anything?"

"What use to ask? It was he that . . . we met his burial-train at Feginsbrekka, as we bore Ulvhild in to Nidaros — "

"Ay," said Ragnfrid. "We had to leave the way — go aside into a meadow. I saw them bear him by on his bier — with priests and monks and armed yeomen. I heard he had made a good end — had made his peace with God. I prayed as we stood there with Ulvhild's litter between us — I prayed that my sin and my sorrow might be laid at his feet on the Last Day — "

"Ay, like enough you did," said Lavrans, and there was the same shade of scorn in his quiet voice.

"You know not all," said Ragnfrid, cold with despair. "Mind you that he came out to us at Skog the first winter we were wedded — ?"

"Ay," answered the man.

"When Björgulv was dying. . . . Oh, no one, no one had spared me. . . . He was drunk when he did it — afterwards he said he had never cared for me, he would not have me — he bade me forget it. My father knew it not; *he* did not betray you — never think that. But Trond — we were the dearest of friends to each other then — I made my moan to him. He tried to force the man to wed me; but he was but a boy; he was beaten. . . . Afterwards he counselled me to hold my peace, and to take you — "

She sat a while in silence.

"Then *he* came out to Skog — a year was gone by; I

thought not on it so much any more. But he came out thither — he said that he repented, he would have had me now, had I been unwedded — he loved me. He said so. God knows if he said true. When he was gone — I dared not go out on the fjord, dared not for my sin, not with the child. And I had begun — I had begun to love you so!" She cried out, a single cry of the wildest pain. The man turned his head quickly towards her.

"When Björgulv was born — oh, I thought he was dearer to me than my life. When he lay in the death-throes — I thought, if he died, I must die too. But I prayed *not* God to spare my boy's life — "

Lavrans sat a long time silent — then he asked in a dead, heavy voice:

"Was it because I was not his father?"

"I knew not if you were," said Ragnfrid, growing stiff and stark where she sat.

Long they sat there in a deathly stillness. Then the man asked vehemently of a sudden:

"In Jesu name, Ragnfrid — why tell you me all this — now?"

"Oh, I know not!" She wrung her hands till the joints cracked. "That you may avenge you on me — drive me from your house — "

"Think you that would help me — " His voice shook with scorn. "And then there are our daughters," he said quietly. "Kristin — and the little one."

Ragnfrid sat still awhile.

"I mind me how you judged of Erlend Nikulaussön," she said softly. "How judge you of me, then — ?"

A long shudder of cold passed over the man's body — yet a little of the stiffness seemed to leave him.

"You have — we have lived together now for seven and twenty years — almost. 'Tis not the same as with a stranger. I see this, too — worse than misery has it been for you."

Ragnfrid sank together sobbing at his words. She plucked up heart to put her hand on one of his. He moved not at all — sat as still as a dead man. Her weeping grew louder and louder — but her husband still sat motionless, looking at the faint grey light creeping in around the door. At last she lay as if all her tears were spent. Then he stroked her arm lightly downward — and she fell to weeping again.

"Mind you," she said through her tears, "that man who came to us one time, when we dwelt at Skog? He that knew all the ancient lays? Mind you the lay of a dead man that was come back from the world of torment, and told his son the story of all that he had seen? There was heard a groaning from hell's deepest ground, the querns of untrue women grinding mould for their husbands' meat. Bloody were the stones they dragged at — bloody hung the hearts from out their breasts — "

Lavrans was silent.

"All these years have I thought upon those words," said Ragnfrid. "Every day 'twas as though my heart was bleeding, for every day methought I ground you mould for meat — "

Lavrans knew not himself why he answered as he did. It seemed to him his breast was empty and hollow, like the breast of a man that has had the blood-eagle * carven through his back. But he laid his hand heavily and wearily on his wife's head, and spoke:

"Mayhap mould must needs be ground, my Ragnfrid, before the meat can grow."

When she tried to take his hand and kiss it, he snatched it away. But then he looked down at his wife, took one of her hands and laid it on his knee, and bowed his cold, stiffened face down upon it. And so they sat on, motionless, speaking no word more.

---

* Blood-eagle, see Note 26.

NOTES

THE BRIDAL WREATH

P. 1.   1. *The Bridal Wreath*

· This was the old Norwegian word (directly borrowed from
the English *garland*) for the gilt circlet which it was the pre-
rogative of maidens of gentle birth to wear, on state occasions,
on their outspread hair. In the title of this book it connotes,
besides that circlet, the wreath of golden flowers with which
the Elf-maiden tempts Kristin (p. 20), and also the bridal crown
(p. 310), which was an heirloom kept to be worn by brides
during the wedding festivities.

P. 2.   2. *Jörundgaard, see Plan*, p. 334

The houses of an old Norwegian manor-farm were generally
grouped in two adjacent squares or oblongs around the
"ind-tun" and the "ut-tun" (the "courtyard" and "farmyard" of this translation). The dwelling-houses and storehouses,
etc., lay around the "ind-tun," and the farm-buildings (barns,
cow-houses, goat and sheep-houses, etc.) round the "ut-tun."
The stable divided the two yards, turning one gable to the
"ind-tun" and the other to the "ut-tun." Small buildings of all
kinds were erected whenever needed, and when a building,
small or large, was no longer needed, it was usually suffered to
fall to ruin by decay, unless its site happened to be needed
for a new building. To this day the buildings on a big Gudbrandsdal farm may number thirty or forty — old grey wooden
houses.

There were usually no fortifications round a mediæval manor,
but the houses were joined together by wooden fences, pierced
here and there by wicket-gates, and there was a larger gate
closing the main entrance to the courtyard. The manor was
approached by a so-called "street" (*gade*) leading up to it
between fenced-in cornfields.

The courtyard was of green sward, and the roofs of all houses
were thatched with turf — fresh, green, and gay with flowers
in wet summers, yellow and dry in dry years, which are common in Gudbrandsdal. All the houses were built of large logs
of fir-wood.

Every house originally contained only one single room (often with the addition of a loft-room in the case of the storehouses described below). Thus the usual word for room (*stue*) was also often used as meaning "house." By the time when this book opens, however, the original single large, log-built room had been supplemented by penthouses (*svale*) made of "staves" (see Note 23), built around it on one, two, three, or all four sides, to shield the timbers of the main room from the weather and to keep out draughts. The penthouse was entered by a porch supported on wooden pillars and arches, and, along one side of the house, was usually divided by partitions into small rooms. One of these was the "outer room" (*forstue*), from which opened the main door of the living-room; others were closets (*kove* or *kleve*), used for the storage of chests, etc., or to hold a bed.

Cooking was done in a separate kitchen-house (*ildstue*), and there were also usually a brew house (*bryghus*), a weaving-house (*vaevstue*) for the looms of the mistress and maids, as well as workshops — for all farming implements were made and repaired on the place. The smithy and the bath-house (for steam baths) were placed some distance off in the fields, on account of the danger of fire.

Across the courtyard from the main dwelling-houses was a row of store-houses (*bur;* in modern times usually built on pillars, for security from rats and mice, and hence called "stabbur") — log-houses, often two-storeyed. The ground-floor of a "bur" was for the storage of all kinds of produce — hides, butter, cheese, and candles, loaves of bread, dried fish, salted meat, etc. A wealthy man, owning several farms besides his home farm, received his rents in kind, and the produce so received, as well as that of the home farm, was stored in these "bure." Hides, wool, fish, and other strong-smelling wares would be kept in one "bur," milk products, flour, and bread, etc., in another.

The most characteristic buildings of the older type were the hearth-room house (*aarestue*) and the storehouses (*bure*).

Page 335 shows a typical "aarestue," the old form of living-room. The two beds (built against the wall) were occupied, one by the master and mistress, often with one or more young children, the other by the elder children, or other members of the family. For those of the family for whom there was no room in the beds, sleeping-places were made up on the wall-benches. On the smaller farms the servants also lay on these benches; but on large places like Jörundgaard there were separate houses for the men-servants and the maids, and a house for the bailiff and his wife (*raadmandsstue*), Jon and Tordis of this story.

The hearth (*aare*) in the middle of the hearth-room was the sacred centre of home and family life. The smoke escaped by a smoke-vent (*ljore*) in the ridge of the roof. A wooden frame, with a pane of bladder or horn in it, could be drawn across this vent, by means of a pole (*ljorestang*), which hung down into the room. As the smoke-vent had to lead into the open air, the hearth-house was necessarily originally a one-storeyed building. The hearth-room, being the warmest room, and therefore the one most used in winter, was sometimes called the winter-room.

The newer type of dwelling-house, such as the "hall" (*höienloftshus*) on Jörungaard (see p. 334), was built in two storeys, the difficulty as to heating being overcome, after a fashion, by the introduction of wall fireplaces in masonry (*murede ovne*) in both the ground-floor room and the loft-room. Such a fireplace was an erection of stone in clay, built into a corner of the room, opening to the room in an arch, with a flat or domed mantel. Usually, in country houses, such fireplaces had no sort of chimney, so that they of course smoked horribly, and came to be known as "smoke fireplaces" (*rök-ovne*). The ground-floor rooms of these new-fashioned buildings often had windows with glass panes, whereas the hearth-room was lighted exclusively from the smoke-vent and the door.

The upper storey of the "bur," known as "bursloft," protruded on the gable front, and the front portion formed a balcony (this, too, was called "svale"), with an open arcade looking down into the courtyard. The "bursloft" was usually reached by an outside staircase leading up into the balcony. The entire "bur" was (and is) the favourite architectural structure of the Norwegian farm, beautifully proportioned, of excellent workmanship, and adorned with fine carvings and wrought-iron locks. The "bursloft" was used for storing the best clothes and the jewellery of the family, spare bedding, weapons, and the arms of the master; but there were also beds in it, so that it could be used as a guest-chamber, or as a summer bedroom for the family, or for the daughters and maid-servants. As the whole "bur" was quite unheated, it was of course hardly possible to use the "bursloft" as a bedroom in the winter.

The space under the overhanging balcony (*bursvale*) is the favourite trysting-place of the lover and his mistress in Norwegian — and Danish — ballads; and their conversation is often overheard by an eavesdropper in the dark balcony above.

The hall (*höienloftshus*) was built much on the same lines as the "bur" as to the overhanging upper storey, the balcony, and outside staircase; but was much larger, turned its side, instead of its gable, to the courtyard, and had its balcony (*svale* or *höienloftsbro*) on the courtyard side. The large loft-

Plan of Jörundgaard

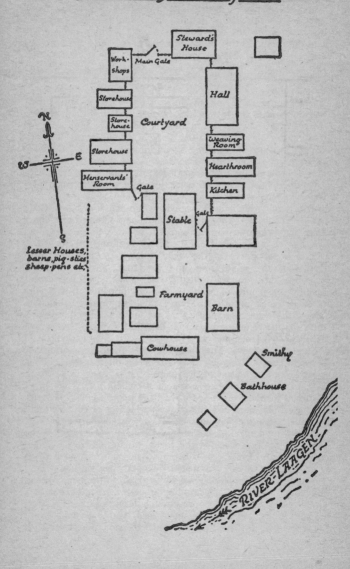

Plan of typical Hearthroom-house.

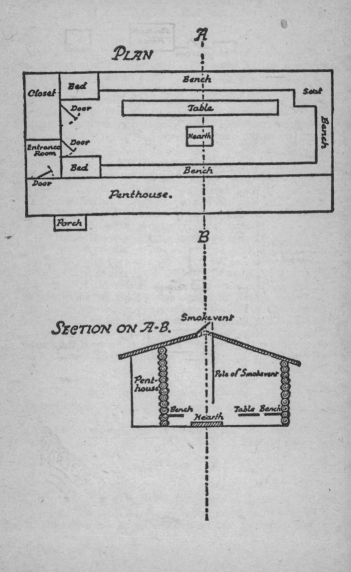

PLAN

A

Closet — Bed — Bench — Seat

Door

Table — Bench

Hearth

Door

Entrance Room — Bed — Bench

Door

Penthouse.

Porch

B

SECTION ON A-B.   Smokevent

Penthouse — Pole of Smokevent

Bench — Hearth — Table Bench

room (the "upper hall" of this translation) was the state-room of the manor. The hall (*stue*) underneath was the new winter living-room of the master and his family, with its wall fireplace and window with glass panes.

P. 2.   3. *Lagmand*

The position and functions of the Swedish "Lagmand," with reference to the Assembly (Thing) of his province, seem to have been closely analogous to those of the Speaker of the early House of Commons in England. He was chosen by the people, presided over the meetings of the Thing, and when the King was present, it was the Lagmand's duty to communicate to him the resolutions of the Thing, and generally to represent the rights of the common people.

P. 2.   4. *King Haakon the Old*

King Haakon the Old is Haakon IV. (*Haakonssön*), the grandson of King Sverre and the hero of Ibsen's *The Pretenders*. The Kings of Norway during the period covered by this book, and that immediately preceding it, were:

Haakon IV.	. . .	1217–1263
Magnus VI. (Lagaböter)	.	1263–1280
Eirik	. . .	1280–1299
Haakon V.	. .	1299–1319
Magnus VII. (Smek)	.	1319–1343

Magnus VII. was the grandson of Haakon V., being the son of Haakon's daughter Ingeborg (the Lady Ingebjörg of this book) by Duke Eirik of Sweden. He succeeded as a minor (see Part III, Chap. II.) to the thrones of Norway and Sweden. The complications arising from the vesting of the two crowns in one person form one of the springs of action in the second part of *Kristin Lavransdatter*, entitled *The Housewife* (*Husfruen*).

P. 6.   5. *Domestic Arrangements of Priests*

For an explanation of Sira Eirik's domestic arrangements, see p. 92.

"Sira" was the title (directly borrowed from the English) of parish priests.

P. 12.   6. *Peasant Guilds*

See Note 17.

P. 20.   7. *Elf-maiden or Dwarf-Maiden*

For the many superstitions connected with the "mountain people" reference may be made to any of the collections of

Norwegian Folk and Fairy Tales, of which the best known is the classical work of Asbjörnsen and Moe.

References to these superstitions occur on p. 28 (where the Hamar Cathedral is likened, in Kristin's imagination, to the mountain folk's hall); p. 57 (where Lady Aashild refers to the tales in which astute mortals get the better of the trolls or dwarfs); and p. 230 (where the phrase translated "she goes around like one bewitched" is in the original "she goes about as if she were come out of the mountain").

P. 37.   8. *St. Sunniva and the Selje-men*

St. Sunniva was an Irish Princess who, to escape the unwelcome attentions of a heathen chief, fled across the sea, with a number of devoted followers, in a vessel without rudder, sail, or oars, and reached the Norwegian coast, where the party landed on the island of Selje. The refugees dwelt in caves of the hills, living on fish. The heathen inhabitants of the neighbouring mainland, missing from time to time some of their cattle left to graze on the islands off the coast, suspected that the strangers were responsible, and sent an armed party against them. On arrival, the party found that the caves occupied by the refugees had been blocked up and their occupants entombed by a great landslide.

Some time afterwards passers-by in boats noticed a strange light streaming from the spot where the strangers had been entombed. The matter reached the ears of the King, Olaf Tryggvesön (then engaged in his attempt to Christianize the land), and he proceeded to investigate, accompanied by a bishop. The caves were opened up, and, while the remains of Sunniva's companions showed their sanctity only by the emission of the supernatural light and of a sweet smell, the body of the Princess herself was found intact and uncorrupted. The King had a church built upon the spot and the body enshrined there. A hundred years later the body was removed to the Bergen Cathedral.

The Mass of the Selje-men was celebrated annually on the 8th July, in honour of Sunniva and her companions.

P. 70.   9. *Sewing chair (Sömmestol)*

An arm-chair with a chest in the seat to hold the needlework, sewing implements, etc.

P. 103.   10. *Birch-legs (Birkebeiner)*

The followers of King Sverre, so called because, in the many wanderings and privations in hills and wastes which eventually led that great adventurer to the throne, they covered their nakedness with garments of birch-bark. See Ibsen's *The Pretenders*.

P. 108.   11. *Hovedö*

The largest of the islands in the Christiania Fjord close to the town. Noted for the Cistercian monastery established there in the twelfth century by monks from Kirkstead in Lincolnshire. See p. 136.

P. 109.   12. *Baron*

Lendermand in original. The lendermand was a high feudal dignitary holding a fief under the Crown in return for certain services to be rendered to the King in war and peace, which do not seem to have been prescribed generally, but were fixed separately in each particular case. Neither title nor fief was hereditary.

The title was changed to "Baron" by King Magnus Lagaböter, but continued to be personal, and not hereditary.

Haakon V., in pursuance of his policy of curbing the growth of the Norwegian aristocracy and preventing the formation of a feudal nobility in the European model, decreed (1308) that no more "barons" were to be made. The office and title thus became extinct.

P. 113.   13. *Commoners (Proventsfolk)*

The "proventsfolk" were what in modern times would be called boarders — laymen and women, chiefly elderly people, who are boarded and lodged by the convent on payment. Both monasteries and nunneries had such boarders, and as, in both cases, the boarders were of both sexes (in spite of the orders of the bishops to the contrary), they were lodged in houses outside the convent gates.

P. 117.   14. *Saint Days and Festivals*

As times and seasons are constantly marked in the text by Church festivals the dates of some of the less familiar of these may usefully be noted:

St. Gregory	13th February.
St. Halvard	15th May.
St. John	21st June.
St. Lawrence (Lavrans)	10th August.
St. Batholomew	24th August.
Birthday of the Virgin	8th September.
Holy Cross Day (Elevation)	14th September.
Michaelmas	29th September.
St. Clement	23rd November.

Pp. 119, 176.

15. *Town "Dwelling-places" and "Yards"*

The word "gaard," which when it refers to country-places, has been translated "manor" or "farm," was also used for the residences of families in towns and for the squares or yards occupied by merchants and shopkeepers. In the former case the word "dwelling-place" has been used, and in the latter the word "yard" (on the analogy of such places as Bell Yard or Tokenhouse Yard in London). In both cases the town "gaard" bore a general resemblance to the courtyard (*ind-tun*) part of a country "gaard," as described in Note 2; *i.e.* it consisted of a number of houses enclosing a square or oblong open space, the houses being connected by fences, and the entrance being through a gate.

Ordinarily several country families would share a town "gaard," each owning one or more of the houses.

Under regulations of King Haakon V. and his predecessors, each important trade was assigned its own "gaard," to which it was confined. Thus Mickle Yard (*Miklegaard*) was the quarter of the shoemakers and leather-merchants.

P. 120.   16. *Money*

What Lavrans gave Kristin as pocket-money was "a mark of silver in counted money." The following is a very brief and rough sketch of the somewhat confusing monetary arrangements of the period:

"A mark of pure silver" (*en mark brændt sölv*) was a *weight* of 215.8 grammes of silver, or rather less than ½ lb. avoirdupois (227 grammes). The divisions of this weight were:

1 mark = 8 öre = 24 örtug = 240 penninger.

But the value of "a mark of silver in counted money" (*en mark sölv i tællede penger*) was only from ⅓ to ⅕ of that of a mark of pure silver.

Thus Kristin's pocket-money was equal in value to (say) ⅓ of ½, or ⅙ lb. = 2⅓ ounces of pure silver – the purchasing power of which was, of course, very greatly in excess of what it would be at the present day.

All sorts of foreign coins (including shillings and florins) were in circulation, being valued according to their weight and fineness.

On pp. 123-4 Kristin bargains with the Rostock men to pay them an "örtug," which, as shown above, was equal to 10 "penninger." We have rendered "örtug" by "silver ducat," a coin said to have had a value of about 3*s*. 4*d*., and "penning"

by "silver penny," which we assume to have been worth
about 4*d*.

On p. 303 Erlend promises "four marks of silver" (*fire mark
sölv*) towards the rebuilding of the church. This was no doubt
"pure silver," so that the contribution was equal in value to
nearly 2 lb. avoirdupois of pure silver — a handsome offering,
considering the high value of silver at the period.

P. 132.   17. *Peasant or Farmers' Guilds*

These included both freeholders and tenants, both men and
women, and were associations for all kinds of mutual helpful-
ness and protection, ranging from insurance against fire (in
times of peace — in war-time the functions of the guild were
partially suspended) to the avenging of the deaths of members,
and providing for the welfare of their souls by prayers and
masses.

The guilds originated in heathen times, but were eagerly
adopted and adapted by the Catholic Church. The various
guilds were assigned patron Saints, and each held a great drinking festival on its Saint's day and the succeeding days. For these
festivals somewhat elaborate regulations were laid down in the
laws of the guilds, with a view to ensuring that they should
be decorous and dignified functions. Thus quarrelling, foul
language, and indecorous behaviour towards women were pro-
hibited; no man was to become so drunk that he could not
behave himself; no man was to bring his dogs or hawks into the
hall; no child under three years old was to be admitted except
in its mother's or foster-mother's charge; guild members were
responsible for the behaviour of any outside guests they might
introduce, etc.

The toasts usually included cups to the memory of the
Saviour, the Virgin Mary, the Saints, and departed guild brothers and sisters.

P. 150.   18. *Mission to Vargöyhus*

Vargöyhus is now the little town of Vardö in the north-east
of Finmark. The mission of Gissur Galle in 1310-1311 had for
its object the regulation of the taxation taken from the Lap-
landers, and the erection or strengthening of a little fort on
Vargöy (Wolf Island), which in the following centuries was
the outpost of Norwegian power against Russian raids into
Finmark.

Pp. 161, 229.   19. *Barons and Wardens*

For Barons, see Note 12.

The word translated Wardens is in the original *sysselmænd*.

The sysselmand was a high official in charge of a district, his duties being those of a chief administrator, military commander, and police officer. The appointment was made by the Crown from among gentlemen of distinction — at the period of this story a sysselmand would be usually, though not always, a knight. He had to maintain a certain number of armed men and subordinate officials. His remuneration varied in different cases — he might be paid directly by the Crown, or remunerated by a share in fines and fiefs.

P. 264.   20. *The Sacred Blood at Schwerin*

Some drops of blood from a bleeding Host preserved in a monastery at Schwerin were much venerated throughout the North, and were visited by many Scandinavian pilgrims.

P. 272.   21. *Marriage Settlements*

According to old Norwegian law and custom the normal marriage settlement was as follows:

The bride brought with her into the partnership her dowry (*hjemmefölge*); and the bridegroom was legally bound to transfer to her in addition an "extra-gift" (*tilgave*) which was fixed at one-third or one-half of the value of the dowry. The dowry and "extra-gift" together were generally calculated to be about one-third of the total joint estate.

This (dowry plus "extra-gift") was the wife's portion of the couple's joint possessions. If the marriage were childless, and the husband survived his wife, her family inherited it; if he died first, her family, in her name, had to see that the husband's heirs paid it over to the widow.

In the case of the wife's adultery, the husband kept the "extra-gift" in stewardship till her death; after which he was bound to pay it to her heirs.

In case of the man's adultery (but only with another man's wedded wife) his wife, if she chose to leave him, might claim that her portion be transferred to the stewardship of her kinsmen.

Husband and wife could not inherit from each other.

The "morning-gift" (*morgen-gave*) was a voluntary gift from the husband to his wife on the morning after marriage. It might often be much more valuable than the "extra-gift," the amount of which was fixed by law. But the bride's parents often let the bridegroom fix the intended "morning-gift" when the marriage-contract was made.

P. 287.   22. *Hatt*

Hatt was one of the incarnations of Odin.

P. 298.   23. *Stave-churches*

The mediæval "stav-kirker," the wooden churches of the inland districts of Norway, were built of "staves," very thick and
heavy pieces of wood, something between a small plank and a
small beam, cut out of the log, and hewn flat, by means of
axes — the use of saws and planes being almost unknown. The
roof was of tarred wooden shingles.

NORWEGIAN STAVE-CHURCH
Period 1150-1200.

To strengthen the building, and shield the walls against storms
and rain, an open arcade or "cloister-way" (*svalgang*), with
low arches opening outwards, ran all round the church, its roof
of shingles being supported on the lower points of the roof
construction of the aisles. It had small porches opposite the
portals of the church. In this covered way men deposited their
axes and swords before entering the church; penitents who
had not received absolution must remain during the elevation
of the mass, etc. It was also very much used as a meeting-place,

for drawing up legal documents, for parish councils, arbitration meetings and the like.

The church had no tower, but a "ridge-turret" — a small turret on the ridge of the roof above the nave. This held the little bell. The great bells were in a separate belfry (*stöpul*) near the lych-gate.

Fine examples of mediæval "stave-churches" still exist, or existed till recently, at Borgund, and at Hitterdal in Telemarken.

The words "stave" and "cloister-way" used in the text have been chosen as the least misleading renderings of the Norwegian "stav" and "svalgang." It should be borne in mind, however, that these "staves," though not unlike barrel staves in shape, were very much larger and thicker; and that the "cloister-way," instead of forming the *enceinte* of a courtyard, as a cloister usually does elsewhere, surrounded a solid building, and was open on its outer, not on its inner side.

P. 303.   24. *Land Measurement*

For "four marks of silver," see Note 16.

"Land to the value of sixty cows" is in the original "et markebol." Landed property in southern and central Norway was calculated in "öresbol" or "markebol" (one markebol = three öresbol). The "markebol" in Gudbrandsdal had a value varying from 16 to 20 silver marks, or from 40 to 60 cows, according to the quality of the land.

In western and northern Norway the unit of measurement was the "maanedsmatsbol," the literal meaning of which is: "as much land as will feed one man for one month."

P. 312.   25. *The Wedded Woman's Coif*

"Hustrulinet" in original. Only maidens wore their hair "down." For every woman who was not a maid, some kind of head-covering was obligatory. Wives tied up their hair and covered it with "hustrulinet" — the "long, snow-white, finely-pleated linen cloth" described on p. 319. See also p. 173.

P. 330.   26. *The Blood-eagle*

A method of execution (*riste blodörn paa ryggen*) practised in the Viking age. The ribs were hewn from the backbone, and the lungs and heart torn out through the wound. Sometimes a man would ask to be put to death in this manner, to show his defiant spirit, and prove his courage. So, at least, the sagas tell us.

ABOUT THE AUTHOR

SIGRID UNDSET (born 1882) grew up in Oslo, Norway, the daughter of a Norwegian archaeologist, whose early death left his family in difficult circumstances. From 1899 to 1909, she supported her family as an office clerk, writing at night, and won her first success in 1912 with her third novel, *Jenny*, the story of an urban working girl. Other modern novels followed during her thirteen-year marriage to a painter, during which she also raised six children. But her interest in the Middle Ages gave rise to her masterpieces: the three-volume *Kristin Lavransdatter* (1920–22), and the four-volume *The Master of Hestviken* (1925–27). She was awarded the Nobel Prize for Literature in 1928. Undset was divorced in 1925, and turning her back on the liberal, feminist circles of her youth, converted to Roman Catholicism the same year. Her later novels (she published fourteen during her lifetime) returned to modern settings and were overtly religious in tone. During World War II, she escaped to the United States, having been a vocal and bitter opponent of Nazism. She returned to Norway to die in 1949.

SPECIAL OFFER: If you enjoyed this book and would like to have our catalog of over 1,400 other Bantam titles, just send your name and address and 50¢ (to help defray postage and handling costs) to: Catalog Department, Bantam Books, Inc., 414 East Golf Rd., Des Plaines, Ill. 60016.

KRISTIN LAVRANSDATTER

by
Sigrid Undset

A sweeping epic of medieval life in Norway, **KRISTIN LAVRANSDATTER** takes its golden-haired heroine from her wondrous childhood in the misty valley of Jorundgaard to maturity and the wisdom of age in a convent far from home. This richly textured trilogy abounds in color and high drama: feasts in the great hall, ancient bridal customs, witchcraft, rape and adultery among nobles, a plot against the crown, childbed agonies and penitential journeys in sackcloth and bare feet. Yet it is most powerful in its portrait of one woman moving through the ordinary events of her life, changing through first love, loss of innocence, marriage, motherhood and age. Ancient in setting, but unerringly modern in its psychological treatment of character, it is as vital today as when it won the Nobel Prize for Literature in 1928.

THE BRIDAL WREATH (Volume I) A novel of passion. Her father's favorite child, Kristin is ready to accept his choice of bridegroom—until she meets the rakish Erlend Nikulausson, a renegade nobleman exiled for living in sin with another man's wife. For Erlend she sacrifices her honor, her father's favor, her own peace, and persists against all obstacles to marry him.

THE MISTRESS OF HUSABY (Volume II) A novel of marriage. A pregnant Kristin weds Erlend and becomes mistress of his neglected estate, Husaby. She bears him seven children, living in years'-long cycles of resentment, rage, reconciliation and renewed passion. Not until Erlend is arrested and sentenced to death for treachery does Kristin fully realize the absolutely fated quality of their love.

THE CROSS (Volume III) A novel of leave-taking and reconciliation. Husband, sons, wealth— all slip away, leaving Kristin alone, but still indomitable. Journeying through a land ravaged by the Black Death, she is chastened by the suffering around her. She ends her days in a cloister, nursing victims of the plague, until she herself contracts the disease, having glimpsed only at the end the spiritual fulfillment she has sought all her life.

Be sure to read all three volumes of **KRISTIN LAVRANSDATTER,** to be available at Bantam Books, wherever paperbacks are sold. **THE MISTRESS OF HUSABY** will be on sale October 1st, **THE CROSS** will be available November 1st.

THE NAMES THAT SPELL GREAT LITERATURE

Choose from today's most renowned world authors—every one an important addition to your personal library.

Hermann Hesse

☐	2906	KNULP	$1.95
☐	11916	MAGISTER LUDI	$2.25
☐	2944	DEMIAN	$1.75
☐	10060	GERTRUDE	$1.95
☐	11978	THE JOURNEY TO THE EAST	$1.95
☐	11796	SIDDHARTHA	$1.95
☐	10352	BENEATH THE WHEEL	$1.95
☐	12509	NARCISSUS AND GOLDMUND	$2.50
☐	11289	STEPPENWOLF	$1.95
☐	11510	ROSSHALDE	$1.95

Alexander Solzhenitsyn

☐	10111	THE FIRST CIRCLE	$2.50
☐	11712	ONE DAY IN THE LIFE OF IVAN DENISOVICH	$1.95
☐	2997	AUGUST 1914	$2.50
☐	11300	CANCER WARD	$2.50
☐	12079	LENIN IN ZURICH	$2.95

Jerzy Kosinski

☐	12465	STEPS	$2.25
☐	12460	THE PAINTED BIRD	$2.25
☐	2613	COCKPIT	$2.25

Doris Lessing

☐	11870	THE SUMMER BEFORE THE DARK	$2.25
☐	10425	THE GOLDEN NOTEBOOK	$2.25
☐	12461	THE FOUR-GATED CITY	$2.95
☐	11717	BRIEFING FOR A DESCENT INTO HELL	$2.25

André Schwarz-Bart

☐	10469	THE LAST OF THE JUST	$1.95

Buy them at your local bookstore or use this handy coupon for ordering:

Bantam Books, Inc., Dept. EDG, 414 East Golf Road, Des Plaines, Ill. 60016

Please send me the books I have checked above. I am enclosing $_____ (please add 75¢ to cover postage and handling). Send check or money order —no cash or C.O.D.'s please.

Mr/Mrs/Miss_____

Address_____

City_____State/Zip_____

EDG—9/78

Please allow four weeks for delivery. This offer expires 3/79.

REACH ACROSS THE GENERATIONS

With books that explore disenchantment and discovery, failure and conquest, and seek to bridge the gap between adolescence and adulthood.

☐	11919	**BONNIE JOE, GO HOME** Jeanette Eyerly	$1.50
☐	2670	**NOBODY WAVED GOODBYE** Elizabeth Haggard	$1.25
☐	2858	**THE UPSTAIRS ROOM** Johanna Reiss	$1.25
☐	8541	**THE FRIENDS** Rosa Guy	$1.25
☐	11239	**RUN SOFTLY, GO FAST** Barbara Wersba	$1.50
☐	12347	**SUMMER OF MY GERMAN SOLDIER** Bette Greene	$1.75
☐	11540	**HATTER FOX** Marilyn Harris	$1.95
☐	10370	**THE BELL JAR** Sylvia Plath	$1.95
☐	12057	**IT'S NOT THE END OF THE WORLD** Judy Blume	$1.50
☐	11912	**I NEVER LOVED YOUR MIND** Paul Zindel	$1.50
☐	12501	**PARDON ME, YOU'RE STEPPING ON MY EYEBALL** Paul Zindel	$1.95
☐	12252	**I KNOW WHY THE CAGED BIRD SINGS** Maya Angelou	$1.95
☐	11799	**RICHIE** Thomas Thompson	$1.95
☐	11605	**MY DARLING, MY HAMBURGER** Paul Zindel	$1.75
☐	11288	**WHERE THE RED FERN GROWS** Wilson Rawls	$1.50
☐	12320	**PHOEBE** Patricia Dizenzo	$1.50
☐	11496	**ELLEN: A SHORT LIFE, LONG REMEMBERED** Roe Levit	$1.50

Buy them at your local bookstore or use this handy coupon for ordering:

Bantam Books, Inc., Dept. EDN, 414 East Golf Road, Des Plaines, Ill. 60016

Please send me the books I have checked above. I am enclosing $_____
(please add 50¢ to cover postage and handling). Send check or money order
—no cash or C.O.D.'s please.

Mr/Mrs/Miss_____

Address_____

City_____State/Zip_____

EDN—8/78

Please allow four weeks for delivery. This offer expires 2/79.
